Her Secret, His Child

MIRANDA LEE
ANNE McALLISTER
CHRISTINA HOLLIS

Published in Great Britain 2013
by Mills & Boon, an imprint of Harlequin (UK) Limited,
Eton House, 18-24 Paradise Road, Richmond, Surrey TW9 1SR

HER SECRET, HIS CHILD © by Harlequin Enterprises II B.V./S.à.r.l 2013

A Night, A Secret…A Child, *One-Night Love-Child* and *The French Aristocrat's Baby* were first published in Great Britain by Harlequin (UK) Limited.

A Night, A Secret...A Child © Miranda Lee 2010
One-Night Love-Child © Anne McAllister 2008
The French Aristocrat's Baby © Christina Hollis 2010

ISBN: 978 0 263 90573 1
eBook ISBN: 978 1 472 00146 7

05-1213

Harlequin (UK) policy is to use papers that are natural, renewable and recyclable products and made from wood grown in sustainable forests. The logging and manufacturing processes conform to the legal environmental regulations of the country of origin.

Printed and bound in Spain
by Blackprint CPI, Barcelona

A NIGHT, A SECRET…
A CHILD

BY
MIRANDA LEE

Miranda Lee is Australian, living near Sydney. Born and raised in the bush, she was boarding-school educated and briefly pursued a career in classical music, before moving to Sydney and embracing the world of computers. Happily married, with three daughters, she began writing when family commitments kept her at home. She likes to create stories that are believable, modern, fast-paced and sexy. Her interests include meaty sagas, doing word puzzles, gambling and going to the movies.

CHAPTER ONE

NICOLAS moved with uncharacteristic slowness as he alighted the cab outside his apartment building. He felt dog-tired and strangely lacking in the buzz that finding and promoting an exciting new talent usually brought him.

Admittedly, standing in the wings of a stage and watching someone else perform had never given him the same adrenalin rush as being out there himself. But being the man behind a successful star or show had come a close second this past decade.

Tonight, however, his pulse rate hadn't risen when his latest musical protégée had brought the highly discerning New York audience to its feet more than once. He was happy for her. Of course he was. She was a nice girl and a brilliant violinist. But he just hadn't felt anything like what he normally did. In truth, he hadn't given a damn.

How odd.

Maybe he was entering a midlife crisis: next year he'd turn forty. Or perhaps he was reaching burnout. Showbiz was a wearing career, both on the performers and the promoters. Lots of highs and lows. And lots of travelling.

Nicolas had grown to hate hotel rooms very quickly. That was why he'd eventually bought apartments in New York and London. His friends called him extravagant. But Nicolas knew he'd chosen well and would never lose money on his purchases. His New York apartment had already tripled in value in the six years he'd owned it. His London town house wasn't quite as spectacular an investment, but he certainly hadn't lost money.

'Everything go well tonight, Mr Dupre?' the night doorman asked as he opened the door for Nicolas. There was a note of concern in his voice. Obviously he'd seen the weariness in Nicolas's body language.

Nicolas flashed the doorman a warm smile. 'Very well, Mike. Thank you.'

The doorman nodded. 'That's good.'

Nicolas might have given him a tip if Mike would have accepted it. But Mike refused to take money from the residents, only guests and visitors. Nicolas always slipped him a card and a nice fat cheque at Christmas, claiming he would be offended if Mike refused to take his Christmas present. Nicolas suspected Mike probably gave most of the money away to someone he considered more needy than himself; he was that kind of man.

The young man on the front desk glanced up as Nicolas entered the foyer. Chad was a third-year law student who worked nights to pay his way through college. Nicolas admired anyone who worked hard and had given Chad more than a little something last Christmas as well.

'There's a letter here for you, sir,' Chad said.

'A letter?'

Nicolas frowned as he walked up to the desk. He never received mail these days. All his bills and bank statements were redirected to his accountant. If anyone wanted to contact him personally they did so by phone, text message or email.

The young man smiled. 'The mailman brought it in this afternoon after you'd left for the theatre. Have to confess we had a bit of a chuckle over it. You'll know what I mean when you see the way it's addressed.' And he handed over a bright pink envelope.

On it was written:

Mr Nicolas Dupre
c/o Broadway
New York
America

'Good Lord,' Nicolas said with a wry smile.

'Nice to be famous,' Chad said.

'I'm not all that famous.' Not nowadays. It was mainly the entertainers who were interviewed on the talk shows, not the entrepreneurs. Nicolas had had one television interview a couple of years back, after one of the musicals he'd produced had won heaps of Tony awards, but nothing since.

'It's come all the way from Australia,' Chad said, and Nicolas's heart missed a beat.

Something—some inner instinct—warned him not to turn the envelope over and look at the sender's name…. Not till he was safely alone.

'Looks like it's from a lady,' Chad went on, obviously dying to know who.

Nicolas, however, had no intention of satisfying the younger man's curiosity.

'An old fan, I imagine,' Nicolas said, and slipped the envelope inside his breast pocket. 'Someone who doesn't know I stopped performing years ago. Thank you, Chad. Good night.'

'Oh…er… Good night, sir.'

Nicolas made it into the privacy of his tenth-floor apartment before he extracted the envelope and looked at the back flap.

His stomach churned as he stared at the name of the sender. It wasn't from her. Had he honestly expected that it would be?

Had he been hoping against hope that Serina had finally come to her senses and realised that she couldn't live without him?

Once he got over his dismay, the letter did, however, evoke considerable surprise and curiosity. Because it was from Serina's daughter, the child whom Nicolas had once briefly thought could be his, but wasn't. Felicity Harmon had been born ten months to the day after the last time he'd slept with Serina, and exactly nine months after her marriage to Greg Harmon.

Nicolas still had trouble accepting what Serina had done that night. It had been cruel of her to come back into his life and raise his hopes where she was concerned.

It had taken him years to get over her initial refusal to go to England with him when he'd been just twenty-one. But he'd finally come to understand and accept—or he thought he had—that her love for her family back in Rocky Creek was much stronger than her love for him. He'd stayed away from home after that, not even returning to visit his mother. Instead, a couple of times a year, he'd send his mother money to travel to whatever part of the world he was in. Why torture himself?

Serina was the one who'd eventually sought him out, several years later.

He'd imagined he was over her by then. There'd been other women, lots of them. The fact he'd never lived with one, let alone married any of them, should have told him that his heart still belonged to Serina, that heart taking off into the stratosphere when he'd spotted her in the audience as he'd been taking his curtain call that fateful night, thirteen years ago. He recalled the date very well because it was the first time he'd performed in Sydney, having stayed right away from Australia as well as Rocky Creek.

When she'd appeared at his dressing-room door afterwards, he'd been incapable of speech. He'd taken one look into her lovely, tear-filled eyes, pulled her inside the room and locked the door behind her. They'd made love on the sofa with a hunger that had been insatiable, before sheer exhaustion had had them both falling asleep in each other's arms.

When he'd woken she'd gone, leaving him a note saying that she was sorry, but she simply hadn't been able to resist the temptation to be with him one last time. She'd begged him not to follow her home. She was marrying Greg Harmon in a few weeks and nothing he could do or say was going to change her mind. He could still recall her final argument, word for word.

'Your life is playing the piano, Nicolas. It's what you want and what you need—to perform. I could see that tonight. What we have when we're together, it's not love, Nicolas, it's something else. Something dangerous. If I give in to it, it will destroy me. You will survive without me, I know you will.'

Well, he had. Survived, that is. Though it had been touch-and-go a couple of times.

Yet it had only taken the arrival of a pink envelope from Australia to make his heart race in that crazy way it always raced when he was with Serina. He'd thought she'd felt the same way about him once. And maybe she had. Looking back, he could see she'd been as powerless to resist him physically, as he'd been her. As lovers, they'd been perfect together, right from the start. Amazing, considering they'd both been virgins.

Nicolas shook his head at the memory of that night. If he'd known what was going to happen he would never have agreed to Mrs Johnson's suggestion that Serina partner him to his graduation ball.

At that time in his life, Nicolas had had no time for girls. His only passion had been the piano.

Not that the girls weren't after him; they were. At eighteen, Nicolas had been tall and handsome, with wavy blond hair and Nordic-blue eyes, which he'd been told were sexy. There'd been any number of girls in his class and in other classes at his high school who would have gladly agreed to go with him to his grad. But Nicolas just hadn't wanted the complications that came with having a girlfriend. His focus had been all on his career back then. All he could think about was becoming the world's greatest concert pianist. He'd already won a scholarship to go to the Conservatorium of Music in Sydney and would be leaving to study there in a couple of months' time. His life in Rocky Creek—which he'd always hated—would soon be over.

But his mother had really wanted him to go to his graduation ball, so he'd given in to his music teacher's suggestion and asked Serina, who was another of Mrs Johnson's piano pupils. Nicolas had reasoned—incorrectly as it turned out—that because she was rather shy Serina was unlikely to become a problem. Conversation wouldn't be difficult, either. They could always talk about music.

Imagine his surprise—and shock—when he went to pick her up in his mother's car and a vision of loveliness came walking through her front door. She was wearing blue, a deep electric blue. Her dress was strapless, its material shiny, with a bell-shaped skirt, and her shoes were high. Her very shapely legs seemed to go on forever.

Up till then Nicolas had only ever seen Serina in her school uniform, with no makeup and her hair either in a plait or up in a pony tail.

Suddenly, with her hair down, her face made up and her amazingly grown-up figure very much on display, she looked much older and extremely sexy. Nicolas took one look at her and was struck by a desire he'd never felt before. He could not take his eyes off her all night. Dancing with her became both a delight and a torment.

He was in quite a frazzled state by the time they left the ball and he drove Serina home shortly after midnight. Her parents had made a condition of her going with him that he wouldn't take her on to any of the after-grad parties, which were well known for being drunken booze-ups and sex-fests. Nicolas didn't mind, since he didn't drink and wasn't into sex. Not as yet, anyway.

Suddenly, however, he wanted Serina even more than he wanted to dazzle the world with his piano playing. But he knew it was out of the question. For one thing, his date was obviously a virgin, like himself.

But just as they were approaching Rocky Creek, Serina's hand slid over and came to rest on his thigh. His eyes flew to hers and what he saw there echoed his own quite desperate need.

'Don't take me home yet,' she whispered huskily.

Nicolas needed no more encouragement, swiftly turning his mother's car off the main road onto a narrow bush track, which he knew would bring him to a very private spot down by the creek.

And it was there that it all began. Just kisses at first, then touching and more touching. Clothes came off and before he knew it he was trying to get inside her. Her gasp of pain didn't stop him, either. By then he was beyond thought, beyond control. Only afterwards did he panic, because he hadn't used a condom.

'Your father's going to kill me if you get pregnant,' he'd groaned.

'I can't,' came her surprisingly calm reply. 'Not tonight, anyway. I've just finished my period. According to a book I read that means I'm safe.'

Nicolas breathed a huge sigh of relief.

'I'll go in to Port and buy some condoms tomorrow,' he replied, and she just stared up at him, her eyes large and dark.

'It'll be better next time,' he heard himself promise.

'I liked it this time,' she stunned him by saying. 'It was lovely. Do it to me again, Nicolas.'

And he did. More slowly the second time, watching with wonder as she came. By the time he took her home around two, Nicolas was totally obsessed with her.

Somehow, they managed to keep their teenage love affair a secret during that entire summer holiday, Nicolas sneaking out of his bedroom every night and running all the way to meet Serina down behind her house. Fortunately, her parents lived on a small farm that had lots of outbuildings where they could make love. Nicolas made Serina promise not to tell anyone about their relationship, especially not any of her girlfriends. He knew that Serina's rather old-fashioned parents would do everything to separate them if they found out what was going on. Publicly, they pretended to their small community that they were just friends, brought together by the fact that they were both pupils of the same music teacher.

It wasn't till later that they began to date openly. By then Nicolas had gone to Sydney to study and the star-crossed lovers didn't see each other all that much. When they did, however, they made the most of their time together. They would tell their respective parents that they were practising the piano together, or going to the movies, or to the beach.

But an unwanted pregnancy and a teenage marriage were not in Nicolas's plans for his immediate future, not if he was going to become the world's greatest concert pianist.

However, he'd always known that Serina was the only girl for him, that one day they would marry, and he would be the father of her children. It had seemed inconceivable to him back then that she would ever be with another man, let alone bear a child.

Yet she'd had another man's child—and that child had just written to him.

Why, for pity's sake?

Nicolas ripped open the pink envelope and out came a white sheet of paper on which was a computer-generated letter.

Dear Mr Dupre
Hi. My name is Felicity Harmon. I live in Rocky Creek

and I am twelve years old. I am captain of our primary school and am helping the teachers organise an end-of-year concert to be held on Saturday afternoon, the twentieth of December this year, to raise funds for our local bushfire brigade.

We are going to have a talent quest instead of a normal concert and need someone to act as judge for the night. It would be nice to have someone famous so that lots of people will come. You are the most famous person to have ever lived in Rocky Creek, and I thought I would write and ask you to come and be our judge. My piano teacher, Mrs Johnson, said you probably wouldn't come because you live in New York now and you don't have family here anymore. But she also said you were once good friends with my mum and you just might come, if I asked nicely. You probably don't know this but my dad was killed not that long ago. He went to help down in the terrible bushfires in Victoria last summer and a burnt-out tree fell on him. He told me the day before he died that our local bushfire brigade needed better firefighting equipment to keep our town safe from bushfires. A new truck would be good. But new trucks cost a lot of money.

I'm sure that if you come and be our judge we would make a lot of money. If you can come, you could stay at our house as we have a spare bedroom. Below is my email address if you think you can make it. I hope you can. Please let me know soon, as the concert is only three weeks away.

Yours sincerely

Felicity Harmon.

PS. I used a pink envelope because I thought it might stand out and have a better chance of finding you.

PPS. If it does, please come!

Please come! That was a laugh. Wild horses couldn't keep him away.

If Greg Harmon had still been alive, Nicolas would not even have dreamt of going back to Rocky Creek. He would politely have declined Felicity's undeniably touching plea, then have posted her a large, disappointment-saving cheque.

But the carrot had been waved, hadn't it? Serina was now a widow. How could he not return?

She'd always been his Achilles' heel. Always driven him crazy. One day, she'd probably be the death of him.

It was a prophetic thought...

CHAPTER TWO

SERINA stared with disbelieving eyes at her daughter. Felicity's bald announcement over breakfast that she'd secured Nicolas Dupre as the judge of her school's fund-raising talent quest had rendered her temporarily speechless.

'But how did you know where to contact him?' she finally managed to blurt out.

Felicity's impossibly smug expression reminded Serina quite fiercely of her father. Her biological father, that was, not the man who'd raised her.

'I didn't,' Felicity replied. 'I wrote him a letter and addressed it care of Broadway, New York. And he got it!'

Serina scooped in a deep breath whilst she prayed for calm. 'And?'

'I gave him my email address and he sent me a reply last night.'

'Why didn't you tell me all this last night?'

'His email didn't come till after you'd gone to bed.'

'Felicity! You know I don't like you being on the Internet after I go to bed.'

'Yeah, I know. Sorry,' she apologised without a trace of guilt in her voice.

Serina glared at her daughter. Felicity was a wilful child and far too intelligent for her own good. On top of that she was a brilliant pianist. Mrs Johnson often said she was the most talented musician she'd taught since…

Serina swallowed. This couldn't be happening to her!

'Felicity, I…'

'Mum, please don't be mad at me,' Felicity broke in. 'I had to do something or no one would've come to our talent quest except for the parents. This way lots of other people will come. We might even make enough money to buy one of those brand-new fire trucks. One which has sprinklers on top like Dad always wanted. I'm doing this for Dad, Mum. He can't do it from heaven, can he?'

What could Serina say to that? Nothing, really. Felicity had adored Greg, had been devastated by his death. She'd been the apple of Greg's eye and he'd never known the truth about his daughter's parentage. Serina had managed to keep her guilty secret from everyone, even Nicolas himself, who'd broached the subject of his possible paternity when he'd returned briefly to Rocky Creek a decade ago to attend his mother's funeral.

Fate—and genetics—had helped her with her deception and denials. First, she'd carried her baby for ten months, something that happened occasionally on the maternal side of her family. Her great aunt had had a couple of ten-month pregnancies. On top of that, her daughter had been born with dark hair and eyes, the same as herself and Greg, not with Nicolas's fair colouring. Also, Felicity had been little more than a baby at the time of Mrs Dupre's death, so she hadn't started taking piano lessons. There was no evidence of her then having taken after Nicolas, nothing at all to make him suspicious. Even now, everyone in Rocky Creek thought Felicity had inherited her musical talent from her. Given that her relationship with Nicolas had broken up years before, this was only logical. Who would imagine that the very respectable Serina Harmon would have gone to Sydney and made mad passionate love with her ex-boyfriend a mere month before her wedding? It was unthinkable!

But then, Nicolas had always made her to do the unthinkable.

She would have done anything for him at one stage. Anything except abandon her family when they'd most needed her.

How could she have gone to England with him after her father's stroke? It had been impossible. Nicolas had been stunned when she'd refused, then furious. He'd claimed she didn't love him enough.

But she had. Too much. In a way, the power of her love for Nicolas had terrified the life out of her. She wasn't herself when she was with him. She became his slave, a nothing person with no will of her own. He only had to take her in his arms and she was reduced to being a robot, incapable of saying no to him.

Knowing this, she'd made her initial stand against him over the phone. Nicolas had just won a concerto competition in Sydney and the prize would take him to England to study and perform. He'd rung her immediately and insisted she accompany him, though there'd not been an offer of marriage, she'd noted. She'd be his travelling companion as well as his personal assistant—and, most of all, his extremely accommodating love slave.

'I can't go with you, Nicolas,' she'd choked out even as the tears had run down her cheeks. 'Not now. I have to stay in Rocky Creek and help run the family business. There's no one else, only me.' She'd had no brothers or sisters to help, having been an only child. And her mother had had to stay home and nurse her father.

Nicolas had raged at her for ages—raged and argued. But she'd stayed firm that time. Much easier with him so far away. When he'd threatened to return to Rocky Creek to persuade her, she'd claimed he would be wasting his time, adding the des-

perate lie that she was sick to death of their long-distance relationship anyway. In truth, since he'd gone to Sydney to study,
she only saw him on the odd weekend when he came home,
and during holidays. He sometimes didn't even come home for
those. More than once he'd gone away to a music camp.

'I want a normal boyfriend,' Serina had wailed. 'One who
isn't obsessed with music. And one who lives in Rocky Creek!
Greg Harmon's always asking me out,' she'd added quite
truthfully.

'Greg Harmon! He's old enough to be your father!'

'No, he's not.' Greg did look older than he was. But
actually he was only in his late twenties, a local fellow who
worked as a teacher in nearby Wauchope High School, where
both Serina and Nicolas had studied. Although she had never
actually been in any of Greg's classes—he taught agriculture
and woodwork—she'd always known he fancied her.

He'd started asking her out the moment she'd graduated
from school.

'He's a very nice man,' Serina had snapped defensively.
'And very good-looking. Next time he asks me out, I'm going
to say yes.'

It had almost been a relief when Nicolas had stormed off
to England by himself. But then she'd never heard from him
again: no letters or phone calls begging her forgiveness;
nothing but a bitter silence.

Serina had taken a long time to get over Nicolas. But, in
the end, sheer loneliness had forced her into saying yes to
Greg's persistent requests to take her out. In the back of her
mind, however, she'd always believed Nicolas would return
one day to claim her. So she didn't sleep with Greg at first,
or accept any of his regular proposals of marriage.

But as time went by and Nicolas didn't return to Rocky
Creek, Serina let Greg put an engagement ring on her finger.
And take her to bed, after which she'd cried and cried. Not

because it was awful. Greg turned out to be a tender and considerate lover. But because he wasn't Nicolas.

Still, in time, she managed to push Nicolas right to the back of her mind and began making concrete plans for her wedding to Greg. Although not ecstatically happy, Serina was reasonably content with her life. She was loved by her fiancé, family and friends, and respected in the community. She was also finding great satisfaction in expanding the family's lumber yard into a more extensive building supply business, local demand increasing as Rocky Creek gradually became a very desirable 'tree-change' destination for retirees and tired city dwellers.

If only she hadn't made that fateful trip to Sydney in search of the right wedding dress... If only she hadn't seen Nicolas's interview on television in her hotel room... If only she'd stayed away from his performance that night at the Opera House...

Serina glanced across the breakfast table at her daughter and wondered, not for the first time, if she'd done the right thing, passing Felicity off as Greg's daughter. It hadn't been a deliberate act on her part. By the time she'd realised she was pregnant, the wedding was upon her and she hadn't had the heart to hurt Greg as she knew the truth would have hurt him. And hurt everyone else: her parents, his parents, their friends.

Life in a small country town was not as simple as people sometimes thought.

No, I made the right decision, she accepted philosophically, *the only decision.*

Greg was a devoted husband and father and I had a good life with him, a nice, peaceful life. I still lead a nice, peaceful life.

But that peace was about to be broken. Big-time.

Fear clutched at her stomach. Fear of what might happen when she saw Nicolas again—this time without the moral protection of a husband in her life. She still hadn't forgotten how she'd felt when she'd seen him at his mother's funeral. That had been ten years ago, when she'd been twenty-seven and Nicolas an incredibly dashing thirty. Greg had insisted they both attend, Mrs Dupre having been a well-loved member in their small community. They'd taken Felicity with them. She'd been around two at the time. It was at the wake that Nicolas had cornered her, getting her alone after Greg had carried their daughter outside to play for a while.

Nicolas had been cold to her, as cold as ice.

She hadn't felt cold, however. Even whilst he'd questioned her about Felicity's birth date in the most chilling and contemptuous fashion, she'd burned with a desire that she'd found both disturbing and despicable. It still upset her to think of what might have happened if Nicolas had made any kind of pass at her.

Fortunately, he hadn't.

But who knew what he might do now that she was a widow. Had Felicity told him Greg was dead? It seemed likely that she had.

'Do you have a copy of the letter you sent Mr Dupre?' she asked her daughter somewhat stiffly.

Felicity looked pained. 'Oh, Mum, that's private!'

'I want to see it, Felicity. And the email he sent back to you.'

Felicity pouted and stayed right where she was.

Serina rose from her chair, her expression uncompromising. 'Let's go, madam.'

Serina found her daughter's letter very touching, till she got to the part where Felicity offered Nicolas accommodation at their house.

'He can't stay here!' she blurted out before she could get control of herself.

'Why not?' Felicity demanded to know with the indignation—and innocence—of youth.

'Because.'

'Because why?' her daughter persisted.

'Because you don't ask virtual strangers to stay in your home,' she answered in desperation.

'But he's not a stranger. He lived here in Rocky Creek for years and years. Mrs Johnson said you were very good friends. She said you dated for a while.'

'Only very casually,' Serina lied. 'And, as I said, that was nearly twenty years ago. I have no idea what kind of man Nicolas Dupre might have become in the meantime. For all I know he could be a drunk, or a drug addict!'

Felicity looked at her as though she were insane. 'Mum, I think you've totally lost it. But you don't have to worry. Mr Dupre refused my offer to stay with us. Here! Why don't you read his email and then you won't say such silly things.'

Felicity did a couple of clicks with her mouse and brought up the email from Nicolas. Serina read it.

Dear Felicity
Thank you for your lovely letter. I was saddened to hear of the tragic death of your father and send my deepest condolences to you and your mother. I have fond memories of Rocky Creek and would be glad to help you with your fund-raising project. You sound like a very intelligent and enterprising young lady of whom I'm sure your mother is very proud. Consequently, I would be honoured to be the judge for your talent quest.
Unfortunately, I have business engagements in New York and London for the next fortnight and cannot arrive in Sydney till the day before your concert. Thank you for your kind offer of a room but I would prefer to arrange my own accommodation in Port Macquarie. I will contact you by phone as soon as I arrive there, at which time you can explain where and when you want me to be the following day. Please confirm this arrangement by return email and include your home phone number.

My regards to your mother and Mrs Johnson. I am
looking forward to meeting up with them both once again.
All the best, Nicolas Dupre.

Serina didn't know what to say. The email was extremely
polite. Too polite, in fact, and a bit pompous. It didn't sound
at all like Nicolas.

Maybe what she'd said to Felicity was right in a way. She
didn't know him anymore. The passing years might have
changed him from the impassioned and rather angry young
man he'd once been into something entirely different.
Someone calm and mature and yes…kind. Maybe he was
coming all this way out of kindness. Maybe it had nothing to
do with her being a widow now, nothing to do with her at all!
Nicolas was just responding to the heartfelt request of a young
girl whose father had been tragically killed.

Serina tried to embrace this possibility but she simply
couldn't. She knew, in her heart of hearts, that his coming
back to Rocky Creek had nothing to do with kindness. It was
all about her.

Not that she believed Nicolas was still in love with her.
He'd made his contempt quite clear at his mother's funeral.
But maybe he'd spotted the hunger in her eyes. Maybe his
plan was to take full advantage of that hunger, to do to her
what she'd once done to him: indulge in a wild one-night
stand, then dump her in the morning.

A shiver ran down Serina's spine, a highly disturbing,
cruelly seductive shiver.

Please, don't let that be his plan. Let him be coming back
for something else. To visit his mother's grave perhaps. Don't
let me be his underlying motive, or his prey. Don't let him be
looking for sexual revenge. Because this time, I have nowhere
to run to, and no one to hide behind…

CHAPTER THREE

NICOLAS could have hired a car in Sydney and driven to Port Macquarie. But that was a five- to six-hour drive, maybe longer, given that his early morning arrival at Mascot would mean he would hit peak hour traffic going through the city. He'd done just that when he'd returned to Rocky Creek for his mother's funeral and regretted it. He'd regretted also hiring a stupid sports car, which hadn't coped too well with the not-so-wonderful roads up that way.

This time, he booked a connecting flight to Port Macquarie that left Sydney at 8:00 am and only took fifty-five minutes. Once there, he planned to take a taxi to his accommodation where the four-wheel-drive vehicle he'd already hired would be waiting for him. He hadn't wanted the bother of picking it up at the airport. Experience had taught him that doing so could be a very time-consuming operation. Having made the decision to come, Nicolas knew that he couldn't bear the thought of anything delaying his arrival in Rocky Creek. The weariness he'd been feeling the night Felicity's letter had arrived was long gone, replaced by the kind of excitement he used to feel just before going on the stage to perform.

Everything went according to plan. The flight from London set down at Mascot only a few minutes late and the connecting flight to Port Macquarie left right on time. Nicolas stepped out onto the tarmac at Port Macquarie airport right on nine. Fifteen minutes later, he and his luggage were speeding towards the centre of town.

'Port's grown since I was last here,' he remarked as he glanced around. 'But it has been nearly twenty years.'

'Crikey, mate,' the taxi driver replied. 'You'll be lucky to recognise anything.'

Not true, however. The town centre hadn't changed all that much, Nicolas thought as they drove down the main street. The rectangular layout was basically the same, the streets straight and wide, with parking at the curb sides and in the middle. The old picture theatre was still there on the corner and the pub across the road. But the evidence of a tourism explosion was everywhere, with all the high-rise apartment buildings and the upsurge in restaurants and cafés.

And of course, the tourists themselves were there in full force. Summer had arrived in Australia and with it the hot weather that sent people flocking to seaside towns. Nicolas was already feeling a little sticky. He'd be glad to have a shower and change into something cooler than the suit, shirt and tie he was currently wearing.

The taxi turned right at the end of the main street and headed up the hill to where Nicolas's choice of accommodation was located, a relatively new boutique apartment block that was several storeys high and made the most of its position overlooking Town Beach. Nicolas had found it on one of the many travel Web sites available and booked one of the apartments from his home in London a couple of nights back.

Although book-in time was officially not till 2:00 pm, Nicolas was soon given his keys. The apartment he'd chosen had not been occupied the previous night. Not surprising, given the hefty price tag and the fact that last night was a Thursday. Added to this was the fact that he'd taken it for a full week.

Nicolas was suitably impressed when he let himself in and walked around, inspecting what his two grand had bought him. There was a spacious living room that combined the sitting and dining areas and opened out onto an equally large, sea-facing balcony, with a barbeque, outdoor furniture and a hot tub. The bedroom was five-star, the bed king-sized, as was the plasma television screen built into the wall opposite the foot of the bed. The en suite bathroom was total luxury with gold taps, crystal light fittings and a spa bath fit for two. The kitchen was superbly appointed with black granite countertops and stainless steel appliances.

Nicolas noted the complimentary bottles of wine in the fridge. Not just champagne, but Chardonnay and Chablis. There were also a couple of bottles of fine Hunter Valley reds resting in the stainless steel wine rack. A bowl of fresh fruit sat on the coffee table and a box of chocolates, too.

Serina had a sweet tooth, he recalled.

Serina…

How would she react to him this time? he wondered as he unzipped the first of his two cases and began to unpack.

She'd been extremely tense when he'd confronted her after his mother's funeral. Fearful, he suspected, that he might say something to her husband. No doubt she'd never confessed to Greg that she'd slept with him not long before their wedding.

His own mood had been vicious. Grief combined with jealousy had not made him ready to be kind, or forgiving. He'd questioned Serina mercilessly about her daughter's parentage, even though his eyes had already told him that the pretty little dark-haired, dark-eyed child wasn't his.

And all the time they were talking together, he'd been fiercely erect. Wanting her. Loving her. Hating her.

She'd looked even more beautiful than he remembered. Black became her. There again, just about any colour suited

Serina, with her dark hair and eyes, and lovely olive skin. Having a child had enhanced rather than spoilt her figure. Her curves were the curves of a woman in her prime. She'd looked luscious, and as sexy as ever.

It had killed him to watch her leave the wake with another man, to see the proprietorial way Greg had taken her arm and led her away.

Nicolas hadn't slept a wink that night. He'd tossed and turned, picturing Serina in her marital bed, in her husband's arms, under her husband's body.

The next morning, a grim-faced Nicolas had given instructions to his mother's solicitor to dispose of the house and all its contents, and forward the proceeds to his bank in London. By noon he'd left Rocky Creek, vowing never to return.

Yet here he was, doing just that.

Of course, he'd never imagined that the extremely healthy-looking Greg Harmon would die so young. Or that Serina's daughter would write to him and practically beg him to come back to Rocky Creek.

Nicolas wondered what Serina felt about Felicity doing that? Would she have been annoyed? Angry? It had been rather bold of the girl to write to him like that. He suspected it had been done without her mother's permission.

The fact there'd been no email from Serina herself had been telling, he thought. The principal of Rocky Creek Primary school had emailed him, checking that his offer was for real, but nothing, however, from Felicity's mother.

Perhaps her silence meant indifference. But he doubted it.

Serina could never be indifferent to him, just as he could never be indifferent to her.

As Nicolas carried his toilet bag into the bathroom, he made another vow. He wasn't going to leave Australia this time till he knew for certain how Serina felt about him and how he felt about her. He was not going to live the rest of his life pining for what might have been, or what might be in the future.

He'd booked this apartment for a full week. Long enough, he imagined, to have all his questions answered…

CHAPTER FOUR

SERINA found it impossible to concentrate at work that Friday morning. All she could think about was the fact that Nicolas was on his way here right at this moment; that soon, he would reach Port Macquarie and call, not Felicity or Fred Tarleton, Felicity's school's principal, but her own sorry self.

Felicity, the precocious child, had informed her of these new arrangements late last night, explaining that she'd given Nicolas her mobile number to contact when he arrived at Port Macquarie, as everyone at the school would be tied up all day, getting the school hall ready for the concert the following evening. Everything had to be perfect for their famous visiting judge.

There had been no use protesting. Felicity was as stubborn as a mule. And Nicolas, it seemed, was uncontactable at that hour, having already boarded his plane in London for the flight to Sydney. It hadn't occurred to Serina till she'd arrived at work this morning that he probably had one of those fan-dangled new phones that received emails, even on planes. Serina had never been overly keen on technology and whilst she used a computer at work and carried a basic mobile phone with her, she didn't have a PC of her own at home and wasn't at all enamoured with the Internet.

Felicity, however, like most modern children, was a real computer buff and could make her way around the worldwide web with ridiculous ease. Over the past fortnight she'd regaled Serina with scads of information about Nicolas that she'd found on the Internet, from his earliest concert playing days right up to the successes he'd had as a theatrical entrepreneur, including that of his latest musical protégée, a young Japanese violinist called Junko Hoshino who was as beautiful as she was talented. Several gossip columnists had them being an item already. It seemed Nicolas had somewhat of a reputation as a ladies' man, a fact that didn't surprise.

Serina already knew quite a bit about Nicolas's life over the past decade. There'd been a segment on *60 Minutes* a couple of years ago back that was like a mini *This is Your Life*, highlighting the accident that had ended his piano playing career, then praising him for the way he'd put such a tragedy behind him and forged a new career in show business.

It had made difficult viewing with Greg by her side on the lounge. She'd wanted to tape the segment and watch it over and over—watch him over and over—but hadn't dared. Greg knew she'd once dated Nicolas, though she'd always down-played their relationship, claiming she hadn't been unhappy when he left Australia to pursue his career. Later that night, when Greg had wanted sex, however, she'd turned him down, because she knew she simply could not bear to make love with her husband with the memory of Nicolas so fresh in her mind.

He was very fresh in her mind again today, not just because he was on his way to Rocky Creek but because of what she'd watched on Felicity's computer last night. That incorrigible child had found an old video of him on a social networking site showing him playing one of Chopin's polonaises at the Royal Albert Hall.

'You have to come and look at this, Mum,' she'd insisted.

Serina had, very reluctantly at first. But then with total con-centration on the screen.

No one, in Serina's opinion, played the piano quite like

Nicolas. She had no doubt that lots of concert pianists—past and present—were more technically brilliant. But none possessed his passion, his panache, or his blatant sex appeal.

Women had swooned over him when he played. She certainly had that fateful night. His performance—even on this grainy video—sent sexual shivers running down her spine.

'Wasn't he an incredible pianist, Mum?' Felicity had raved.

'Yes,' Serina had agreed huskily, her tongue thick in her throat.

'And to think he can't play anymore! I cried when I read about his hands being burned like that. But it was very brave of him to do what he did, wasn't it?'

'Yes,' Serina had agreed again, this time in a more composed voice. 'Very brave.'

Which it had been. Apparently, he'd been walking along a street in central London very late one night—not long after his mother died—when a passing car had careered out of control on a corner, hit a brick wall and burst into flames. The driver—a woman—had been knocked unconscious. Nicolas had raced over and dragged her out. He'd just pulled her clear when he'd heard the baby crying. It had taken him some considerable time to undo the seat belt and extricate the baby from its capsule in the backseat, during which time his hands had been burned, his left hand so badly that his left thumb had had to eventually be amputated.

Serina had cried, too, when she'd first heard about Nicolas's burnt hand. It had been widely covered in the news at the time. Greg had found her weeping over it in her bedroom, but thought she was crying over her inability to conceive another child. She'd let him think that. For how could she explain her distress over Nicolas's accident?

She'd felt guilty, though. She'd felt guilty a lot during her marriage. That was the one thing that Greg's death had released her from. Feeling guilty.

There was no guilt in Serina today. The guilt had been replaced by the most excruciating nervous tension.

Her eyes kept going to the clock on the wall. Only ten-fifteen. If he was driving, Nicolas couldn't possibly be in Port yet. His plane didn't touch down in Mascot till six-thirty this morning. By the time he got through customs and rented a car he would have hit peak hour traffic in Sydney. It would take him till well after nine to get out of the city and onto the freeway. Once you included a couple of stops for food and nature calling, plus all the delays caused by the road works around Bulahdelah and Taree, his estimated time of arrival would be around three or four this afternoon.

But, of course, he might not be driving up. He might have taken a connecting flight. She herself had never flown anywhere from Port. When she went to Sydney by herself that one time, she'd taken the train from Wauchope. Then, after her marriage to Greg, on the few occasions they'd gone to Sydney, they'd driven down. But she knew there was a flight from Sydney that got in around ten. If it was on time, it would take Nicolas about half an hour to collect his luggage and get to wherever he was staying in Port. Which meant she could expect a call anytime now.

Serina had just finished this mental calculation when her phone rang. Not her work phone but her mobile.

'That'll be him!' Allie called out from the reception desk.

'If it is then he couldn't have driven,' Serina said.

'Of course not!' Emma said impatiently from her nearby desk. 'A man like that. He wouldn't drive all this way when he could fly.'

Both the girls who worked with Serina in the office knew everything about Nicolas's visit—and the man himself—courtesy of Felicity dropping by every second morning to give them an update, including this morning. Fortunately, neither of the girls were old enough to have been at high school with either Serina or Nicolas, so they believed everything Serina told them about her relationship with the famous entrepreneur.

Nonetheless, being typical females, they were quick to suggest that her 'just good friends' status with the famous Nicolas Dupre might develop into something more once he got to see her again. Both Allie and Emma were openly admiring of their boss's looks and style, and had recently begun to try to matchmake her with every single man in Rocky Creek. Unfortunately—or perhaps fortunately—there weren't too many local men around Serina's age who weren't already married, or Mumma's boys, or simply too unattractive for words.

In truth, Serina had no interest in getting married again. Or even in dating.

But Allie and Emma didn't believe her.

'For pity's sake, Serina,' Allie snapped. 'Will you stop staring at that darned phone and just answer it!'

Serina winced as she swept up her phone from where it was vibrating all over her desktop.

'Hello?' she croaked out.

'Serina? Is that you?'

It was Nicolas. His voice was extremely memorable, being rich and deep and as smooth as melted chocolate.

Serina cleared the lump in her throat. 'Yes, yes, it's me, Nicolas,' she went on, hopefully sounding more like the calm, confident woman she usually was around the office. 'So where are you?'

'In Port Macquarie.'

'Oh. You flew, then. So where are you staying?'

'The Blue Horizon Apartments.'

The newest and most luxurious in Port. Trust Nicolas to choose the best. That segment she'd seen on TV had been filmed in his New York apartment, which was like a show home and probably worth millions.

'Did you have a good flight from London?' she said, well aware of Allie and Emma listening in.

'Great. I slept all the way.'

Which was more than could be said for herself last night.

'I always take a sleeping tablet on overnight flights,' he added. 'And I travel first class, which helps.'

'I'm sure it does.'

Serina grimaced. Did that sound waspish? She hoped it didn't, because that betrayed emotion and she was determined to remain cool around Nicolas. On the surface, anyway. She'd vowed during the long hours she'd lain awake last night that she was not going to let him get to her in any way.

But that was last night and this was now. Serina had an awful feeling that any vows she'd made where Nicolas was concerned would not stand up once they were face-to-face. Bad enough just talking to him. Her heartbeat had already doubled and her hand—the one clutching the phone—felt decidedly clammy.

Of course it was hot today. The forecast was for thirty-six degrees. But their office was air-conditioned. There was no reason for her to have sweaty palms.

'Have you hired yourself a car?' she inquired. *Please don't let him say that he hasn't.* The last thing she wanted was to have to chauffeur Nicolas around.

'Of course,' he said rather drily. 'But I learned my lesson from last time and rented an SUV.'

'What do you mean, last time?'

'When I came home for Mum's funeral I hired a sports car.'

'Oh, yes, I remember,' she said. All the girls in town—and the boys—had practically salivated over the yellow sporty number parked outside the church that day. Greg had made some caustic remark. Serina had done the wise thing and ignored it.

'I presume the potholes on Rocky Creek Road are still as bad as ever,' Nicolas said.

'I'm afraid so,' she replied.

'Port's changed a lot.'

'Well, it has been a long time, Nicolas. Everything changes with time.'

'Some things not for the better,' he said rather brusquely. 'Now, as soon as I shower and change, I'll drive out to Rocky Creek and you can show me when and where I have to go tomorrow. Then I thought I'd take you to lunch.'

'Lunch?' she practically squawked before she could think better of it. A nervous glance over at Allie and Emma showed them both nodding vigorously. To refuse would have seemed not only inhospitable, but also worthy of suspicion.

'Is there some reason why you can't do that?' he was already saying.

'Well I…I'm at work at the moment,' she hedged.

'Ah, still the demands of the family business. But surely you're the boss by now. Or did your father eventually recover from his stroke?'

Serina swallowed. 'No, no, Dad never recovered. He… um…passed away a couple of years back. Another stroke.'

'I'm so sorry, Serina,' he said softly. 'I know how much you loved him. How's your mum coping?'

Serina blinked at this surprising sensitivity from Nicolas. So different from the last time they'd spoken. At his own mother's wake, he'd been full of bitterness and anger. There'd not been one shred of understanding, or forgiveness. Maybe she was wrong about why he'd come back. Maybe he had grown mellow with age. Maybe he was well and truly over what she'd done to him all those years ago.

She hoped so. She really did.

'I think Mum was almost relieved when Dad died,' she told him. 'His quality of life was never good. He couldn't speak, you know, or walk. Therapy didn't work. The damage to his brain was too great.'

'I didn't realise that.'

Well, of course not. He'd never asked. And she'd never told him. Not that she'd had much opportunity after his stormy departure for England. There'd been no contact between them after that till the night Felicity was conceived, where their brief reunion had not exactly been filled with conversation.

Oh, why did I have to start thinking about that night?

Serina's head began to whirl. What had he just asked her? Something about her mother. Oh, yes…

'Mum's fine,' she said. 'She sold the old farm and moved into a villa in a new retirement village closer to town. She's even started working here again at the weekends, which is very good. It gives me more time to spend with Felicity.' She didn't add that all this had come about after Greg's death, when Serina hadn't felt capable of going to work for a while.

She had loved her husband. Maybe not with the type of grand passion she'd once felt for Nicolas, but it had been a very true affection.

Nevertheless, she had to confess that once she got over her initial shock and grief, Serina had experienced a strange measure of relief, the same kind of relief, no doubt, that she was sure her mother had felt after her husband had died. Her mother had become very depressed over the years, looking after her husband's needs and having little pleasure in her own life. Serina's life with Greg hadn't been as bad as that. But there was no denying her marriage had not been entirely happy. There'd been too much guilt in Serina's heart. And one very big secret, which sometimes weighed heavily on her conscience.

Now that she was widow, Serina had imagined that that secret was safe.

Till this moment…

What would Nicolas think, she suddenly worried, when he watched Felicity play the piano? And he would tomorrow night, when she performed in the talent quest. Thankfully, Felicity still looked nothing like her real father. But she had developed certain physical mannerisms when she played. Mannerisms that were horribly familiar. The flamboyant way she attacked the keys; the flourish with which she lifted her hands once she'd finished a piece; the way she tossed her hair…

It was a worry, all right.

Just when she was beginning to feel slightly more relaxed over Nicolas's motives in coming home.

'Could your mum pop in to work now, do you think?' Nicolas asked. 'Give you some time off?'

'Oh…er…no, she can't. She had to take Mrs Johnson down to Newcastle. To the John Hunter Hospital to see a heart specialist.'

'Mrs Johnson's not well?'

'Generally speaking she's very well. But she's an old lady, Nicolas. When she had a bit of a turn a few weeks back, Mum decided she should have a few tests. After what happened to Dad, she's become a strong believer in prevention being better than cure. But she won't be back till late today.'

'I see. So you're stuck at work for the rest of the day.'

'No, no, I can get away for a while,' she said when Allie and Emma started making exasperated noises. 'I have very good help here in the office. And business is rather slow at this time of the year. Not much building going on this close to Christmas.'

'That's great. I'll see you in about an hour then.'

'Fine. You know where to go?'

'I presume the lumber yard's in the same place it's always been. On the left, just past the garage at the far end of the main street.'

'Yes, that's right.' Serina could not help a wry smile pulling at her mouth. In the ten years since Nicolas's last visit to Rocky Creek, the town—plus her family's business—had changed almost as much as Port had. She would rather enjoy seeing the shock in Nicolas's eyes when he saw the changes for himself.

'You've changed, too,' she murmured not quite so happily as she inspected herself in the powder room mirror a few minutes later.

On the surface she was still an attractive woman. She hadn't put on any weight over the years. And her hair hadn't yet started turning grey. But her skin no longer held the bloom of youth. She had some lines at the corners of her eyes. And now that she looked closely, there was definitely some slackness around her jaw line.

Serina put her palms on her cheeks and her thumbs on her neck and pulled upwards, tightening her skin. That was what successful New York women did when their faces began to sag. They had facelifts and injections.

Serina dropped her hands away from her face with an exasperated sigh. She was being silly. And vain. All because of Nicolas.

Normally, she didn't wear much makeup to work, just a touch of mascara and lipstick. This morning, however, she'd surrendered to temptation and used a little foundation and some eyeliner. She'd also worn a new outfit, bought at one of the boutiques in Port Macquarie the previous weekend, one of two outfits purchased with Nicolas's visit in mind.

Feminine pride had demanded she look her best and not like some country bumpkin.

Serina's hand trembled as she went to retouch her lipstick, her fingers freezing when her eyes met her own in the mirror.

They were bright. Too bright.

'Oh, Serina, Serina, be careful,' she whispered.

She'd claimed to Nicolas that time changed everything. But

nothing had changed for her where he was concerned. She still wanted him. She would always want him.

But she would not let him know that. She could not let him know that. For if she did, who knew what might happen…

CHAPTER FIVE

NICOLAS'S mind wasn't on his surroundings as he set out for the half-hour drive to Rocky Creek. It wasn't as though he didn't know the way. There was only the one road which connected Port Macquarie to Wauchope: the Oxley Highway. His thoughts were on Serina's attitude on the phone.

She hadn't seemed too upset by his return, though clearly she hadn't wanted to be personally involved with it. She'd sounded rather reluctant to go to lunch with him today. But she couldn't really say no, not without being rude.

Her daughter would not have been pleased with her mother if she'd been less than hospitable, something Nicolas was well aware of when he'd rung.

Nicolas smiled when he thought of the emails he'd exchanged with Felicity. What a delightful and intelligent child she was. But very strong-willed, if he was any judge. A handful for a widowed mother. What Felicity wanted, Felicity would contrive to get.

Nicolas knew first-hand about wilful children: he'd been one.

His own mother, who'd been a widow of sorts, had given up with him entirely by the time he was thirteen. After which he'd run his own race, on the whole, very successfully.

Only with Serina had he failed. Twice he'd let her get away. The first time through fate. Her father's stroke had made it very difficult for her to leave Australia with him. He had eventually understood that, as he'd understood how loneliness might have forced her into the arms of someone else. He hadn't exactly lived a celibate life over the years himself.

The second time he'd let her get away, Nicolas had blamed himself entirely. He should have gone after her, regardless of what she'd said in that note. He should have rocketed back to Rocky Creek, made a scene and demanded she marry him instead. He should have left no stone unturned in trying to win back the woman he loved.

Because, of course, he'd still loved her back then.

It seemed totally illogical that he still wanted her today.

But he did, heaven help him.

'And you're not going to let her get away this time, Nick, my boy,' he muttered determinedly.

Nicolas suspected, however, that Serina wasn't about to fall into his arms the way she had that night in Sydney. Thirteen years had gone by since then, thirteen long years, and ten since they'd last met. Though one could hardly count that occasion, with her husband hovering in the background.

But there was no husband now. No one to plague Nicolas's conscience if he was reduced to using sex to win her, which he might have to.

The Serina he'd spoken to just now was a lot more self-assured than the teenage Serina who'd willingly gone along with his plans.

But she was still his Serina. She might not think that there was anything left between them but she was wrong. The girl who'd never said no to him—at least where sex was concerned—was about to be awakened once more.

Nicolas's flesh stirred as he recalled the things they'd done together. In the beginning, their lovemaking had been extremely basic. But with time and practice they'd gradually known no bounds. Sometimes when he'd come home from

Sydney for the weekend and Serina's parents had been out playing golf, they'd spent the whole afternoon making love all over her place…though never in her parents' room.

Nowhere else, however, was deemed sacrosanct from their increasingly erotic activities: the guest bedroom where there was a brass bed; the large squashy sofa; the rug in front of the fireplace; the coffee table…

And she'd been with him all the way.

It had been amazing—and highly addictive.

Which was why she'd come to him that night less than a month before her marriage. Because she hadn't been able to forget how it had been between them. Because she'd missed the way he'd been able to make her lose herself whilst making love.

She'd called it self-destructive, what they'd shared.

Maybe it had been. Because he'd never been totally happy with any other woman. Now that he thought about it, Nicolas suspected Serina hadn't been happy with her husband, either. The day of his mother's funeral, Serina's tension had been more than fear that she might expose what she'd done to her husband because that old chemistry had been there simmering between them.

That was what he wanted to believe, anyway. And until he had proof otherwise, Nicolas was going to believe it.

Damn it all, he had an erection now. He really had to stop thinking about sex with Serina, or things might become embarrassing.

The temperature outside was hovering around thirty degrees already. He'd boarded the plane in chilly London wearing a suit, cashmere topcoat and scarf. In Sydney, however, he'd had to start taking things off, after having to board the connecting domestic flight by exiting the air-conditioned terminal and walking across a short space of much warmer tarmac. It had been even hotter by the time he'd landed at Port Macquarie, with the clear blue sky promising an even higher temperature later in the day. Which was why he'd changed into light trousers and an open-necked shirt rolled up to the elbows.

When he'd first climbed into the rented four-wheel drive for the trip to Rocky Creek, Nicolas had felt both refreshed and relatively relaxed.

Not so anymore.

Grimacing at his discomfort, he bent forward to turn up the air-conditioning to the max. Some very cold air blasted forth and it helped clear his mind from thoughts of Serina so he could concentrate on where he was going.

Wauchope loomed up ahead, the town closest to Rocky Creek, where Nicolas had attended high school and where most of the people in Rocky Creek came to shop. He glanced around left and right, not noticing the kind of major changes he'd seen in Port. The railway crossing was still the same, as was the main street. It wasn't till he was heading out of town along the highway that he could see that the houses went farther out than they had before. There was also a big new shopping centre opposite the Timber Town tourist park.

Wauchope's prosperity had once relied solely on the timber from the surrounding forests. The trees would be cut down and the logs brought out of the hills by bullock trains, then floated down the Hastings River to Port Macquarie. Not so anymore. But you could still see demonstrations of the old ways at Timber Town, as well as buy all kinds of wood products.

Nicolas was thinking about the wooden bowl he'd once bought his mother for her birthday when he drove right past the turn off to Rocky Creek. Swearing, he pulled over to the side of the road, having to wait for several cars to go by before he could execute a U-turn. Finally, he was back at the T-intersection and heading for home.

No, not home, he amended in his mind. Rocky Creek had never been his home.

Nicolas had been born and bred in Sydney, the offspring of a brief affair between his forty-year-old mother—who'd been working as wardrobe mistress for the Sydney Opera Company at that time—and a visiting Swedish conductor who'd had a wife and family back home and a roving eye whenever he was on tour.

The conductor's eyes had landed on Madeline Dupre, who'd still been an attractive-looking woman at forty. Her lack of success so far in relationships, however, had left her somewhat embittered about the male sex, giving her a brusque manner that men had found off-putting. She'd been rather taken aback, but secretly elated, by the conductor's interest in her and had happily comforted him in bed during his stay in Sydney, deliberately deceiving him about being on the pill. She'd waved him off a few weeks later at the airport, well satisfied with her rather impulsive but successful plan to have a child by a man who would be conveniently absent from her life, but who was both handsome and intelligent. She hadn't realised at the time that raising a child by herself—especially one like Nicolas—would be so difficult.

After quitting her job during her pregnancy, she'd set about earning her living as a dressmaker. That way she could be home to look after her son. She'd already had the foresight five years earlier to get into the property market, purchasing a small though rather run-down terraced house in the inner-city suburb of Surry Hills. The deposit had taken her life savings and there was a twenty-five-year mortgage, but it had given her a sense of security. She'd patted herself on the back now that she was having a baby.

Sydney, however, was a harsh city for a woman alone. Madeline's parents had passed away—longevity did not run in her family—and her only brother had moved to western Australia to find work and had not exactly been a good communicator. All her friends had drifted away when she stopped being part of their working and social life, leaving her increasingly lonely. All she'd had in the world was her son, who'd proved to be more than she'd bargained for.

When Nicolas had been eleven—and becoming more difficult to control with each passing day—she'd made a dress for a regular client's sister who was visiting from a small town on the north coast called Rocky Creek.

'If there was a dressmaker of your skills in my home town,' the woman had gushed, 'she'd never be out of work.'

Madeline had often thought about living in the country, but just hadn't found the courage to make such a big change. She herself had been born in Sydney and had known nothing else but city life. But the problems she was encountering with Nicolas—he was getting in with a gang of boys who roamed the streets at night—forced her to look seriously at getting him away from the bad influences in the less than salubrious suburb where they lived.

Assured that she'd be able to buy a house in Rocky Creek for half of what her Surry Hills place was worth, Madeline made the massive decision to up stakes and move from Sydney to the country.

Nicolas had been furious with her. He was a city boy through and through. He didn't want to live out in the sticks. He didn't want to go to a school that had less than sixty children. He complained—and played up—at considerable length.

Till Mrs Johnson—and the piano—came into his life.

Despite being known as Mrs Johnson, the piano teacher was actually a childless spinster who lived in the house next door to the small cottage in Rocky Creek that his mother had bought. She gave private piano lessons for a living and had reputedly once been a not so very famous concert pianist. As fate would have it, her music room was just over the fence from Nicolas's bedroom. He could not help hearing the music. For ages, Nicolas had not understood why he liked it so much. Up till then his musical taste had stopped at rock and heavy metal. One day—he'd just turned twelve—he hadn't been able to resist the pull of the music any longer, so he'd asked his mother if he could have piano lessons.

Despite not having any spare money for music lessons— or a piano—a delighted Madeline Dupre had quickly come to an agreement with Mrs Johnson, who would teach Nicolas for nothing if Madeline made her a dress whenever she needed one. As for a piano, Mrs Johnson had also agreed that Nicolas could practise on hers whenever it was free. Once she'd realised she had a prodigy on her hands, the ecstatic teacher had even gave him a front door key so that he could let himself in when she was out playing bridge.

Soon Nicolas was practising every chance he got. He'd rarely done any of his homework but he'd excelled at the piano. At the age of fifteen he'd passed seventh grade with honours. By seventeen he'd received his Licentiate Diploma of Music, the highest musical exam one could take in Australia. During his last year in high school he'd sat for—and won—a scholarship to the Sydney Conservatorium of Music.

Mrs Johnson had been extremely proud of him, as had been his mother. But no one else in Rocky Creek had cared all that much. Why? Because he was an outsider. He'd always been an outsider, not a true local. At school, he'd never joined in, or played sports, made friends, had a girlfriend. All he'd cared about was playing the piano.

Serina was the only girl he'd ever bothered to speak to.

Serina again…

Nicolas scooped in a deep breath, then let it out very slowly. It was a toss-up, he decided, who had seduced whom that first night. Serina had confessed to him once that she'd had a wild crush on him since their paths had crossed when he was twelve and she was only nine. She'd told him she used to organise her own music lessons so that they came after his.

She would arrive early and sit in Mrs Johnson's lounge room and listen to him play. He'd hardly noticed her back then. Gradually, however, they had exchanged a few words and in the end he'd quite looked forward to their conversations. Once, Mrs Johnson had taught them a duet, which they'd performed at the Rocky Creek annual fete to much applause.

Though not as good as he was, Serina had been an accomplished pianist. It did not surprise him that her daughter was taking piano lessons now. What did surprise him was that Mrs Johnson was her teacher. She'd have to be about a hundred years old by now.

Well, at least over eighty. She must have been about sixty twenty-five years ago. Or so Nicolas had thought at the time. Still, when you're young, anyone over forty seems old.

Now he was almost forty himself. The years were flying by. And so was this rotten damned road.

Hitting a pothole reminded him to slow down and to put his mind on his driving. He slowed down even further to negotiate a series of hairpin bends, which he knew would take him down into the valley and Rocky Creek.

It had always been a pretty little town, he'd give it that, and quite conveniently located, being only ten minutes from the train line at Wauchope and half an hour from Port Macquarie, with its beaches and airport. But it was too small for his liking. Too small in size and in thinking. Everyone knew everything about everyone in Rocky Creek. He hated that. He loved the privacy—even the anonymity—that cities like London and New York could provide. Not to mention the wide range of entertainment. He could not imagine ever living anywhere else.

So what are you doing here, Nicolas? came the sudden thought.

Serina's not still in love with you and she's never going to come with you. Not ever. You know that. She is a local and so is her daughter.

You're wasting your time.

It was a bitter pill to swallow, the truth. But swallow it, Nicolas did. He also faced another truth, the real reason why he'd come, why he'd rented that luxury apartment. Why he'd contrived to be alone with her today.

Because he just had to be with Serina one more time.

Nicolas glanced at his scarred and thumbless left hand and remembered how it had been for him, accepting that he would never play the piano again. For a while he'd been in total despair. But in the end he'd had to accept it, because he couldn't change that. He couldn't grow another thumb.

But he could be with Serina again. Maybe only for a few hours, but it was possible. And whilst it was possible, nothing short of death was going to stop him from achieving that end.

The road swung round one last bend before straightening and heading down a more gentle incline. The thick bush on either side thinned out a little and Nicolas caught a glimpse of house after house between the tall trees.

Nicolas's eyebrows arched. They certainly hadn't been there ten years ago. His surprise increased as he drove slowly over the wooden bridge that forded the creek and led straight into the main street of Rocky Creek. Now his eyes widened as he noted the massive number of shop fronts. There was a tea house he'd never seen before, an antique shop and a very swish-looking beauty salon. There was another new café, with alfresco tables and chairs on the foot path. Even the old general store—which had been built in 1880—had been modernised with a separate fruit-and-vegetable shop next door to it.

The butcher was basically the same, as was the bakery.

But everything looked brighter and more prosperous.

The old garage at the end of the main street had received a facelift as well. But none of those things prepared him for the changes to Ted Brown's Lumber Yard.

Firstly, it wasn't called that anymore. The new sign facing

the road shouted Brown's Landscaping and Building Supplies
in bold red letters. The old shed, which had once housed a
ramshackle office, had been replaced by a smart cream brick
building. To the right of this building sat huge piles of sand,
gravel, coloured stones and mulches of various kinds. To the
left was a large array of brick, tiles and paving samples to
choose from. In front was a tarred car park, the parking spaces
neatly marked out with lines, a far cry from what had once
been a dirt paddock with a rutted driveway that turned to mud
in the wet weather. Visible over the roof of the cream building
stood the timber supply section, which had to be double the
height and size that it used to be.

Nicolas smiled a wry smile as he angled his vehicle into
one of the parking spaces. Serina could have warned him. But
he supposed seeing the changes for himself was worth a
thousand words.

A sudden and not very nice thought popped into his head.

Maybe Rocky Creek wasn't the only thing that had made
massive physical changes during the past ten years. Maybe
the Serina he remembered had changed, too. Maybe she'd put
on weight. Maybe she'd cut her lovely hair short and started
wearing polyester tracksuits.

'Surely not,' he muttered as he switched off the engine and
extracted the key. It wasn't in her nature to let herself go. She
was a perfectionist, like him. He only had to see what she'd
done with the family business to know that she'd become a
right little powerhouse in her own way. A woman like that
would still look after her appearance.

Feeling relieved, Nicolas pushed open the driver's door,
only to be met by a great whoosh of warm air.

It's hot, he thought as he climbed down from behind the
wheel. Swelteringly, blisteringly hot.

Admittedly, his blood was thick because he'd been living
in the northern winter. But still…how had he stood it here

every summer? None of the houses or shops in Rocky Creek had had air-conditioning back then.

Nicolas shook his head and moved quickly over to the cream brick building, grateful to see two cooling units sitting by the side wall.

The girl behind the rather high and very long reception desk looked up as he entered the chilled space, her plump, plain face lighting up into a welcoming smile.

'You must be Mr Dupre,' she said chirpily.

'I am,' he agreed.

'I'm Allie. He's here, Serina,' she called out over her shoulder into the open-plan office.

Nicolas stepped closer to the chest-high counter and followed the direction of Allie's eyes.

And there she was.

His Serina, sitting behind a wide, wooden, sun-drenched desk.

His heart virtually stopped when she stood up and made her way across the room. She hadn't lost her gorgeous figure, he noted as his gaze raked her body from head to toe. She was just the same as she'd looked at his mother's funeral: lush and beautiful.

This time, however, she wasn't wearing black. Far from it. Her dress was extremely bright, emerald-green with large multicoloured flowers printed around the hem of the gathered skirt. The top was sleeveless and square-necked, a wide white belt cinching in her waist, highlighting her hourglass shape. As she walked, her hair, which was slightly shorter at shoulder length, swung like a sleek dark curtain around her slender shoulders.

The only thing that had really changed was her face. It was the face of a woman now, a woman who was clearly determined not to be bowled over by an old flame hitting town. Her eyes were decidedly cool as she approached, and there was a hint of annoyance in the firm set of her lips.

'You got here more quickly than I thought you would,' she said.

'I was anxious to see my home town again. Which, I might add, is looking wonderful. As are you,' he added, and looked hard at her mouth, that same mouth that had known every inch of his body.

Her lips pressed even more firmly together. 'You're looking very well yourself,' came her somewhat stiff reply. 'Look, I'll just get my handbag and we'll go straight over to the school, where you can meet everyone and find out where and when you have to go tomorrow.'

'Fine,' he replied, not sure what to make of her impersonal manner. 'And then we'll drive to Port for a long lunch by the water,' he added whilst he had her where he wanted her—in public. 'We can catch up on old times. That'll be all right, won't it, girls?' he said, smiling at Allie then at the other girl he'd spotted sitting at a desk not far from Serina's. 'You can cope without the boss for the rest of today, can't you?'

'Absolutely,' they chorused, beaming back at him.

'Great,' he said, and totally ignored Serina's scowl.

'Your handbag?' he prodded with a smooth smile when she just stood there, glowering at him. Sucking in sharply, she spun on her heels and stalked back to her desk.

'I'm Emma, by the way,' the other girl piped up during the time it took Serina to collect her bag.

She was the more attractive of the two, though Nicolas could have guaranteed that she was not a natural blonde. Her short spiked hair had decidedly brassy ends with dark roots.

'Lovely to meet you, Emma. And you must call me Nicolas,' he said to both of them. 'So will you two girls be at the talent quest tomorrow afternoon?'

'Are you kidding?' Emma answered. 'We wouldn't miss it for the world. Everyone in town's going, and quite a lot of people from the surrounding areas. Felicity's done a great job at promotion. She printed out hundreds of fliers on her computer and she and her friends delivered them to every post-box for miles.'

'Yes, and it cost me a small fortune in paper,' Serina grumbled on rejoining him. 'Come on, let's go.'

'See you tomorrow night, Nicolas,' Emma called after them.

'Looking forward to it,' he called back...

CHAPTER SIX

SERINA gritted her teeth as both of them stepped outside, steeling herself for a very difficult day.

'I'd forgotten how hot it can get here in the summer,' Nicolas said. 'I should have put shorts on.'

His comment drew her gaze, not just to his trousers—which were beige and elegantly cut—but his overall appearance. He'd aged very little during the last ten years. There was no extra flab to spoil his tall lean body and only a few extra lines around his eyes and mouth. No one would believe he was almost forty. He cut the same dashing figure whom she'd faced at his mother's funeral, and who'd once wowed the audiences at his concerts. He still wore his blond wavy hair down to his collar, she noted irritably, still had ridiculously long eyelashes and the bluest of blue eyes—eyes that had always set her heartbeat racing even when she was a young girl.

Her heart was racing now. It had started the moment he'd walked into the office.

Her automatic response to him annoyed the hell out of her. One would have thought that the years would have brought her more control—and a lot more common sense. All she could hope for was that her feelings weren't written all over her face.

'No need really,' she replied crisply. 'I presume your hire

car has air-conditioning?' She nodded towards the dark grey SUV parked opposite them.

'Of course.'

'Then let's go get in,' she suggested, her voice cool and confident but her insides anything but.

It wasn't till they were inside the vehicle, with the engine and air-conditioning on, that she dared glance across in his direction once more. Even so she didn't look at his face. She found her decidedly uptight gaze landing on his hands as he placed them on the steering wheel.

'Oh, Nicolas!' she exclaimed before she could stop herself.

'What?' His head jerked round, his blue eyes alarmed.

'Your...your hand.'

'Ah,' he said knowingly, and lifted his left hand from the wheel, turning it this way and that as though it was a long time since he'd looked at it himself.

There was no thumb, not even a small stump, the digit having been amputated at the second knuckle. But that wasn't all. The back of his hand was heavily scarred, the skin puckered up in places. His right hand had a few scars as well, she noted, but nothing like his left.

'Lovely, isn't it?' he said drily, and placed it back down on the wheel, his remaining knuckles showing white when his fingers curved tightly around the rim. 'Unfortunately, there are no compositions suitable for thumbless concert pianists. And to think I used to be able to span ten keys. But not to worry. It probably worked out for the best. The life of a concert pianist is very limited and limiting. I've done well enough out of my change of career.'

'Yes, I know,' Serina said, quickly pulling herself together and resolving not to go all mushy over him just because of his hand. 'I saw you being interviewed on television a couple of years ago,' she went on matter-of-factly. 'You looked very successful in your New York apartment and very prosperous.'

He gave a small laugh. 'That's the pot calling the kettle black. Just look at what you've done. Turned your dad's rather ramshackle lumber yard into a thriving business. I can see where your daughter gets her entrepreneurial skills from.'

Serina didn't know what to say to that. It took all her will-power not to look guilty.

The sound of her mobile phone ringing saved her from further embarrassment. Serina fished it out of her handbag and flipped it open.

'Yes?' she answered.

'Has he rung yet?' her daughter demanded to know in impatient tones. Too late, Serina remembered that Felicity had asked her to ring her as soon as she'd heard from Nicolas. Felicity had begged for her own personal mobile phone for her tenth birthday. And, being somewhat spoiled by Greg, she had got what she wanted.

'Yes, Felicity,' Serina said with a sigh. 'He's rung and he's here in Rocky Creek and we're on our way to the school right now. Okay? See you shortly.' And she hung up.

Nicolas smiled over at her as he fired the engine. 'That daughter of yours is quite a handful, isn't she?'

'How did you guess?' she replied frustratedly, and he laughed.

'So,' he said as he drove out of the car park and turned left. 'Is the school in the same place?'

'Yes.'

'What? No more surprises?'

'Maybe a few.'

'Perhaps you should elaborate whilst I drive. Save me from having egg all over my face. Though I suspect that's what you had in mind when you didn't warn me over the phone how much Rocky Creek had gone ahead.'

'Huh! I didn't see any egg over your face back at the office. You had those girls eating out of your hand and you know it.'

He shot her a smile that curled both her toes and her heart. 'I have learned the art of charming the ladies over the years.'

Serina was grateful that he'd reminded her in time what kind of life he'd been leading since leaving Rocky Creek. Not pining for her, that was for sure. Not even before their final but brief encounter thirteen years ago.

According to the many tabloid articles Felicity had uncovered about him on the Internet, he'd wined and dined some of the most beautiful women in show business. No doubt he'd slept with most of them as well. The Nicolas she knew would not have been living the life of a monk. Not likely!

'I am relieved,' she said in chilly tones. 'Just make sure you don't use up all that much-learned charm before tomorrow. I would hate you to turn into one of those judges who think they have to be cruel to be kind.'

Although Nicolas was slightly taken aback by her sarcasm, he was also heartened, as he had been by her obvious annoyance back at her office. She was trying very hard to be cool but her frosty politeness didn't fool him for a minute. He could feel the sexual tension that she was desperately trying to hide. If he hadn't had at that moment turned in to the street where the school was, he would have pulled over to the side of the road and kissed her senseless.

'Now, as you can see,' she went on as he drove along the tree-lined road, 'the old school is still there. But when our enrolment trebled a few years back, the government finally built us a new school next to it that incorporates an office, several classrooms and a great big school hall, which has a decent stage and room for five hundred seats. That's where we're holding the talent quest.'

'With air-conditioning?' he inquired.

'Of course,' she said haughtily. 'Gus paid for that.'

'Gus?' Nicolas echoed. 'Surely you don't mean old wino Gus.' Old Gus had been a harmless drunk who'd slept in the sports shed and whom the kids had looked after with food, blankets and clothes.

'Yep. Turned out he was a secret millionaire. When he died back in 2005, he left all his money to the Rocky Creek Parents' and Citizens' Association. We don't touch the capital, which is wisely invested. But, with the interest so far, we've air-conditioned the school, kitted out a great computer room, cleared some of the bush behind and built a soccer field and two netball courts. Now we're saving up to put in a swimming pool.'

'We? Does that mean you're on the committee of the P and C?'

'Of course I am,' she told him. 'I'm the treasurer.'

Nicolas tried not to be dismayed by her involvement with the community, but failed. The more she told him, the more he realised that nothing was going to get Serina away from Rocky Creek. She was entrenched here.

But then you knew that, didn't you, Nick, my boy?

It was why she'd rejected you, not once, but twice. Because she preferred life here to the life you craved. Because she loved her family—and Rocky Creek—more than you.

Maybe if she'd been a childless widow, he might have stood a chance. But she wasn't. She was a mother. Mother love, Nicolas knew from experience, was much stronger than anything he could ever evoke in her.

But alongside his dismay lay the same kind of determination with which Nicolas had always faced life and life's challenges. He might not have any future with Serina. But no way was he going to leave Australia without holding her in his arms once more, without experiencing one more time their unique brand of chemistry—and it was unique. Nicolas had never felt anything like it. They'd once shared a stunning degree of physical intimacy and sexual pleasure that could never be forgotten. He hadn't forgotten it and he was damned sure Serina hadn't. She was just pretending that she had.

But he would remind her during their lunch together.

First, however, he had to get this visit to the school over and done with.

Nicolas pulled the SUV into the curb outside the school's front gate, and stared up at the ancient sign, which said it had been established in 1870. The old school was made of wood, a rectangular building with a highpitched roof and a north-facing verandah that had pegs on the wall where the children could hang their hats and school bags. There'd only been four classrooms when he'd gone to school there, with composite classes the order of the day.

Admittedly, he'd only attended Rocky Creek primary for one year, but he hadn't been happy there. He'd still been sulking because of their move from Sydney and he hadn't yet discovered the joys of the piano. He recalled going on a hunger strike at one stage, giving all his food to a very grateful Gus. When no one appeared to care whether he starved or not, he started eating again.

Nicolas was not one to bash his head against a brick wall for long. Once reality sank into his head, he accepted it and moved on. Which was probably why he hadn't pursued Serina those two times she'd rejected him. He'd actually believed her when she'd said she didn't want him. Believed there was no point in going after her. Pride hadn't been the only issue.

But there was wanting and wanting. Her love for him had obviously been found wanting. But what of her lust?

The speed with which she bolted out of the SUV once he'd stopped suggested she hadn't enjoyed being alone with him in a confined space.

'You might as well leave your bag behind,' he suggested as he climbed out from behind the wheel and slammed the door. 'We're going to lunch together shortly, remember?'

Her body language showed extreme irritation with him. She clutched the bag even more tightly in her right hand and threw him what could only be described as a wintry look. 'I don't recall agreeing to do any such thing.'

The possibility of her not even going to lunch with him did not sit well with Nicolas. 'It will look odd, if you don't. Emma and Allie won't be pleased. Neither will Felicity. What are you afraid of, Serina? That I'll throw you across the restaurant table and have my wicked way with you right in front of everyone?'

'Don't be ridiculous,' she snapped. 'I'm well aware that the days of my being your sexual cup of tea are long gone. This way,' she said coldly, and marched off through the front gate and along a path that led past the old school and across to an L-shaped cream brick building sitting where the playground had once been.

An increasingly frustrated Nicolas stalked after her, grudgingly noting that the surrounds of the new Rocky Creek primary school were a credit to the P & C. Covered walkways ran everywhere, protecting the children from rain as well as the hot summer sun. The gardens and lawns were both immaculate and alive, obviously having an excellent watering system.

'Very nice landscaping,' he remarked.

'Gus's money also pays for a gardener,' she said.

'Good old Gus.'

'There's no need to be sarcastic!'

'I wasn't,' Nicolas denied, although he recognised his mood had shifted to a darker place, that place where he was propelled when things didn't go his way, or when he looked like he was failing at something.

Serina stopped walking and whirled to face him, her dark eyes stormy. 'Look, I know what you think of Rocky Creek. It's written all over your supercilious face. No matter how much the town's progressed, you still think of it as a backwater with nothing here to interest you. Which is absolutely true. We don't have an opera house or theatres galore, or mansions full of the rich and famous who hold dinner parties every day of the week. We don't have expensive art galleries, museums or designer boutiques. We certainly don't have super highways where you can drive at two hundred kilometres an hour in your two-hundred-thousand-dollar sports cars. What we do have, however, is people who care about each other. People who are loving and loyal, people who look after each other when times are tough and who are prepared to make sacrifices. Who don't always think of their own selfish selves!'

Nicolas stood there, stunned by the savagery of Serina's tirade.

She seemed a little stunned herself. 'I'm sorry,' she said at last, if a little grudgingly. 'I guess that was rude of me. The thing is, Nicolas, I just don't understand why you agreed to come all this way for a silly little talent quest. Other than your brief visit when your mum died, you haven't darkened the doorstep of Rocky Creek for over twenty years!'

He looked deep into her eyes and ached to tell her the truth.

I came because I still want you, Serina. Because I wanted to make love to you again. I came because I just couldn't stay away, not once I knew you weren't married anymore.

But it wasn't the right time, or the right place. It might never be the right time, or the right place, he realised grimly. Not if she felt this viciously about him.

'I came,' he said instead, quite truthfully as well, 'because of your daughter's very touching letter.'

And, right on cue, Felicity came flying down the path towards them.

Nicolas knew she was Felicity because it was like seeing Serina at that age, so great was the resemblance.

'You're here!' Felicity squealed as only a twelve-year-old girl can squeal. She didn't stop there, either, literally throwing herself against him so hard that he lurched backwards a step.

'Oh, thank you, thank you, thank you!' she blurted, hugging him tightly around the waist before abruptly disengaging herself and throwing him a sheepish look from under her long lashes. 'Sorry. I get a bit carried away sometimes. Don't I, Mum…?'

CHAPTER SEVEN

SERINA would have loved to turn tail and run at that point. It had already been getting to be too much for her, seeing Nicolas again. That had been why she'd let fly at him just now, because she'd needed some outlet for the tension building inside her.

Serina had expected today to be difficult. And she'd been right. But nothing had prepared her for what she'd just witnessed.

Seeing her daughter hug her biological father had produced a mixture of emotions that threatened to overwhelm her. Perversely, she almost felt jealous of Felicity. How she would love to hug Nicolas with such unashamed delight! At the same time a great wave of guilt twisted at her insides. She should never have passed Felicity off as Greg's daughter. Never! She should have told the truth from the start. Instead, she'd locked herself into a secret that was going to crucify her now till her dying days.

Because she'd seen the flash of joy in Nicolas's face when his daughter had wrapped her arms tightly around him, seen the gently indulgent way he'd smiled down at her. He was still smiling at her.

The unexpected realisation that Nicolas might have been a good father to Felicity was shattering.

But it was too late now. It had been too late from the moment she'd walked down that church aisle with Greg all those years ago. Her secret had to continue. Because in Felicity's mind, Greg Harmon was her father, not Nicolas. She'd loved Greg, and she loved Greg's parents—they were her adored Nanna and Pop. No, the secret had to be kept.

She had to pull herself together and not act like some guilt-ridden, broken-hearted fool, even if what she wanted to do was fall in a crumpled heap on this path and cry.

Amazing what a mother could endure when faced with the possibility of her child's unhappiness. So Serina found a smile from somewhere and a voice that sounded close to normal.

'There's nothing wrong with being enthusiastic, Felicity,' she said. 'But it might be wise not to be too familiar with Mr Dupre. Otherwise people might say there's favouritism if you come first in the talent quest tomorrow night.'

Too late Serina wished she hadn't brought up that subject.

'I've already thought of that,' Felicity returned. 'So I've decided not to enter.'

'I think that's a wise decision,' Serina said, hiding her relief behind a genuinely warm smile.

'But I was looking forward to hearing you play,' Nicolas protested.

'Oh, you'll still hear me play,' Felicity informed him quite happily. 'I'm giving a special performance at the end of the talent quest. I don't want to tell you too much except that it's a tribute to a certain concert pianist who sadly can't play anymore.'

Serina smothered a groan of despair. Not only was Felicity going to play for him, but she was also sure to choose one of Nicolas's favourites, maybe even the Chopin Polonaise both of them had heard him play on the Internet. If today was proving difficult, tomorrow loomed as a nightmare!

'Come on, Nicolas,' Felicity said. 'It's time for you to meet everyone else.'

'Felicity!' Serina protested. 'You shouldn't be using Mr Dupre's first name.'

'It's perfectly all right, Serina,' Nicolas remarked.

'No, it's not,' Serina protested. 'It is my job to teach my daughter respect for her elders.'

'In that case she can call Mrs Johnson, Mrs Johnson,' Nicolas shot back, his face irritated. 'I'm not yet forty and don't consider myself an elder just yet. So if you don't mind, I'd prefer to be called Nicolas. Lead on, Felicity, my dear,' he concluded, and actually took his daughter's hand.

Felicity beamed with smug satisfaction whilst Serina felt like strangling her. And Nicolas. Perhaps it was a survival mechanism, but suddenly her mood changed from one of distress to a simmering fury. Whereas before she hadn't been looking forward to having lunch with him, now she was. It would give her the opportunity to say all the things she'd bottled up about him over the years. Her brief tirade of a minute ago was just the tip of the iceberg. There were lots of questions she'd always wanted answered. Specifically why, if he'd loved her so much, he hadn't come back for her from England all those years ago? Why at least he hadn't written!

But the critical question was why hadn't he pursued her after their last extremely passionate encounter. Any man as in love as he'd expressed himself to be that night should have ignored her letter and come after her anyway.

No wonder she'd married Greg!

Clenching her teeth, she trudged up the path after Felicity—and her daughter's unsuspecting father—and into the school hall, where she pasted a plastic smile on her face and watched with growing resentment whilst Nicolas charmed the socks off everyone there.

There were lots of people in the hall that morning. All the teachers, all of the mothers who didn't work, a few husbands who'd taken time off to help put all the plastic chairs in rows and quite a number of children. Serina might have marvelled at Nicolas's social skills if she hadn't already witnessed him in action back at the office. He hadn't always been Mister Warmth and Charm. But there was no doubt he'd learned how to deal with people over the years. He was smooth, very smooth.

He'd been smooth during that television interview a couple of years back, she recalled. But that wasn't the same as seeing him in action in the flesh. In no time he had everyone eating out of his hands. Felicity, especially.

'Isn't he awesome, Mum?' she gushed at one stage when Nicolas was off to one side, chatting with the principal. 'And so good-looking. Do you think he has a girlfriend back in New York?'

'I would imagine so,' Serina said, surprised that this thought hadn't entered her mind earlier. Surprised, too, at the hurt it brought.

'Probably that Japanese violinist,' Felicity went on, blissfully unaware of her mother's agitation. 'She's very pretty. I'll ask him.'

'Don't you dare!' Serina snapped. 'That would be very rude.'

'Oh. Do you think so? Well you could ask him, Mum. Later, when you're at lunch together.'

Serina rolled her eyes. 'Who told you I was going to lunch with him?'

'Nicolas did. Just now.'

'I see,' she said with an exasperated sigh. 'I suppose I might be able to find out. But why on earth do you want to know?'

Felicity's expression turned a little sly. 'Well, I was thinking that if he didn't have a girlfriend, then you and he might… you know…get together again. I mean…you were once boyfriend and girlfriend.'

'For pity's sake, Felicity, how many times do I have to tell you that we only dated a few times!'

'That's not what Mrs Johnson said. She told me you were

as thick as thieves in the old days. And Nana said you cried for weeks after he went to London to study.'

'You know, Felicity, you shouldn't listen to small-town gossip. Nicolas and I were just good friends, like I told you. We were not romantically involved. As for my crying when he went overseas, Mum's mistaken about that entirely. It was around that time that your grandpa had his stroke and I was very upset. My crying had nothing to do with Nicolas leaving Rocky Creek. You've got it all wrong, missy. So please don't try to do what those two silly girls in my office are doing and matchmake me up with every eligible man who happens to cross my path. I loved your father very much and I don't wish to date, or get married again, especially not to Nicolas Dupre. Do I make myself clear?'

Felicity had the good grace to hang her head at this dressing down. Unfortunately, this allowed Serina a direct view over the top of her daughter's drooped head right into Nicolas's piercing blue eyes.

'I'm all finished here,' he said, his facial expression bland.

Hopefully, he hadn't heard that last, rather savage remark. But Serina suspected that he had.

'Mr Tarleton said I was to be here tomorrow at one-thirty,' Nicolas went on crisply. 'Is that early enough, Felicity?'

'Heaps early enough. The talent quest doesn't start till two. You'll stay for the party afterwards, won't you?'

'Of course. Now I'm off to take your mother to lunch. We're going to spend the afternoon in Port Macquarie, catching up on old times.'

Serina flashed him a sour glance before smiling at her daughter. 'I'll be home no later than four, sweetie,' she said. 'Will you be finished setting up the hall by then?'

'Oh, yes. Easily. We're almost done now. But Kirsty wants to rehearse her acts for tomorrow. I'm going to practise as well. One of the pieces I've chosen to play is really hard.'

'You're making me very curious over what you're going to play,' Nicolas said.

Felicity looked smug. 'Sorry. Can't tell. And you're not to tell him, either, Mum.'

'How can I when I don't know myself?' Serina replied somewhat starchily.

'That's good,' Felicity said with a brilliant smile. ''Bye now. See you when you get home.' And she ran off to join her friends.

'I suspect you do know what she's going to play,' Nicolas said as he clamped a firm hand around her right elbow and started steering her towards the side door. 'And you're not happy about it for some reason. The same way you're not happy about my returning to Rocky Creek.'

'I see no reason why I should be happy?' she retorted once they were outside and out of earshot of other people.

'Maybe not,' he bit out. 'But there's no reason why it should overly bother you, either. There's no husband to object to our reunion. Or any new boyfriend, from what I just overheard.'

Serina wrenched out of his hold and ground to a halt. 'Our reunion?' She glared up into his eyes. 'We are not having any kind of reunion here. If I had my way we wouldn't even be having lunch together. But you manipulated things so that I couldn't say no without being rude. As for catching up on old times…don't go thinking that's ever going to happen, Nicolas Dupre. I wouldn't let you touch me again if you were the last man on earth!'

Serina knew the second that last statement fell out of her mouth that she'd gone too far. Way too far.

A cruel smile began at the corners of his eyes. His coldly glittering blue eyes.

'I'll remind you what you just said later today. But for now, I would suggest that you shut that beautiful mouth of yours. Because whilst you might not want to date me ever again, or

God forbid, marry me, I'm pretty sure you do want to go to bed with me. In fact, I'm absolutely certain of it.'

Serina's mouth gasped open. She was on the verge of hotly denying his arrogant statement—despite it being appallingly true—when she spotted a couple of the mothers standing at one of the school hall windows, staring over at them. The time to do battle was not right now, she quickly appreciated, and snapped her gaping mouth shut.

'Glad to see you've finally found some common sense,' he ground out. 'And some honesty. Let's go.' And taking forceful possession of her elbow once more, he propelled her along the path that led them past the old school and back to the parked SUV…

CHAPTER EIGHT

NICOLAS knew—as one always knew deep down—that he'd just crossed a line; that line that you didn't step over if you were a gentleman.

But then he'd never been a gentleman. And he never would be one, despite having smoothed away most of his rough edges over the years. He spoke like a gentlemen these days and dressed like one. His town house in London was the home of a gentleman. His New York apartment, however, reeked of new money, the kind made by men who hadn't been born rich, but who'd made it in the world by talent and tenacity. Men who were winners, men who knew what they wanted and went after it.

What he'd just said to Serina had been provocative in the extreme, provocative and presumptuous. And risky. By speaking up so boldly, he'd ruined any chance of a romantic seduction.

But in that moment before she'd been able to hide the truth, when her body and mind had still been reeling from the shock of his words, he'd glimpsed her ongoing sexual vulnerability to him. What he'd just said had been right. She did want to go to bed with him.

Serina didn't say a single word during the short time it took to steer her back to the car. But her body language reeked of rebellion. Nicolas's own body was consumed by something else....

* * *

Serina snatched her arm away from his hold before climbing up into the SUV and banging the door shut behind her. She refused to look at him as he got in behind the wheel, refused to speak. Instead, she stuffed her handbag at her feet and crossed her arms, glaring balefully out of the passenger window.

'You'd better put your seat belt on,' Nicolas advised as he did so himself then started up the engine.

She did so huffily, still not looking his way, Rocky Creek well behind them before her simmering fury found a path to her tongue.

'I was right all along,' she blustered, her head finally turning in his direction. 'You didn't come back out of kindness, or generosity. You came back for revenge!'

Her accusation produced a startling result, Nicolas's eyes leaving the road at an inopportune time, since they were on a sharp corner at the time. The left-side wheels slid off the narrow strip of tar, spitting gravel out behind them. The back of the vehicle began to slide, Nicolas swearing as he struggled for control.

The adrenalin of fear and panic had Serina gripping her seat belt whilst visions of their careering off the road and into a steep gully—or the bone-crunching trunk of a gum tree—flashed before her mind.

'And I was right,' Nicolas snarled when he finally had them safely back on the road. 'You're going to be the death of me one day. I think I'll find a place to stop before we continue this rather amazing conversation.'

Serina didn't object. She was still shaking inside when he pulled over into a lay-by and turned off the engine.

'Now,' he said firmly as he undid his seat belt and turned towards her. 'What's all this nonsense about revenge?'

Serina stared into his beautiful blue eyes and saw nothing dark or deceptive. Only confusion. Which confused her.

'Revenge for what?' he demanded to know.

'For…for what I did that night,' she spluttered.

'Ah,' he said, and nodded. 'You're still feeling guilty about that, are you?'

'Of course! What I did that night…it was very wrong.'

'Are we talking about what you did to me? Or what you did to your husband?'

Serina stiffened. 'Greg wasn't my husband at that stage.'

'That's semantics, Serina, and you know it. You were unfaithful to your soon-to-be husband that night. And you deceived me.'

A guilty frustration swamped her, making her head whirl and her heart twist. 'I didn't mean to do either,' she blurted out. 'I…I just couldn't help myself.' Tears of dismay and despair filled her eyes. 'It all happened by accident.'

Nicolas's expression was sceptical. 'You just happened to be at my concert. Is that what you're saying?'

'No. Yes. I mean…I came to Sydney for a couple of days shopping for my wedding and I saw you being interviewed on television. One of those morning programs. I heard you were playing at the Opera House that night and I thought… what would be the harm? I just want to see him one more time,' she choked out, as though she were talking to someone else. Confessing, perhaps, to a priest. 'But then I watched you perform and I…I knew I had to do more than just see you….' The tears spilled over then and trickled down her cheeks. 'I couldn't help it, Nicolas. I'm not a bad person. And I'm sorry, truly sorry.'

He reached over and gently wiped the tears from her face. 'I won't say that what you did didn't hurt me. It did. Terribly. But I can see that I hurt you, too, by staying away in the first place. I should have come back for you earlier.'

'Why didn't you?' she said with a tormented groan.

'Male pride, mostly. You said you didn't want me.'

A small laugh escaped her lips. 'And you believed me?'

Nicolas smiled a rather sad smile. 'Yes, Serina, I believed you. But that's water under the bridge now, isn't it? We can't go back and undo anything in the past. All we can control is the here and now. So let me redress something I told you a little while ago, about why I'm here. Yes, it was because of your daughter's letter. But not for the reason I let you think. I haven't come all this way to help Felicity raise money for your local bushfire brigade. I could have easily sent a cheque to do that. I came because your daughter told me that her father—your husband, Greg—is now dead. I came because of you, Serina. Let's not have any misunderstandings about that.'

Serina tried to work some saliva into her suddenly dry mouth. It was what she both craved and feared.

'But it's too late,' she told him.

'Too late for what?'

'For us…'

'It's never too late, Serina. Not whilst we're still alive.'

'You don't understand.'

'Are you saying that you don't want me anymore?'

She could not help the sensual shudder that rippled down her spine.

'You have to give me another chance, Serina,' he proclaimed.

'I won't leave Rocky Creek,' she insisted wildly. 'I won't, I tell you.'

'I'm not asking you to,' he said. 'Just come back to Port Macquarie for the afternoon.'

She stared at him, her eyes wide.

'I can't!' she protested huskily.

His smile was sexy. 'Of course you can. We're already going there for lunch.'

'You're not talking about lunch, though, are you?'

'No. No, Serina, I'm not.'

The image his words evoked took her breath away. 'You're wicked. You were always wicked!'

'Oh, come now, Serina, don't go all holier-than-thou on me. I never did a single thing you didn't want me to. Or beg me to.'

'I never begged!'

'Then perhaps it's high time you did. Shall I make you beg this afternoon, my love?'

Serina knew she had to fight the insidious desires that were already invading her. For if she gave in to what he wanted…

She shuddered to think of the consequences, both to her life and her future happiness. Not to mention the happiness of her child.

'How can you possibly put words like *love* and *beg* in the same sentence?' she argued fiercely. 'You have no idea what love is, Nicolas Dupre. You never really loved me. I meant no more to you than your piano. I was just an instrument to be mastered. You practised making love to me the way you used to practise your scales. Till your technique was perfect. But you never cared for me enough to make me any kind of priority. Your career always came first. When our relationship became difficult, you chose your career over me and moved on. You did the same thing when fate intervened and cut short your concert career. You moved on. Very successfully, too. Yet if you'd truly loved playing the piano, that accident would have come close to destroying you. But it didn't, did it? You rose again, like the Phoenix, and made an even greater success of your life. Which is commendable in a way. But it shows a certain ruthlessness of character, which I know I can't live with. Or love.'

Her stomach contracted a little at this last lie. Because, of course, she did love Nicolas. Always had and always would. But the other things she'd just said weren't lies. He was not the kind of man a woman could rely on to make her happy. Serina hadn't reached the age of thirty-six without becoming a reasonable judge of character.

Nicolas was selfish and self-centred. He might not have come back for revenge, but he had come back to win. She was the one who'd got away. That was why he'd been so angry with her at his mother's funeral. Because she'd rejected him, not once but twice. A man like Nicolas didn't take rejection lightly, a fact made obvious by the expression on his face.

'So you won't give me another chance,' he said grimly.

'I don't see any point, Nicolas. Your life is in New York, or London, or wherever your latest show is being staged. My life is here, in Rocky Creek, with my daughter and my family. We have nothing in common anymore, not even the piano.'

'We have this in common, Serina,' he growled, and in the twinkling of any eye, he captured her startled face in his hands and swooped with his mouth.

No! She might have screamed aloud if she'd been able to scream. But actual screaming was impossible with his lips clamped to hers and his tongue already pushing past her teeth. All she could manage was a low groan, which sounded more like the sound of surrender than any kind of protest.

It was a brutal kiss, punishing and powerful, demanding and devouring, irrefutable and irresistible.

Serina knew, soon after Nicolas started kissing her, that she didn't have a hope in Hades of resisting him. Her body had always had a mind of its own when it came to Nicolas. From the first moment he'd touched her, she'd been his. Whenever they'd made love, he'd evoked feelings in her—both physically and emotionally—that had both consumed and enthralled her. Being with him had quickly become an obsession and an addiction, which only the tyranny of distance had put a halt to. Whenever he'd come home, she'd been there, waiting for him.

So when his head finally lifted, she didn't bother to voice any further protest. She just looked up into his eyes and said breathily, 'All right, Nicolas. You win. I'll go to bed with you one more time. But that will be the end of it,' she added before he could look too triumphant. 'The end of us. There will be no more.'

'Are you quite sure of that, Serina?' he murmured, his hands turning soft and seductive around her face.

'Quite sure,' she lied in steely tones...

CHAPTER NINE

NICOLAS was taken aback by Serina's tough stance. This wasn't the girl he remembered. She would have just melted into his arms and agreed with whatever he wanted.

But then he remembered the Serina who'd come to him that night at the Opera House. She'd melted all right. For a while. But she'd solidified quickly enough after she'd had what she wanted.

'So it's just sex you want from me again, Serina,' he growled, his fingertips tightening on the soft skin of her flushed cheeks.

Something flickered through her large brown eyes. A momentary shame, perhaps. But she didn't look away. Her gaze stayed steady, and strong.

'That's all you're good for, Nicolas,' came her stunningly hurtful words.

He did his best not to show any visible distress, finding a slow smile from somewhere. 'If you think insults can save you, Serina, then think again. I haven't come all this way to go home without seeing the way you look when you come. And I will make you beg for it this time, sweetheart.'

Her eyes glittered wildly in return. 'You'll be the one doing the begging, lover,' she spat back at him.

His fingers slid down to caress her throat. 'Is that a challenge?'

'It's a promise.'

His eyes narrowed whilst hot blood rushed along his veins. 'I suggest you ring that daughter of yours and let her know that you won't be home by four,' he snarled.

'And I suggest you stop making suggestions and just drive!'

As Nicolas glowered down into her flushed but feisty face, it came to him that the adult Serina was exciting him much more than the teenage girl ever had. Or even the wildly frustrated creature who'd come to him that night thirteen years ago.

She was a woman now, he saw, more experienced and confident. More...interesting.

He smiled again.

'Excellent idea,' he pronounced, and turned his attention to doing exactly what she'd suggested. Thirty seconds later, he was whizzing along the Oxley Highway, pushing the speed limit to the max as he sped towards their destination.

Serina leant back in the passenger seat and turned her head away to stare blankly through the passenger window.

She'd done it now. Not only had she agreed to have sex with him again, but she'd also challenged him and provoked him.

Nicolas was not the sort of person one challenged, or provoked. As a teenager he'd been one angry young man, with tunnel vision and a quick temper. He'd hated being teased. Hated anyone who told him he couldn't do something. As an adult male, she had no doubt that, down deep, he wouldn't have changed all that much.

But it was too late now. It had been too late the second he leant over and kissed her. There was nothing to do but to go through with what she'd agreed to. Which, of course, she secretly wanted. She wanted it so much she was already trembling inside.

Suddenly, and with typical female thinking, Serina was glad that she'd taken trouble with her appearance today. Glad she'd shaved her legs last night and painted her nails, and worn a pretty set of lingerie under her new dress.

Not that she'd be wearing any of it for long. Nicolas had never been fond of making love under or around clothes. Her accusation earlier that Nicolas was wicked was probably right. But if he was wicked then so was she. She felt wicked now—and terribly turned on.

The next fifteen minutes went agonisingly slowly, despite Nicolas not keeping to the speed limit. Once he reached the outer parts of Port Macquarie, however, the traffic forced him down to sixty, his frustrated mutterings echoing her own feelings.

'I'm not stopping anywhere for lunch,' he growled once he turned the corner that led into the main street of Port. 'I don't want to waste any of the miserably short period of time I have with you.'

Serina said nothing. What was there to say that wasn't shameful?

I don't mind, Nicolas. All I want to eat is you.

'You won't have to starve,' he went on. 'There's wine in the apartment, and fruit and chocolates. I presume you still like chocolates?'

She still didn't speak, or look his way.

'There's no need to sulk,' he snapped. 'You want this as much as I do.'

Her head jerked round, but any smart crack she might have made disappeared once she saw the raw passion in his face. This was the Nicolas she remembered, the Nicolas she'd fallen madly in love with. All of a sudden it seemed stupid to spoil their last time together. If she was going to do this—and it seemed she was—she would do so willingly. But on her terms, not his.

'I won't deny it,' she stated matter-if-factly. 'If I did, you'd find out soon enough I was lying. But let's get one thing straight, Nicolas. This afternoon is our swan song. There will be no encore performance. Once that talent quest is over tomorrow night I want you to leave Rocky Creek and never come back.'

'And what if I don't want to do that?' he retorted. 'I'll have you know I've rented this apartment up here for a week.' And he nodded towards a tall, grey-blue cement-rendered building just ahead on their right that Serina hadn't actually seen before, though she knew of it. Blue Horizon Apartments had opened recently with a big colour spread in the local newspaper.

'I'm sure they'll give you a refund,' she replied as he pulled in to a driveway just to the left of the building.

Once the SUV was stopped in front of the car park security gate, Nicolas glared over at her. 'What gives you the right to make demands like that?'

'I don't have any right,' she admitted. 'But if you do what I ask, I'll do whatever you want for the next four hours. If not, then you can turn around and take me home.'

Nicolas could have called her bluff, the way he had a short time ago. But really, there was no point. All his questions had been answered now. Serina didn't love him anymore. Maybe she'd never loved him. That night thirteen years ago hadn't been about love, it'd been all about lust. As was this afternoon.

She still wanted him. Quite badly, if he was any judge. Which explained why she was so anxious to get rid of him, because she was afraid of what she might do.

Nicolas suspected he could seduce her into going away with him, if he tried hard enough. But he wasn't that ruthless, despite what she thought of him. He could see that her life here meant the world to her, as did her daughter. To take her away from Rocky Creek would be cruel and truly wicked, which he was not.

Which left him with the harsh reality that this afternoon would be the last time he'd be with her.

Four miserable short hours.

It just wasn't enough.

'Make it six hours,' he counteroffered. 'Call Felicity on her mobile and tell her to go to a friend's place till then.'

'I can't do that. People will talk.'

'Serina, they're going to talk anyway. But if I leave town for good the day after tomorrow, they'll soon forget.'

'If you leave town?'

'That's conditional on your staying with me for six hours. And what was it you offered? Doing whatever I want.'

'That's blackmail!' she protested.

Nicolas laughed. 'No, my darling heart. That's negotiation. So what's it to be?'

'I…I'll ring Felicity later. But not right now. Closer to four.'

'Fine.' Satisfied for the moment, he leant out of the driver's window and swiped the key card across the security unit attached to the wall. As the gate slowly lifted, Nicolas glanced at his watch.

It was noon. High noon.

He smiled a wry smile.

What have I done? Serina agonised when she saw Nicolas smile.

You've sold your soul to the devil, that's what you've done. No, not my soul. My body. My soul is still mine.

But this last thought was little consolation. Serina's hands curled into tight fists in her lap as Nicolas drove slowly down the ramp before angling the bulky vehicle into an empty parking space in a dimly lit corner of the basement car park. The moment the engine died, a nervous sigh shuddered from her lungs.

'There's no need for that,' he said with surprising tenderness, and reached over to take her tense hands in his. 'I don't mean you any harm, my darling,' he murmured, and lifted her hands to his mouth, where he kissed the whitened knuckles one after the other. 'I just want to make love to you the way I used to. Not what we shared that night at the Opera House.

That was way too fast and furious. I want to enjoy you at length the way we did in the beginning. Remember how it used to be between us?'

How could she forget?

Already she was trembling inside.

'You used to do whatever I asked. Whatever I wanted. Be like that with me one more time and I'll leave like you asked me to.'

A soft moan escaped her lips when he uncurled one of her fingers and pushed it deep into his mouth. She closed her eyes as he began to suck, her mind filling with memories of all the things he'd done to her in the past. Nothing had been taboo in the end. Everything had been tried, everything enjoyed. Even...

Serina snapped open at that particular memory.

'You...you do have protection with you, don't you?' she blurted out.

Slowly, his head lifted, leaving her finger wet and tingling.

'Of course,' he said softly.

Of course. Nicolas had always been a thinker and a planner. Only twice had he not practised safe sex with her. That first time. And then during that wildly impassioned encounter at the Opera House, for which she only had herself to blame.

His head turned at the sound of a group of people walking across the car park and getting in a nearby car.

'Time, I think,' came his oh-so-cool words, 'for us to go upstairs...'

CHAPTER TEN

SERINA'S knees felt like jelly during their short walk to the lift well. She was glad that no one joined them there, leaving them alone for the ride up to Nicolas's floor. She didn't want anyone to see the state she was in. Though nothing much was visible on the outside, nothing except for her possibly haunted eyes and her rock-hard nipples. An outsider could not see her wildly whirling thoughts, or the shocking wetness between her legs.

Nicolas, on the other hand, to all appearances had regained total control of himself. There again, he hadn't touched her since alighting from the SUV, going about his business with the key card in the lift without even glancing her way. So maybe he wasn't quite as cool as he was pretending to be.

Once they left the lift, he did take her elbow, steering her across a grey carpeted foyer and down a corridor to a door marked number seventy-three in silver numbers. A quick swipe of the key card and a green light came on in the silver door handle, Nicolas swiftly pushing the door open.

The apartment was, she saw immediately, not run-of-the-mill holiday accommodation. The living room into which she first walked was very spacious, the décor expensive. The walls and ceilings were painted a soft off-white, with the furniture, floor and accessories in various shades of blue, ranging from the palest of grey-blues to quite bright blues to the darkest navy, with the odd splash of turquoise thrown in.

'Very nice,' she murmured, and dropped her handbag onto a large navy leather armchair before moving across the room to the sliding glass doors, which led out to the balcony.

'It's locked,' she said when the door wouldn't slide open.

Nicolas strode over, lifted the latch then locked it again.

'Oh,' she said, feeling totally flustered and confused.

Nicolas cupped her face and forced her eyes up to his. 'If you think you're going to waste time out there looking at a view you've seen a million times before, Serina, then think again. I didn't bring you up here to play pretend tourist. Now, as pretty as this dress is that you're wearing,' he said, his hands dropping down to the wide belt around her waist, 'it has to go.'

Serina's first instinct was to object. But her second thought was to stay silent and just let him get on with it. After all, this was what she'd agreed to. And what she'd often dreamt about over the years. To somehow be able to go back into the past when they were teenagers and so very much in love.

Which they had been.

Not once had Serina ever felt that the intimacies they'd shared were just acts of lust. It had always been lovemaking, not sex. Nicolas had never made her feel used. Yes, he was dominant and domineering, but he was also tender and loving. He never stopped telling her how much he loved her and how beautiful she was.

Her stomach twisted at this last thought. Would he still think her beautiful? She was not as young, or as firm. She'd had a child. Her breasts drooped a bit and her belly, though without stretch marks, was soft and rounded.

'Nicolas,' she choked out.

His eyes flashed impatience at her. 'What now?'

'Tell me that you love me.'

'What?'

'You don't have to mean it. Just say it. I want to hear you say it.'

Nicolas just stared at her. He would never understand women. Why couldn't she just be honest? She didn't want his love, so why ask for fake words?

'You said you wanted to make love to me the way you used to,' she went on before he could say anything. 'Well, you used to tell me how much you loved me all the time. And how beautiful I was. It made all that we did together…seem right.'

Nicolas was totally unprepared for the wave of emotion that her words evoked. It choked him up, a huge lump forming in his throat.

'You think I'm silly, don't you?' she said in a broken voice, which almost brought him undone.

Somehow he managed to hold himself together, though he had to clear his throat before answering her. His words weren't critical, but his tone was brusque and uncompromising.

'You're a woman, and women look at things differently to men. We don't need the justification of love to make sex acceptable. There's nothing wrong with a man and a woman enjoying each others' bodies. Which we have always done, Serina. More perhaps than most men and women. I can honestly say that I have never forgotten what we shared. It was, indeed, unforgettable. It's why you came to me that night at the Opera House, and why you're here now. Why I'm here. There is a chemistry between us that refuses to die, or even fade. We will take it to our graves. But we're all grown up now,' he said as he removed the belt from her waist and tossed it aside. 'There's no need to say things we don't mean.'

A type of relief claimed Nicolas once he stopped talking and started seriously undressing her. It had taken a supreme effort of will not to say what she wanted him to say. Because, to be brutally honest, he wasn't sure that he did.

Emotions could be deceptive. Especially desire.

He wanted her the way he'd always wanted her. But was that love?

Maybe. Maybe not.

Even if it was, there was no point in loving her. She didn't love him back. He'd overheard what she'd said to her daughter. She'd loved Greg Harmon. She didn't want anything to do with him, except in this most basic way. He'd been right when he said she was just trying to justify her feelings with romantic words. The bottom line was she was here because she wanted sex.

Nicolas's teeth clenched down hard in his jaw, his last thoughts hardening his heart towards her. She wanted sex, did she? Well, he'd give her sex. And he'd make her beg. He hadn't forgotten his earlier threat. If nothing else, he would reduce her to that. And he'd make her say that she loved him.

She'd accused him of coming back for revenge. Who knew? Maybe he had…

CHAPTER ELEVEN

SERINA could not remember Nicolas undressing her quite this quickly before. In the old days he'd liked to take his time over everything. She suspected that their first rushed encounter had seriously embarrassed him, stinging the perfectionist in his nature. But nothing was ever rushed. The undressing, the foreplay, the act itself. He would sometimes spend up to an hour playing with her body's erogenous zones, using his hands mostly, but also his mouth. He'd loved making her climax over and over before he entered her, loved watching her eyes, loved the feel of her wet heat when his own flesh finally fused with hers.

She knew all this because he would tell her, his constant stream of hot words turning her on, and keeping her turned on.

Even that fateful night thirteen years ago, when they'd fallen upon each other like wild beasts, he'd talked incessantly, telling her how much he'd missed her; how much he loved her. He'd only become silent when he fell asleep.

Today he was stripping her in total silence, almost roughly, not bothering to linger as he once would have. In no time she was nude before him, trembling with nerves and tension.

He stepped back at that stage and just looked at her, his eyes both hot and cold at the same time. Serina had no idea what he was thinking. He seemed angry for some reason, which upset her.

'What is it, Nicolas?' she blurted out. 'What's wrong?'

'Why should anything be wrong?' he snapped and reefed his shirt out of the waistband of his trousers.

Suddenly she understood. He'd come all this way, hoping that they could find each other again. Maybe he'd even hoped she would finally go away with him. One afternoon of reliving old times was not what he had in mind.

Her heart twisted with dismay. *Oh, Nicolas, Nicolas, why didn't you come back for me sooner? Why did you wait till it was too late?*

But at least he'd come. She had that to be grateful for. She would not die without knowing that she'd meant as much to him as he had to her.

'Let me do that,' she said softly when he started wrenching open the buttons on his shirt.

As she stepped forward to take his hands away, she gazed up into his undeniably startled eyes. 'I always wanted to undress you. But you never would let me. You might find you like it.' She started slowly undoing his shirt buttons one by one, satisfied when she heard his breath catch in his throat.

It was exciting, taking control, something she'd never done, either with Nicolas or with Greg. Her husband had been a conventional lover with simple sexual needs and definite expectations of her as his wife. He'd interpreted her initial reluctance to sleep with him as an indication that sex was not a high priority with her. Serina had never led him to believe otherwise. She rarely said no to him when he approached her in their marital bed. But the pleasure he gave her, whilst pleasant enough, never came even close to what she'd experienced with Nicolas, which she knew she would experience today. Already her heart was racing with anticipation of what lay ahead.

Nicolas could not believe he was doing this, letting her undress him. It was not his usual modus operandi when it came to sex. There was, however, affection in Serina's lovely dark eyes as she undid the buttons on his shirt. Seeing that affection stirred both his body and his soul. It was no use. He couldn't pretend this was just about sex. Maybe it was for Serina. She'd obviously come a long way in experience over the years. As much as it killed him to admit it, Greg Harmon had obviously been an excellent lover. Nicolas couldn't imagine Serina falling in love with any man who didn't please her sexually.

But Greg Harmon is dead, he reminded himself in his usual pragmatic and rather ruthless fashion, *and I'm here!*

No way was Nicolas going to let jealousy ruin the next few hours. Serina was his again, for now. And he was going to enjoy her to the full.

'You've looked after yourself, haven't you?' she said admiringly when she finally pushed his shirt back off his shoulders.

He had. Not because he was obsessed by his body image, but because he'd found working out was an antidote for the depression that had seized him after the accident. After a while, going to the gym several times a week had become a habit. He was glad now that he had, glad that she could look at him and like what she saw. He certainly liked what he saw. Serina was even more beautiful for having had a child. Her body was curvier and sexier. *She* was sexier.

'I always loved it that you didn't have much body hair,' she murmured as she ran her fingertips provocatively over his smooth chest muscles. His nipples tightened under her touch. It wasn't the only physical change she was evoking. He'd thought his flesh couldn't become harder. But he was wrong.

'Serina,' he bit out warningly.

'Mmmm?'

'Move on,' he advised thickly.

She smiled. It was a woman's smile, sweet and sexy at the same time.

When her hands dropped to the waistband of his trousers, Nicolas had to use all of his willpower to take control of his body.

He managed to get through her undressing him without disaster striking. But the moment her hand reached out to touch him down there, he simply had to stop her.

'No,' he growled, and grabbed her hand in his.

Serina stared up at him, her dark eyes startled.

'You only have yourself to blame,' he said drily as he scooped her up into his arms and carried her into the bedroom. 'You are way too beautiful to last long this first time.'

She didn't say anything, just gave him a look that implied he was lying. Which he wasn't, of course.

'But never fear, my darling,' he went on as he laid her down on top of the soft blue quilt. 'Things won't always be this rushed.'

'You're...you're not wearing protection?' she sputtered when he went to join her on the bed.

His teeth clenched down hard in his jaw with frustration. 'See? I've totally lost my head over my desire for you. Won't be long.' And he walked off in the direction of the en suite bathroom.

Serina just lay there, staring after him and wondering if he'd deliberately tried to have sex with her without a condom.

Surely not! But if not, then what? The thought that he had been overcome with desire for her was flattering in the extreme.

Don't go there, Serina, she warned herself. *He does not love you. This is all about winning, not love.*

He came striding back into the bedroom, looking like a Viking warrior intent on ravagement. The sight of his intense desire inflamed her own once more, making her belly tighten and her thighs tremble. Suddenly, it didn't matter why he'd come back. He was here: her Nicolas, her one true love.

'Nicolas,' she choked out, holding out her arms and opening her legs at the same time.

He groaned, then fell upon her, much like he had that night at the Opera House, his flesh fusing with hers like a sword being slid roughly into its scabbard. She gasped and clung to him, her arms wrapping around his back, her legs lifting to wind tightly around his waist. She whimpered as he surged into her again and again, her head threshing from side to side.

'No, don't,' he said with a groan when she went to shut her eyes. 'Look at me, Serina, look at me.'

So she looked at him, and came immediately, her mouth falling open as she sucked in some much-needed air. He kissed her then, kissed her and came at the same time, without missing a beat of his merciless rhythm, Serina wallowing in the pleasure and power of his twin possessions, thrilling to the way her body responded to both. She would have stayed that way forever, if it were possible.

But his climax finally ended and his head finally lifted.

She stared up at him as he stroked her hair back from her sweat-beaded forehead, her eyes searching his face as she tried to read his mind. But nothing of his inner feelings showed on his face this time. The stormy passion she'd glimpsed earlier had obviously been sated, at least temporarily.

'I feel a lot better now,' he said. 'Don't you? No, you don't have to answer that. I felt your climax right down to my toes. You have to admit that some things never change, my darling. You still come quicker than any girl I've ever been with.'

Her heart curled over in dismay that he could be so cold and cruel whilst he was still inside her. But it was good, in a way, for him to show his true colours. It would stop her from harbouring silly thoughts, the kind that had filled her soul when she'd held out her arms to him.

'I'm rather hungry,' he went on in that coolly casual fashion that she was sure she would soon hate. 'I dare say you are, too. Time I think, for some refreshments. And perhaps some refreshing. Good thinking, Nicolas,' he said, and withdrew from her body with such abruptness that she gasped.

He smiled down into her bereft face.

'Sorry, darling heart,' he said, patting her patronisingly on the cheek. 'But needs must. Once I have the spa bath full and all our goodies lined up in there, it will be all systems go again. Meanwhile, let me tell you again how beautiful you are.'

'Don't say that!' she snapped. 'You don't mean it. I know you don't.'

His smile, when it came, was extremely sardonic. 'I'm saying it to make all that we're going to do this afternoon seem right.'

Suddenly, she was afraid. Of this cold, cruel Nicolas, but mostly of herself. Because she was still turned on by him. Even now. 'What...what are we going to do?'

Sexy blue eyes glittered down into her.

'Whatever I want you to do,' he said. 'That was the deal, wasn't it...?'

CHAPTER TWELVE

'ANOTHER chocolate, my sweet,' he said, and leant forward to pop one of the deliciously creamy delicacies into her mouth.

No point in objecting, Serina thought. No point in objecting to anything he suggested. The bitter truth was she simply didn't have the willpower to resist him, or the desire.

Besides, she was ravenously hungry, having not eaten a thing since a very light breakfast—just coffee and one slice of toast.

So she ate the chocolate and washed it down with a mouthful of champagne, all the while wondering why he hadn't suggested something more decadent than their current positions in the spa bath. They were sitting at opposite ends, only their feet touching occasionally.

It was not what Serina had envisioned. What she had, perhaps, secretly hoped for.

This wasn't the first time they'd shared a bath. In the old days he would have placed her across his lap, his swollen sex deep inside of her whilst they lay back in the water like two spoons. His hands would have covered her breasts and he would be whispering hot words of love and passion into her ears.

'What time is it, do you think?' she asked suddenly.

'Haven't got my watch on,' he replied. 'But my guess is it's just after one. Plenty of time left. We could even waste a little of it talking.'

'Talking?' she echoed in startled tones.

'You don't want to talk? Too bad, Serina. It's not your choice. So tell me, was your marriage happy?'

The last thing she wanted to talk about was her marriage. Serina sipped some more champagne in an effort to find composure.

'Like most marriages,' she said at last, not quite meeting his probing gaze, 'it had its ups and downs. But on the whole we were happy.'

His head tipped slightly to one side in that way people did when they were trying to detect if someone was lying to them.

'Why only one child?' he went on, blue eyes boring into her.

Serina's stomach tightened, but she managed a nonchalant shrug. 'We tried for more. It just didn't happen.'

'Your fault or his?'

'Neither. We were perfectly healthy, the doctors said.' Now this was not totally true. Greg had discovered quite a few years back that he had a low sperm count, possibly because he'd had mumps as an adolescent. Technically, he had been still capable of fathering a child, but conceiving had not been easy.

'I see,' Nicolas said. 'Well at least you have Felicity. She's a delightful child.'

'Delightful,' Serina agreed. 'But difficult.'

Nicolas smiled an indulgent smile. 'Yes. I can see that she might be that.'

Serina knew she had to get off that topic and quick.

'And what of you, Nicolas?' she countered. 'Have you anyone waiting for you back in New York? That pretty little Japanese violinist perhaps.'

His eyebrows lifted. 'You know about Junko?'

So he was sleeping with her!

'I know of her. Felicity did an Internet search and showed me what you'd been up to over the years.'

'I see.'

'You've had a lot of beautiful women, by all accounts.'

'True,' came his cool reply.

Dear heaven, but he was annoying.

'You never wanted to marry any of them?'

'Yes. Once. But it didn't work out.'

'When was that?'

'Years ago,' he responded nonchalantly, as though it was of no importance. 'Look, I can see that making idle chitchat is not our forte. Not this afternoon, anyway. Let's get out of this bath and back to what we do best together.'

He rose up through the water, soapy bubbles clinging to various parts of his body—his shoulders his chest...

She stared up at it, then up at him.

'As you can see,' he said drily as he stepped out of the bath and reached for a towel, 'I have recovered sufficiently to continue. Now put down that champagne, beautiful. I need someone out here to dry me, someone who knows just how I like it done.'

Serina's heartbeat quickened at his command, her head whirling with hot jabs of desire. At last it was going to begin again. At last, she could touch him as she'd been dying to touch him.

Foolish man, Nicolas was to think thirty seconds later. She didn't dry herself at all, her beautiful body glistening with moisture as she proceeded to dry him, slowly, sensuously, dabbing at his arms, shoulders and back, then moving around to press the towel against his buttocks before slowly running it down the back of his legs. His gut tightened when she began to move the towel up between his legs.

'Delay,' he'd read in the last chapter of an old sex manual he'd once bought, 'is the best way to increase the intensity of one's climax.'

Serina had obviously learned that lesson well. She pulled

the towel away and walked round to face him. There, she stood before him and rubbed the towel slowly over her own body, her dilated eyes showing him that she was just as turned on as he was.

'Throw the towel away,' he groaned.

She did.

'Kneel down.'

She obeyed once more. Without question, without hesitating.

'Now tell me that you love me.'

Her head tipped backwards as her eyes flew up to his.

'You don't have to mean it,' he ground out, his hands reaching to tug her hair down from where she'd wound it up on top of her head, out of the reach of the bath water. 'Just say it. So that it makes what you're going to do seem right.'

'Nicolas, don't,' she croaked out.

'Don't what, my darling?' His fingers splayed through her hair, spreading it out onto her shoulders. 'Don't humiliate you this way? How can it possibly be humiliation when you want this as much as I do?'

Her sob filled him with self-loathing. But nothing was going to stop him. Not her distress, or his conscience.

'No one has ever done it better than you, Serina,' he crooned.

When her head drooped and her hands lifted from her sides, he thought she was about to burst into tears. Instead, she reached up and touched him, enfolding delicate fingers around his aching penis and pressing the tip against her lips.

His whole body shuddered as though lightning had struck it. She didn't stop there, however. She opened those soft sweet lips and took him into the wet heat of her mouth. He stared down at her as her head lifted and fell in a slow but merciless rhythm. He wanted to cry out, to scream. He wanted, more than anything, to hate her.

And he did hate her in that moment when he knew he could no longer contain his desire. For as his body raced towards a climax, the victory suddenly felt like hers. She was the one in control here. She was the one doing the using and the rejecting once again.

Serina wanted him gone from her life. And she was prepared to do anything—even this—to achieve her goal.

Such thoughts brought bitterness and a dark desire, not to witness his own ragged release, but hers. She was the one he wanted to see out of control. Had she forgotten his threat to make her beg? He was hardly achieving that this way.

At the last moment he found the strength to pull free of her, glorying in the glazed and confused eyes she raised up to his face.

'I'll take a raincheck on that, my love,' he said as he lifted her onto unsteady feet. 'I have other things in mind for this afternoon. And for you…'

CHAPTER THIRTEEN

NICOLAS shook his head ruefully as he gazed down at Serina's sleeping form. So much for his intention to indulge in a whole afternoon of vengeful sex, where she'd have lost control and begged for mercy.

If only he hadn't brought her back to bed.

The bed had been a mistake, as had his unsuccessful attempt to arouse her so much with his own mouth that she'd plead for release. She'd been aroused all right, he was pretty sure of that. But not as much as he had been. Before he knew it he was reaching for another condom. Even worse, he'd taken her in the spoon position, which meant he hadn't even been able to see her face when she came. If she had, that is. Men could never be too sure about such things, he'd discovered over the years. All in all, things hadn't gone according to plan. Afterwards, she'd fallen asleep.

A glance at his watch showed it was just on three. Of course he could wake her up and start all over again, this time reliving a few of the more erotic foreplays and positions that they'd explored at length all those years ago.

The possibilities were endless. But he just didn't want to. He didn't want to feel what he felt every time he touched her.

It wasn't hate at all.

Nicolas knew that he could not face another three hours of

this emotional torment. It was time to call a halt before his thoughts and feelings got the better of him.

'You're a sad case, Nick, my man,' he muttered to himself as he rose from the rumpled bed and headed for the bathroom.

Five minutes later, a dressed Nicolas was shaking Serina's right shoulder.

She moaned softly, rolling over onto her back and stretching voluptuously before blinking open her eyes.

Nicolas was glad he was fully dressed. His body was still, unfortunately, on a different wavelength to his mind.

'Time for me to take you home, sweetheart,' he said, his voice as hard as his poor tormented flesh.

She blinked and sat up, her full breasts moving in a most provocative way. 'What?'

'You heard me. It's time for me to take you home.'

Alarm filled her face. 'It's six o'clock already? Why didn't you wake me? Oh no, I didn't ring Felicity.' She glanced at the digital bedside clock before throwing him a confused look. 'But...but...it's only just after three o'clock!'

'I've changed my mind about the length of this afternoon's activities,' he interrupted in a cold, crisp voice. 'I've had enough.'

'Enough?' she echoed rather blankly.

'Did I not make myself clear? Then let me put it another way. You're still one heck of a good lay, but I can see that you were right. Our relationship, such as it was, is dead in the water. All that was left was some lingering flames. This afternoon snuffed out the last of those flames, good and proper. For which I am grateful. Now I can go back to my life the day after tomorrow and not give you a second thought. And you, my love, will surely do the same.'

Serina was grateful that he turned away from her at that point. For her face had to have betrayed her shock at this last statement.

Not give him a second thought?

Was he insane, or just seriously deluded?

'Better shake a leg,' he said over his shoulder as he strode from the bedroom in the direction of the living room.

She stumbled out of the bed, only then realising that her clothes were out in the living room. Where he was.

To walk out there naked after what he'd just said sent a shiver running down her spine. Not once, in the past, had Nicolas referred to her as a 'lay', either good or otherwise. The word was repulsive in her eyes. Didn't he know how much she still loved him? Hadn't he felt the love in her lips? In her willingness to do whatever he wanted?

Of course not. Why would he? She'd acted like a tough cookie on the way here, saying that sex was all he was good for. She only had herself to blame for the way he was treating her.

But, oh…it had been wonderful for a short while. She'd been able to pretend that nothing had changed, that they were young lovers again, where nothing existed for her but the heat of the moment. She'd wallowed in the thrill of obeying his commands; in playing the role of his love slave.

But the time for pretence was over now, she realised as a bleak dismay filled her heart. It was time to go back to the real world and her real life. Time, too, to get a grip.

Gathering herself, she hurried into the bathroom, where she grabbed a towel and was wrapping it tightly around her nakedness when she caught a glimpse of her reflection in the vanity mirror.

Goodness, she could not go back to the office looking like that! Her hair was a mess, her lips looked puffy and her eyes…

If eyes were the windows to one's soul, then her soul was in big trouble!

Steeling herself once more, she hurried out to the living room where she found Nicolas making himself a cup of coffee in the kitchen. Ignoring his sharp, top-to-toe glance, she set about scooping up her clothes from the floor. Finally, and without a single word, she snatched up her handbag as well and bolted back to the bathroom.

Serina had just made herself look respectable when her mobile phone rang. She stiffened before rifling the handset out of the bottom of her bag and whisking it to her ear. Since the terrible call about Greg's death, she experienced a rush of anxiety whenever her mobile rang at odd times. Felicity knew not to ring her on it unless there was an emergency. But who else could it be?

'Yes?'

'It's only me, Serina,' her mother replied somewhat wearily. 'Not Felicity. You have to stop worrying about that child, dear. She's extremely capable of looking after herself.'

'Yes, Mum. I do know that. So what's up? It's not like you to ring me on this phone.'

'I tried the office number but it was engaged. That's why I rang you on your mobile. I thought you might like to know how things went with Mrs Johnson today.'

'Oh, yes, yes, I would. But can you tell me quickly? I'm still in Port Macquarie, and I told Felicity I'd be home by four.'

'What are you doing in Port?'

Serina swallowed. 'Having lunch with you know who.'

'Who? Oh, you mean Nicolas Dupre. Really? I'm surprised. I got the impression you weren't too pleased with Felicity for securing his services as judge for the talent quest.'

'I wasn't. And I didn't want to have lunch with him, believe me,' she said. 'But he asked me in front of those silly girls in my office and they made it impossible for me to refuse.'

'You're right. They are silly, those two. But nice girls all the same. So what's he like these days? Still handsome, I would expect.'

'Mum, could this conversation wait till later? I'm running out of time and I can't talk whilst I drive.' It seemed wise to let her mother think she had her own wheels.

'It will have to be much later. I haven't left Newcastle yet.'

'So how is Mrs Johnson?'

'Healthy as a horse. The doc gave her some mild blood pressure pills and told her to lay off the sherry.'

'Which she won't.'

'I doubt it. Anyway, dear, off you go and I'll ring you when I get home.'

'Please do.' And she hung up.

'Who were you talking to in here?' Nicolas said as he flung open the door.

'My mother,' she replied brusquely, and dropped the phone back into her bag. 'She rang to let me know how Mrs Johnson is.'

'And?'

'She'll live till she's a hundred. Now, if you don't mind, I need to get back to Rocky Creek.'

'You're the one who's been taking your time. Let's go.'

The drive back to Rocky Creek was excruciating. Neither of them spoke, not a single word.

Serina stared through the passenger window and tried not think about what she'd just done. If her mother ever found out she'd jumped into bed with Nicolas within hours of his returning, she would not believe her. Of course, her mother never knew about the highly sexual nature of their teenage affair. She probably thought her dear darling daughter had gone to her wedding night a virgin.

Serina would have liked to confide in her mother. To confess everything. But she couldn't. Her mother would not understand. She would be totally shocked, and bitterly ashamed.

I'll have to do what I've always done, Serina thought wearily. *Keep my mouth shut and all my dark dirty secrets to myself.*

Just after they'd gone through Wauchope, Nicolas's own brooding silence began to seriously bother her. If he considered their relationship dusted and dried, as he'd claimed, then why was he so angry with her?

And he was. She could feel his anger hitting her in waves.

They were just coming down the hill towards the bridge that crossed Rocky Creek when she decided to speak up.

'There's no need for this, Nicolas,' she said with more calm than she was feeling. 'It's childish.'

'What's childish?'

'Giving me the cold-shoulder treatment. Look, I'm sorry if things haven't worked out the way you might have imagined. I'm sorry I'm not the girl you remember. Like I said, things change. So do people.'

His sidewards glance showed a reluctant flash of admiration. 'You've certainly grown up a lot.'

'Marriage and motherhood has a tendency to do that.'

'Are you saying I haven't grown up?'

'Not at all. But parenthood has a way of forcing a person into early maturity, and into being less selfish.'

'Ah, so you're saying that I'm selfish.'

'Don't put words into my mouth, Nicolas. You would know better than me if you're selfish or not.'

Nicolas nodded. 'I suspect that I am. My mother always said I was.'

They both fell silent again as he drove into town. Despite knowing she would see Nicolas again the next day, Serina didn't want this day to end badly.

'Can't we part friends, Nicolas?' she asked, her voice cracking a little.

He did not reply at first. But then he nodded. 'If that's what you want.'

Oh, yes, of course it wasn't what she wanted. But what she wanted—what she'd always wanted—just couldn't be. She'd made her bed all those years ago. And now she had to lie in it, till the end of her days.

'It's what I want,' she said.

He pulled into the car park of Brown's Landscaping and Building Supplies, but didn't bother to park, just drove straight up to the front door. The face he turned towards her was totally unreadable.

'Friends, then,' he said, and bent to give her a peck on the cheek. 'See you tomorrow.'

Her eyes met his for a long moment. She almost said it.

I love you.

I've always loved you.

But only almost.

When tears pricked at her eyes, she did the only thing she could do. She smiled, then got out of the car and waved him off.

She didn't go into the office. She could not bear to make conversation right at that moment, couldn't bear any more pretending. She went straight to her own car and drove straight home.

Felicity wasn't there yet, thank heavens. Her daughter wasn't renowned for punctuality. Just as well, because by then serious tears were threatening. Serina just managed to get herself inside before the floodgates opened.

'Oh, Nicolas,' she cried as she sank down to the floor, her back against the front door, her head dropping into her hands. 'Why did you have to come back?'

An equally distraught Nicolas was thinking exactly the same thing as he drove back to Port Macquarie. If he hadn't promised Felicity to judge that stupid bloody talent quest tomorrow he would have taken the first available flight back to Sydney. He didn't want to see Serina again. He didn't want to have to pretend to everyone that they were just 'good friends'. His life had been much easier when she was just a memory, one which had occasionally tormented him but which he'd been able to put aside, most of the time.

Impossible to put aside a flesh-and-blood woman in the same room as him, one who only a short time earlier had been kneeling, naked, before him.

Nicolas shuddered.

He had to stop thinking about that. Had to stop thinking that he'd never meant anything more to her than just a piece of meat.

But she'd said as much, hadn't she?

Sex is all you're good for, Nicolas.

They were her very own words.

She'd also said he was childish. And selfish.

As Nicolas drove back to Port Macquarie, he mulled over everything she'd said and done that day. By the time he let himself back into his apartment he'd come to the conclusion that Serina was right. He was childish and selfish. And extremely egotistical to think she might still love him. Which of course was what had brought him here in the first place. That vain hope.

Very vain.

It saddened him to face the truth, but it had to be faced. He'd lost his chance with Serina twenty years ago. That episode at the Opera House had meant no more to her than a one-night stand. As had this afternoon.

Opening one of the wine bottles, Nicolas poured himself a long glass and sat down to drink. Think of tomorrow as a job, he lectured himself. A series of auditions for a show. He'd always liked auditions. Liked the anticipation of discovering someone with real talent. Who knew? Maybe someone in Rocky Creek primary school has real talent…

CHAPTER FOURTEEN

NICOLAS sat down at the judge's table and kept his eyes glued to the stage. That way he wouldn't be tempted to look over at Serina, whom he knew was sitting in the first row of seats, a little to his left. He'd managed to avoid her in the main, although even a short hello and a few miserable glimpses had burned her appearance into his poor besotted brain.

She was wearing white, pure virginal white. Unfortunately, she looked anything but, her dress being halter-necked with a deep V neckline, a tightly belted waist and a gathered shirt that emphasised her hourglass figure and gave rise to the kind of erotic thoughts she always evoked in him.

Felicity walking onto the stage was a good distraction. He hadn't forgotten that she was going to play at some stage this afternoon and he was really looking forward to it, though he rather suspected Mrs Johnson's effusive praise earlier over Felicity's abilities as a pianist might be exaggerated.

'Reminds me of you, Nicolas,' the old lady had said.

Unlikely, given Felicity was a girl and only twelve. Although she looked older standing there in a pale blue dress and shoes that had heels. Her long dark hair swung around her slender shoulders the way Serina's did when she walked. She was, however, taller than her mother. There again, her father had been tall.

'Act number one,' Felicity announced into the microphone, 'will be Jonathon Clarke. Jonathon is in fourth grade and he's going to juggle. Jonathon?' She waved towards the wings and a skinny, nervous-looking boy with short brown hair and glasses emerged. Some taped music started, but Jonathon didn't. Whoever was behind the scenes stopped the tape, then started again.

Nicolas had a feeling that he wasn't seeing the winner.

Rocky Creek Primary School didn't have a great deal of talent, Nicolas accepted by the time he'd sat through eight very mediocre acts. But what the kids lacked in talent they made up for in enthusiasm. There was a real buzz in the hall, which was full to the brim with parents, locals and some concert-goers not so local.

None of them seemed disappointed with the acts so far, applauding wildly at the end of each. Nicolas, who appreciated he'd been spoiled by years of seeing top performers all over the world, put aside his super-critic hat and kept his comments on the kind and constructive side. The audience seemed appreciative of his ability to find praise for even the worst performance.

So far he'd endured the hapless Jonathon, who'd dropped more clubs than he caught; a gymnastic-style dance troop of fifth-grade girls whose movements often got out of sync; a poetry reading of 'The Man From Snow River', complete with stick horses thundering across the stage in the background; two separate country and western singers with absolutely no originality; a twelve-year-old magician whose magic was straight out of a do-it-yourself manual; an Elvis impersonator, who'd been hilarious, because he was so atrocious. And last but not least, a ten-year-old boy named Cory, playing the spoons.

Actually, he wasn't half-bad. If no one better came along, Nicolas was going to give Cory first prize.

Only two to go, according to the program. A twelve-year-old hip-hop dancer named Kirsty. And an eleven-year-old girl—her name was Isabella—singing 'Danny Boy'.

He should have known 'Danny Boy' would get in there somewhere.

Kirsty was somewhat of a pleasant surprise. She was darned good. But Isabella was clearly the star act of the night, the audience falling silent the moment she opened her mouth, her voice as pure and as clear as a bell.

Everyone clapped wildly when she finished, Nicolas included. He didn't have to think too hard over who would win, or who would be runner-up. He'd make that second prize a dead heat between Kirsty, the hip-hop dancer, and Cory, the spoon boy. It would be simple to add a bit of money to the prize pool himself, if need be.

But before any of this could happen, however, there was one event left: Felicity's special performance.

Nicolas found his heartbeat quickening when she walked back out onto the stage.

Surely he couldn't be nervous for her.

But he was, nervous as hell.

Nicolas had never been nervous himself before a performance. He used to be excited. He could not wait to get out there, to show what he could do, to blow his audience away with his brilliance.

But then he'd always been super confident when it came to playing the piano. Girls—especially young girls like Felicity—rarely possessed that kind of confidence.

Yet as he watched her cross to the centre of the stage, there was no hesitation in her stride. She stopped there for a moment, faced the audience and bowed, at the same time throwing him a smile that wasn't just confident. It was super confident.

'Wait till you hear this,' Felicity's principal whispered from where he was sitting beside Nicolas at the judge's table. 'Felicity would have won hands down if she'd entered, you know.'

It was a telling remark, coming so soon after Isabella's almost faultless rendition of 'Danny Boy'.

Nicolas watched, his mouth drying as Felicity moved over to the piano that had not been used as yet that night, Isabella having sung unaccompanied and the dancers using recorded music.

Another smile came his way after she sat down on the stool and lifted her hands to the keys.

'I have chosen to play this medley of pieces in honour of our very special guest here tonight,' she said to the audience. 'I cannot hope to play them as well as he once did. But I will do my best and hope he forgives my mistakes.'

What mistakes? Nicolas was to think numbly thirty seconds later as Felicity's fingers flew over the keys. He'd never heard Rimsky-Korsakov's 'Flight of the Bumblebee' performed any better by one so young. In no time the fast, flashy piece was over, Felicity switching with effortless ease and surprising sensitivity into the haunting adagio from Beethoven's 'Moonlight Sonata'. Lastly, just as everyone in the audience was almost in tears, she launched into Chopin's very showy polonaise 'Heroic', a piece requiring great technical brilliance and showmanship.

Chopin was a favourite choice of composer amongst concert pianists, especially his polonaises. This particular one had been a staple of Nicolas's list. He watched, totally amazed, as Felicity attacked the wild sweep of notes with the same kind of panache and passion that he'd possessed, which the critics had loved. She never looked up at any sheets of music because there were none there. She was playing from memory as he'd always done.

Nicolas could not believe it. Only twelve and already she could play like this. Why, she could take the world by storm in a few years!

Felicity finished the polonaise with a flourish, bending

over the keys in a long, dramatic pause before slowly lifting her hands. She tossed her hair back from her shoulders as she stood up, taking her time to turn and bow to the audience, all the while with a 'Yes, I know I'm good' expression on her face.

It was then that she broke into a grin and winked at him.

The cheeky minx, Nicolas thought as he jumped to his feet, clapping and shouting 'Bravo!' as European audiences sometimes did. Everyone else in the hall started doing likewise and Felicity finally began to look a little embarrassed. It was left to the principal of the school to hurry up onto the stage and bring some order back into proceedings.

'Wasn't that just wonderful, folks?' he said, and gave a by then embarrassed-looking Felicity a shoulder squeeze. 'Not only is our school captain a great little pianist, but she's also a great little organiser. We have her to thank for the presence here tonight of our esteemed guest and judge, Mr Nicolas Dupre. For anyone who doesn't know, Mr Dupre was Australia's most famous concert pianist till a tragic accident cut short his career a decade ago. But you can't keep a Rocky Creek lad down for long. He then went on to become an equally famous theatrical entrepreneur. Some of you might have seen the segment about him on TV a few years ago. Anyway, we are most grateful that he found the time to be with us here tonight. He came a long way. Now…we come to the most important part of the evening. Will Mr Dupre please come up onto the stage and announce the winners?'

Nicolas rose, and made his way forward to some ear-splitting applause.

Serina wasn't clapping, however, her hands twisting in her lap as she watched Nicolas mount the short flight of steps then walk across the stage to where Felicity and Fred Tarleton were standing.

He looked magnificent, dressed in a charcoal-grey suit

which must have cost a small fortune. Not only did it fit his body to perfection, but there also wasn't a single wrinkle where the sleeves met his broad shoulders. His shirt was blue, about the same colour as his eyes. His tie was dark blue and grey striped. Only his collar-length blond hair spoiled his image as a millionaire businessman. That, and the inherent sensuality in his face.

Serina heard a few soft sighs from the women in the audience.

In a way, those sounds provided a degree of comfort. How could she blame herself for being besotted by the man when perfect strangers were affected by him?

But it wasn't his sex appeal that was causing her hands to be wrung. Or her stomach to be hopelessly in knots. It was the fear that he might have seen the truth during Felicity's astounding performance just now.

Surely he must have seen what was so obvious to her. That this was his own flesh and blood playing up there. His genes, not Greg's.

She leant forward in her seat to get a closer look at the expression on his face when he approached Felicity. When his daughter smiled up at him, he smiled back, just as happily, without hesitation, without even a hint of distress or anger.

He hadn't seen! He didn't even suspect!

Perversely, any relief Serina felt was tinged by a bitter resentment. What was it about men that they had no sensitivity, or intuition? He should have seen what was obvious. But no, they only saw what they wanted to see. Or what their male ego let them see, and believe.

Nicolas had believed she didn't love him all those years ago, and he believed it once again today. Yet she'd shown him in that bedroom this afternoon how much she did.

She shook her head and sank back into her seat.

'He hasn't changed much,' Mrs Johnson said from where she was sitting on the right side of Serina.

'No,' Serina agreed with considerable irony. He was still a blind fool!

'Hush up, you two,' her mother said impatiently from the other side of Serina.

Nicolas took the microphone from Fred Tarleton and faced the audience.

'Firstly,' he said, 'my heartiest congratulations, Felicity, for what was, indeed, a spectacular performance. I know I could not have done better myself at your age. Such prodigious talent is a tribute to the dedication and skill of her teacher, Mrs Johnson, who was my own first teacher. Mrs Johnson…' He bowed gallantly towards the old lady. 'I salute you.'

'I take that back,' Mrs Johnson murmured. 'He has changed. The boy I taught had no charm whatsoever.'

A swift sidewards glance showed Serina the old lady was preening under his praise and that well-learned charm.

Her teeth clenched down hard in her jaw.

She sat there, silently fuming—which was insane!—as he went through the process of allotting the prizes, exerting more of his charm and gaining more approval from the audience as he awarded not one but two runner-up prizes. It had been a foregone conclusion that once Felicity was out of the running that Isabella would win. Not that Serina minded that. Isabella was a delightful girl with a truly lovely voice.

Serina tried telling herself she should be grateful that Nicolas hadn't twigged to the truth. Possibly she would be, in time.

Just not right now!

'I have one last presentation to make before today's event comes to a close,' Nicolas said, everyone in the hall falling silent and snapping to attention. 'Felicity, I think you should be the one to receive this.' And he extracted from the breast pocket of his suit jacket what looked like a cheque. 'It was your lovely letter that brought me here. A touching letter, folks, about her dad's tragic death in the Victorian bushfires.

As you all know, this afternoon was a fund-raiser for the local bushfire brigade of which her dad was president. Now as much as you have all turned out in wonderful numbers and paid your money at the door, I made enquires about what it would cost to buy just one of those new firefighting trucks that Felicity told me about and I don't think you're going to make it today, not unless I give things a helping hand. So here you are, dear girl. I think it should be enough.'

Serina watched her daughter's eyes widen as she stared at the cheque, watched her daughter then throw her arms around Nicolas. By the time Nicolas disengaged her, Felicity's big brown eyes were dancing with happiness.

'It's for three hundred thousand dollars!' she shouted to everyone.

Everyone began to clap. Everyone, that is, but Serina, who was crying. Her mother put an arm around her shoulders.

'There there, love. I know. It's still hard. But I'm sure Greg must be happy tonight, looking down at his daughter from heaven. Happy and proud.'

Serina cried all the harder…

CHAPTER FIFTEEN

THE after-concert party was in full swing, with Nicolas being bombarded with both finger food and conversation. People kept coming up to him to congratulate him on a job well done and to say thank you, the girls from Serina's office included— though not Serina, he noted ruefully. She kept her distance, even when her own mother and Mrs Johnson were chatting to him.

Felicity brought along her paternal grandparents, Franny and Bert Harmon, whom he'd never met before. They looked like they were in their late seventies and rather an odd couple: Bert was tall and thin whilst Franny was very short and plump. But both of them had grey hair and dark, gentle eyes.

'Nanna and Pop bought your old house, you know,' Felicity said after she'd introduced them.

'Really?'

'And your old piano. That's what I first learned to play on.'

Nicolas was quite startled by this news. He'd imagined that her having piano lessons had been Serina's doing, that Felicity would have learned to play on her mother's piano. Serina had had her own instrument long before Nicolas acquired his, courtesy of a competition he'd won. Till then he'd always practised on Mrs Johnson's piano.

'Whenever I went to stay at Nanna and Pop's,' Felicity went on, 'I could hear the kids having lessons next door at Mrs

Johnson's. Her music room was just over the fence from my bedroom window. I used to love to lie in bed and listen.'

Nicolas could hardly believe what he was hearing. Talk about coincidence!

'Then, one day, when I was about three,' Felicity continued, 'I can't actually remember this…but Pop tells me he came downstairs and I was trying to play. He decided then and there I should have lessons. To tell the truth, Mum wasn't all that keen but Dad was, even though he wasn't musical at all.'

'Tone deaf Greg was,' Franny said with a nod. 'But he was so proud of you, love. I'm sure he would have been very proud of you tonight. The way you played. Nicolas was right. You were quite magnificent.'

'If you moved to Sydney to attend the conservatorium of music,' Nicolas said to her, 'you would become an even better pianist. In a few years, you could be giving concerts all over the world.'

Felicity looked very taken aback. 'But I would hate that,' she said very forthrightly. 'I love playing the piano, Nicolas, but I don't want to do it for a living. Good heavens, no! I'm going to become a vet.'

'A vet,' he echoed blankly.

'Golly, yes. Who'd want to be a concert pianist?' she went on with the tactlessness of youth. 'I can't think of anything more boring. Playing the piano is fun, but not all the time. Oh, sorry, Nicolas,' she added, suddenly realising what she'd just said. 'I forgot for a moment. Still, I'll bet you enjoy yourself a lot more doing what you're doing now than thumping away on the keys for hours and hours every day. Which is what I'd have to do if I wanted to become a concert pianist. I know because Mrs Johnson said so. "If you want to make a career of the piano, Felicity,"' she pronounced in a perfect imitation of Mrs Johnson's somewhat haughty voice, '"you have to practise, practise, practise." Well I practised like mad for weeks for tonight's performance and I can tell you I've had more than enough of that piano for a while. I'm not going to touch a key over the Christmas holidays. Now, I really do have to go help the others with the food and stuff, or they'd think I'm slacking. Thank you again, Nicolas,' she said as she gave him a peck on the cheek. 'Don't go without saying goodbye.'

'A vet,' Nicolas muttered drily as he watched Felicity hurry away to join her friends. What a horrible waste of talent!

'She's animal mad, is our Felicity,' Bert piped up. 'Not domestic animals so much. Wildlife. She and Kirsty—who's her very best friend, the one who did the hip-hop dance—they're always hunting around in the bush looking for injured animals and birds. Kirsty's folks have an acreage just out of town.'

'I see,' Nicolas said politely. Though he didn't at all. All he could see was that she was wasting a musical talent that was beyond exceptional.

'To tell the truth, Mr Dupre,' Bert went on, 'Mother and I are glad Felicity wants to be a vet. That way, even if she goes away to study for a while after leaving school, she'll eventually come back to live in this area. She's all we have now that our son has gone. Greg was an only child, you see. We always hoped that he and Serina would have more kiddies, but that wasn't to be.'

'His having had the mumps as a young lad had something to do with that,' Franny added. 'He had some tests done when Serina didn't fall for a baby again and they said he had a low sperm count. So we're lucky to have one grandchild. We'd be totally lost without Felicity, wouldn't we, Bert? She brings us such joy. Do you remember the day she was born? She was amazing from the word go. Didn't look like a newborn. Why, she could have passed for three months old. And she was so beautiful. Nothing like Greg when he was born. He looked like a wizened-up monkey for weeks. Of course she's taken after Serina with her looks and her musical talent. Not so much in nature though. Felicity's a real little goer, as I'm sure you've gathered, but extremely stubborn. It's thankful she has a good heart to temper her ambitions. But I know Serina has trouble with her sometimes. We help as much as we can. And Serina's mother does, too, of course. The girl really needs a father figure. Greg was wonderful with her, not too indulgent. He recognised she needed direction. Felicity adored him. Oh dear,' Franny said suddenly, her eyes suddenly filling with tears. 'Sorry. I thought I was over doing this.'

Somehow, Nicolas managed to murmur something sympathetic. But his mind was whirling with the things Felicity's grandmother had just told him.

If she was Felicity's grandmother, Nicolas began thinking with a sick, hollow feeling forming in the pit of his stomach... Surely Serina wouldn't have done that? Surely not? But the evidence he'd just heard suggested differently.

His eyes started to scan the room, searching for her.

'Come on, Mother,' Bert said gently as he took his weeping wife's arm. 'Let's go get you a nice cup of tea. Lovely talking to you, Mr Dupre. And thanks once again for donating that terrific sum of money. You've made Felicity one extremely happy girl tonight.'

Serina knew, the moment her eyes met Nicolas's across the crowded hall, that what she'd feared would happen ever since she heard Nicolas was returning to Rocky Creek had just happened.

Never had she seen Nicolas look at her like that. There wasn't just anger in his eyes, or disbelief... There was sheer unadulterated horror.

'God help me,' she muttered under her breath as he came striding towards her, where she was thankfully standing by herself behind the drinks table.

'We need to talk, Serina,' he growled. 'Now!'

'What about?' she asked with feigned innocence whilst her heart was thudding wildly behind her ribs and nausea swirled in her stomach.

His eyes narrowed on her, his expression uncompromising in the extreme. 'I think you know what about.'

'Not unless you tell me.'

'You really want me to say it here? To shout out to all and sundry that Felicity is not your husband's daughter, but mine,' he hissed. 'Because I will if you don't make some excuse and come with me right here and now.'

Serina thought she was going to faint as she saw her whole world crashing around her. Not just her world, but her daughter's as well. And lots of other people's.

But he can't know, came the saving thought as she gripped the edge of the table, steadying her body as well as her mind. *He just suspects. You can bluff this out, girl. You have to bluff it out.*

'I can't imagine what Franny and Bert said to you to make you think such an outrageous thing,' she said with superb calm. 'But you're dead wrong. Felicity is Greg's daughter. Not yours.' Which she was, in every way but biologically.

'I don't believe you, Serina,' he challenged. 'Now are we going to argue about this here, or are you going to come with me?'

'Come where?' Not his apartment. No way was she going to go there again!

'Somewhere private,' he spluttered.

Felicity's bouncing up to her mother right at that moment with Kirsty by her side was both a blessing and a curse.

'Kirsty wants me to go to her place for a sleepover,' she said. 'Can I, Mum? Can I, please?'

'Felicity, I…'

'Oh, please, Mrs Harmon,' Kirsty begged. 'Mum says it's okay. Then we could spend tomorrow together.'

Serina knew there would be no dissuading them, not once

they ganged up on her. On top of that, it provided her with the perfect solution over where to take Nicolas. She would feel much safer facing him in her own home; safer, and stronger.

'All right, then,' she said, relenting. 'What about clothes?'

'She can borrow some of mine, Mrs Harmon,' Kirsty said. 'We're exactly the same size.'

'Fine. Just don't go doing anything silly.'

'Like what?'

'Like going too far into the bush looking for more sick koalas. The weather forecast for tomorrow is very hot, even hotter than today, and windy—perfect bushfire weather. Promise me you'll stay close to Kirsty's place.'

'We promise,' the two girls chorused.

'You could go out with Nicolas again tonight, if you wanted to,' Felicity added, and Kirsty giggled.

It didn't surprise Serina that her daughter was still trying to matchmake her with Nicolas. That girl never let up, once she got a bee in her bonnet. If only she knew!

'What a good idea,' Nicolas said immediately with a coldly cryptic smile. 'I enjoyed the time I spent with your mother today very much. We've always been great mates. We could go the movies, Serina, like we used to.'

Serina felt all the blood drain from her face. Because of course they never went to the movies in the past. They just told their parents that was where they were going. They always spent the time making love.

If he thought he could somehow coerce her into having more sex with him, then he was sadly mistaken. But then an appalling thought popped into her head. What if he said he'd tell everyone in Rocky Creek he was Felicity's father if she didn't do just that?

Surely he wouldn't do a wicked thing like that. Surely not!

Nicolas saw her moment of realisation. Saw, also, the way her chin rose, her eyes spearing his with tigerish fury.

'I'm way too tired to go to the movies,' she returned coolly. 'But you can come back to my place for some coffee, if you like.'

He didn't like. He didn't want to go where she'd played happy family with Greg Harmon with his daughter. But he could hardly make a fuss in front of Felicity and her friend.

Frankly, Nicolas wasn't sure what he was going to do as yet. Except make Serina suffer for a while.

She deserved to suffer, if what he suspected was true.

'An excellent idea,' he said crisply.

'I can't leave straight away,' Serina said once Felicity and Kirsty ran off together. 'I have to help clean up here. As you can see, the party's coming to a close and there's lots of mess. All the plastic chairs have to be stacked up and put away as well.'

Nicolas controlled himself with difficulty. He was used to getting his own way with things, used to people jumping to do his bidding.

Serina was clearly past doing his bidding. It came to him suddenly that she'd only appeared to do so this afternoon because she had a secret agenda. To get him out of Rocky Creek as soon as possible. As much as she might have seemed to enjoy his love-making, she was probably faking it, the same way she'd faked her mad passion that night at the Opera House. All to get him to have sex with her without protection. All to conceive the child that she knew Greg Harmon couldn't give her.

A dark fury—and even darker desires—filled his soul as he thought about that night. What a fool he'd been! A blind besotted fool! But he would have her again—tonight. And she'd let him. Because that would be his bargain. One more night of sex in exchange for his silence, plus his departure tomorrow...

CHAPTER SIXTEEN

SERINA expected him to argue with her. But he didn't.

'In that case, I'll help,' he said. 'That way, you'll be finished more quickly.'

Which was true. Nicolas, the celebrated entrepreneur, was also a splendid organiser. Within thirty minutes everything was cleared away, the floors swept, the chairs stacked. Fortunately, during this time, her mother had left to take a tired Mrs Johnson home and Felicity had gone off with Kirsty and her parents.

Night was just falling when they emerged from the hall at eight-thirty, by which time Serina had her arguments all fixed firmly in her mind. She clung to the fact that Nicolas had no proof, just suspicion.

'It's still very hot out here,' he complained straight away. 'I hope your place has air-conditioning. If it doesn't we'll be going elsewhere.'

Serina kept her temper with difficulty. 'It has air-conditioning. On a timer, which I set for eight. The house should be nice and cool by the time we get there. But even if it wasn't, I wouldn't be going anywhere else with you, Nicolas Dupre.'

'Is that so?' came his cold reply. 'That's a matter to be seen. My wheels are over here.' And he took a hold of her arm.

She would have wrenched her arm away if other people hadn't been nearby. 'I have my own wheels, thank you very much,' she said and extracted herself carefully from his grasp. 'It's the white car over there. You can follow me home, it's not far.'

'How far?'

'Less than a kilometre. I live up at the top end of Winter Street. Remember the old strawberry farm? Well, developers bought it, tore down the dump of a farmhouse and turned it into a very nice estate. Greg and I bought a block of land there not long after we got married.'

Nicolas really didn't want to hear about Serina's life with Greg Harmon. He was still finding it hard to believe what she'd done. The girl he'd known—and loved—wasn't capable of such deception. There again, the girl who'd come to him that night at the Opera House hadn't been that same girl. She'd been engaged to Greg Harmon by then. Madly in love with him, obviously, and ready to do anything for him.

But what she'd done had been downright wicked!

If that was what she did, another voice piped up in his head. One that wasn't quite so ready to condemn. One that was still connected to reason. *You might be wrong, Nicolas. Not about Felicity being your daughter, but about how and why she was conceived. Serina might not have planned anything. Maybe it just...happened.*

But if that was the case, then why did she go through with marrying Harmon? Why didn't she come to me? I would have married her. I loved her.

No, he was right the first time. She'd planned it all right.

He knew women could do such things. His own mother had.

His heart hardened once again towards Serina. She had to be made to tell him the truth. Okay, so he probably wouldn't blackmail her back into his bed. Even he could not condone that kind of outrageous behaviour, much as his dark side relished the idea. That had just been his anger talking and a primal urge for vengeance.

By the time Serina pulled in to the driveway of a cream, cement-rendered, ranch-style home, Nicolas had himself come halfway to reason. But only halfway. He wasn't in the mood for any bulldust from her.

'I hope you're not going to keep on denying it,' were his first words on joining her on the neat front porch.

She ignored him and went on unlocking the front door.

'Watch your feet,' she finally said when she pushed the door open. 'I have a cat who just loves to wind herself around your legs. Her name is Midnight.'

Nicolas wasn't one for pets, but he didn't mind cats. He quite liked their independence.

Not that Serina's cat seemed to be displaying much of that. She almost tripped both of them up in her rush for attention. Serina eventually scooped the big black cat up into her arms and carried her down the cream-tiled hallway into an open-planned living area that combined the kitchen, dining and sitting rooms.

'Yes, yes,' she said soothingly, stroking the cat's glossy black fur for a while before dropping her onto the kitchen floor. 'Mummy's home. I suppose you're hungry.' And she turned away to open the refrigerator door.

Nicolas could see that any hope of conversation was nil till the cat was attended to. So he sat down on one of the cane stools that fronted the breakfast bar and shut his mouth whilst he watched Serina fix her pet's food.

Eventually, however, his eyes strayed to his immediate surroundings.

For a house that hadn't looked all that large from the street, the inside was extremely spacious, especially this section where there was enough room for a couple of loungers, a huge television, lots of side tables and a large, oval-shaped dining table that would easily seat ten people. The floor was tiled in the same cream tiles as the hallway, but with well-placed rugs for warmth and comfort. The walls were cream, the furniture in various shades of brown and green. It was a well-designed area, perfect for family living and gatherings.

Before he could stop himself, Nicolas began thinking of all the family get-togethers that would have taken place in this room: the birthdays parties, the anniversaries, the Christmases.

He stared at Serina and wondered if she'd ever felt guilty over what she'd done. It seemed impossible that she hadn't given him a second thought over the years. He was her daughter's father, for pity's sake.

There again, this whole situation seemed impossible.

Suddenly, her fussing over Midnight annoyed the hell out of him.

'If you've finally finished with that damned animal,' he snapped, 'do you think we might get back to the subject at hand?'

She stood up and glared at him, her shoulders as straight as her gaze. 'Look, I already told you. Felicity is Greg's daughter, not yours. I can't imagine what Bert and Franny told you to make you believe otherwise.'

'Several things,' he shot back at her. 'Firstly, they expressed their gratitude that their son had been lucky enough to have at least one child. It seems having mumps as an adolescent can lead to sterility.'

'Greg was not sterile,' she countered quite firmly, 'and I can prove it. We had tests done when we didn't conceive another child. He did have a low sperm count. But he could still have become a father.'

'But not of a musical prodigy,' Nicolas snapped. 'Serina, do you think I'm totally blind? How many twelve-year-old girls can play like Felicity did tonight? She didn't come from some tone-deaf father!'

'She's my daughter, too, you know,' Serina argued, her face becoming quite flushed. 'I wasn't half-bad at music.'

'You were merely adequate.'

Her hands found her hips. 'Oh, thank you very much.'

'You can snap and snarl all you like. But I know what I know. Felicity is my daughter.'

'In that case, how can you explain her birth date, which can also be verified? Felicity was born exactly nine months after our wedding day, ten months after I slept with you that night. Since you're such a genius, you should be able to do the maths. She couldn't possibly be your daughter!'

Nicolas had been waiting for this argument to surface.

'I fell for that argument once before, Serina,' he retorted, finding calm in the face of her growing hysteria. 'But not tonight. Bert and Franny also waxed lyrical about how beautiful Felicity looked when she was born. Nothing like their son, who'd been all wrinkly. Not like a newborn at all, Franny said.'

He watched as Serina struggled to find something to say. But failed.

'She was late being born, wasn't she?' he charged. 'Very late.'

'Don't be ridiculous!' she spluttered. 'No doctor worth his salt would let a mother go that late these days. He would have given me an induction.'

'The doctor probably didn't know you were that late. Because you gave him the wrong dates. Now let me guess. You didn't have an ultrasound during your pregnancy. You made up some excuse about being superstitious about them. Maybe I could ask your mother and verify my suspicions.'

Serina crossed her arms. 'What you're saying is just so much rubbish! I don't know if you're mad, or just delusional.'

'If you keep denying it, Serina, I will have a DNA test done and then there will be no further arguments.'

Her arms fell open, as did her mouth. 'You can't do that! Not without my permission.'

'Oh, yes I can. Trust me. All I need is a good lawyer and a

court order. Soon, I'll have what you've denied me for twelve years. Proof of my paternity, then access to my daughter.'

'Don't do this, Nicolas!' Serina cried, coming forward to grip the edge of the countertop.

'Don't do what?'

'Don't destroy your daughter's life.'

'So she is my daughter.'

There was a stricken silence from Serina, then a long shuddering sigh as her head drooped. 'Yes,' she confessed brokenly. 'Yes, she's your daughter!'

Nicolas felt like someone had struck him. It was one thing to suspect something, quite another to hear it from the only person who knew. He was sitting there, stunned, when her head lifted, her eyes flooded with tears.

'I'm sorry, Nicolas,' she choked out, 'so sorry.'

'She's sorry,' he repeated numbly.

'I never meant to hurt you. I never meant any of it. What I did...it was wrong. But not intentional.'

'Not intentional,' he repeated, all the while trying to control the emotions welling up inside him. Not fury so much anymore. In its place was a deep sadness, and a dreadful, dreadful emptiness.

'By the time I found out I was pregnant,' she cried, 'the wedding was upon me and I...I didn't have the courage to just walk away.'

'You should have told me,' he said bleakly.

'I should have. Yes.'

'But you didn't.'

'No.'

'You didn't love me. You loved him.'

Again, she fell silent, shaking her head from side to side.

'Did you know Harmon couldn't have kids when you slept with me? Did you do it to give him the child you knew he couldn't have.'

Nicolas could not deny the shock that filled her face. 'No! No! I would never do a thing like that. And Greg could have children. I told you. He just had a low sperm count.'

'If that's the case, when did you know she was mine?'

'Oh, God,' she sobbed, then snatched a handful of tissues from a box on the counter, turning away from him as she blew her nose.

'I'm waiting for an answer, Serina,' Nicolas said with barely held patience.

Her sigh was weary, her eyes haunted. 'I knew all along,' she confessed. 'I...I hadn't slept with Greg during the last couple of months of our engagement. He wanted to make our wedding night special, he said.'

'And was it?' Nicolas asked bitterly.

'I'm not going to answer that.'

'You'll answer anything I ask you. And you'll do anything I ask you. Or you know what will happen. I'll tell everyone in Rocky Creek the truth and to hell with you.'

'You wouldn't do that. You're not that cruel.'

'How do you know? Like you said earlier today, we don't know each other anymore.'

'What is it that you want me to do?' she asked him, her eyes fearful.

'That depends on what you want me to do. Spell it out for me, Serina. That way I won't be under any further illusions about you.'

'I...I don't want you to tell anyone. Ever. I want you to keep my secret. Not for my sake. For Felicity's. And for her extended family. You must have seen how much Greg's parents love her. It would break their hearts—and Felicity's—if you tell them Greg wasn't her father.'

'And what about my heart? Or don't you think it can be broken?'

'Oh, Nicolas, Nicolas, do be honest. It's only your ego that is hurt by this. You don't have any bond with Felicity. It's not as though you want to come back to Rocky Creek and be her father for real. You hate it here. Your life is in New York and London.'

Amazing how the ugly truth could rub one raw. Though it was going a bit far to say that only his ego was hurting.

'She could come with me,' he said stubbornly. 'I could help her become a truly great pianist. She has the talent.'

Serina pulled a face. 'You don't know your daughter even a little bit if you say that. She doesn't want to be a concert pianist. She wants to be a vet.'

'Yes, I know,' he said grimly. 'She told me.'

'See? There's nothing to be gained by telling her that you're her father. She would end up hating you for it, believe me.'

'And you, Serina? Would you end up hating me? Or do you already hate me?'

Her eyes carried extreme frustration. 'I never hated you, Nicolas. But I could, quite easily, if you do this.'

'Are you talking about my telling everyone Felicity is my daughter? Or what sexual favours I might demand in exchange for my silence?'

'Oh, Nicolas, Nicolas,' she said, her soulful eyes chastening, then infuriating him.

'It's not too much to ask, surely,' he bellowed at her. 'One miserable night for a future lifetime of silence? You might even enjoy it. You seemed to this afternoon.'

She went very pale. But her chin went up and she eyed him with the same strength of character with which she'd eyed him all day.

'This afternoon was something else entirely.'

'Really? You mean you didn't agree to do whatever I wanted in bed in exchange for my rapid departure tomorrow?'

'I know it probably looks that way...'

'I can't see how it can look any other way. So, if I asked you for a repeat performance tonight, you'd agree?'

She just stared at him, her eyes reproachful.

'If I must,' she said at last.

Her answer took all the breath from his lungs. And struck a vicious blow to his conscience.

It came to Nicolas then just how much Serina loved their daughter. It was a love that transcended pride; that would endure any humiliation to protect her child from harm, or unhappiness.

His own mother had loved him that way.

His father, however, had not given a damn about him. Nicolas had caught up with him a few years ago and told him he was his son. The man had not only denied it, but he'd also spoken disparagingly about his mother, inferring she was some kind of sleep-around slut, which Nicolas knew wasn't true. Nicolas hadn't expected his father to love him. But he could have been kind, not cruel. Could have been decent.

He had the chance to be kind now…to be decent.

'It's all right, Serina,' he said with a weary sigh of his own. 'I won't ask that of you. You win. I'll walk away. And I won't say a word about being Felicity's father.'

She immediately burst into floods of tears.

'Don't cry,' he snapped. 'I'm not doing it for you. But for her. For my daughter.'

Serina lifted her head from her hands, her wet eyes beseeching. 'You just don't understand anything, do you? I loved you, Nicolas. I loved you so much. I thought you loved me, but you didn't. You left me when I needed you. And you never came back. I couldn't forgive you for that. But I couldn't forget you, either.'

They stared at each other for a long time.

Nicolas was the first to speak.

'Did you love Harmon as much as you loved me?'

'I learned to love him,' she said. 'He was a good man. But my heart has always been yours, Nicolas. You were my first love, my first and only grand passion.'

As she was his.

'Spend the night with me,' he said, his voice breaking a little.

Her eyes showed total disbelief.

'I won't put any conditions on your doing so. I promise I won't say anything to anyone about Felicity whether you say yes or no. Please, Serina, I just want…' He broke off before he broke down.

'What, Nicolas?' she asked with a tortured groan. 'What is it that you want?'

'Just you. In my arms. One more time.'

'You don't know what you're asking,' she choked out. 'If I do this, I'll fall hopelessly in love with you again and I won't want you to go. I've never been able to resist you in bed, Nicolas. You must know that by now.'

'It is some small comfort,' he returned. 'So what's it to be, my love? Yes, or no?'

'Oh…' She shook her head from side to side before lancing him with a despairing look. 'Not here,' she blurted out.

Nicolas took that as a yes. So did his body.

'I'll follow you back to your place in Port,' she said, her eyes already glittering brightly. 'But I won't be staying the whole night.'

Nicolas nodded….

CHAPTER SEVENTEEN

When Serina woke, a pre-dawn light was filtering through the window above the bed head.

So much for my resolve not to stay the whole night, she thought ruefully as she glanced at her wristwatch and saw that it was five past six. Sighing, she very carefully lifted her leg off Nicolas's still-sleeping form and rolled onto her back next to him.

She'd been right to be fearful of staying the night with him. Nicolas in passionate mode was difficult enough to resist; Nicolas, the tender lover, was impossible to resist.

She hadn't fallen hopelessly in love with him again. How could she when she was already in love with him? But she'd begun to have foolish hopes where he was concerned, very foolish hopes, indeed.

Down deep, she knew that he wasn't going to come back to Rocky Creek to live. Neither was he going to marry her. The most Serina could hope was that he'd stay for the week that he'd booked. And perhaps come back for the odd visit over the coming years.

But more than likely he was going to get on that plane today and never return.

Last night had had goodbye written all over it.

Her heart turned over at this last thought. How was she going to be able to stand losing him again?

You'll just have to, came the harsh voice of reason. *You have no other choice. Mothers can't afford to have mental breakdowns. Now get your butt moving, get dressed and go home before all the neighbours wake up and see you driving past still dressed in the clothes you were wearing last night.*

Such thinking propelled her out of bed like a shot. Her clothes, fortunately, weren't strewn all over the place as they had been yesterday afternoon. Nicolas had undressed her here, with care, in the bedroom. Scooping them up, she hurried into the bathroom, where she climbed into the shower. Five minutes later, she was out, dried and dressed.

That was another thing mothers learned to do: be quick.

Having rinsed her mouth out with cold water, she was finger-combing her hair into place when the bathroom door opened and there stood Nicolas in all his naked glory.

'And where do you think you're going at this hour?' he asked.

Serina thought her nonplussed expression was of Oscar-winning standards. 'Home, of course,' she said coolly.

'But why? Felicity's not there. And you don't go into the office on a Saturday.'

'I have to this morning,' she returned crisply. 'Emma's having the day off. She's going to a wedding.'

'You still don't have to go this early. It's only ten past six. Have coffee with me first. I have something I want to discuss with you.'

Her heart leapt, not with hope, but with fear. Surely he hadn't changed his mind about not disclosing the fact he was Felicity's biological father? 'What about?' she asked somewhat warily.

'Nothing for you to worry about. Look, I'll go put on the kettle,' he said, and turned away, giving her a perfect view of his perfect rear.

'Only if you put some clothes on first?' she called after him.

He just laughed.

By the time she dared to leave the bathroom and join him in the living area he'd pulled on a pair of black satin boxer shorts.

'So what is it you want to talk to me about?' she asked whilst he opened a couple of the coffee bags supplied and popped them into mugs.

'I've been thinking,' he replied slowly, then stopped to pour in the boiling water.

'About what?'

'You take milk and one sugar, don't you?'

'Yes,' she said grudgingly. 'Now what's all this about?'

'My, my, but you are not such a happy chappy in the mornings, are you?' he said as he proceeded to take his time, getting the milk out of the fridge then slowly opening a packet of sugar.

'Nicolas, you're driving me mad! I have to get going. The neighbours will wake up soon and they'll see me coming home still dressed in this.' And she indicated the white dress she'd worn the night before.

His eyebrows lifted. 'Oh, I see. I forgot that people noticed such things in Rocky Creek. Not only noticed, but cared. Now don't blow a gasket,' he added when he saw a dark frustration fill her face. 'This won't take long. The thing is, Serina, I've changed my mind.'

Oh, no, she thought in a panic.

'It's not what you're thinking.' He frowned suddenly. 'Why must you always think the worst? What I've changed my mind about is leaving today.'

'But last night, you said…' She broke off, not sure if she was happy now with his change of heart. Amazing how things could work out in your head when they were romantic fantasies. Everything became much more complicated in real life.

'I know what I said. But I've had more time to think things

through and there's no reason for me to leave today. Look, I'm not going to say anything about being Felicity's father. I gave you my word on that. I can see how cruel that would be, and pointless. Felicity would probably hate me, as you said. And you, too. Which is not what I want. Not at all,' Nicolas added, then came forward to draw her into his arms. 'You said there was a danger you'd fall hopelessly in love with me again last night. Dare I hope it might have happened? Or is that just wishful thinking on my part?'

Serina groaned as her heart began to battle with her head. To tell him that she loved him was a big step and, perhaps, a foolish one at this juncture. After all, he hadn't said he loved her and he'd had plenty of chances last night.

'Nicolas, I can't afford to have my heart broken by you again,' she said carefully.

'You think I would do that?'

'I don't know what you'd do. Like you said, we don't know each other anymore. On top of that, we come from different worlds.'

'That's not quite true. We're both Australians. If you'd ever spent time living overseas, you'd realise that Australians are a breed apart. Look, I appreciate that you think I hate it here in Rocky Creek and that I prefer living in New York, et cetera, et cetera et cetera,' he said as he pushed her coffee across the kitchen counter towards her. 'But do you know what? I'm not so sure I hate Rocky Creek as much as I thought I did. Frankly, I enjoyed yesterday's talent quest more than I've enjoyed anything in years. But all that pales into insignificance against what we have together. Do you honestly think I'm going to let you get away from me for a third time? Okay, so I probably wouldn't like to live here full-time,' he went on. 'But there's no reason why I can't visit on a regular basis. No reason why you can't visit me as well. I'll pay all your expenses, of course.'

Of course, Serina thought, an unexpectedly sour taste filling her mouth. That was what wealthy men did for their mistresses: they paid.

Becoming Nicolas's part-time, long-distance mistress was not the stuff Serina's romantic dreams were made of. Especially since he hadn't even said he loved her. On top of that, to have him visit her in Rocky Creek on a regular basis was still a risk.

Her face twisted with the reality of that risk. 'You promise you won't say anything about you-know-what? Not ever? Even if you get angry with me for some reason?'

'I give you my solemn word.'

'So what, exactly, am I to tell my family? Especially my mother. She's going to ask questions if you stick around for another week.'

'Tell her the truth. That I've fallen hopelessly in love with you again and can't bring myself to leave just yet.'

Serina's mouth fell open. It was still open when Nicolas kissed her.

Nicolas leant over the railing of the balcony, calling and waving to Serina as she crossed the road to where she'd parked her car. When she glanced up and threw him a kiss, he threw one back.

'I'll ring you later,' he shouted, and she smiled.

It made him feel good, that smile. She made him feel good.

Okay, so she didn't quite trust him enough to tell him that she loved him, too. But he'd felt her love last night, and in her kisses just now. Soon, she would say the words he wanted to hear. Meanwhile, he'd begin making concrete plans for their future together, sensible ones that he could live with on a permanent basis.

There was no doubt in Nicolas's mind that existing 24/7 in Rocky Creek was beyond him. He would eventually miss the things which had become an integral part of his life. Going to stimulating dinner parties, the theatre, the opera. Serina was right about that.

But one didn't have to go to London or New York for such cultural diversions.

There were plenty of cities in Australia that could cater to his occasional need for such activities. Sydney especially, which was only a short flight from Port Macquarie. It might take some time, but he would sell his apartments in London and New York and buy a place in Sydney, as well as one in Port Macquarie. He would inquire if there was an apartment for sale in this building, he thought as he walked back inside and set about making himself a fresh cup of coffee. That way he could commute between both places with ease, and without feeling like he had no home. He could even continue his career as a producer and promoter, if he felt so inclined. Just because he hadn't brought shows to Australia in the past didn't mean he couldn't in future. Sydney had several theatres large enough to hold even the most lavish musicals. And the Opera House administrators were always trying to persuade the world's top singers and musicians to come Down Under.

Admittedly, he'd been growing a bit bored with that part of his life lately, but Nicolas was old enough to know that he might grow unbored at some future date. Showbiz was in his blood. To suddenly drop it from his life would be a recipe for disaster. He'd seen many a marriage flounder because of one or either party thinking their spouse would change after the wedding.

And he meant to marry Serina.

He hadn't mentioned the M-word yet—fearing it was a little premature—but she wasn't going to get away from him this time.

He'd done a lot of thinking overnight. He still loved her. And he'd finally come to the sensible realisation that he was crazy to feel any jealousy over her life with Greg Harmon. Her marrying another man was entirely his fault. If he'd been there for her in the first place, if he'd shown her by his actions that he truly loved her, instead of letting his stupid male pride ruin everything, then she would never have married Harmon. Her statement that she'd learned to love her husband had been very telling. She'd never been in love with Harmon the way she had with him.

He could spend the rest of his life tormenting himself over what might have been. But what would be the point of that? If nothing else, Nicolas was not the kind of man to cry over spilt milk. When things got tough, he got even tougher.

With his fresh coffee finally made, he carried it back out onto the balcony where the morning sunshine wasn't yet too fierce, just pleasantly warm. It was, after all, only six-thirty in the morning. But the day promised to be a sizzler: high thirties, someone had said last night.

Now that was one thing he'd have to get used to again: the long hot summers.

Thank heavens for air-conditioning and cool balconies that faced the sea....

CHAPTER EIGHTEEN

'WELL, well, well,' Allie said with a knowing smile when Serina walked into the office shortly after nine. 'We didn't expect to see you in here this morning. We thought you'd be home in bed, catching up on the sleep you didn't get last night.'

Serina tried not to look either guilty or surprised. 'Don't tell me,' she said drily as she walked past a grinning Allie. 'The Rocky Creek grapevine has been at it already.' She'd thought she'd managed to sneak back home without her neighbours seeing. Obviously that hadn't been the case.

'No need to get defensive, love,' her mother piped up from where she was sitting at Emma's desk. 'Everyone's pleased as punch that you've finally decided to get out and enjoy yourself a bit. Did you have a nice time?'

Serina wasn't sure what to make of her mother's attitude. She would have expected more disapproval. She decided to play it cool and see what happened. There was no way she could follow Nicolas's advice and just blurt out that they were madly in love. Her mother, for one, would think she was crazy!

'Very nice, thank you,' she said as she crossed the room to her own desk. 'We went to a club for a while and I'm afraid I had too much to drink. So Nicolas let me bunk down on his sofa till I sobered up. Next thing I knew the sun was coming up.' Serina suspected this story just might be believed. She had a reputation for being stand-offish with men, so it would seem unlikely that she'd jump into bed with Nicolas so quickly.

'I suppose he's staying in a pretty snazzy place,' her mother said. 'A man like him.'

Serina dropped her bag on a nearby filing cabinet before pulling out her office chair. 'I thought I told you the other night. He's rented an apartment in the new Blue Horizons building.' She sat down and turned on her computer. 'Maybe I didn't.' She'd been very distracted during that phone call. Spending the afternoon in bed with Nicolas did that to her. 'Yes, it's a very snazzy place with a lovely view. He's decided to stay on there for another week.'

'Another week! But he told Mrs Johnson and me just last night that he was leaving today.'

'He was going to. But he's changed his mind and extended his booking. Since he'll still be in Port for Christmas, Mum, I…er…thought I'd ask him to join us on Christmas Day.'

'Are you sure that's a good idea? I mean…Christmas Day is for family.'

Serina's heart turned over. If only her mother knew. Nicolas was family. He was her granddaughter's father. 'Family and friends, Mum,' she said firmly. 'I'm sure Franny and Bert won't mind. And Felicity will be delighted. She likes Nicolas a lot, you know.'

'Yes, I know. She never stops talking about him.'

'Then there's no problem, is there?'

'I guess not,' her mother said. Suddenly, she didn't look so approving, confirming Serina's suspicion that any relationship she had with Nicolas might be frowned upon. She could not imagine her mother being pleased with her daughter becoming any man's mistress.

'Can I come for Christmas, too?' Allie piped up with a mischievous grin.

Serina smiled. 'I don't think your parents would be too pleased with that idea.'

'Darn. Oops. Incoming call. Browns Landscaping and Building Supplies,' she trilled. 'Oh, Mr Dupre! We were just talking about you. Yes, yes, all right...Nicolas... Yes, she does that sometimes. Just a sec. Serina,' Allie called out. 'Nicolas said you've got your cell phone turned off and could you please turn it back on.'

Serina tried not to look flustered as she stood up and retrieved her phone from her bag. There she'd been, handling everything quite well, she thought, then bingo, Nicolas called and she was immediately in a state. In a way, she wished he hadn't told her that he loved her this morning. It could make her go crazy, if she let it. Crazy with wanting and hoping and...and just plain crazy!

'Tell him it's turned on now,' she said a little stiffly.

'It's turned on now, Nicolas. 'By-ee,' Allie finished, her voice having gone all soft and simpering.

Serina suppressed a sigh.

Ten seconds later, her vibrating mobile phone was dancing over the desktop. Serina snatched it up to her ear, telling herself all the while to stay cool. Her mother was listening and so was Allie. She had to be careful not to say anything that would contradict what she'd told them about last night.

'Hello, Nicolas,' she said. 'Sorry about the phone. It's a habit of mine. So what's up?'

There was a short sharp silence at the other end of the line, then Nicolas laughed. 'I get it. Your mum's there, isn't she?'

'Yep.'

'And you haven't told her about us.'

'Not exactly.'

'You bad girl, I'm going to have to take you in hand.'

'Yes, please.'

'Ooh, you are a bad girl. So when can I take you in hand? This afternoon too soon?'

'I'll have to see what Felicity is doing first. I'll give her a call and then get back to you.'

'Don't make me wait too long. I'm not a patient man. Not when I want something.'

Serina almost opened her drying mouth to ask him what he wanted. Fortunately, common sense won and she remained silent.

He laughed again, softly, sexily. 'You can't talk. I get it. Shall I tell you what I want in minute detail, with accompanying sound effects?'

'Not right now, Nicolas.'

'Oh, I love that schoolmarm voice you have at times.'

'I'll call you back after I've contacted Felicity, all right?'

He sighed. 'Spoilsport.'

Serina finally began to find some amusement in the situation.

'Yes, I know it's terribly hot,' she said. 'Why don't you go have a swim and cool down? 'Bye now. I'll call back soon.'

She hung up, but her mind was already on the time when she could be with Nicolas again, when he could take her in hand.

'Serina…'

Serina blinked, then turned her head towards her mother.

'You were going to call Felicity,' her mother reminded her.

'What? Oh, yes. I forgot for a moment.'

'I can see that….'

Serina resented the note of disapproval in her mother's voice. Heavens, it wasn't as though she was a neglectful mother.

Felicity answered straight away.

'Hi, Mum. How's things? You have a good time last night?'

'A great time,' Serina admitted. 'And you? I suppose you and Kirsty stayed up all night.' Sleepovers between girlfriends never involved much sleep.

'We passed out on the lounge around two, didn't we, Kirsty?'

'So what time do you want me to pick you up today?' Serina asked, knowing full well that it wouldn't be anytime soon. When those two got together, wild horses couldn't drag them apart.

'Not till dark,' Kirsty replied straight away. 'How about eight o'clock?'

'I don't like driving along that road in the dark.' Kirsty's place was a few kilometres out of town along a narrow winding road that had no lighting whatsoever. 'Could we make it seven?'

Serina heard some fierce negotiations going on in the background. 'Look, Kirsty's mum said I could stay for another night, if that's all right with you.'

'Are you sure? I think I should talk to her.'

Janine, Kirsty's mother, came on the phone and it was finally agreed that Felicity could stay another night.

'How's the weather out your way?' Serina asked.

'Very hot,' Janine said. 'And windy.'

'Don't let the girls go too far into the bush, okay?' Kirsty's place was on the edge of a state forest that was simply huge and very thick.

'Will do. Oh, and Serina?'

'Yes?'

'I thought you looked really lovely last night.'

'Why thank you. What a nice thing to say!'

'A little bird told me you went out with Nicolas Dupre after the party?'

'My, my, that little bird flies fast.'

Janine laughed. 'That's Rocky Creek for you. So is it true?'

'Yes.'

'And is it also true that he's an old flame of yours?'

Kirsty's family only moved into the area a few years ago, so they knew nothing of the time when Nicolas Dupre and Serina had been teenagers. Serina decided that she was tired of denying that they had some kind of relationship in the past. But she wasn't about to admit too much.

'Yes, he was,' she said.

'Lucky you. Do you think anything will come of it this time? I mean, is he sticking around or is this just a whirlwind visit?'

'I'm not sure yet, Janine.'

Which just about said it all. She wasn't sure. About anything.

The adrenalin rush that she'd felt earlier when Nicolas called had totally dissipated by the time she hung up. Was she being a fool, thinking they could make a lasting relationship this time?

'Serina…'

Serina blinked then turned to face her mother.

'What?'

'Could you come outside for a minute? I want to speak to you about something. Privately,' she added softly with a surreptitious glance Allie's way.

The heat hit them both the moment they stepped outside the door.

'Better make this quick, Mum,' Serina said as she moved back into the shade of the building's eaves. 'Or we're going to melt away.'

'I'm not sure I can be quick. To be honest, I'm not sure where to even start.'

Serina was taken aback before the penny dropped. Her mother wanted to say something to her about last night but didn't have the courage. She'd never been one of those mothers to voluntarily bring up the subject of sex. If it had been left up to Margaret Brown, then Serina would never have learned the facts of life. She grew up, grateful that she lived in the country, and had been able to work things out for herself. Her father had been of a similar ilk, a shy man who wasn't given to conversations or confidences about private matters. Serina wasn't surprised that she was an only child.

'I'm beginning to get worried about you and Nicolas,' her mother blurted out at last.

'In what way?'

Her mother's face twisted into a mask of concern. 'I'm worried he's going to break your heart again. And don't go telling me that he didn't break your heart all those years ago. You can lie to Felicity if you want to. I wouldn't expect you to tell your daughter the truth.'

Serina's heart skipped a beat. 'The truth?'

'About you and Nicolas in the old days. I knew you were way more than just good friends. I knew you were sleeping together, right from the first night you went out with him. It was there, in your eyes, the next morning. You looked…different. Older.'

'Mum, I…'

'Oh, it's perfectly all right,' her mother interrupted. 'I'm not judging you. I never judged you. I understood exactly what you felt for that boy.'

'You did?'

'I felt the same way about a boy when I was around the same age. I was simply mad about him. Couldn't keep my hands off him.'

'Goodness!'

'There was nothing good about him, I can tell you. He was a wicked lad and he broke my heart. I was never the same after he dumped me. I couldn't bear for another boy to touch me for years. And then I met your father.' Tears filled her eyes. 'If it wasn't for your father I would never have gotten married, or had you. His tenderness was my saving grace. Plus his shyness. He was nothing like Hank. For which I was eternally grateful.'

'What… What happened to this Hank?'

'Got killed on his motorcycle when he was twenty-one. I still cried when he died. But I think it was more for my own sorry self than for him.'

'Oh, Mum. I had no idea.'

'How could you? I never told you. I've never talked to you at all much about myself, or even about you. When Nicolas left Rocky Creek I knew you were heart-broken. But I was afraid to talk to you. Afraid you might tell me what you'd been doing together. Afraid I might tell you what I went through. And I didn't want you to know. I didn't want you to be ashamed of me.'

'Ashamed of you! Why would I be ashamed of you?'

She flushed a beetroot red. 'The things I did with Hank. They were wicked.'

'Were they really, Mum? You loved him, didn't you?'

'More than I thought was ever possible.'

'There, you see?' She put her arms around her mother's shoulders and held her close. 'Not wicked at all. Just in love. Like Nicolas and I were. Like we still are.'

Her mother lifted wet eyes to Serina's. 'He loves you? He said that?'

'Just this morning, before he kissed me goodbye.'

'And he's going to stay this time?'

'Only for the next week. But he's promised to visit often.'

'Do you think you might get married one day?'

'No, Mum. I don't think that's ever going to happen.'

'You're a very brave girl, Serina, very brave and very strong. Did I ever tell you that?'

She had, actually. At Greg's funeral. But Serina thought it wasn't quite the right moment to mention that. Instead, she steered her mother back inside, where she made her a cup of tea, after which she surreptitiously carried her mobile phone into the ladies' and called Nicolas back.

'I thought you were never going to call,' he said sharply. 'I was getting worried.'

'No need. Everything's fine. Felicity's going to stay another night at Kirsty's. And I'm going to ask my mother to hold the fort for the rest of the day so that I can spend it with you.'

'Wow! They say all good things come to those who wait, but I've never believed it till now.'

'Oh, and there's one more thing.'

'What?'

'I love you....'

CHAPTER NINETEEN

NICOLAS had experienced several moments of happiness in his life.

But this moment surpassed all others: it was true happiness. He was stunned to feel tears pricking at his eyes. Never in all his forty years had he cried with happiness.

'Well you've done it now,' he choked out.

'What do you mean?'

'I'm never going to let you go now, Serina. Not if you love me.'

'I still won't go overseas with you, Nicolas. Well, I would…briefly. Just not permanently.'

'Even that small compromise shows me you do really love me.'

'You doubted me?'

'Might I remind you that you were the one who said I was only good for one thing.'

'Oh, Nicolas…I'm so sorry I said that. That wasn't nice. But you only have yourself to blame. A girl tends to forget a man's other qualities when one stands out.'

'You should be grateful that it stands out at all. When a man approaches forty…'

She laughed. It was a delightful laugh.

'When can you get away?' he asked.

'Soon.'

'How soon?'

'Very soon,' she said softly.

An hour later, Nicolas was pacing the pavement outside Blue Horizons, impatiently waiting for Serina's car to arrive. The temperature had risen dramatically during the last sixty minutes and a hot wind was whipping down the street. He'd finally dressed sensibly in shorts and T-shirt but was still feeling uncomfortably warm.

Suddenly, there she was, pulling up to the curb opposite. Nicolas raced over and wrenched the driver's door open.

'Why has it taken you so long?' he demanded to know. 'I could have flown back to Sydney in that time.'

She smiled up at him as she climbed out of the car, looking cool and pretty in cream Bermuda shorts and a lemon blouse.

'I was held up for a while with a builder who wasn't happy with the timber we'd delivered to him. Sorry, but Mum isn't at her best dealing with difficult customers, and Allie's useless.'

Nicolas wasn't in the mood to be mollified. 'I thought you'd had an accident. You could have called me. That's what mobile phones are for.'

'I said I was sorry.' Her smile widened. 'My, but you're not a happy chappy when you have to wait for something,' she said, echoing his words of that morning. 'Now why don't you just kiss me and stop being obsessive compulsive?'

'Takes one to know one, sweetheart,' he growled, and pulled her into his arms. His kiss was deep and long and brought several toots from horns of passing motorists.

'I have something I want to show you,' he said when he finally came up for air.

'Not down here, I hope,' she teased. 'I don't want to be arrested for indecent exposure.'

'Very funny. No, it's nothing like that. I want you to come upstairs with me.'

She laughed. 'I already gathered that.'

Nicolas gave her a droll look. 'Will you get your mind off sex for the moment?'

'You mean you want to actually do something else?'

'No, I don't want to do something else. I just thought it might be wise to show you that I can do something else.'

'Such as what?'

'If you'll just be quiet for a minute or two,' he said as he steered her across the road, 'I'll show you.'

'I'm already speechless.'

Serina laughed when he ground to a halt and speared her with a fierce narrowed-eyed glance. 'You will be punished later for your sarcasm!'

'Oooh. Is that a promise or a threat?'

'Another twenty lashes for Madame!'

'Are we on the *Bounty* here, or in one of those old war films? You keep changing characters.'

'I am the master of disguise.'

'Good grief,' she said, laughing. 'It's Boris Karloff!'

'I'm not that old!'

'You're nearly forty.'

He pretended to look horrified. 'You must not mention the dreaded F word. Not unless you want to be punished.'

'That depends on the punishment.'

'You will be tied naked to my bed for the rest of the day.'

Her face fell in mock disappointment. 'Oh…is that all?'

'I will rub your entire body with oil.'

Her eyebrows arched coquettishly. 'What kind of oil?'

'What other kind is there?' he countered, flexing his biceps like Popeye. 'Olive oil!'

'You'll ruin the sheets.'

He waved nonchalantly. 'There are plenty more sheets where they came from. But first, we must ride up to the penthouse.'

'The penthouse! You've moved apartments?'

'Not as yet. But I'm thinking of buying the penthouse. It's for sale.'

'Oh, my!' Serina exclaimed as soon as she walked inside. 'This place is out of this world. But it must be worth a small fortune.'

'It's on the market for three-point-five million. But in this current economic climate, I think I can close the deal for three.'

'Far be it for me to persuade you otherwise, Nicolas,' Serina said as she wandered from the extensive and expensively furnished living area into the equally lavish master bedroom. 'But can you afford it?'

'My apartment in New York is worth five times that much. I also own a town house in London worth at last two and a half mil. Pounds, that is. Neither have mortgages. So yes, I can afford it.'

She just stared at him. 'I didn't know you were that rich.'

He shrugged. 'I've been very fortunate. And very astute, when it comes to investments. I know there's a line in the show *The Producers* that says to never put your money in the show. But if you put your money in the right show, then the sky's the limit when it comes to profits. I've put my money into two super successful musicals. And I manage some extremely successful musicians. So yes, I'm very rich.'

And very used to getting his own way, Serina appreciated. It had to be very corrupting to be that rich, to be able to buy whatever you wanted.

Does he really love me? Serina suddenly worried as she gazed at the king-sized bed. *Or does he just want me?*

His hands curling over her shoulders startled her. She hadn't seen him move behind her.

'So what do you think, my darling?' he murmured as his lips brushed over her hair. 'Should I buy it, or not?'

Serina swallowed when he pulled her back against him and

she felt his hardness. 'It seems a lot of money for a place you'll hardly ever be in.'

'Oh, I don't know about that,' he said, taking his hands off her shoulders and moving them down under her arms and over the swell of her breasts. 'I have a feeling I'm going to be here quite a lot.'

Serina sucked in sharply when he started undoing the buttons on her blouse. 'What…what do you think you're doing?'

'What do you think I'm doing? You know I don't like making love with clothes on.'

'But we can't… Not here… Someone might come in…'

'Why would they? The girl on the desk said I could take all the time I wanted inspecting the place.'

'But someone still might come in…'

'I very much doubt it.'

Her blouse and bra were quickly disposed of.

'But they might,' she protested even as he unzipped her shorts.

'We'd hear them before they came in here. Ah. That's better,' he said as the shorts fell to the floor. 'Mmm. Very sexy panties but I prefer you without them.' Her underwear went the same way as the shorts, leaving her naked except for her sandals.

His right hand smoothed over her stomach, then dipped between her legs.

'Nicolas…please…I…I don't think I can relax.'

'I don't want you relaxed.'

She gasped when his other hand started playing with her extremely erect nipples.

'I want you as turned on as I am.'

When Serina moaned, he stopped what he was doing.

'Lie back across the bed,' he ordered her thickly. 'And touch yourself while I get naked.'

Why did she do it? Why?

Because she loved obeying him as much as she loved him. It was like a drug, the way he could make her feel.

'Yes, that's the way,' he said as he hurriedly stripped off his clothes. 'Open your legs a little wider, darling. You look so beautiful like that.'

Beautiful? More like brazen. For she no longer cared if anyone came in.

'Beautiful,' he said again as he knelt between her legs and lifted her hand away….

CHAPTER TWENTY

'SEE?' Nicolas said some considerable time later. 'Nobody came in.'

'Just as well,' she muttered.

'I'd like to get up and get dressed now,' she said, her will-power having returned.

'Are you sure you want to?'

'Nicolas! Get off me, please.'

'Oh, very well.' And he levered himself up off her body. 'Fancy a shower together?'

Serina winced. 'Haven't you had enough?'

'Of you? Never.'

'I wish you wouldn't say things like that.'

'Why?'

'Because it's unrealistic.' She scrambled to her feet and reached for her clothes. 'I need to go to the bathroom,' she snapped. 'Alone, if you don't mind.'

Nicolas frowned as he watched her go. She still didn't trust him, he realised, didn't trust his love for her, or his commitment to her.

What could he do to reassure her? Ask her to marry him?

It seemed a premature move to Nicolas. But women saw things differently to men. An offer of marriage conjured up all sorts of romantic connotations for women. It spelt out love in ways that mere words couldn't.

Nicolas decided then and there to do just that. Tonight, over a candlelit dinner. He'd have to buy her an engagement ring first, of course, a really nice one. Port Macquarie was sure to have some decent jewellery shops. Tourist towns catered to people who had money and time on their hands to shop. It meant he would have to make some excuse to have a couple of hours alone this afternoon. He would say that he was tired and needed a nap before their night out. Sounded a bit lame but he couldn't think of anything else.

Meanwhile, he would have to get dressed, quick smart, so as not to annoy Serina further when she emerged from the bathroom. She hadn't been too pleased with his having his way with her a little while ago. But she only had herself to blame, kissing him the way she had when she arrived, then flirting with him so outrageously. Still, he would make sure that in future he kept their lovemaking to places where there was no possibility of their being disturbed.

He'd just pulled on his shirt when she opened the bathroom door, looking just a little wary. Till she saw he was properly dressed.

'I was thinking we might go for a drive around the beaches for the rest of this morning,' he said straight away. 'Then have a spot of lunch somewhere cool, overlooking the water.'

'Sounds good,' Serina said, feeling somewhat guilty for her attitude earlier. It wasn't as though he'd forced her to have sex. She'd been more than willing in the end.

'Great! But before we go, come and take a look at the view from the terrace. It goes for miles.'

It certainly did, from the horizon out to sea to the mountains in the west. The only minus at that moment was the heat and the westerly wind that whipped Serina's hair across her eyes as she tried to take in the full, 360-degree panorama.

'This would be superb on a warm winter's day,' she said as she struggled to hold her hair back. 'Or a balmy summer evening.'

'But not today,' Nicolas said. 'I agree. I just wanted you to see it. Let's get going.'

As Serina turned away from the glass security fence that surrounded the terrace, a whiff of smoke suddenly teased her nostrils. Frowning, she anchored her hair back from her face more securely and stared in the direction the wind was coming from.

West.

'Nicolas!' she said sharply. 'Come over here.'

He hurried to her side. 'What is it?'

'Over there,' she said, pointing towards the mountain range in the distance. 'Can you see it?'

'See what?'

'Smoke.'

Nicolas narrowed his eyes against the glare of the sunshine and peered hard in the direction of Serina's finger.

'Yes. I can see it,' he confirmed.

'Oh, my God! It's a bushfire, isn't it? Over Rocky Creek way.'

'There's no need to panic. From what I can see it's only small and probably in the state forest. The one beyond Rocky Creek. They used to have fires in there practically every summer, but they never reached the town.'

She turned to him, her eyes full of worry. 'But you don't understand. The town has spread. And the people Felicity's staying with this weekend, they live right on the edge of that state forest. With this wind, the fire won't be small for long and it could be upon them before you can say boo.'

'Surely the rural fire service would evacuate them, if there was any danger.'

'Like they did in Victoria?' she countered despairingly.

'Even if we had the resources, which we don't, things can go very wrong very quickly. In extreme weather conditions like this, sometimes there's not enough time to evacuate everyone. There are lots more people living out in the bush now than when you lived in Rocky Creek. Kirsty's parents live farther away than most. And there's only one access road. What kind of stupid mother am I to let Felicity stay there this weekend? I knew the weather forecast. And I know the dangers. Greg drummed them into me. If anything happens to Felicity…' she cried, her face going ashen at the thought.

Nicolas had faced several crises in his life but none had ever affected him the way this had. Serina claimed he had no real bond with Felicity. That clearly wasn't true. The rush of love and protectiveness he felt for his daughter was very real indeed. As was his fear for her safety. But he had to keep a cool head. Nothing was to be gained by panicking.

'We can't be sure yet where the fire is, Serina. Or how close it might be to Felicity. But let's not dillydally. Let's go get your daughter.'

Serina lifted her big brown eyes to his.

'Our daughter,' she choked out.

Keeping a cool head suddenly became more difficult. Action came to Nicolas's rescue.

'We'll take the four-wheel drive,' he asserted. 'You can phone the people that Felicity's staying with on the way. Do you have their number?'

'It's in my menu. Yes.'

'Good.'

Her mobile didn't work till they were out of the basement car park and on the road.

'There's no answer,' she said, alarm in her voice.

'That might be good news, Serina. They might have made the sensible decision to get out early.'

'Then why didn't they put a message on their answering

machine? And why didn't they call me? No, this doesn't feel right. Something's wrong. I'll try Felicity's mobile.'

It rang but there was no answer.

'I feel sick,' Serina said.

'That makes two of us,' Nicolas said. 'But we have to try to stay calm, Serina.'

'Yes, that's what Greg used to say.'

'Sounds like a sensible man. Now what else would he have advised in this situation?'

'He'd say to ring the local bushfire brigade. Find out exactly where the fire is. Now why didn't I think of that earlier?'

'Do you have their number?'

'Yes. Greg used to be president, remember?'

'Then hop to it.'

The fire was in the state forest, she was advised, but not near any dwellings at this time. The wind was changeable, however, and people were advised to keep a sharp watch, and to keep in contact with the authorities for advice.

'We'll still go and get Felicity,' Nicolas said.

'We certainly will,' Serina agreed.

'Try ringing Kirsty's mother again,' Nicolas advised.

This time Janine answered.

'Oh, Janine! I'm so relieved. I tried ringing earlier but there wasn't any answer.'

'I was outside, looking for the girls.'

That sick feeling came rushing back into Serina's stomach.

'And did you find them?'

'No, I didn't. I made them promise not to go into the forest today but you know those two. They have minds of their own.'

'But isn't there a bushfire out your way?'

'Yes. That's why I went to find them. Ken's just phoned me to tell me to be ready to leave at a moment's notice. He's been out helping fight the fire all morning. He said there wasn't any imminent danger, but in this weather he didn't want us to take any chances. I was just about to call you when you rang me.'

'I'm on my way to your place now.'

'Look, I'm sure the girls will be back any minute. They wouldn't want to stay out long in this heat.'

'You don't think they could be lost?'

'Heavens, no. They know that place like the back of their hands. Besides, all the walking tracks are well marked.'

'I tried to ring Felicity on her mobile but there was no answer. Does Kirsty have her mobile with her?'

'I'm afraid not. I found it lying on her bed.'

'Darn. We'll be another fifteen minutes getting to your place, Janine. We're coming from Port Macquarie.'

'Who's we?'

'Me and Nicolas Dupre.'

'Oh...I see.'

Serina doubted it.

'You have my mobile number, don't you?'

'Yes.'

'I won't ring anyone. Call me the moment they get back.'

Serina hung up on a deep shuddering sigh.

'Where have the little devils gone?' Nicolas demanded to know straight away.

'Into the forest.'

He swore. Then swore again, banging the steering wheel at the same time. 'I'm going to strangle that girl.'

'You'll have to get in line,' Serina quipped.

They both laughed but they were just fear-covering laughs. They quickly fell silent, Nicolas putting his foot down every chance he got. Soon Wauchope was behind them, then Rocky Creek. Serina kept staring at her mobile, which she was gripping tightly in her lap, but it didn't ring. With each passing minute, her fear increased, horrible thoughts entering her head. She could not bear it if she lost Felicity. It would be the end of her.

'This is one hell of a road,' Nicolas said as the SUV hit another pothole.

'It's not the best.'

'Much farther?'

'A couple more corners. Slow down. Their driveway is coming up on the left. There! Between those two gum trees.'

'Hell on earth,' Nicolas grumbled as he drove up the gravel road to the house that, though perched on a cleared rise, was virtually surrounded by trees. 'These places are disasters waiting to happen. Why haven't they cleared the trees farther back from the house?'

'They're not allowed to cut down any natives without permission from the local council. And getting permission is a minefield of red tape.'

'Insanity!'

'I agree. But Janine's place is safer than most. Ken's cleared out all the immediate scrub and undergrowth, which is where bushfires get their fuel. They also have sprinklers built into the roof and a fireproof cellar. Oh, look, there's Janine on the verandah. She doesn't look too happy. The girls can't have come back yet.'

Nicolas pulled the vehicle to a rather ragged halt in front of the steps and they both jumped out. The heat and wind by then was atrocious, and the thick smell of smoke on the air very worrying. So was the big black cloud on the horizon above the treetops.

'No sign of the girls yet?' a worried Serina said as she hurried towards Janine.

'Not yet. I…'

'Mum—Mum!'

Both women turned in the direction of the girl's voice. It was Kirsty, running like mad across the wide front lawn.

'Where's Felicity?' Serina demanded to know immediately.

'She's still in there,' Kirsty said, pointing back towards

the forest. 'We were on our way back when we heard this crying sound not far from the track. It was a fox who'd fallen down a rabbit hole and broken its leg. We tried to get it out but it was in a right panic and slipped farther down into the hole. I told Fliss to leave it. I could tell that the fire was getting closer. But she wouldn't. You know what she's like, Mrs Harmon.'

'Yes,' Serina said with a groan.

'I didn't know what to do, Mum,' Kirsty said, a sob catching in her throat. 'I…I couldn't make her leave so I thought I'd come and get help.'

Nicolas looked at the way the fire was leaping from treetop to treetop on a nearby hilltop and realised there was no time to lose. 'Can you show me where she is, Kirsty?'

'My daughter's not going back in there!' Janine said, and hugged her child to her side.

'We don't expect her to,' Nicolas said. 'We just need to know which way to go.'

'Please, Kirsty,' Serina begged.

'It's all right, Mum,' Kirsty said, getting control of herself. 'I'll show them. She's not all that far in.'

'In that case, I'm coming, too,' Janine said.

They all ran towards the forest and the fire.

'Along here,' Kirsty said, and dived into the forest, with everyone in hot pursuit.

Despite following a well-trodden walking track, Nicolas was astonished at how quickly the forest seemed to close in around them, blocking out the light. Of course it didn't help that the sky above was filling with black smoke. Get off this trail, however, and you'd be lost in seconds.

Lost and cooked.

Nicolas had not forgotten how it had felt, being burned. Yet he didn't feel afraid for himself. His fear was all for his daughter.

'She's just in there,' Kirsty said, stopping and pointing

through some thick bush on her left. 'Fliss, are you there?' she yelled out.

'Yeah,' Felicity yelled back. 'This bloody fox is stuck. Come and help me, will you?'

'I'm going to kill her,' Serina said, and was about to launch towards her daughter's voice, when Nicolas grabbed her arm.

'You go back to the house. I'll get her.'

Serina set rebellious eyes upon him.

'Take her back, Janine,' Nicolas snapped before she could say a word. 'Now!'

They all heard it then. The sound of the flames, roaring towards them.

'No!' Serina screamed, and wrenched out of Nicolas's hold. 'I won't go back without Felicity. I won't!' And she plunged into the forest, calling out to her daughter.

'You go back!' Nicolas screamed to Janine and Kirsty as he raced after her. 'I'll get them. Don't worry.'

And he would, he vowed. No way was his family going to die here today. No way!

He found them both quite quickly, Serina trying to pull her stubborn daughter away from the rabbit hole and the fox she was insanely intent on saving. Even in that short time, the intensity of the heat had grown. Nicolas couldn't see the fire yet, but he could feel it coming.

'Felicity,' he said firmly. 'You have to come with us now, or we'll all die.'

Felicity lifted startled eyes at his voice. 'Oh, it's you, Nicolas. Look, maybe you can get the fox out. You have longer arms than me.'

'Leave the damned fox, girl!'

Felicity speared him with a mutinous look. 'I will not leave the damned fox!'

'Felicity! For pity's sake!' Serina screamed at her daughter. 'Just do what your father says!'

Nicolas gaped at Serina's immediately stricken face, then at Felicity, who looked more than a little confused.

'Silly woman,' Nicolas said straight away. 'Doesn't know if she's Arthur or Martha at the moment. It's Nicolas here, Serina, not Greg. Still, it's a shame Greg isn't here, given his wealth of experience with bushfires. So tell me, Felicity, what would your dad have done at this moment?'

'He'd have saved my fox if I'd asked him to,' she replied, her eyes suddenly filling with tears. 'But he's not here, is he? He's dead.'

'That's true,' Nicolas agreed. 'But I think he'd save his lovely daughter, too, wouldn't he? So let's get your fox out of that hole and get us all safely out of this forest.'

The fox wouldn't cooperate. Pain and fear were making it panic. Nicolas lifted it out of the hole in the end, though not before the animal had bitten him on the hand.

Not that he cared. Nothing mattered but getting the people he loved to safety.

When Felicity hesitated to leave again, he glared at her. 'What now?' he demanded to know.

'My mobile phone. It's at the bottom of the rabbit hole.'

Nicolas almost swore. Instead, he gritted his teeth and prayed for patience. 'I'll buy you another phone,' he said. 'A better one. Now go, girl. And take your mother with you,' he said, only then noticing that Serina was still standing there in a shocked silence.

This time Felicity did as she was told, grabbing her mother's arm and pulling her towards the trail, Nicolas hot on their heels carrying the fox.

Not that they were out of the woods yet. The winds had whipped the fire into a fireball that was moving at tremendous speed towards them through the bush.

'Run,' he screamed at Felicity and Serina. 'Run faster.'

They made it, just, bursting out onto clear ground with the

flames licking at their heels. Even so, they didn't stop running till they reached the house where Janine and Kirsty were waiting for them with anxiety on their faces.

'I'm so glad you're all right,' Janine said, then shot Nicolas a rueful glance. 'I see you brought the fox.'

Nicolas shrugged. 'Felicity wouldn't leave it behind.'

'He was wonderful,' Felicity said. 'Here, Nicolas. I'll take the fox now. I know what to do with it. Kirsty and I have a makeshift hospital in one of the sheds.'

'Excuse me, missy,' Janine said firmly, nodding towards where the fire had reached the grassy surrounds of the property. 'But we're all going down to the cellar till this fire is under control. Ken's just rung. He said they're on their way here and they're bringing a couple of water-bombing helicopters, but he doesn't want us taking any chances. My husband's one of the volunteer firefighters,' she explained to Nicolas.

'Well, the fox comes, too,' Felicity insisted. 'Kirsty, we'll need a beach towel to wrap her up in. And a dish of water for her to have a drink. She'll be very thirsty.'

'We're all pretty thirsty,' Nicolas said, and wrapped a tender arm around Serina. 'Aren't we, sweetheart?'

'What?' she asked, her voice somewhat vague.

Still in shock, he realised.

'I said we're all thirsty.'

'Oh. Yes, I suppose so.'

'There are drinks down in the cellar,' Janine informed him. 'And a cupboard full of food. But no toilet. So anyone who wants to use the bathroom had better do so now. We might be down there for a while.'

No one did. Possibly because they were all dehydrated.

It was a large cellar, with a wine rack along one wall, an old sofa along another, boxes and bits and pieces stacked along another and several chairs around a table in the centre. Temperature wise, it was lovely and cool.

Nicolas pulled out a chair for Serina at the table whilst Janine got some cans of drink from an ancient bar fridge. Felicity sat next to Kirsty on the sofa with the towel-wrapped fox in her lap, stroking its ears and singing some kind of song. There was not a peep out of the mesmerised animal.

'I've spawned Doctor Doolittle,' Nicolas muttered under his breath when Janine moved away to give Kirsty and Felicity their cans of Coke.

'Hush up,' Serina said sharply.

Nicolas sighed. 'Serina, you don't have to worry. No one heard me and I covered your earlier blunder.'

'But what if you hadn't been able to? What if Felicity had guessed the truth?'

'She didn't.'

Serina just shook her head. 'You just don't understand, do you?'

Janine came back to sit at their table and Nicolas lifted his can of drink to his mouth.

Janine gasped. 'Nicolas! Did you know your hand was bleeding?'

'What? Show me!' Serina said.

'It's nothing much. The fox bit me.'

'There's a first-aid kit here somewhere,' Janine said, and went in search of it.

'What kind of person am I?' Serina said bleakly. 'I didn't notice that you were bleeding. And I haven't even thanked you for what you did out there. I'm a terrible person.' And she burst into tears.

'What's wrong with Mum?' Felicity asked straight away, her voice worried.

'She's just in shock,' Nicolas replied as he held a weeping Serina against him with his non-bleeding hand. 'You must realise how worried she was, Felicity. She thought that you were going to die, too. Like your dad.'

'Oh… Oh I see.'

'I hope so, Felicity,' Nicolas said firmly. 'Next time, think before you risk your life. Your mother needs you just as much as that fox.'

'Found the first-aid kit!' Janine piped up.

'What do you need the first-aid kit for?' Felicity asked.

'Nicolas's hand is bleeding. Your fox bit him.'

'Your good hand or your bad hand?' she asked him.

'My bad hand,' he replied.

'Oh, that's all right then.'

He laughed whilst Serina wept on. If it hadn't have been funny he might have cried, too.

Nicolas's hand had been properly attended to and Serina had stopped crying when suddenly, there were sounds overhead and all eyes simultaneously went upwards. The cellar door was flung open and daylight flooded down the steps. Fortunately, there was no smell of smoke, and no other evidence of the fire having reached the house.

'Everyone okay down here?' called a deep male voice.

'Yes, Ken,' Janine said, jumping up onto her feet and racing over to the bottom of the cellar staircase. 'How's the house?'

'Right as rain.' Ken, a big brawny guy dressed in his yellow firefighting suit and holding a hard hat, came down the steps. 'The wind changed again and sent the fire back in the direction it came from, which was a bonus. So!' He smiled broadly as he gathered his wife into his arms then glanced over at Felicity and Kirsty. 'I see our own little rescue team has been busy. What do you have this time, girls?'

'A fox,' Kirsty said as both girls struggled to their feet. 'It has a broken leg.'

'We'll have to take it to the vet,' Felicity said, and looked straight at Nicolas.

He was taken aback. Why look at him? Why not Ken, or her mother?

'Dad always took all my sick and injured animals to the vet for me,' she said, her voice just a little shaky.

Nicolas's heart turned over.

'You'll have to give me directions,' he said. 'I have no idea where the nearest vet is.'

'I'll show you,' Felicity exclaimed, her pretty face breaking into a smile….

CHAPTER TWENTY-ONE

'I HOPE the fox will be okay,' Nicolas said.

He was sitting with Serina in the vet's waiting room, Felicity having taken her patient into the consulting room fifteen minutes earlier. Although the hospital wasn't open for surgery for another hour, there'd been a bell on the front door to ring for emergencies, and luckily the vet—who lived at the back of the building—had been at home.

'I'm sure it'll be fine,' Serina replied. 'Ted's a good vet.'

'Let's hope so. Felicity's somewhat obsessive about saving wildlife, isn't she?'

'Mmmm.'

'Do you think she has any idea of the risks she took today?'

'I doubt it.'

'She needs a firm hand, Serina, and a protective one.'

'I do my best, Nicolas.'

'She needs a father.'

Serina gave him a panicky look. 'You promised you would never tell her.'

'And I won't. But how about a stepfather?'

'Stepfather?' Serina echoed, her eyes blinking wide.

'Yes, Serina, stepfather. I was going to wait till tonight to propose to you over a candlelit dinner with a big diamond ring in my pocket. But I doubt you'll come out with me tonight after what happened today. I also doubt that a big diamond ring would impress you, anyway. So I'm asking you now—will you marry me?'

Serina just kept on staring at him.

Nicolas sighed. 'I can guess what you're going to say,' he went on before she could argue with him. 'We come from different worlds. We don't really know each other anymore. We've left it too late. Well I have the perfect answer for all of that and it's balderdash! All that matters is that we love each other. We've always loved each other. If there's anything that today should have shown you, it's that all life is a risk. We could have fried in there today. All three of us. Instead we're alive and well. Look, I promise you that I won't ask anything of you that would make you unhappy. I won't ask you to move, or change, or anything. We can make this work, Serina. I'll make it work. Trust me, darling, and just say yes.'

Serina closed her eyes for a long moment. When she opened them again, they were awash with tears.

Nicolas thought they were tears of happiness.

But he was wrong.

'Oh, Nicolas…if only you'd asked me to marry you twenty years ago. Or that night at the Opera House. Or even yesterday. Yesterday, I might still have said yes. Though of course that would have still been a big mistake. What happened today showed me that I can't marry you. Ever. Neither can I have a relationship with you. Not one around here, anyway.'

'What? But why?'

'Because I couldn't bear it.'

'Couldn't bear being what?'

'Couldn't bear keeping another secret. Couldn't bear being afraid all the time of the truth coming out. It was bad enough when I was married to Greg. I coped because I was the only one who knew. And because you were another world away. I nearly died today when I said what I said. I felt ill. I still feel ill, thinking about it. Because if Felicity ever found out Greg wasn't her real father, she'd never forgive me. She'd hate me. Yes, life is a risk, but I can't risk that, Nicolas, no matter how much I love you. I'm sorry.'

Nicolas just sat there. Stunned, hurt, devastated.

He struggled to find the right words to say. The right questions to ask.

'When you said you can't have a relationship with me around here, what exactly did you mean?'

'You know very well what I meant, Nicolas. I'll visit you overseas every now and then, but I don't want you coming here. Not anymore. Because one day, one of us might say something in front of Felicity—or someone else—like we did today.'

Nicolas's head understood her reasoning. But his heart reacted very badly. 'I offer you marriage,' he said, bitter resentment in his voice, 'and that's what you offer me in return? Well I'm sorry, too, Serina, but a dirty weekend here and there is not enough for me. I love you and I want to spend quality time with you. I also love my daughter. That's something I discovered today. I would never do anything to hurt her. I gave you my word that I would never tell her I was her father, and I will keep my word. But I want to be able to play some kind of role in her upbringing. I want to watch her grow up. I want to watch over her. It seems, however, that you're going to deny me even that.'

'Nicolas, I…I…'

'Please don't say another word,' he snapped. 'The subject is now closed. We are now closed. Finito.' He made a chopping gesture across his throat as he stood up. 'I will wait outside for you. Then, when Felicity is finished, I will drive you both home and say my goodbyes with our daughter present. That way I can be assured that I will not say anything further that I might later regret. No, Serina,' he snarled when she opened her mouth again. 'Do not waste your breath. I have always been a very black-and-white person. You don't love me the way I love you. You never have. So please, let's just leave it at that.' And whirling, he stalked out of the waiting room.

Serina stared after him, her head whirling, but her heart like lead in her chest. *He doesn't mean it,* she reasoned. *He's just angry with me. He can't mean it.*

But he did mean it, she was to discover to her despair. He'd meant every word.

He drove them home and said his goodbyes, Felicity quite upset by his decision to leave Port Macquarie the following day.

'But I was hoping you'd be with us for Christmas,' she said plaintively. 'Mum, tell him he has to stay.'

Serina just shook her head. She could already see that Nicolas was not about to change his mind. And she couldn't trust herself to speak.

'I have to go, Felicity,' he said, and gave his daughter a quick hug. 'I'm needed back in New York. The show must go on, sweetheart. Look after your mother for me. And give my regards to Mrs Johnson.'

Felicity waved him off from the front porch, her goodbye smile fading once he was gone.

'I don't see why he had to go back to New York in such a hurry,' she grumbled whilst Serina set about feeding a noisily complaining Midnight. 'Unless, of course, he does have a girl-friend back there. Did you ever ask him, Mum, if he was dating that Japanese violinist?'

'Yes.'

'And?'

'He said he wasn't.'

'I didn't think so. Kirsty and I reckon he's still in love with you.'

'What makes you think that?'

'The way he kept looking at you.'

'What way is that?'

'Like he adored the ground you walked on.'

Serina swallowed the great lump in her throat, then forced out a small laugh. 'You two girls. You're just like Allie and Emma, incorrigible romantics. If he adored the ground I walked on then what's he doing going back to New York? Look, could you put this cat food away for me, love? I have to go to the bathroom.'

She just made it into the bathroom before the tears came.

It was not the first time she was to cry uncontrollably during the following few days.

She cried when the mobile phone arrived for Felicity, posted from Sydney airport. Then again when she had to go into Port Macquarie to buy Christmas presents. And again when she passed the spot where Nicolas had pulled the SUV off the road and kissed her.

She dreaded Christmas, fearing she would not get through the day without breaking down, especially since that year they were holding their family celebrations at the Harmons, in the house where Nicolas had lived. Serina managed to keep it together till Felicity's grandparents requested Felicity do an encore of the medley she'd played at the talent quest…on Nicolas's old piano, no less.

Serina started weeping shortly after her daughter started playing and she just couldn't stop.

Fortunately, Greg's parents didn't connect her distress with Nicolas. They thought she was still grieving for their son.

In the end, Serina had to go home where a very upset Felicity demanded to know what the matter was.

'It's Nicolas, isn't it?' she said when Serina didn't enlighten her. 'He's broken your heart again like Grandma said he did once before. You still love him, don't you?'

Serina just couldn't bring herself to lie.

'Yes,' she confessed brokenly. 'Yes, I still love him.'

'But he doesn't love you?'

'Oh, yes, yes, he does. Very much.'

'Then why did he go back to New York?'

Serina looked deep into her daughter's eyes.

'Because I asked him to go,' she admitted.

'Mum! But why?'

'Because I was afraid…'

'Afraid of what?'

Serina's face twisted, her courage failing her once more. 'I can't tell you.'

'Of course you can, Mum. You always say that we can tell each other anything!'

'If I tell you, you might hate me.'

'I would never hate you, Mum. You are the best mother in the whole wide world.'

'Oh. Oh, dear…'

'Mum,' Felicity said firmly. 'You have to tell me what's making you so unhappy and we'll work it out together.'

Could she really tell her? Dared she?

Serina thought of Nicolas, all alone in New York and wanting so much to be a part of their lives. And then she thought of herself, living the rest of her life the way she'd felt this past week. Not just lonely, but horribly guilty. More guilty than she'd ever felt when she'd been married to Greg.

No more guilt, she decided. No more secrets.

Serina said a little prayer first, then started talking….

CHAPTER TWENTY-TWO

THE snow had stopped falling by the time Nicolas alighted the cab outside his apartment block, but the air was bitterly cold.

'Don't know how you stand it, Mike,' he said to his favourite doorman as he hurried up the front steps.

'I'm used to it, Mr Dupre. But then I'm a New Yorker. Not an Aussie like you. Better get yourself inside now, before you catch your death.'

An Aussie, Nicolas was thinking as he stepped into the invitingly warm lobby. He'd actually stopped thinking of himself as Australian. Till his recent return to the country of his birth.

Now he couldn't stop thinking about the place. And the daughter he had there. The daughter he would never see again.

He'd once loved Christmas in New York. He'd even loved the cold. This year he'd hated it all. He'd wanted to be back there in Rocky Creek, with Serina and Felicity. He'd wanted to shower them both with gifts. Wanted to kiss them and hug them and just…be with them.

Instead, he'd spent the day, alone, in his apartment, having refused several last-minute invitations to Christmas dinner. He hadn't even bought any presents, though he did give his usual cash gifts to Mike and Chad. He spent Boxing Day alone as well, and the twenty-seventh.

Today, he'd forced himself to go out. He'd attended the matinee show of a play that had just opened—and he found deadly dull—after which he'd had a bite to eat before heading home. What he would do tomorrow he had no idea. Go jogging in the park, maybe… Something that would put a bit of life back into him.

Because he felt dead. Dead inside.

I should never have cut Serina out of my life like that, he realised grimly. *Being bloody black-and-white was a recipe for depression of the worst kind.*

'Mr Dupre!' Chad called out to him as he made his way with his head down across the lobby.

Nicolas took a deep breath as he ground to a halt. *Don't take it out on the lad,* he lectured himself. *It's not his fault that you want to strangle him, just for talking to you.*

He tried not to scowl as he turned back in the direction of the reception desk. 'Yes, Chad?'

'There's another pink letter for you. From Australia.'

'What?'

A stunned Nicolas hurried over to the desk where Chad was indeed holding out a bright pink envelope to him. It was exactly the same as the last one. Though there were several important differences. There was nothing written on it except his name.

He flipped it over. Nothing on the other side as well.

'I don't get it,' he said, totally thrown. 'How did you know this was from Australia? There's no stamp on it or any sender's name and address. In fact, there's no damned address on the front, either. So how on earth did it even get here?'

Chad looked a little sheepish. But not too worried. 'It was…um…hand-delivered.'

'Hand-delivered?'

'Yes,' a woman's voice said behind him. 'By me.'

Nicolas's chest tightened. Dear God, he knew that voice.

He whirled and there she was: his Serina.

'Felicity sent me,' she said simply as she walked slowly towards him from the lobby's lounge area. 'That's from her.' And she nodded towards the pink envelope.

'I don't understand….' And he didn't. But the beginning of a wonderful hope was clawing its way into his, till then, dead heart.

Serina glanced over his shoulder at Chad, who, no doubt, could overhear their conversation.

'Come over here,' she said quietly, and drew him towards a lounge in a far corner of the lobby, next to which sat a small suitcase and a very large handbag.

Nicolas's heart was pounding in his chest by the time they were sitting down together.

'Tell me what's going on, for pity's sake!'

'I told Felicity the truth, Nicolas. I told her you were her father.'

Nicolas literally stopped breathing at this astonishing piece of news. 'And?' he choked out.

Her smile would have melted the arctic. 'She didn't hate me.'

'What…what about me?' Never in his life had Nicolas stammered the way he did at that moment.

'Oh, Nicolas, how could she possibly hate you? None of it was your fault. The guilt was all mine.'

'That's not true, my darling,' he said as he took her hands in his.

'Oh, yes it is. Please, Nicolas, let me own my sins. I should have told you, way back then. I took the easy way out. But I paid for it and so did you. Felicity took me to task for the way I've treated you.'

'She wasn't too upset about Greg not being her real father?'

'She was very upset at first. But I made her see that Greg was her father, in every way but genetically. A wonderful father.'

'Which he was,' Nicolas agreed.

'Yes. I hope you don't mind, my darling, but neither of us want to tell anyone else the truth, especially Greg's parents. They'd be shattered.'

'Yes, they would be. I could see that.'

'They're very elderly, you know. There will come a day in the not too distant future when it won't matter so much who knows the truth.'

'I don't mind other people not knowing,' he said, 'as long as my daughter knows.'

'She asked me to ask you to open that letter in front of me.'

'Did she now?' He ripped open the pink envelope with some trepidation. The letter was computer-generated as before.

Dear Nicolas

   Sorry, but I don't feel right calling you Dad. I already have a dad. But I think it's kinda cool that you are my father. No wonder I play the piano a bit like you. Anyway I'm glad Mum told me the truth, because I reckon I might have figured it out some day. Now look, Nicolas, it's Mum I'm really writing to you about. She's been very sad since you left. I mean seriously seriously sad. She still loves you and she says you still love her. Which I sure hope is true, because if it's not, I will never speak to you again as long as I live. Which would be a tragedy of the highest order as I like you heaps. So please please ask her to marry you again. And come back to Australia to live.

Bye for now,

Your secret daughter,

Felicity Harmon.

PS. Please email me the very second Mum says yes. (Which she will.)

PPS. I'd like a baby brother or sister please. ASAP.

PPS. I still don't want to become a concert pianist.

Nicolas couldn't help laughing.

'What is it?' Serina demanded to know. 'What did she say?'

He just handed her the letter.

Serina groaned. 'Oh, dear. She is terribly precocious, isn't she?'

'I think she's marvellous,' Nicolas said.

'She's the one who found out your actual address. From that program you did on television a few years ago. She got the phone number somehow as well and rang the desk to make sure you were staying here and not in London before she booked my flights. She insisted I come in person. She said it would be cowardly of me to just email, or ring.'

'You're no coward. I think you are the bravest lady I've ever met. So will you marry me, my darling?'

'Need you ask?'

'Had to. Or my daughter said she wouldn't speak to me for the rest of her life.'

'Then yes, Nicolas. I'll marry you.'

He smiled then hugged her. 'So what do you think about her other request for a baby brother or sister, ASAP?'

Serina's eyes sparkled. 'I'm willing, if you're willing.'

'In that case I think we'll go upstairs and get started on that project straight away. But first… Chad!' he called out across the lobby as he stood up. 'Am I right in assuming you and Serina are already acquainted?'

'Er…yes, Mr Dupre. We had quite a long chat earlier on. That's how I knew she was from Australia. Though I already guessed, from her accent.'

'We're getting married, Chad.'

'That's wonderful news, Mr Dupre. Mike will be thrilled. He's been a bit worried about you. I'll go tell him right away.'

'You do that. Now we've got something we've got to do straight away,' he said to Serina as he picked up her luggage.

'Yes, I know,' she said, standing up, too. 'The email.'

'The email can wait. I can't. Come on.'

They reached the lifts, where Nicolas was about to press the up button, when Serina stopped him. 'There's something I want to say first.'

'Do you have to?'

'Yes. I want to say that I love you, Nicolas Dupre. I've never stopped loving you. When I was a young girl, before you even noticed me, I used to dream that one day we would get married, and have a family together. And now that dream is going to come true. Thank you, Nicolas. For still loving me. And for asking me to marry me again. Thank you.'

Nicolas couldn't speak for a long moment.

He dropped the luggage and reached out to curve his hands over her shoulders.

'It's I who should be thanking you,' he said, his voice husky. 'For still loving me, after all these years. Do you remember my saying that there was a woman once whom I wanted to marry but it didn't work out?'

Serina nodded.

'You were that woman, my love. You. Never anyone else.'

'Oh, Nicolas...'

'No. No more tears. From now on we're not going to look back. Our new life together is just beginning. We're going to be the happiest couple to ever live in Rocky Creek.'

Serina's eyes widened. 'Rocky Creek?'

'Yes, damn it. Rocky Creek. If we're going to have more children, I can't really drag them all over the world all the time, can I?'

'But you won't be happy living in Rocky Creek all the time!' Serina protested.

'Who said?'

'You said.'

'True. Okay, I'll buy that penthouse in Port Macquarie and do a bit of commuting. That sound feasible enough for you?'

'Very feasible. Felicity wants to go to school in Port Macquarie next year. They've not long opened a new high school there. It has a great reputation already. It is rather expensive. But she said you could afford it.'

'What? That girl! She's incorrigible!'

'Indeed. I wonder where she gets her ruthlessness from?'

'Hey, don't blame me for everything. She has half your genes, you know.'

'You didn't say that about her piano playing! You claimed all those genes.'

Suddenly, Nicolas grinned. 'We're arguing over our kid already.'

'Parents always argue over their children.'

'Do they? I rather like it.'

'You won't once the boys start calling. Which will be any day now.'

Serina almost laughed at Nicolas's horrified expression. 'She's not old enough for boys.'

'She'll be thirteen next year. In two years she'll be fifteen. I was fifteen when I went to your graduation.'

'My God. Where is she now? Who's she staying with whilst you're over here?'

'Kirsty's parents.'

'What? She's back out there in bushfire land?'

'We can't mollycoddle her, Nicolas.'

'Oh, yes I can. I'm her father. I can mollycoddle her all I like! You're going home, Serina, and I'm coming with you.'

'Really, Nicolas, are you quite sure about that?' And sliding her arms up around his neck, she kissed him.

They didn't fly home till after the New Year.

EPILOGUE

Christmas Day, one year later...

NICOLAS sat at the head of the huge dining table, with Serina on his right, and three-month-old Sebastian lying in his boun-cinette between them.

'How about a toast, everyone?' Nicolas said, and lifted his wineglass high.

There were eight other people seated around the table. Ken, Janine and Kirsty; Bert and Franny; Margaret, Serina's mother; Mrs Johnson; and of course, Felicity.

This was what a Christmas should be, Nicolas realised. Not presents so much—though he had gone over the top a bit this first year—but friends and family all gathered together.

'Happy Christmas!' he said, and clicked his wineglass against Serina's.

'Happy Christmas!' everyone chorused.

Sebastian responded to the noise by rocking madly back and forth in his bouncinette, flapping his arms and laughing his highly infectious laugh.

Everyone laughed with him, then got on with eating. Everyone except Serina, who wanted to take a moment to drink in, not the wine, but her happiness.

What a year it had been! So much had happened, everything orchestrated by Nicolas with speed and efficiency. They'd married by special licence in the middle of January, at the old Rocky Creek church, then honeymooned in both New York and London, during which both Nicolas's properties were sold. By the time they returned home to Australia in early February, Serina was well and truly pregnant. She'd actually fallen during the first week she'd spent with Nicolas in New York but kept that news to herself for a while.

On returning to Australia, Nicolas decided that the penthouse apartment—which he'd put a deposit on—wasn't suitable for family living. So he pulled out of that contract, then took Serina and Felicity house-hunting. They ended up buying, not just a house, but a small acreage not far from the Port Macquarie racecourse. It had belonged to a horse trainer who'd decided to go farther north.

Both Felicity and Serina had fallen in love with the place at first sight, Felicity because of the stables—extremely suitable to house sick animals in!—and Serina because of the house, which, though only five years old, was in the design of a colonial farmhouse with a high pitched roof and verandahs all around. Although much larger, it reminded her of the house she'd been brought up in and where she'd always been very happy.

And it was from this new and much-loved home that Nicolas had driven her to the hospital to have their baby.

Her pregnancy was the only worry that this year had brought Serina. Despite being thrilled at falling so quickly, she had been secretly concerned that she might have to endure another ten-month pregnancy before popping out a clone of Felicity. The news during her four-month ultrasound that she was having a boy eased her mind somewhat, but she was still a little nervous over what her baby might look like, especially if his birth was delayed.

She need not have worried. Right on her due date her water

broke, and after a thankfully short labour, Sebastian came into the world, the spitting image of his father. Nicolas had been over the moon and everyone who came to visit oohed and aahed over the babe's angelic appearance.

Serina had anticipated that Nicolas would be besotted with his son. And he was. She hadn't been quite so sure about Felicity's reaction. After all, Felicity had been top dog in the family for thirteen years.

But Felicity quickly became just as besotted with Sebastian as his father. She spent every spare second with her baby brother, playing with him and playing to him. On the grand piano Nicolas had bought her. She told Serina in secret one day that she knew Nicolas was disappointed that she didn't want to become a concert pianist, so she was determined to program Sebastian into fulfilling his father's wishes.

'You're not eating your dinner, Serina,' Nicolas said with a frown in his voice. 'I hope you're not on some silly diet.'

'Good heavens, no.' And she picked up her knife and fork. 'I'll be having seconds later. I love turkey.'

She'd taken several mouthfuls when Felicity suddenly stood up from where she was sitting at the other end of the table.

'I have a toast I want to make, too,' she said, and lifted her glass of Coke. 'To Nicolas. The best stepfather in the whole world.'

Serina's heart squeezed tight.

'To Nicolas,' everyone said, then drank.

'One more thing,' Felicity added. 'I've talked this over with Nanna and Pop and they think it's a good idea. The thing is...I don't want to have a different surname than my brother. So I'm going to be known as Felicity Harmon Dupre from now on. If that's all right with you, Nicolas.'

Serina saw the muscles working overtime in Nicolas's throat.

'Absolutely all right,' he finally managed to say.

'And you, Mum? You don't mind?'

'Not at all, darling. I think it's an excellent idea.'

'What a lucky girl you are, Felicity,' Serina's mother said as Felicity sat down. 'To have been blessed with two wonderful fathers.'

'Felicity is a lucky girl,' Nicolas told Serina as they lay in each other's arms that night, their son asleep in the cot next to their bed. 'But no one is more blessed than me. I have everything any man could ever want.'

Serina glanced up from where she was snuggled against his bare chest. 'You don't miss show business?'

'Not at the moment. But if I ever do, I can always buy a place in Sydney and get back into it. This is all I want to do right now. Spend every day with you and my children.'

'You'll eventually get bored.'

'Maybe. Meanwhile, what say we make another baby?'

Serina's breath caught. 'So soon?'

'The sooner the better. I didn't realise how much I would enjoy having a baby. The last three months have been the best three months of my life.'

'You might change your mind once Sebastian learns to walk. And talk. Haven't you heard of the terrible twos?'

'All the more reason to start a baby straight away, before I get disillusioned.'

'But if I have another baby I might have to give up work.'

'What a good idea! Then you can stay home all day every day with yours truly.'

'You are a wickedly selfish man.'

'It is a failing of mine. But you love me, just the same.'

'I don't know why.'

He showed her why.

Then he showed her again, just to be sure.

AUTHOR'S NOTE

Some of you may have read that I was born in Port Macquarie. So you will know already that Port is a real seaside town, on the mid North Coast of New South Wales, Australia. Wauchope—pronounced Warhope—is also a real town. Rocky Creek, however, is a place of my imagination.

For the first ten years of my life I lived on Rawdon Island, which is in the middle of the Hastings River, between Port Macquarie and Wauchope. My father was the school teacher there, my mother a dressmaker. Every Thursday we went to Wauchope to shop, and every Saturday to Port Macquarie, where my parents played golf and my two brothers, my sister and myself went to the movies. That was where my love of story began.

I recently revisited Port Macquarie to see what it was like nowadays. Yes, the old picture theatre is still there. And so is an old house with steep terraced lawns where I used to roll down whilst my mother was inside, doing dress fittings with the lady owner. There is no apartment block called Blue Horizons. At least, not one like mine. But it is real in my mind, as are my characters and their wonderful love story. Very real. Hopefully, they are now real in yours.

ONE-NIGHT LOVE-CHILD

BY
ANNE McALLISTER

Award-winning author **Anne McAllister** was once given a blueprint for happiness that included a nice, literate husband, a ramshackle Victorian house, a horde of mischievous children, a bunch of big, friendly dogs, and a life spent writing stories about tall, dark and handsome heroes. 'Where do I sign up?' she asked, and promptly did. Lots of years later, she's happy to report the blueprint was a success. She's always happy to share the latest news with readers at her website, www.annemcallister.com, and welcomes their letters there, or at PO Box 3904, Bozeman, Montana 59772, USA (SASE appreciated).

For Anne Gracie who kept my head above water

For Nancy, Cathy and Steve
who shared the journey

And for Kimberley Young, whose editorial
comments made this a better book

CHAPTER ONE

THE letter arrived out of the blue.

"I don't know what it is, my lord." Mrs. Upham sniffed, then dangled the smudged and tattered pale-blue envelope from between two fingers with clear disapproval. "It's very… dirty."

She had put the rest of the post on Flynn's desk in neat sorted stacks as she always did. Estate business—the biggest stack. Fan mail and book business—the midsize stack. Personal letters from his mother or brother—neither of whom seemed to believe in phones or e-mail—in the third.

All very tidy and organized—as if she could do the same to Flynn's life.

Good luck, he thought.

As his life currently consisted of Dunmorey, a dank and crumbling five-hundred-odd-year-old castle full of portraits of disapproving ancestors who looked down their noses at Flynn's efforts to literally keep a roof over their heads, its attendant farms, lands and tenants, as well as his horse-mad brother, Dev, who had great plans for reviving the Dunmorey stud but no money to accomplish it, and his mother, whose mantra since his father's death seven months ago had been, "We need to find you a bride," Flynn didn't think Mrs. Upham was likely to find any joy in it at all.

The only joy he could give her would be to tell her to throw it out.

His father certainly would have.

The late eighth earl of Dunmorey had no patience for anything that wasn't proper and traditional. He had once thrown out a letter Flynn had scrawled on a piece of a paper bag from a war zone where he'd been working on a story.

"If you can't be bothered to write a proper letter, I can't be bothered to read it," his father had informed him later.

It would have been nice if the late earl had stopped saying things like that since he was dead. But the fact was, Flynn spent most days trying to deal with all of Dunmorey's demands while inside his head he heard the virtually unceasing drone of the dead eighth earl saying, "I knew you couldn't do it."

Save the castle, he meant. Be a good earl, he meant. Be dutiful and responsible and Measure Up, he meant.

If you can.

The implication had always been that Flynn couldn't.

"My lord?" Mrs. Upham persisted.

His jaw tight, Flynn glanced up. He needed to run these figures again, to see if somehow—this time—there was enough to put the new roof on and still get the stables in order by the time Dev brought his new stallion home from Dubai.

There wouldn't be.

He had more chance of hitting the *New York Times* bestseller list with his new book coming out in the States next month. At least he had a talent for hard-hitting interviews, for insightful stories, for the written word.

It was what he'd done—what he'd been good at—before the earldom had changed his life.

But he was not going to give up on Dunmorey, even though the battle to keep the grim old Irish castle from crumbling to bits under his watch was fierce. It was his obligation, not his joy. And frankly, as a younger son, he had never expected to have to do it.

But like everything else in his life these days, he'd inherited while he was making other plans.

His late father would have said it served him right.

And maybe it did.

It wasn't what he would have chosen, but by God, he was determined to show the old man—dead though he was—that he could do it right.

"Everything you need to deal with is here, my lord," Mrs. Upham said. "I'll just throw this nasty old thing out, then, shall I?"

Flynn grunted and started again at the top of the column.

"May I bring you a cup of tea, my lord? Your father always liked a cup of tea with his post."

Flynn ground his teeth. "No, thank you, Mrs. Upham. I'm fine on my own."

He had learned rather quickly that while in Mrs. Upham's eyes, he would never be his father—and thank God for that, Flynn thought—he did have his own version of the Voice of Authority.

Whenever he used it, Mrs. Upham got the point.

"Very good, my lord." She nodded and backed out of the room. He might as well have been the king of England.

He did the figures again. But they still didn't give him the total he wanted. He sighed and slumped back in his chair, rubbed his eyes and flexed his shoulders. He had an appointment with a contractor at the stables in an hour to see what else needed to be done before Dev brought the stallion home in a fortnight.

As the horse was a proven winner and thus a money-making proposition, the stables were an absolute priority. Stud fees and book royalties didn't seem like enough to keep Dunmorey afloat.

The castle had been in the family for more than three hundred years. It had seen better times, and, hard though it was to believe, it had seen worse times as well. To Flynn it was the physical embodiment of the family motto: *Eireoidh Linn*, which he knew from his Irish schooldays meant, roughly, We Will Succeed Despite Adversity.

His father had always told English-speaking guests it meant, We Will Survive!

So far they had; though since the castle was no longer entailed, it could be sold.

They hadn't had to sell it yet. And Flynn was damned if he was going to be the one to lose the fight.

But the post brought more renovation estimates that were depressingly large, and bills that were equally so. They'd borrowed against the castle to get the money to get the stud up and running. When it was, things would be better. If his book did well, they would certainly improve. In the meantime…

Flynn shoved back his chair and got up to prowl the room, cracking his knuckles. It was on his return to the desk that his eyes were drawn to the spot of blue paper in the bottom of the bin.

It was every bit as dirty and crumpled and unappetizing as Mrs. Upham had said. And yet it intrigued him.

It wasn't another bill or another set of estimates. It wasn't a circular about a farm auction or an invitation to Lord and Lady So-and-So's house party. It wasn't stuffy. It wasn't embossed.

And it was, he could see, addressed half a dozen times over, to him. A call from his old life.

"Junk," his father would have said, dismissing it.

But he had never been his father, as they all well knew.

Flynn reached down and fished it out. The original address had been sent to him in care of *Incite* magazine in New York City.

His brows lifted at that. Once upon a time he'd done entertainment personality pieces and feature articles for them. But he hadn't written articles for *Incite* in years. Not since he'd covered what had been dubbed "The Great Montana Cowboy Auction" in tiny Elmer, Montana, six years before.

His father had always called those articles "fluff" and said it was a pity Flynn hadn't been good enough to write real news about something that mattered.

In fact, he had been. And the succession of addresses crossed out on the envelope were pretty much a record of where he had proved exactly that: Africa, the East Indies, west central Asia, South America, the Middle East.

One hot spot after another, each one hotter than the last.

Now he stared at the envelope, caught up in a flickering cascade of memories—of excitement, of challenge, of life.

He studied again the firm but neat feminine handwriting beneath the others. He didn't recognize it. He was amazed that the letter had caught up with him at all. It must have been a labor of love or sheer stubborn perseverance on the part of the world's post offices. The single U.S. domestic postage stamp had first been canceled in November five years before.

Five years?

Five years ago last November Flynn had been in the middle of a South American jungle, writing a "real news story" on twenty-first-century intertribal warfare—by experiencing it firsthand.

"You sure you want to do this?" His editor in London had been skeptical when Flynn had announced he was going. "You've already been shot once this year. This time you could get yourself killed."

That had been the general idea at the time.

His older brother, Will—"the heir," his father had always called him—had died just months before. And depending how you looked at it—certainly if you looked at it the way the earl did—Will's death had been Flynn's fault.

"He was going to the airport to meet you!" the earl had railed, feeling only his own pain, never even acknowledging Flynn's.

"You're the one who had to come home to recover! You're the one who got shot!"

But not the one who'd died.

That had been Will—steady, sensible, responsible Will who had stopped on the way to the airport to help a motorist change a flat tire and got hit by a passing car.

In a matter of an instant, the world changed—Will was gone and Flynn had become "the heir" in his place.

It was hard to say who was more dismayed—Flynn or his father.

Certainly when he'd recovered from his gunshot wound received pursuing one of those "real news stories that mattered"—the one he'd come home to recuperate from when Will had been killed—no one, least of all his father, had objected when he'd left for the intertribal warfare in South America.

No one had objected when he'd pursued increasingly danger-ous assignments after that.

But no matter how dangerous they were, no matter that he got shot again, more than once, Flynn hadn't died. He'd still been the heir when his father had dropped over from a heart attack last July.

Now he was the earl. He wasn't traveling the world anymore. He was stuck at Dunmorey Castle.

And a five-year-old letter that had chased him around the world and finally tracked him down seemed far less demanding—and much more appealing—than thinking about any of that.

Flynn slit it open. Inside was a single sheet of plain white paper. He took it out and unfolded it. The letter was brief.

Flynn. This is the third letter I've written you. Don't worry, I won't be writing any more. I don't expect anything from you. I want nothing. I just thought you had a right to know.

The baby was born this morning just after eight. He was

seven pounds eleven ounces. Strong and healthy. I'm naming him after my father. Of course I'm keeping him. Sara.

Flynn stared at the words, tried to understand them, put them in a context where they would make sense.

Expect…nothing…right to know…baby.

Sara.

The paper trembled in his fingers. His heart kicked over in his chest. He started again—this time with the signature: Sara.

An image of intense brown eyes, flawless ivory skin and short-cropped dark hair flickered through his mind. A vision of smooth golden skin and the taste of lips that spoke of cinnamon and spice teased his thoughts.

Sara McMaster.

Dazzling delightful Sara from Montana.

Good God.

He stared at the letter as its meaning became clear.

Sara had been pregnant. Sara had had a baby.

A boy…

His son.

It was Valentine's Day.

Sara knew this because last night she had helped her five-year-old son, Liam, print his name laboriously on twenty-one Valentine cards complete with cartoon-art mutant creatures saying, "Be Mine" and "I'm 4 U."

She knew it because together they had covered a shoe box with white paper and red hearts to be his own "mailbox" at kindergarten and because she had baked cupcakes—chocolate ones with chocolate frosting and red and white candy hearts on them—as right before he went to bed Liam remembered he had volunteered to bring the cupcakes for the class party today.

And she knew because—for the first time since Liam was born—she actually had a date.

Adam Benally had asked her to dinner. He was the foreman out at Lyle Dunlop's place. He had come to the valley a few months ago from Arizona. A widower with a past he didn't often talk about, he was at least candid about "trying to outrun his demons." He'd brought the ranch accounting work in for Sara, and that was how they'd got to know each other.

No stranger to demons herself, Sara thought she and Adam might have a lot in common. He at least was getting past his demons. It was about time she got past hers.

"You can't be a recluse forever," her mother, Polly, had told her more than once. "Just because you had one bad experience…"

Sara let her mother talk because that's what Polly did. A lot. And her mother was probably right about the recluse part. It was the "bad experience" part that was the sticking point.

It hadn't been bad. At least not while it was going on. While it was going on it had been the most amazing three days of her life. And then…

Nothing.

That was the bad part. That was the part that made her gut clench every time she thought about it. The part that spooked her, that made her hesitant to ever open up to another man, to ever try again.

But finally she'd said yes. She'd made up her mind to try again with Adam. A dinner date. A first step.

"About time," Polly had said when Sara told her the plan. "I'm glad. You need to banish some ghosts."

No. Just one.

One Sara saw in miniature—right down to the tousled black hair and jade-green eyes—every time she looked at her son.

She shoved the thought away ruthlessly. Now was not the time to be thinking about that. About *him.*

Liam might be a reminder, but *his father* was past. Ordinarily she went whole days without thinking of him at all. It was just today—because it was Valentine's Day, because she'd accepted Adam's invitation, determined to kill two memories with one night out—that he kept plaguing her thoughts.

"Don't," she told herself out loud. The past was over. She'd rehashed it often to kill it from over scrutiny. It had done no good. Now she needed to concentrate on the future—on Adam.

What would Adam expect? She paced the kitchen, made tea, thought about what to wear, how to be charming and make conversation. Dating was like speaking a foreign language she had no practice in. It was something she'd done very little of before—

No! Damn it. There she went again!

Determinedly she carried her mug of tea to the table and laid out files so she could work. If she could get the hardware store accounts finished before Liam got home from school, then she could take a break, maybe go out and build a snowman with him, have a snowball fight. Do something to distract herself.

Liam was going to spend the night at her aunt Celie's who lived up the street with her husband, Jace, and their kids.

"Why all night?" she'd demanded when Celie had offered. "We're only going to dinner. I'm not spending the night with him!"

"Well, you might want to invite him in after," Celie said innocently. "For a cup of coffee," she added with a smile. It wasn't what she meant.

Sara knew it as well as she knew that she wasn't up for anything beyond dinner. Not now. Not yet.

How on earth could she have let six years go by without a single date?

Well, really, she rationalized, when had she had time?

She'd spent the first three years after Liam's birth finishing a degree in accounting, then setting up in business. Between her son and her schooling and the jobs she'd taken to make ends meet, she'd had no time to meet eligible men.

Not that she'd wanted to.

Once burned, twice shy and all that. And while she supposed there was wisdom in the notion of getting right back on a horse once you'd been thrown, there was also wisdom in being a damn sight more cautious the second time around.

She'd been too reckless the first time. This time she was taking it slow and easy and that meant dinner, perhaps a quick peck on the lips. Yes, she could do that.

But first she had to get to work.

One of the pluses of her job as an independent certified public accountant was that she could set her own hours and work from home. That made it easier to be home when Liam was. The downside, of course, was that it was easy to get distracted—like today. There was no boss to crack the whip, to make demands. It was more tempting to think about checking her closet to see what she wanted to wear or to put in a load of laundry, make a cup of tea and talk to Sid the cat when she really needed to focus on work.

So she started again, made herself settle down at the kitchen table, which was also her desk, and spread out the accounts from the hardware store. Adding columns of figures required that she pay close attention and didn't allow her mind to wander, to anticipate, to worry.

A sudden loud knock on the front door made her jump. She slopped tea all over her ledger sheet. "Damn!"

She went to the sink and grabbed the dishrag, mopping up the spill, cursing the delivery man, who was the only one who ever came to the front door. He left her office supplies when she ordered them. But she didn't remember—

Bang, bang, bang!

Not the delivery man, then. He only knocked once, then,

having awakened the dead, he always jumped back into his delivery truck and drove away. He never knocked twice.

Bang! Bang! Bang!

Let alone a third time.

"Hold your horses," she shouted. "I'm coming!"

She stalked to the door and jerked it open—to the ghost of Valentine's past.

Oh, God.

She was hallucinating. Panicking at the notion of dating again, she'd conjured him up out of the recesses of her mind.

And damn her mind for making him larger than life and more appealing than ever. Tall, rangy and narrow-hipped, but with shoulders even broader than she remembered. And just for reality's sake, her brain had even dusted his midnight hair with snowflakes. They should have softened his appearance, made him seem gentler. They didn't. He looked as pantherish and deadly as ever.

"Sara." His beautiful mouth tipped in a devastatingly appealing lopsided grin.

Sara knew that grin. Remembered it all too well. Had kissed the lips that wore it. Had tasted his laughter, his words, his groans, his passion.

Her face burned. Her whole body seemed suddenly consumed by a heat she'd tried to forget. She glanced at her hands knotting together, astonished that they didn't have steam coming off them, the memory of him was so powerful.

"Speechless, *a stór*?" His rough baritone with the light Irish inflection made the tiny hairs at the back of her neck prickle. It felt as if a ghost had run a finger down the length of her spine.

"Go away," she said fiercely, closing her eyes, resisting the hallucination, the memories—the man. It was agreeing to go out with Adam that had done this to her. It had tripped a trigger of memories she'd bottled up, stored away, refused to take out and look at ever again.

She screwed up her eyes and shut them tight. Counted to ten. Opened them.

And felt her stomach plummet to her toes at the sight of him still standing there.

He wore jeans, a black sweater and a dark-green down jacket. He hadn't shaved in a day or two. His cheeks and jaw were stubbled. His eyes were bloodshot. But his impossibly long lashes blinked away snowflakes as he watched her with amusement. And when he grinned a little more at her befuddlement, she saw that he had chipped a tooth. She didn't think she would have hallucinated the chipped tooth.

So he was real. He was everything she remembered.

And worse.

Six years ago Sara had dreamed of this moment. Had held on to the hope that he would come back to Elmer, to her. For nine months she had planned and hoped and prayed. And he'd never come. Had never called. Had never written.

And now—out of the blue—he was here.

Sara's heart turned over, and at the same time, she felt the walls slam down. A fury of pain so fierce engulfed her that she had to swallow and swallow again before she could find her voice.

And when at last she did, she prayed it sounded as flat and disinterested as she wanted to be as she acknowledged him. "Flynn."

Flynn Murray. The man who had taken her love, given her a child and left her without a backwards glance.

It had been her fault. She knew that. He'd never promised to stay. Had never promised anything—except that he would hurt her.

And by God, he'd done that.

At the time, of course, she hadn't believed he could. She'd been nineteen, naive, foolish and in love beyond anything she'd ever dreamed possible. She'd met Flynn unexpectedly when he'd come to their small town to cover the human-interest angle of a celebrity cowboy auction. It had been strange, serendipitous, and almost like finding the other half of herself.

She'd always been practical, sensible, driven. She'd had goals since she was old enough to spell the word. Meeting and falling in love with Flynn had turned them upside down. He'd come to her tiny town and changed her world.

Flynn had made her want things she'd never dreamed of wanting—and for a few days or weeks she'd believed she could have them.

She knew better now.

She knew about hurt and pain and getting past them. She knew she wasn't letting it happen again. Ever.

"You look beautiful," he told her. "Even more beautiful than I remember."

Sara's jaw tightened. "You look older," she said flatly.

And harder. The lines and angles of his face were sharper, his features almost gaunt. He was still handsome, of course. Perhaps even more handsome, in a rough-edged harsher way. At twenty-six Flynn Murray had been all smooth easy smiles, pantherish grace and spontaneous Irish charm. At thirty-two he looked rugged and ragged and battle weary, like a man come home from war.

There were surprising flecks of gray at his temples. And a scar creased his temple and disappeared into salt-and-pepper hair.

Had some jealous boyfriend attacked him when Flynn had charmed a local girl?

Sara wouldn't have been surprised. Living a fast-lane life must be tougher than she'd ever imagined. How hard it must be, Sara thought mockingly, tracking celebrities all over the globe.

Flynn's mouth tipped ruefully and he shrugged. "You know what they say—it's not the years, it's the miles."

"And you've gone quite a few, I'm sure," Sara said acidly. And he could keep right on going. She didn't need him here now. Didn't need him upsetting her life, her hopes, her son.

Oh, God, Liam. A shaft of panic shot through her. He couldn't have ignored Liam for five years just to turn up now, could he?

"What are you doing here?" she demanded.

And as if he could read her mind as well as disrupt her life in every other way imaginable, Flynn said, "I want to meet my son."

CHAPTER TWO

SARA'S jaw set. She steeled herself against his words, his intent and, mostly, against the green magic of his eyes.

"You're a little late," she said through her teeth. About five and a half years.

"I am." He nodded gravely. "I just found out."

Just found out? She blinked her disbelief. "Yeah, right." There wasn't enough sarcasm in the universe to flavor her response.

But Flynn didn't seem to notice. He was rummaging inside his jacket, pulling a small manila business envelope out of an inner pocket. He opened the envelope and extracted a dirty creased faded blue one. Wordlessly he held it out to her.

Sara stared at it. Then, slowly, she reached out and took it from him with nerveless fingers.

The paper looked as if it had been trampled by a herd of buffalo. She turned it over and saw at least half a dozen addresses printed and scrawled and scratched out, one on top of another. One word caught her eye: *Ireland.*

That was a surprise. Six years ago he'd been delighted to be out of the land of his birth.

"Nothing for me there," he'd said firmly.

Like her ancestors 150 years ago, she'd supposed. Her dad had often told handed-down stories about their own family's desperate need to leave and find a better future for themselves. Though Flynn had never said it, she had no trouble believing it had been true of him, too.

Now, curious about his change of heart, she glanced from the envelope to the man. But his green eyes bored into hers so intently that her own skated away at once back to the envelope.

It had originally been a pretty robin's-egg blue, part of a set with her initials on it that her grandmother had given her at high school graduation. Sara hadn't had the occasion to write many letters. She still had some sheets of it left.

But this letter she remembered very well.

She had written it only hours after Liam was born. She had known that there was little chance Liam's father would heed it. He hadn't paid any attention to her previous two letters, not the first one telling him she was pregnant, not the later one telling him again in case he hadn't got the first one.

He'd never replied.

She'd understood—he wasn't interested.

But still she'd felt the need to write one last time after Liam's birth. She'd given him one last chance—had dared to hope that news of a son might bring him around. She wasn't proud. Or she hadn't been then.

Now she was. And she was equally determined. He wasn't going to hurt her again.

"I didn't know, Sara," he repeated. He met her gaze squarely.

"I wrote you," she insisted. "Before this—" she rattled the envelope in her hand "—I wrote. Twice."

"I didn't get them. I was…moving around. A lot. I wasn't writing for *Incite* anymore. They sent it on. So did others. It kept following, apparently. But I didn't get it. Not until last week. Then I got it—and here I am."

Sara opened her mouth, then closed it again. After all, what was there to say? He'd come because he'd discovered his son. It still had nothing to do with her.

It shouldn't hurt after all this time. She'd known, hadn't she, that she didn't matter to him the way he'd mattered to her. But hearing the words still had the power to cut deep.

But she was damned if she was going to show him her pain. She crossed her arms over her chest. "So? Should I applaud? Do you want a medal?"

He looked startled, as if he hadn't expected belligerence. Had he thought she'd fall into his lap with gratitude, for heaven's sake?

"I don't want anything," he said gruffly, "except the chance to get to know my son. And do whatever you need."

"Go away?" Sara suggested because that was definitely what she needed.

Flynn's scowl deepened. "What? Why?"

"Because we don't need you."

But even as she said it, she knew it was only half-true. *She* didn't need him. But Liam thought he did.

"Where's my dad?" he'd been asking her for the past year.

If he wasn't dead, why didn't he come visit? Even divorced dads came to visit, he told her with the knowledge of a worldly kindergartner. Darcy Morrow's dad came to see her every other weekend.

"He can't," Sara said. "If he could, he would." It wasn't precisely a lie. Even though she'd believed Flynn had deliberately turned his back on them, she knew telling Liam that would be absolutely wrong. It wouldn't be wrong to say his father would come if he could. He simply couldn't—for whatever unknown reason. End of story.

Fortunately, Liam hadn't asked why. But when told at school that Thanksgiving was a family holiday, he'd wondered again why his dad wasn't there. And then he'd said, "Maybe he'll come at Christmas!"

"Don't get your hopes up," Sara had cautioned. But telling Liam that was like telling the sun not to rise.

"I'll take care of it," he'd said, and when they went to the mall in Bozeman, mortified Sara by marching right up to Santa, telling him that for Christmas he wanted his father to come home.

Sara had been prepared for tears on Christmas morning when no father appeared. But Liam had been philosophical.

"I didn't get my horse at Grandma and Grandpa's right away, either," he'd said. "I had to wait till spring."

Because, of course, the colt hadn't been born till spring. And now? Sara could just imagine what Liam would say when he came home this afternoon.

"He should have a father," Flynn said now. "A father who loves him."

There was something in his voice that made Sara look up. But he didn't say anything else.

"He's fine," she insisted. His life might not be perfect, but whose was? "You don't need to do this."

"I do," he said flatly.

"He's not here."

"I'll wait." He looked at her expectantly. She didn't move.

He cocked his head and studied her with a look on his face that she remembered all too well. A gentle, teasing, laughing look. "You're not afraid of me…are you, Sara?"

"Of course I'm not afraid of you," she snapped. "I'm just… surprised. I assumed you didn't care."

The smile vanished. The look he gave her was deadly serious. "I care. I mean it, Sara. I would have been here from the first if I'd known."

She didn't know whether to believe him or not. She did know

she wasn't going to be able to shut the door on him. Not yet. She was going to have to let him in, let him wait for Liam, meet his son.

And then?

He was hardly going to be much of a father if he was in Ireland. But at least Liam would know he had one who cared.

But first she would need to set some ground rules. So, reluctantly, she stepped back and held the door open. "I suppose you might as well come in."

"And here was I, thinking you'd never ask." He flashed a grin, the one that said he knew he'd get his way.

Sara steeled herself against it—and against the blatant Irish charm. She stepped back to let him pass—and to make sure not even his sleeve brushed hers as he came in.

But as he passed through the doorway, he stopped and turned towards her. And he was so close that she stared right at the pulse beat in his throat, so close that it wasn't his sleeve, but the chest of his jacket that brushed against the tips of her breasts, so close that when she drew in a sharp breath, she caught a whiff of that heady scent of woods and sea that she remembered as purely and essentially Flynn. Her back was against the wall.

"Did you miss me, Sara?" he murmured.

And Sara shook her head fiercely. "Not a bit."

"No?" His mouth quirked as if he heard the truth inside her lie. "Well, I've missed you," he said roughly. "I didn't realize how much until right now."

And then quite deliberately he bent his head and set his lips to hers.

Flynn Murray had always known how to kiss. He had kissed her senseless time and time again. She'd tried to forget—or at the very least tried to assure herself that it was only her youthful inexperience with kissing that had made her body melt and her knees buckle.

She'd told herself it would never happen again.

She'd lied. And this kiss was every bit as bad—and as marvelous—as she had feared.

It was a hungry kiss, a kiss determined to prove how much he'd missed her. And it was—damn it all—mightily persuasive. It tasted, it teased, it possessed.

It promised. It promised moments of heaven, as Sara well knew. But she wasn't totally inexperienced now. She knew it also promised years in the aching loneliness of hell.

She lifted her hands to press against his chest, to push him away, and found her hands trapped there, clutching at his jacket, hanging on for dear life as every memory she'd tried so hard to forget came crashing back, sweeping her along, making her need, making her ache, making her want.

Exactly as she had needed and ached and wanted before. Only, then she'd believed he felt the same.

Now she didn't. Couldn't. Not and preserve her sanity. Not if she didn't want to be destroyed again.

Flynn had come, yes. But he'd come because of his son—not because of her.

And despite his kiss—the sweetness, the passion, the promise—and because of his kiss—its ability to undermine her reason, her common sense, her need for self-preservation—she had to remember that.

She'd loved him six years ago, and he had left her.

He'd made no promises, but she'd trusted. She'd given him her heart and her soul and her body. He had known her on a level no one else ever had. She'd believed he loved her, too. She'd believed he'd come back.

He never had.

Not until today. Not until he'd found out about Liam.

He wanted his son. Not her.

Finally she managed to flatten her hands against his chest and give a hard, furious shove.

He stumbled backwards awkwardly and, to her amazement, fell against the nearest chair. "Damn it!"

But it wasn't her he directed the words at. He muttered them to himself as he staggered, then winced and shifted his weight onto his left leg. Sara didn't know which stunned her more—the kiss or the fact that he was clearly favoring one leg and moving with none of his customary pantherlike grace.

Still trembling from the kiss, she asked, "What happened?"

"I got shot." The words were gruff and dismissive.

She felt as if they'd gone straight to her heart. "Shot?" She gaped, then told herself it probably served him right. Maybe he'd played fast and loose, loved and left a woman who got angrier even than she had. "Take advantage of one too many women?" she asked. Given the fast-lane celebrities he wrote about, it seemed all too likely.

"Assassin."

"What?"

"He wasn't trying to kill me." He shrugged. "I was in his way."

Sara swallowed, then shook her head. "I don't understand." She wasn't sure she wanted to, but it was better to be distracted by assassins than kisses. She shut the door and stepped around him into the room.

"I was in Africa." He mentioned a small unstable country she'd barely heard of. It made Sara blink because there certainly weren't any celebrities there. "He was trying for the prime minister. He missed. At least he missed the prime minister. Gave me a little souvenir to remember him by." His mouth twisted in a wry smile.

None of it made sense to Sara.

The Flynn she'd known went to New York and Hollywood and

Cannes, not Africa. And even if he had gone there, prime ministers were hardly the sorts of celebrities he wrote about. He wrote features about starlets and rock stars, actors like her stepdad and, at a stretch, soccer stars and tennis pros.

But she didn't have a chance to ask anything else.

She hadn't heard the back door open, hadn't heard the footsteps pound across the kitchen floor, hadn't heard anything until the door into the living room and dining room flew open.

And Liam burst into the room.

CHAPTER THREE

DEAR God, the boy was Will all over again.

And the sight of him would have sent Flynn reeling if kissing Sara hadn't already done so.

She'd given him a shove, of course, and, with his bad leg, that had been enough to send him off balance literally. But emotionally just the sight of her had already rocked him. And the kiss, well…Flynn had kissed his share of women over the years, but none of them had been like kissing Sara.

He wanted to think about his reaction—and hers—analyze it, understand the effect she had on him. But there was no time. Not now.

Now he stood stunned and staring at this vital bouncing ball of energy, this miniature version of his dead brother.

Intellectually Flynn had known that his son would likely resemble his Murray forebears. But actually seeing it was astonishing.

The boy—Lewis, if she'd named him after her father—was the spitting image of his brother. The same black unruly hair, same fair skin, same spattering of freckles, same thin face and pointed chin. Same build, too. Wiry. Slender. There was a coltish boniness even beneath the boy's winter jacket and jeans.

The boy didn't spare him a glance. He came hurtling into the room, with no regard for the stranger in the living room. His eyes—as green as Will's and Flynn's own—went straight to his mother.

"Look!" He wriggled off his backpack at the same time he was thrusting a white box covered with hearts into his mother's hands. "I musta got a skillion Valentines! An' I got a real fancy one from Katie Setsma. She must like me!" He flung his backpack onto a chair, then scrambled up on it to pull off his boots.

Sara shot Flynn a quick glance, as if she were trying to gauge his reaction to this astonishing little person. The words in a crumpled letter and the living breathing bouncing reality were two entirely different things. He wondered if he looked as dazed as he felt.

"Of course she likes you, Liam," she said to her son.

And that nearly did Flynn in.

"Liam?" he said hoarsely. The Irish shortened form of *William*? Flynn's hand groping blindly for the back of a chair to steady himself.

At his voice, the boy stopped jerking off his boots and, for the first time, looked at Flynn curiously.

Instantly wary, Sara stepped between them. "That's what we call him," she said firmly. "I told you I named him after my father, Lewis William. But he's not my father. He's his own person." She said this last fiercely as if defying him to argue.

He didn't. Couldn't. Could barely find his voice—or words. "I…yeah. I'm just…surprised." He sucked in a hard breath and tried again. "It was my brother's name—William. Will. We called him Will."

Sara caught the operative tense. "Called? Was?"

"He died." Flynn ran his tongue over suddenly parched lips. "Almost six years ago."

Their gazes met, locked. Sara looked shocked then, too. And there were a thousand unasked questions in hers. He couldn't answer them. Not now at least.

"I'm sorry," she said quietly. And there was the sound of real regret in her voice. "I didn't know."

It made Flynn's throat tighten. He gave a jerky nod. "I know that. It's just—" he gave his head a little shake "—one more surprise."

And then the room went silent. No one moved. No one spoke. Finally he grew aware of the sound of Liam sliding off the chair and coming around by Sara. He stopped and looked up at his mother, as if trying to figure out what was going on, as if hoping she would tell him. But she didn't speak, didn't even seem to see him, and her gaze never left Flynn.

The boy's gaze followed hers. Will's eyes—Dear God, they really were—fastened on him, then narrowed a little in the same way Will's always did when he assessed something or someone new.

There was no doubt the boy had picked up on the current of apprehension that pervaded the room. He was like a fox scenting danger, Flynn thought.

And then, apparently deciding what was necessary, he deliberately moved in front of Sara, his back to his mother's legs as if he would protect her. His chin jutted out as he contemplated Flynn. There was no sparkle now. Just the hard unwavering green gaze that generations of Murrays wore when protecting their own.

"Who're you?"

It was the question Flynn had been anticipating since he'd made up his mind to come to Montana. It was the question he'd been longing to answer.

And suddenly he found the words stuck in his throat. After a hundred—hell, after a *thousand* at least—visualizations of the moment when he would meet his son, he didn't have the spit to say a word.

He opened his mouth and nothing came out. For the first time in his entire life, Flynn Murray had no words.

Sara, too, was staring at him expectantly, waiting for him to say something. He couldn't. He shook his head.

Maybe she realized he couldn't—or maybe she simply decided that taking charge herself was a better idea. Her hands came down to rest on the boy's shoulders and squeezed lightly. When she spoke, her voice was soft.

"He's your father, Liam."

Liam's eyes flew wide open. So did his mouth. He stared at Flynn, then abruptly his head whipped around so he could look up at his mother. His whole body seemed quiver with the unspoken question: *Is that true?*

Sara's smile was faint and a little wary. But she gave the boy's shoulders another squeeze, then nodded.

"He is. Truly," she assured him. "He's come to meet you."

For a long moment Liam still searched her face. But then, eventually, he seemed satisfied with what he saw there. He turned back to Flynn. His gaze was steady and level and curious as he stared at his father in silence. The silence seemed to go on—and on.

And then, finally, in a slightly croaky but determined voice, Liam asked, "Where've you been?"

Absolutely mundane. Absolutely reasonable.

Absolutely devastating.

Flynn swallowed. "I've…I've been a lot—" he cleared the raggedness out of his throat, glad he at least had a voice now. He started again "—a lot of places. All over the world. I'd have been here sooner. But…I didn't know about you."

Liam's gaze jerked around to challenge his mother's. "You said you wrote to him."

"She did," Flynn answered for her. This wasn't Sara's fault. "Your mother wrote me before you were born. She wrote me later when you were born…but I didn't get the letter. Not for a long time. Years." He picked the envelope up from the top of the bookcase where Sara had set it and held it out. "Take a look. It's been everywhere. But I didn't get it until last week."

Liam's gaze shifted from Flynn's face to the letter in his outstretched hand. But he stayed where he was, so Flynn moved closer.

Still the boy didn't reach out right away. But finally he plucked the envelope from Flynn's fingers and turned it over in his hands, then studied the multiplicity of addresses on it.

"I was working a lot of different places all over the world," Flynn explained awkwardly. "It must have missed me everywhere I went. It finally caught up with me back home. In Ireland."

Liam didn't look up. He was rubbing his thumb lightly over the words on the envelope, staring at the writing, which, Flynn realized suddenly, he wouldn't be able to read yet. He wasn't old enough. "All those addresses are places I was," he explained.

Then Liam looked up at him. "You live in a castle?"

Flynn blinked. He *could* read?

Apparently so, for Liam was pointing at the one address on the envelope that hadn't been scratched out. "That's what it says." He scowled at it, then sounded out, "Dun-more-ee castle." Liam read it out slowly then looked up again. "That's your house?"

"No, dear," Sara began, but Flynn cut in.

"It is. Dunmorey Castle."

He heard Sara's sharp intake of breath. Liam's eyes went so wide that his eyebrows disappeared into the fringe of black hair that fell across his forehead. "You live in a *real* castle? With a moat?"

"I live there. And it is a real castle in name," Flynn qualified, looking at Sara for the first time, seeing accusation in her gaze. "Mostly it's a huge drafty old house," he went on. "Over five hundred years old. Mouldering. Damp. And it does have a turret and some pretty high walls. But it doesn't have a moat."

"Well, that's something, I guess," Sara muttered.

"No moat?" Liam's face fell. His brows drew down. "What makes it a castle then?"

"It was a stronghold. A really old fort," Flynn explained. "Where people could go if they needed to defend themselves against invaders. And it was where the lord of the lands lived. The boss," he added in case that made more sense. "That's what makes it a castle."

Liam digested that. "Can I see it?"

"Of course you can."

"A picture, he means," Sara said hastily. "Can he see a picture? Of your *castle*." Her tone twisted the word as if she were blaming him for it.

The damn place was no end of trouble. Flynn shook his head. "Not with me," he told Liam. "But I can get you some. Even better, I can take you there. You can see it in person."

Liam gaped. "I can?"

"No!" Sara said sharply.

Liam twisted around to look up at her. "I can't?"

"It's in *Ireland*," she explained, shooting Flynn a furious glance. "That's clear across the ocean. Thousands of miles."

"I could fly on a plane." Liam was undaunted. "Couldn't I?" He glanced around at Flynn for confirmation.

"You could," Flynn agreed. "Best way to get there, in fact. We'll talk about it." He smiled at Sara.

Sara's mouth pressed into a tight line. "I don't think we'll be talking about it anytime soon." She turned to her son and said firmly, "He can tell you all about his castle, Liam. But do not expect to go zipping across the ocean."

"But I've never seen a real castle."

"You're five. You have plenty of time," Sara said unsympathetically. "And in the meantime you can make them out of Legos."

Liam brightened. "I already did." He spun towards Flynn. "It's sort of real. But it doesn't have a moat either. Wanna see it?" He was all eagerness now, hopping from one foot to the other now, looking up at Flynn.

The expression on his face now didn't remind Flynn so much of Will as it did of the young Sara—when he had first met her. She'd had that same sparkle, that same eager, avid, intense enthusiasm.

Right now she was glaring at him, her jaw locked.

He had made a living out of reading people, picking up their body language, understanding when to move in, when to back off. He had no trouble reading Sara. She wasn't thrilled to see him and, he supposed, he didn't blame her. He hadn't been here when she needed him.

But he'd come when he found out, hadn't he? They'd get it sorted. They had to. But they weren't going to do it now in front of their five-year-old son. So he gave Sara a quick smile that, he hoped, appeased her for the moment, then turned to Liam. "I'd like that."

"C'mon, then!" And Liam was off, pounding up the stairs.

Flynn looked at Sara. She glared. Then she shrugged. "Oh, hell, go with him. But don't you dare encourage him to think about jetting off to Ireland!"

"It's possible, Sar'. Not immediately but we should discuss—"

"No, we shouldn't! Damn it, Flynn, you can't just pop up and disrupt our lives. It's been *six* years!"

"I didn't know—"

"And you didn't *want* to know," Sara said, "or you'd have come back."

"I thought—"

"I don't care what you thought. You knew where I was. I didn't leave! If I'd mattered at all, you'd have come back. You never came!"

"You were going to med school."

She stared at him. "Do I look like I went to med school?"

He blinked, then shook his head, dazed. "What do you mean? How should you look?"

"I got pregnant, Flynn. I had two and half years of university left for my bachelor's. I had a baby. It was all I could do to get through that. I didn't go to med school."

"But—"

"Circumstances change. Plans change."

"Yes, but—" He couldn't believe it. She'd been so driven. "Is that why you're so ticked at me?"

She stared. "What? Because I couldn't go to med school? Of course not! I don't care about that. I got my degree. I have my own business. I'm a CPA—certified public accountant. I like my work. I like numbers in boxes. I like adding things up and having them come out right. I like knowing the answers! Speaking of which, what the hell is this about you living in a castle?"

He shrugged, still trying to come to grips with Sara as a CPA, not a doctor as he'd always imagined. Sara as a mother had been tricky enough. But Sara changing her determined plans boggled his mind. She'd been so committed, so determined. She'd said flat-out that nothing was going to stop her.

"Castle?" she prompted, when he didn't answer immediately.

"I inherited it," he said dismissively.

"You told me there was nothing for you in Ireland!"

"There wasn't. I wasn't supposed to inherit, I didn't want to. My brother died." He got angry all over again just thinking about it. Sometimes he wanted to strangle Will—except he wanted his brother alive. That was the whole problem.

"Will," she said, making the connection.

"Will." It always felt like a lead ball hitting him in the stomach when he said his brother's name.

Sara pressed her lips together. "Well, I really am sorry about that. It was…a shock, I gather."

"An accident. Coming to get me at the airport."

A mixture of pain and sympathy flickered across her face. "Oh, God."

"Exactly."

Their gazes met again. The connection that had been so strong seemed to be flickering back to life—and Flynn couldn't believe how astonishingly happy that made him feel.

And then, as if she shut the light off, Sara's expression went blank. "You'd better go see the castle," she said, pointing through the door to the kitchen. "Just through there and up the stairs."

Thank goodness he went after Liam.

Sara didn't know how much longer she could have stood there and talked rationally—well, almost rationally. Her heart was hammering. Her hands were trembling. She had to get a grip. Had to stop flying off the handle at him. Had to stop caring!

For years she'd managed to convince herself that she didn't—that her three days of aberrant behavior with Flynn Murray had been some sort of alchemical reaction that would never be repeated.

And all it had taken was the sight of him standing on her doorstep and she was in meltdown all over again.

It was the shock, that was all. He was the last person she'd expected to see when she'd opened the door this afternoon. And the sizzling awareness she'd felt when she'd seen him had caught her off guard.

She didn't even want to think about what had happened when he'd kissed her!

But thinking about him with Liam wasn't much better.

They were so much alike.

Sara had always known that Liam resembled his father. But without pictures—and try as she had to find any of him among

all those taken during that hectic February weekend, she'd discovered none—she'd told herself Liam simply had his father's
coloring. After all, she occasionally saw glimpses of herself, her
own father, her mom, even her brother Jack in her son.

But when Liam and his father were in the same room, she didn't
only see glimpses of Flynn in her son. He was almost a clone.

But even more than Liam's features, it was his body language
that was so much like his father's. He moved like Flynn, with the
same intensity of purpose. And when he was stymied, he even
prowled around rooms like Flynn.

Both Flynn and Liam were edgy, intense, determined. When
Liam wanted something—like building a castle or learning to
read—he went after it. Like his father. And while Liam was still
occasionally little-boy clumsy, Flynn, even with his limp—dear
God, she still couldn't believe he'd been shot!—was clearly
powerful, controlled and in command. Sara was sure that Liam
would be exactly like that one day, too.

She wondered if Flynn saw it.

She wondered exactly what Flynn did see—and what he was
really doing here. To see his son, yes. She could accept that. But
what else did he want? What *more?*

He wasn't going to waltz in here and try to take her son away
from her, was he?

Just because he lived a in castle now, he didn't need to think
he could take over her son.

Or was it just her son he had in mind?

The memory of that kiss snuck back in to torment her—the
memory of his lips on hers, the possessive hunger of that kiss!
Surely he didn't want her again?

Of course he didn't. If he had, as she'd told him, he'd have
come back long before this. God knew he could have had her then.

But this had been a power play, pure and simple. He was just proving he could still make her react, could still—let's face it, Sara, she said to herself—turn her on.

And yes, damn it, he could. He had! He'd nearly swept away her reason, had made her weak with longing, with wanting him exactly the way she'd wanted him all those years ago.

But at least this time she'd managed—barely—to resist. And she would not let it happen again. It could only happen, she assured herself, if he caught her unawares.

But there would be no more "unawares." Now she was forewarned. Flynn Murray had burned her once. There was no way she was letting him do it again!

Thank God she was going out with Adam tonight.

All of a sudden her lukewarm attitude towards their Valentine's Day date had undergone a definite change. Focusing on Adam would be far better than spending the evening at home thinking about Flynn.

She glanced at her watch. It was quarter to four. She didn't know how long he expected to stay, and she didn't want to follow them to Liam's bedroom and ask. Even from the kitchen she could hear Liam's excited chatter and Flynn's low baritone responses. She could hear that blasted Irish lilt in his voice. God, it was seductive. Even now—forewarned, forearmed—it had the power to raise goose bumps along her spine and make the back of her neck tingle.

"Adam," she said aloud. "Think about Adam." She had to get ready to go out with Adam.

Resolutely she climbed the stairs. At the end of the hall she could see into Liam's room, could see Liam darting past the doorway, talking a mile a minute, could see Flynn's long legs stretched out as he sat on Liam's bed.

She did not want to think about Flynn in the same sentence with the word *bed*.

She got her clean clothes from her own room, then headed for the bathroom, calling out as she went, "I'll be in the shower."

It was only to let them know where she was. She hoped to heaven Flynn didn't think it was an invitation!

Of course he didn't. But it didn't stop her face from flaming. She was mortified to see how red it looked when she glanced in the bathroom mirror. "Stop it," she commanded herself. "Stop thinking about him."

Of course, that was easier said than done. She showered quickly—and used mostly cold water, not wanting to think why it seemed suddenly such a good idea. She washed her hair and blew it dry. Then she dressed in the black velvet pants and red cashmere sweater that her sister Lizzie had given her for Christmas.

She had worn a red sweater the night she had gone to Flynn's motel room. And the memory almost had her pulling the sweater back over her head and looking for something else. But to do so would give him more power over her than he deserved.

He deserved no power at all.

Besides, she thought with all the dispassion she could muster, he probably wouldn't even have the vaguest notion of what she'd worn. He hadn't cared about her the way she had about him.

Flicking a brush through her hair, then putting on some lipstick that she dared hope she would not gnaw off, she gave herself one last stern look, then opened the bathroom door.

It was completely quiet. There was no sound of Liam's eager chatter now, no Irish lilt from Flynn. The light in Liam's room was off.

Had Flynn had enough already and left?

It was a happy thought—followed immediately by, *Then where was Liam?*

She hurried downstairs. No one was in the kitchen, either.

"Liam?"

She got no answer. He'd better not be playing hide-and-seek without telling her. When he was four he'd thought it fun to dart into the closet and stay still as a mouse while she went nuts looking for him. But he was five now—nearly five and a half—and she'd told him off in no uncertain terms. He knew better. He'd moved on to other sins—like sneaking in TV cartoons when he thought she wouldn't notice.

"You'd better not be watching television, young man," she said, marching across the kitchen and sticking her head around the door to look in the living room, expecting to find him in the semidarkened room with the sound turned down.

But only Sid the cat was there, sleeping on the couch. He raised his head and gave her a baleful look before closing his eyes again.

Sara was not given to panic. She had learned not to. But now her heart began to pound. She spun back into the kitchen.

"Liam!" Her voice rose.

Where *was* he? He wasn't supposed to go anywhere without telling her. Another of his sins. He'd been in trouble for going to Celie's during Christmas vacation without telling her he was leaving. She'd come down on him like a ton of bricks. He wouldn't do it again.

Would he?

Now she saw that his jacket was gone. His boots were gone.

And so was Flynn.

No!

He wouldn't! He'd never—

I'll take you to Ireland, he'd said. And she'd refused to discuss it.

He couldn't have just walked in and taken off with her child!

She ran to the back door and jerked it open. "Liam!" She was desperate now, frantic as she ran out onto the snow-covered porch. *"Liam!"*

"What?" The small surprised voice came from around the side of the house. It sounded quite close and completely bewildered.

Oh, God. The surge of relief nearly melted Sara's bones. Her legs wobbled and she gripped the pillar at the top of the stairs as, a second later, Liam's head poked around the corner.

"You don't have to yell. I'm right here," he said indignantly.

"So I…see." She was still gasping for air. Her heart was still slamming against the wall of her chest. "Where's Flynn? Where's your…father," she amended, still breathing hard.

"Right here." Liam jerked his head towards the side yard. "We're buildin' a castle." He gave Sara a thumb's-up and grinned broadly. "Like Dunmorey."

Sara was still gulping air, still bashing down the panic, when Flynn came around the corner of the house. It had begun to snow again and his midnight hair was dusted with sparkling white snowflakes. He looked rugged and handsome and gorgeously reminiscent of the first time she had seen him.

She started trembling.

His intent green gaze fixed on her. "Something wrong?"

"No. I just—" she dragged in a breath "—didn't realize you'd gone outside." Her fingers still gripped the porch pillar. "I thought…"

But she couldn't admit what she'd thought, couldn't acknowledge aloud her terror at the belief—even for a split second—that he'd done the most devastating thing of all: taken her son.

She shook her head. "I didn't know where he was. I thought… never mind. Just…carry on." And with those words she turned abruptly and hurried back into the house, shaken, relieved and shattered all at the same time.

She shut the door and sank down into one of the wooden kitchen chairs, trying with trembling fingers to peel of her snow-soaked socks.

The back door opened, and Flynn strode in.

"You thought I'd taken him." His words were flat. His eyes accused her.

She tried to quiet the shaking and forced herself to concentrate on peeling off the socks before she would answer. Then she stood up, needing to be on a level with him, needing to find her self-control before she could reply. "I didn't know what you'd done."

But she couldn't deny her panic—it was still there in her voice and she was sure he could read it on her face.

Flynn's jaw tightened. He pushed the door shut behind him.

Sara shot a glance towards the side yard. "Liam—"

"He's building the turret. I told him I wanted to see it when he was done. And I will see it," he said firmly, "but not before we get this straightened out."

Sara swallowed and straightened, not liking his tone. "Get what straightened out?" Her voice was steadier now. She wished her nerves were.

"What you obviously think. I did not come to steal my son away from you."

She bristled at the words "my son." But she knew he was just making a point. "I didn't imagine—"

"You damned well did!"

"All right, fine. I did. But only because he was gone! And you'd said you'd take him to Ireland! What was I supposed to think? I'd finished showering and dressing and you weren't there!"

"What sort of man do you think I am?" His eyes were stormy now, a turbulent sea green.

He didn't wait for her to answer that. She wasn't sure she could have, anyway. She didn't actually know what sort of man he was, did she? Once she'd thought she had, but that had been all wrong.

"We talked about Dunmorey," Flynn said patiently, as if explaining things to a small, not-too-bright child. "And we talked about forts and building castles and it was snowing and we decided it would be fun to build a snow castle. Okay? We didn't go to Ireland. We were in the garden."

Sara nodded numbly, knowing she should feel foolish, still feeling the residual effects of her momentary panic. "You didn't say," she mumbled.

"I didn't realize you wanted me to stick my head in the bathroom and announce it." A corner of his mouth quirked, and the way his eyes slid over her made her wish she had a suit of armor on, not a cashmere sweater and velvet pants.

She wrapped her arms across her chest. "Of course not!"

He didn't reply for a moment, as if considering what to say. Then he shook his head gravely. "I'm sorry you were upset. It never occurred to me to tell you. I thought you'd figure it out."

"Well, I didn't. I didn't know what you'd do. I don't even know you."

"You did," he said quietly, and the serious husky tone of his voice sent those goose bumps skittering down her spine again.

She hugged herself. "No."

But he nodded. "You did, Sara." His tone was insistent. "I think you knew me better than anyone else on earth."

"Then why—" The anguished words burst from her before she could stop them. But fortunately she managed to shut her mouth before she sounded like a pathetic twit. And thankfully, the phone chose that moment to ring.

She spun away from him and grabbed for the phone on the countertop. "Hello?"

"Oh, dear. You already know." It was Celie, sounding worried and apologetic.

"Know?" Sara echoed. She braced a hand against the counter. Celie wasn't going to tell her about Flynn, was she? The Elmer grapevine being what it was, that was distinctly possible.

"About Annie." Annie was Celie's four-year-old. "I thought you must from the tone of your voice. You sound…weird. Upset. Because I can't babysit tonight. She's running a fever. They sent her home from preschool. She's vomiting now. You don't want Liam here tonight."

"No, I—"

"I'm so so sorry."

"It's all right," Sara said. "I'll work something out."

"Maybe Jace could come down when he gets back from Billings, but it won't be until late and—"

"No, really, it's fine. Don't worry. I…have to go. Hope Annie's better soon." She hung up and stayed facing the cupboard for a moment, getting her equilibrium back before she turned around. It would be all right, she assured herself. She just wouldn't go.

"Trouble?" Flynn asked when she finally turned around.

Sara shrugged. "Celie was going to babysit Liam tonight. Now she can't."

"Where were you going?" There was something so proprietary in Flynn's tone that it set her back up.

"On a date."

His brows drew down. "With who?"

"Obviously, you wouldn't know him. His name is Adam. He's the foreman at one of the ranches nearby. And he's a sculptor, too," she added. It was true and it was definitely impressive. She'd seen some of Adam's work.

Flynn's jaw tightened. "Is it serious?"

"His sculpture?"

His eyes narrowed. "No, damn it. You and him. Adam." He fairly spat the name.

Sara blinked. "What difference does it make?"

"I want to know how things stand."

He wasn't the only one, Sara thought. Only, what she wanted to know about had nothing to do with Adam. "We're dating," she said ambiguously. "And it is Valentine's Day," she added, because why not let him think it was more serious than it actually was?

Besides, Adam was a chivalrous sort of guy. He probably wouldn't mind her hiding behind her date with him. All of a sudden going seemed far smarter than staying home.

"Excuse me now," she said, reaching for her little local phone list. "I need to find a babysitter." She picked up the phone and began to punch in the number.

Flynn took the phone out of her hand. "I'll watch him."

"Don't be ridiculous."

"What's ridiculous about it? He's my son."

"No."

"Why not?"

"He doesn't know you."

"He wants to. He told me he asked Santa for me." Flynn grinned.

Sara wanted to spit. "He's five. And curious."

"So, fine. Let him get to know me. Let me spend time with him. What better way?"

It sounded like the way to perdition to Sara. She shook her head. "It's too soon."

Flynn scowled. "Oh? And when is it not going to be too soon, Sar'? Tomorrow? Next week? Next year?"

"You've been here two hours, if that!"

"And I would have been here sooner if I'd known," he said evenly. "I'll say it again—as many times as it takes—I didn't know. And if you're worried about whether he'll stay with me, ask him."

"What?"

"Ask him if he minds. If he doesn't want me to do it, I won't." Flynn raised his brows, met her gaze, threw down the gauntlet again. "Ask him."

As if on cue, Liam yelled from outside, "Dad! C'mon! What're you doin' in there? Aren'tcha comin'?"

Sara winced at the eager tone, winced at the memory of her son striding up to Santa and saying, "I want you to bring my dad home."

Flynn's gaze remained fixed on her. His expression said all it needed to. But then he added, "Does Adam make you hot when he kisses you, Sara?"

"Fine," Sara snapped. "Babysit. I wish you the joy of it!"

CHAPTER FOUR

FLYNN wished for the joy of it, too.

Babysitting his son while his son's mother went out with another man was not what he had planned.

He'd planned—at some point after Sara had opened the door and bowled him over—to charm her and tease her as he once had done. And then, when he'd soothed her ruffled feathers, he'd intended to take her and Liam to dinner.

He had never considered how high Sara's defenses would be—and how much work he might have to do to make her remember how good it had been between them.

God knew, he remembered. And he was remembering more every minute.

He hadn't let himself think about her—about their time together—for years. What point would there have been?

They had met coincidentally, had clicked instantly. But in truth they had been ships passing in the night—Sara resolutely on her way to medical school and then to save the world, and he determined to shake the dirt of Ireland and Dunmorey off his boots and then to prove to his old man that he wasn't the useless fool the old man seemed to believe.

Just because he wasn't the solid, dutiful lord-of-the-manor type that Will was, didn't mean he didn't have his own talents, his own gifts. Not, Flynn thought wearily, that he had ever managed to convince the old man.

He had an uphill fight convincing Sara that he meant to do right by her and Liam, too. He didn't suppose that grabbing this Adam jerk by the throat and throttling him would go very far in making that point. Sara had never been especially impressed by the caveman approach, as he recalled.

So, fine. He could wait. He could even let her go out with another man—especially one whose kisses didn't make her go up in flames. And this guy's clearly didn't. She wouldn't have been so furious at his question if they had.

But he wasn't going to sit by and let the guy think he had a clear field. No way. So when he heard the knock at the back door and heard Sara open it, he stood up from where he'd been sitting on the sofa looking at old photo albums with Liam.

A few moments later she came into the living room by herself. The Date was apparently on his own in the kitchen.

"He doesn't even come to the front door for you?" he asked Sara as she grabbed her coat from the front closet.

"No reason. He's used to coming in the back door," she said, turning and swishing away towards the kitchen.

Used to? How often did he come in, for God's sake? Flynn's jaw tightened. "Here," he said. "Let me help you with that." He reached for her coat.

"It's all right," she began, still moving. But he twitched it out of her hands and shook it lightly, then held it out for her to slip her arms into.

She tossed him a quelling look over her shoulder, but then stuck one arm into one sleeve and the other into the other. He stepped forward and settled the coat on her slim shoulders, came close enough to breathe in the scent of her shampoo, to catch a whiff of that mixture of spice and sunshine that he'd never smelled anywhere or on anyone but Sara.

It was an intoxicating blend of wholesomeness and seduction. He wondered if she had any idea how enticing she smelled. He bent his head forward to let his nose brush against her hair, to dare to touch his lips to the back of her neck.

She jumped and jerked her head around to look at him, to glare at him.

He smiled guilelessly. "What?"

Her cheeks were almost as red as her sweater. "Nothing," she muttered, rubbing at the back of her neck. "I just—never mind." She stepped away quickly and began to talk rapidly. "I left my cell phone number on the pad on the kitchen table," she said in a businesslike fashion. "You can call Celie if you need anything immediately."

Like to be murdered, Flynn imagined. If Sara wasn't glad to see him, he had no illusions about how her family must feel. "Thank you," he said politely. Then, before she could leave him behind in the living room, he said, "I'd like to meet this guy."

"Why?"

"Color me curious," he said lightly.

"Well—" She hesitated.

"Ashamed of him?"

She shot him a furious look. "Fine. Come and meet him." Then she turned to Liam "No television," she told him firmly. "It's a school night. Get into the bath by eight. I put clean pjs on your bed. I want you in them and in bed at eight-thirty."

"I know," Liam grumbled. Then he looked up calculatingly, "What if Dad says I can stay up later."

"He won't," Sara said, fixing Flynn with a hard stare. "8:30," she repeated to Liam. She bent to give him a kiss, then straightened and looked at Flynn again. "And I mean it."

"Of course." He smiled and she looked at him suspiciously.

"I don't have to go," she said fiercely. "If you think for one minute you're going to undermine—"

Flynn raised his hands and shook his head. "Relax, Sar'. It'll be fine. We'll be fine. Won't we, bud?"

Liam nodded vigorously. There was another knock on the door.

Sara looked as if she would have liked to stay and argue the point further, but finally she just shook her head and turned to go through the door into the kitchen.

"Back in a sec," Flynn promised Liam, and followed Sara.

"I'm all ready," she said briskly to the man standing by the door. And Flynn knew she would have opened the door and disappeared into the night without looking back unless he said something.

"Sara."

She turned back, looking annoyed. "What?"

"Aren't you going to introduce us?" Flynn asked silkily.

One more hard look, but then she shrugged. "Of course." She opened the door wider and put her hand on the sleeve of a very handsome man, who had straight black hair and dark piercing eyes.

"Adam," Sara said in a soft smiling voice that set Flynn's teeth on edge. "You'll never guess who turned up today. This is Liam's father." And then she turned to Flynn. "This is Adam Benally."

So Adam had a name but *he* was simply "Liam's father"?

I don't think so, Flynn thought grimly and, doing his best to minimize his damned limp, strode across the room to claim the kitchen as his territory, offering a hand to Sara's surprised suitor. "Come in," he invited. "I'm Flynn Murray."

The other man's hooded eyes widened fractionally and his gaze flicked toward Sara for a moment before coming back to settle on Flynn. His grip was lighter than Flynn's own, but his hand was hard and callused.

"About time," he said mildly.

The reproach made Flynn stiffen. But if this Adam thought Flynn was going to back down, he was out of luck.

"It is," Flynn said smoothly. "But I'm here now." So back off, he felt like saying. He remembered a story about one of his less-than-civilized ancestors locking his beautiful bride away in the turret to keep her from being ogled by the countryfolk. All of a sudden he felt a certain sympathy with the blighter. And he knew for a fact that he'd never felt this possessive about Dunmorey.

"Can you believe he just got the letter I wrote him five years ago telling him about Liam?" Sara broke in quickly.

Adam looked skeptical. "You don't say."

Flynn didn't. He just stood his ground, met Adam's gaze wordlessly and proprietarily until Adam said, "We have reservations for seven. We need to get going." He looked expectantly at Flynn.

"That's the other thing," Sara went on. "Annie's sick, so Celie can't babysit tonight. Flynn has offered to stay with Liam."

"Flynn?"

"Got a problem with it?" Flynn demanded. "Liam's my son."

Adam looked at Sara. "Are you sure you want—"

"She's sure," Flynn cut in. It was the tone of voice that made Mrs. Upham jump and say, "Yes, my lord," every time he used it.

Adam didn't jump, but Sara did, maneuvering them both out the door. "If we need to be there by seven, we'd better go. You have my number," she told Flynn. "But I'm sure you won't need it."

It was less a comment than a command.

Flynn ignored it. He followed them to the door and stood glowering at them as they went down the steps and along the path towards Adam's fancy pickup truck. "Sara?"

She turned.

He smiled. "I'll be waiting up for you."

* * *

It was Valentine's Day—a time for soft music, warm hearts, tender glances, romance with a capital *R*.

And Sara spent it with Adam—thinking about Flynn.

It made her crazy. *He* made her crazy. He—Flynn. Not he—Adam.

Adam was charming and easy to be with, a man of many talents and definite sex appeal. And tonight he exerted himself to be a good dinner companion, a witty conversationalist, a terrific date.

But it was Flynn whose smile she remembered, Flynn whose words echoed in her brain.

"I'll be waiting up for you," he'd said, that lilt, that charm, that innuendo in his tone!

Well, of course he would be, she rationalized, because he had to be. He was babysitting their son.

But was that what he'd meant? Or was he implying something else? Was he hinting that something would happen when she got home?

Her mind flicked back instinctively to their kiss that afternoon. She shoved it away, tried to focus on Adam. Managed it for all of thirty seconds. But then a thought of Flynn would intrude again. And a memory of the kiss. Flynn, kiss, Flynn, kiss, Flynn, kiss. It happened over—and over—again.

It was not the most spectacularly successful evening.

And when Adam yawned and said he had to be up early to feed cattle, Sara was ready to leave.

The snow had stopped. The night was clear and sharp and cold as they walked back to the truck. They walked so close together that their shoulders brushed. If it had been Flynn, no doubt sparks would have flown. Adam opened the door for her and she climbed in.

They rode back to Elmer in silence. And Sara knew she'd been a disaster of a date. "I'm sorry," she began as he pulled around the corner behind her house.

Adam shrugged. "Now we know."

Did they? Sara supposed they must. She felt guiltier than ever and wondered if she should offer to pay for her half of dinner.

The porch light was on. Was Flynn standing in the kitchen looking out from between the crack in the curtains?

No, that wouldn't be his style, Sara decided. If she didn't immediately come inside, he'd probably open the door and come out and stand on the porch. Jerk!

She climbed out of the truck without waiting for Adam to come around and open the door for her. He raised a brow. She shrugged.

"Because we know," she explained.

"Are you and he—?"

"We're Liam's parents. That's all," Sara said firmly.

"I don't think he's convinced," Adam told her.

"Well, he's going to have to be." She turned to face him. "Thank you for tonight."

"Do you need me to come in?"

She shook her head. "It will be fine." Certainly better than if they reenacted the gunfight in the *OK* kitchen which seemed to be the direction in which Flynn had been headed earlier.

Adam looked doubtful. "You're sure?"

"I'm sure." And then she lifted up to brush a kiss on Adam's cheek. As a thank-you, nothing more.

"Take care of yourself," he said gruffly.

Sara nodded. Heaven knew she was going to try.

She expected to see Flynn in the kitchen, sprawled in one of the chairs, smirking at her, checking his watch and chuckling at how early she'd returned from her date.

But only the cat was waiting. He looked hopefully at his food dish and meowed, but the packet of food she'd set out for him had vanished, so she knew Liam had done his job.

"You're fine," she told Sid who meowed a denial, but who purred when she bent to scratch his ears. "Where is everyone?"

Well, she knew where Liam was. Had Flynn fallen asleep on the couch?

She pushed open the door to the living room so she could hang her coat in the closet and have an excuse to see if Flynn was there. But it was empty, too. The family photo albums he and Liam had been looking at earlier were gone from the coffee table, though. He must have taken them up to look at them with Liam.

Sara hung up her coat, then climbed the stairs. Everything upstairs was dark and silent. Only the night-light in the hall and the one in the bathroom were on.

Had he fallen asleep with Liam, then?

She peeked into Liam's room. Her son lay, as always, on his back with one arm outflung, the comforter wadded up over his middle, the quilt half on the floor. He was the only one there. Carefully, she covered Liam up again and bent to kiss his forehead and his silky hair.

Then, frowning, Sara went back out into the hall. Surely he hadn't left. Even Mr. Here-Today-Gone-Tomorrow Flynn Murray wouldn't be that irresponsible!

"Flynn?" She called his name softly.

She heard a sound. Muffled. Faint. From down the hall.

"Flynn?" She moved back towards the stairway, then heard it again.

And suddenly realized where it was coming from!

How dare he! Sara stalked down the hall to the only other bedroom—hers!—and shoved open the door.

Flynn Murray was sprawled, fast asleep in her bed.

CHAPTER FIVE

SARA stopped dead in the doorway. Her breath caught in her throat.

She was furious—and curious—at the exact same time.

She wanted to stalk straight in there and shake him, wake him and send him on his way. And she knew damned well that shaking him awake would be the worst possible thing she could do.

Confronting a tousled gorgeous Flynn Murray who was already in her bed was a disaster waiting to happen. She needed to turn around and walk away right now.

Every sane sensible cell in her body screamed at her to do exactly that.

But when had she ever been sane and sensible where Flynn Murray was concerned?

Sara clutched the edge of the door frame to keep herself anchored right where she was. But it didn't help. The mere sight of him drew her.

And it wasn't as if she expected anything from him, she thought. She had already used up a lifetime's worth of dreams on this man. She was under no illusions now. She could look with impunity.

Well, maybe not with total impunity, but she knew better than to hope—or dream.

In fact it might be salutary to look at him. It could bolster her immunity to him, help to steel her against any aberrant, tempting thoughts that threatened to undermine her resolve.

And so, carefully, she peeled her fingers away from the door frame and edge closer. Just to look. To see more clearly what the previous six years had done to him.

It was easier—safer—to look at him when he had his eyes closed and was sound asleep.

And so she did. She looked. Then she moved closer still. She stood by the bed and drank in the sight of him. Couldn't help it. She'd dreamed of him so long.

He lay sprawled on his stomach, one arm flung out, his tousled hair midnight dark against the white of the sheet. The shadow of stubble on his jaw was less obvious now, but she remembered the soft scratch of it against her skin six years ago. And the tips of her fingers itched to reach out and brush across it, to feel its roughness now.

Sara clenched her fists, as if she needed to keep them under control, make them behave. *She* needed to behave.

But she couldn't stop staring at him.

For all that she had Liam to remember him by, she had so few other real memories. They'd had three days together—and one amazing night. And since much of that night had been spent in lovemaking, she'd had little opportunity to simply feast her gaze on the man she loved.

Had loved, she corrected herself sharply. *Had.* Past. Very past. No longer.

She didn't love him now. Didn't. Did N.O.T.

She tried to think about Adam, to say his name over and over in her head—but it was no use. He was a lovely man, but not for her. They would doubtless have discovered that anyway. Flynn's presence tonight had merely made it clear much sooner.

She glared at him now—hating him for spoiling all other

men. Hating him for being able to simply walk back into her life after six long years and turn her world upside down.

Hating him for being sound asleep, dead to the world, completely unaware—and making her want him even now.

As if aware of her thoughts, he sighed and shifted—took up even more of the bed. His muscular body was flung across her bed with the same abandon as his son's. His features were a grown-up version of his son's. But the similarities ended there.

Liam was wriggly and cuddly. His father was strong and powerful, even in sleep. His bare shoulders were broad, his arms were well muscled. How a man could get those kind of muscles writing articles absolutely amazed her. He moved restlessly, and the quilt slipped lower.

Was he naked in her bed?

Sara sucked in a sharp breath. Her palms felt suddenly damp and her heart skipped a beat. Quickly she backed up a step. But she didn't flee.

Still she watched. Wondered.

Playing with fire, she cautioned herself. At any moment he could wake, open his eyes and find her staring down at him. He could rise and shed the quilt that covered him and draw her down into his arms.

She wouldn't go! She wouldn't. She hoped.

Still she swallowed carefully, as if the noise of the muscles in her suddenly dry throat would wake him.

She tried to think logically. A part of her wanted to shake him awake, to say, "I'm home. You can leave now." A part of her wanted to crawl in beside him.

She wasn't going to do either.

She had heard him tell Liam he'd flown from Dublin to Seattle, then to Bozeman, and then had driven to Elmer. She couldn't imagine how many hours he'd been awake. It was no wonder he'd crashed.

But in her bed!

Did he expect she would just blithely slide in with him?

Probably he did. After all she supposed he'd simply think that they had shared a bed before. So it would be no big deal. Besides he had to have realized that afternoon that she still wasn't indifferent to his kiss.

Which was exactly the reason she wasn't about to do it.

But she couldn't make him drive back to his motel room in Livingston, either—not after he'd babysat—not to mention smacking a bit too much of obvious self-preservation.

So she crept around the bed, snagged her flannel nightgown off the hook inside her closet door, careful not to step on the floorboards that creaked. Unfortunately, the closet door squeaked despite her best efforts.

At the sound Flynn muttered and rolled onto his side. Sara held her breath, then, when he didn't move again, she grabbed her robe, too, and tiptoed out of the room.

In the bathroom, she stripped off her clothes and pulled on her nightgown. She was shivering and would have loved a hot bath, but the noise of the pipes was legendary.

It would surely wake Flynn. And she had no desire to confront him sleepy and in his underwear—provided he was wearing any. It was far too reminiscent of the night she'd gone to his hotel room. He'd been in a T-shirt and boxers then, not expecting company. He'd looked stunned to see her, had told her it was a bad idea.

And fool that she was, she hadn't believed him.

Now she did. And so she made sure she was as quiet as possible. She brushed her teeth, washed her face, then crept back down the hall into Liam's room where the spare bedding was stored in an old chest. From it she dragged out a patchwork quilt that her great-grandmother had made before her own daughter was born, and then gathering it in her arms, went back downstairs.

Sid met her at the bottom with a curious "Mrrrrow?"

"Shh." She bent and scooped him up on top of the quilt and carried him across the icy kitchen floor, through the dining room and into the living room.

There she dropped him onto the Morris chair, then settled on the sofa and tugged the quilt around her. It didn't win any prizes for comfort.

Sara was only five feet five. The sofa was less. She bent her knees and cursed her stupidity for having declined Sloan and Polly's offer of a new sofa last Christmas.

"Sure you don't want a sleeper sofa?" her mother had asked. "One of us might want to come and stay with you," she'd suggested with a grin.

"Exactly why I'm keeping the one I've got," Sara had retorted, also grinning.

They both knew that Celie's house had more than enough room to put up however many extraneous McMasters and Gallaghers might turn up in Elmer and want a place to stay. Besides, Sara didn't like having things handed to her.

Now, though, she thought she might have made a mistake. The sofa had lumps, too, and—

"What the hell are you doing?"

Sara jerked bolt upright at the sight of Flynn's dark form silhouetted in the doorway. She grabbed the quilt and clutched it like a shield against her chest.

"What does it look like I'm doing? I'm going to sleep."

"Here?"

"Where else? You were in my bed!"

"Noticed, did you?" A slash of white teeth grinned at her. There was a hint of amusement in his voice now, but Sara wasn't laughing. She felt too vulnerable.

"I noticed," she said stiffly. "And I realized you were probably jet-lagged, so I let you sleep. Instead of waking you up and sending you on your way," she added righteously, scooting back farther into the sofa because Flynn was no longer in the doorway. He was coming toward her.

"Very kind, I'm sure. But entirely unnecessary. Come to bed, Sara." His voice was low and husky and sent a shiver of longing down her spine.

"I'm in bed," she said firmly.

"The sofa is too short to sleep on."

"Did you try it?" she challenged.

"Anyone longer than Liam wouldn't fit. Besides—" he loomed over her now "—I wanted to be in your bed."

Sara's heart slammed. She tugged the quilt up higher and folded her arms across it as if that would keep it from leaping right out of her chest.

"No comment?" Flynn queried. "It seemed like a grand idea to me."

"Why?" Sara said gruffly, hating that she sounded breathless.

"Because I was dead tired." He paused. "And because I didn't want that cowboy getting into your bed."

"Oh, for heaven's sake! You thought I would go to bed with Adam? With Liam in the house?" She was outraged at the very notion.

"Obviously not. What about at his place?" The teasing tone was gone now.

She wrapped her arms tighter across her chest. "That is none of your business."

He studied her in the darkness, then shook his head. "You wouldn't," he decided. Then, "You haven't," he added, sounding supremely satisfied.

"How do you know?" Sara demanded indignantly. It was one thing to be particular about who she slept with. It was another to have Flynn act like it was all on account of him. Even if it was.

He smiled down at her. "Because deep down you're still the Sara you were six years ago." She could see the whiteness of his T-shirt and boxers in the moonlit reflections that poured in the windows off the snow. The rest of him was, by contrast, still shadowy and dark. But he was close enough that she could have reached out and touched him. Her fingers clenched around the quilt.

She glared up at him. "And how do you know that?"

He waved a hand at her. "Look at you. You're trying to sleep on a couch the size of a walnut. You're sitting there, uptight as a fireplace poker, that quilt wrapped around you like it was armor. If sex were casual for you, you wouldn't have hesitated getting in bed with me."

"Just because I did once—" she said bitterly.

"You loved me."

"Did," she agreed because there was no denying it. "The more fool I. Besides, I was a child."

He shook his head. "You weren't. You were one hell of a woman, Sara."

In a perverse way his words nourished a part of Sara—the womanly needy part of Sara, the part that had always felt he'd left because she'd failed him—the way rainfall fed a desert land.

But another part—the rational sensible part—heard the same words for the "Here be dragons" warning that she really needed to heed. Whether or not she'd been—or still was—one hell of a woman, she didn't need to get swept away by this man again.

Once was all any sane woman could stand.

"Go away, Flynn," she said wearily. "Go back to bed. Get some sleep. Or drive to Livingston if you're awake enough."

"I'll be staying then," he said easily, "as you've invited me."

"I didn't—"

"'Go back to bed,' you said. 'Get some sleep.' And I will." He held out a hand. "Come with me."

"Not on your life."

"You can't sleep here."

"Yes, I can."

"You'll be miserable. You won't get a wink of sleep lying on this thing." He nudged the sofa with his foot and offered his hand again. "Come on. I won't touch you."

"You couldn't not touch me! The bed's not that big."

"Fine. I'll touch you. But I won't make love to you. Is that what you want? Will you ever get a better offer?" he said mockingly.

It wasn't what she wanted. But what she wanted—Flynn Murray's undying love—she could never have.

"Go away, Flynn," she said past the lump in her throat.

He stood, hovering above her, not going away at all. And she had the panicky feeling that he might just pick her up and carry her up the stairs. But then she thought with the relief of reflection, he couldn't do that. His leg wouldn't let him.

"Damn it, Sara," he muttered, and she got the feeling the thought had crossed his mind, too—and so had the realization that he couldn't just do what he wanted anymore.

Even so, he didn't turn and stalk back upstairs the way she wanted him to, either. In fact, neither of them moved. The grandfather clock ticked loudly, but no louder, Sara thought, than her heart was pounding.

The cat jumped up on the sofa, startling her. "Oh!"

He butted her with his head, then stepped onto her knees, determined to knead them into a sleeping spot. His claws poked her through the quilt and her nightgown. Still she didn't move.

Neither did Flynn.

Then suddenly he turned around and Sara breathed a sigh of relief—until he flung himself down on the sofa next to her!

"Right, then," he said expansively. "We'll just stay here."

She sat up straight and scrunched herself against the arm of the sofa. It was barely more than a love seat. The words took on new meaning. "Flynn, stop it! Don't be an idiot!"

"Eejit," he corrected her. "That's the way we say it in Ireland. At least get the pronunciation right." He slanted her a grin, then stretched out his long bare legs, crossing them at the ankle and spread his arms along the back of the sofa. A male animal staking his territory, a green-eyed panther taking over a den, making himself at home.

In her home! And Sara knew that if she moved back even a fraction of an inch, she would end up leaning against him.

But he didn't touch her.

He'd said he wouldn't—and he wasn't. She wanted to kill him.

The clock ticked. The cat purred. She and Flynn sat in silence. The only other sound was of them both breathing.

Sid kneaded her thighs, then turned and kneaded some more. She gritted her teeth against the sharpest claws in Montana. Or maybe it was just that right now she had the most heightened senses in Montana.

She could feel the heat emanating from Flynn's body. He was that close. So close that she could stick out a finger and run it down over his ribs. She could loosen her grip on the quilt and touch his bare thigh.

She couldn't let herself think like that!

Finally Sid settled down, and the purring grew even louder. It seemed to take over the room.

She and Flynn sat in silence on the sofa. And Sara wondered if they would stay like this forever. Would Liam come down in the morning and find the two of them stiff as boards?

Probably. Because Flynn seemed determined to wait her out.

And he had, by far, the more comfortable seating arrangement. He had three quarters of the sofa, too, though he wasn't using it.

A hiss of annoyance passed through Sara's teeth.

Flynn gave a jaw-cracking yawn, then looked her way. "I'm not responsible if I touch you when I fall asleep," he informed her.

"Go upstairs."

"Not without you."

"For heaven's sake! This is ridiculous."

"It is," he agreed solemnly, "as there's a nice comfortable reasonably good-size bed upstairs just waiting for someone with half an ounce of sense to use it."

"Some*one*," Sara said pointedly.

"Some*ones*," Flynn corrected himself. He reached across his body with his left hand and scratched Sid behind the ears. His hand was now right over her lap. But he wasn't touching her. Just the cat.

Sara didn't breathe. Or move.

"Maybe even a cat if he's lucky."

He would let the cat come, too?

She darted a quick glance in his direction. In the moonlight she could see the shadows of his profile, the hard planes and sharp angles of his face. She could also see a shadowy crease of a scar on his jawline that she hadn't noticed before.

"Another gunshot?" she asked before she could stop herself.

Flynn lifted his hand from Sid's head and ran it along the edge of his jaw and nodded. "That it was. You came very close to never seeing me again at all."

He said it lightly enough, but she realized he was serious and that truly terrifying things had happened to him during the six years she'd imagined him covering all sorts of gossipy entertainment news.

"Why did you do it?" she demanded, needing to know. The

questions she hadn't asked seemed to bubble up urgent but unbidden now.

Flynn shrugged. "Because I was young and stupid and thought I was invincible and immortal." His hand stilled for a moment, then he drew a long breath and went back to scratching Sid's ears. But he stared straight ahead, his gaze fixed on something in the unknowable darkness. "And because I needed to prove I could."

"Not to me," Sara said quickly.

She did not want to be responsible for him nearly dying, thank you very much.

"Not to you," he agreed. "Though I will say you were something of an inspiration."

"I never—"

"You were such an idealist. So bloody determined. Life wasn't a lark to you."

But it had been to Flynn. She knew that. It was one of the things that had so appealed to her about him. He had energy and determination, but he didn't take everything as seriously as she did. He'd made her smile. He'd made her laugh. He'd taught her that there was more to life than duty and determination. There was also love.

For all the good it had done her.

"You inspired me," he told her. "But it was my old man I was showing."

Sara could understand that. She and her mother had not always had the most genial of relationships. Polly had always been casual and scattered and easygoing. Far too easygoing, Sara had thought for many years.

It was only since she'd got pregnant and become a mother herself that she'd begun to understand that Polly's apparent lack of concern wasn't any such thing. It was a matter of prioritizing and not obsessing about things—and people—who could take care of themselves.

She didn't know what Flynn's issues with his father were.

For all that they had spent three days focusing almost entirely on each other, she realized now that she had been the object of most of their discussing. And while Flynn had told her about his life and his likes and dislikes, he'd never talked about his family besides mentioning an uncle who was a priest in New York. She didn't think he'd talked about his father at all.

"Did your father live in the castle?" She could see why having a father who lived in a castle might make a person feel the need to live up to something.

"He did. It's where I grew up."

"Good heavens." He must think her house was a shack.

His mouth curved. "It's not exactly your typical storybook castle. No moat, as I told Liam. It's more of a Renaissance-age fortress. Of sorts."

She wasn't sure what a Renaissance-age fortress of sorts connoted. But it sounded foreboding. "And you live there now?"

He nodded. "I do. As Murrays have these five hundred years."

She couldn't help staring at him. "You're joking."

He gave a shake of his head. "I'm not."

Sara stared in astonishment. "How come you never mentioned it…last time?" She didn't want to think about "last time" but she couldn't help saying that.

Flynn shrugged. "Because it wasn't my problem then. I was my own man. It had nothing to do with me. But then Will died. He was the heir," he explained. "To the earldom. I was the spare—then."

"Earldom?" Sara echoed. She felt suddenly hot and cold and totally disoriented.

"The earl of Dunmorey," he said wearily and rubbed a hand over his face. "The ninth earl, as a matter of fact. The old man was the eighth. He died last summer."

Sara sat in stunned silence. Nothing—absolutely nothing!—

was the way she'd thought it had been. And then she rounded on him indignantly, not even caring that her knees bumped into his thigh. "You lied to me."

"I did not!"

"You said you'd come to America to seek your fortune!"

"And so I had. I wasn't the heir. I had to make my own way. The old man had his ideas of how I ought to live my life. The priesthood was mentioned. Medicine. Something Worthy." He nearly spat the word. "All fine and good, but not for me. He didn't approve of anything I did. I didn't give a damn. We had row after row. And I walked out. Came over here to find my own way, make my own life."

She had never heard so much emotion from Flynn. She wondered now that she'd thought she'd loved him—or that he'd loved her—when it seemed she hadn't really known him at all.

"And did you find it?" she asked after a moment.

"I thought so. I was spinning my wheels, though, when I came here. You challenged me."

"I?" Sara was incredulous.

He nodded. "Made me want something more valuable. Made me want to use my talents—my writing—but do it right. And I was. I still will. I'm a writer. That's what I do. It's how I earn my living. And that won't change. But—" he sighed "—I have other duties now. Other responsibilities."

"Because you're the earl?"

"Because I'm the earl."

He said the words as if the weight of the world lay upon them—and on him. The quicksilver Flynn of six years ago was gone. She wondered now if he even existed or if he'd just been a figment of her girlish imagination.

They had been so wrapped up in each other those few days— and yet they didn't seem to have really known each other at all.

The only thing Sara knew now was that his attitude towards the castle, the earldom—his duties and responsibilities—echoed the way he'd sounded this afternoon when he'd announced he was here to see his son.

"Liam's not a castle," she said, her voice adamant.

Flynn had been staring straight ahead, but at her words his head snapped around and he stared at her. "What?"

"I mean it. He is not a responsibility you need to shoulder. An obligation. A duty to be taken care of. He's a child. A little boy. A real live person!"

"I know that, damn it!" His tone was clipped. Angry almost.

Sara tried to search his face, to see what she could read in his expression. But there wasn't enough light to see clearly. He was the one sitting rigidly now, and she shifted, shrugging her shoulders, inadvertently touching his arm where it lay along the back of her sofa. She stayed where she was, turned to face him. "I just…need to be sure."

"Rest assured. I know all about not being a person," he said grimly. "You don't need to ever remind me about that."

She wanted him to explain. Was he talking about his relationship to his father?

There was so much about him she didn't know. And was afraid to ask for fear she would want to know more. And more. Because for all that she realized now that she hadn't really known him well at all six years ago—despite what he'd said—she knew her feelings for him made her vulnerable.

And that hadn't changed. If she weren't careful, she would find herself right back in the same place she'd been six years ago—in love with a man who didn't really love her, who was only interested in their son.

She pressed her lips together and turned away to stare out the window. It was all shadows of silver and gray, nothing clear. Nothing definable. Like her life. Mere hours ago she'd known exactly where she was going and what she was doing. And now she knew....

She didn't know what she knew.

The silence grew...and grew.

Then Flynn said, "I don't see Liam as just a responsibility. He is, of course. Mine as well as yours, but I want more than that."

Sara stiffened.

"I want to be a real father to him. The kind of father mine never was."

"You live in Ireland!" Sara pointed out. "You're an earl."

"Not my fault," Flynn said roughly, "though my father might disagree. And being an earl does not automatically disqualify me from being a good father."

"You are not taking him to Ireland!"

"I told you I am not taking him away from you. We can all go—"

"No!"

He didn't say anything then. Just sat there in silence. Watched her in the darkness. Made her wary. Made her suddenly weepy. Made her want—want things she'd hoped she was over wanting. Why had he come back?

And if he had had to come back, why now? Why not five years ago when she could have believed he loved her? Or why not five years from now when she might have met another man and fallen in love with him, married him, had his children?

Why *now?*

"Don't worry about it, Sara," he said quietly. And there was a tenderness to his voice that made her ache even more.

"I'm not worried," she said gruffly against the lump in her throat. "I'm fine."

"Of course you are." Still gentle, as if he was trying to soothe a skittish horse.

Sara would have bristled, but she was suddenly too tired. She felt drained, exhausted. Her muscles hurt from sitting up straight so long, and she allowed herself to sag back just a bit. Her back touched his arm. But as he made no move to wrap it around her, she just stayed where she was.

"Go to bed," she muttered.

"When you do," he said with a smile. He didn't move.

She shot him an irritated look.

He shrugged. "Up to you."

"Then I'm staying here," she said stubbornly.

"As am I," Flynn replied and flexed his shoulders, then settled in more comfortably.

"I mean it," Sara said.

"As do I."

But before it could become any more ridiculous, there was a sudden sound from beyond the kitchen. "Mama! Mom?"

Liam's panicky shout from the top of the stairs brought her straight to her feet. She dropped Sid to the floor as she stumbled over the quilt.

"It's all right, Liam. I'm downstairs," she called, already running up them.

He was standing at the top, clutching the Curious George monkey that Jack had given him when he was two. He wasn't crying, but he gulped before he spoke.

"Where were you?" His breathing was rapid, his voice broke.

"I told you. Downstairs." She wrapped her arms around him. "It's all right. Did you have a bad dream?"

He shook his head. "Nuh-uh. I woke up an' I went to look out an' see the castle we built—in case I dreamed it. But I didn't. It's there." He hiccupped.

"Yes, I know." She cuddled him close.

"An' my dad." Another hiccup. "I thought I'd dreamed my dad."

"No, Liam. You didn't dream him."

"I…I know. On account of the castle an' the king." He bobbed his head. "Didja see the king?"

"King?"

"I was gonna show you, but when I went to your room, you weren't there."

"I know. But I'm here now."

He sniffled and rubbed his nose on his pajama sleeve. "Good. C'mon. I'll show you the king. You can see him from my room." And, trauma receding, Liam took her hand and led her down the hallway into his room. He pushed open two slats in the blinds. "See?"

Sara knelt beside him and looked down at the castle that he and Flynn had built in the afternoon. In front of it she saw now that they'd built a snowman, as well.

"A king. See?" Liam pointed. "He's got a crown an' a…an' a…" he groped for the word.

"Sceptre," Flynn said from behind them.

Liam spun around, a grin splitting his face. "You're here!" He gave a little wriggle of happiness.

"I am here," Flynn said firmly.

Liam's joy and the obvious bond they'd begun to build were both evident.

"Time to go back to sleep," Sara said firmly and drew Liam to his bed and tucked him in firmly. "If you don't you'll be all groggy and begging to stay in bed when it's time to get up for school."

Liam shook his head adamantly. "Nope. I gotta go to school. I gotta tell 'em my dad's here."

"Fine, you do that," Sara said. She bent and gave him a kiss, then straightened and brushed a hand over his hair.

"Dad, too," Liam insisted. And he held up his arms for a hug.

And Flynn, understanding the body language, bent awkwardly into their embrace, his injured leg off-balancing him. But he ignored it, hugging the boy hard and giving him a kiss, too.

Sara, watching, felt something very like a pain deep in her chest. Because it was so wrong? Or because it was so right? She wished she knew.

"Go to sleep now," Flynn said gruffly.

"You'll be here in the morning?" Liam demanded

"I'll be here," Flynn promised.

"I thought you were goin' to Livingston."

"I stayed."

Liam looked at his father for a long moment, then his head swiveled so his gaze met Sara's. She didn't have to see the light shining in his eyes to know it was there.

"Don't—" she began.

"Don't worry about a thing, Liam." Flynn cut in. "Just go to sleep now." And he reached over and would have grasped Sara's arm as if to draw her out of the room.

But Sara was having none of that. She stepped away and bent over Liam to give him a kiss. "Do not get any ideas," she told him firmly.

"But—"

"None." She tapped him on the nose with her fingertip, then straightened and marched out of the room, leaving Flynn to follow her.

He did. But before she could go past her own room and head back down the stairs, he caught up with her, took her arm and drew her in, then shut the door firmly behind them.

"What do you think you're doing?"

"You want him to go to sleep?" Flynn leaned against the door so she couldn't get past him. "Then get in your own bed. If you go back downstairs he's going to wonder what's going on."

Sara opened her mouth to argue, but knew it was true. If she went back downstairs now, Liam would be out of his bed in a flash, coming after her, sensing that all was not as it should be.

He would expect her to go into her own room to sleep.

But not with Flynn!

Although that probably wasn't even true, Sara realized grimly.

In Liam's world, mothers and fathers shared beds. Grandma and Grandpa did. Aunt Celie and Uncle Jace did.

So why wouldn't she and Flynn?

She sighed, trapped.

"It'll be all right. I'll even go downstairs if you want," Flynn told her. "Once he's gone to sleep."

Sara hesitated, shivering, though whether from the cold or something else she couldn't have said.

Flynn noticed. "Come on, Sar', you're freezing." And he pushed away from the door and somehow herded her backwards until the backs of her knees bumped against the mattress and abruptly she sat down on the bed.

He sat beside her and took her cold trembling fingers in his hands and chafed them between his. "Get under the covers."

"I don't—" she began.

But he didn't let her finish her sentence. He picked up her legs and shifted her into the bed beneath the covers, then settled himself alongside her, spooned his body against her back and wrapped an arm around her waist to draw her hard against him.

"There," he muttered. His mouth was so close that the word stirred the hair against the back of her neck.

"You said you wouldn't touch," Sara grumbled.

"And you said I wouldn't be able to help it. You were right." He snuggled closer, tucked his arm more tightly around her. "Now shut up and go to sleep."

"I can't."

"Then shut up and let me go to sleep." And she felt him burrow closer, settle in.

"Flynn—"

"Shh." He sighed. Snuggled. His breathing slowed.

Sara lay there, tense and trembling. Mostly disbelieving. She was in bed with Flynn Murray?

To sleep? Oh, sure. She held herself rigid and unmoving.

"Sara." His lips tickled her ear. "Relax."

As if. But she couldn't hold herself as stiff as a barge pole forever. Unconsciously her muscles began to ease. Flynn moved again experimentally, settling against her.

"Better," he sighed. His breathing slowed. His arm that curved over her waist relaxed, his fingers opened. Yet all the while his body pressed hard and warm and enticing against hers.

Any second now Sara knew he would make his move. He would nibble her ear. His hand would curve possessively over her belly or would move up to brush against her breasts. He would touch. He would tease. He would torment.

And she would resist, Sara was determined. She would resist!

And then Flynn emitted a soft faint noise. And then another. He was asleep.

He hadn't slept so well in years.

Flynn sighed and stretched and shifted, coming around slowly, savoring the feel of it, of the soft sheets and comfortable mattress, the cold air and warm quilt. He didn't know where he was, only that he felt better than he had in…well, "forever" didn't seem too much of a stretch of things.

He wasn't at Dunmorey.

He knew that without even opening his eyes.

There, his first conscious awareness was always of the sound of rain dripping in the pails in the hallways or of the icy dampness of the room that he couldn't afford to heat or of the oppressive weight of responsibility for it that he wasn't meeting. He didn't feel that now.

He wasn't in any of the thousand-and-one hotels, rooming houses and dirt bunkers he'd lived in while in pursuit of a story, either. There the sense of edgy urgency always made him shoot out of bed almost before his eyes were open.

He felt settled. At home. Centered.

And as if someone was watching him.

His eyes flicked open.

Green eyes peered into his.

"Will?" he croaked, and instantly realized his mistake, felt the pain of loss and the joy of realizing who this really was all in an instant. "Hey, Liam."

His son.

Liam broke into a broad grin. "I knew it! I knew you'd be awake. I told Mom you'd be up before I went to school. An' I gotta leave in ten minutes, so you'd better hurry!"

Before he could reply, Flynn heard quick footsteps coming up the stairs.

"Lewis William McMaster! You'd better not be—" Sara was hissing the words as she came to a halt in the doorway. Her gaze skated right over her son and collided with Flynn's.

He smiled at her, realizing now exactly why he felt so good. Her cheeks were flushed. Her short dark hair was tousled. She was wearing jeans and a sweater and a scowl—definitely well armored—but he remembered her curves and the softness of her, under the thin cotton of her nightgown.

The truth was he remembered a whole hell of a lot more than that from six years ago. And he knew he wanted it again. Wanted Sara again. Badly.

But he probably shouldn't let himself think about it too intently—not if he wanted to get out of bed anytime soon.

"Liam! I told you—"

"He was awake, Ma," Liam protested. "I didn't wake him up. Did I?" He turned to Flynn, his expression imploring.

Flynn shook his head, his eyes still on Sara. "He didn't wake me up."

"But he's gotta get up," Liam said urgently, "or he won't be able to come to school with me."

"Don't be ridiculous. He doesn't need to go to school with you." Sara stood, hands on hips, glowering at Liam. Flynn thought she looked gorgeous.

"It's show 'n' tell," Liam wailed. "I'm not gonna take my stupid dump truck I built with Legos when I got a father nobody's ever seen!"

"I'll go with him." Flynn started to throw back the covers, then thought better of it. "Go on down with your mom now," he said to Liam. "Let me get dressed. I don't suppose you have a razor?" he said to Sara.

"Disposable ones in the drawer in the cabinet in the bathroom. Not what you're used to, I'm sure. Extra toothbrushes, too." She didn't look at him, and she didn't look pleased, either.

"Come on, Liam," she said impatiently, and she reached out and grabbed his hand when he got close enough so she could tug him out the door. "You don't have to go with him," she said over her shoulder.

"Yes," said Flynn. He knew it in his bones. "I do."

Because he needed to. Because he wanted to be part of this family. He wanted Sara, yes. In his bed, yes. But more than just in his bed.

In his life.

CHAPTER SIX

THERE was no justice in the world.

Flynn Murray, even stubble-jawed and tousled, looked disgustingly refreshed and rested, while Sara, gritty-eyed and decidedly unrested, felt as if she'd been run over by a snowplow.

It was what came of lying awake most of the night.

But how on earth was she supposed to have slept?

Flynn might have had enough jet lag to knock him out like a light. But she wasn't so lucky.

She was still wired from everything that had happened that day—right from the moment she'd opened the door to find him there, to his encounter with his son, to the mind-blowing revelations he had made in the darkness before Liam had woken up.

All that alone would have been enough to keep her awake for hours. But then she'd ended up in her bed in Flynn's arms!

Sleep?

Not in this lifetime!

She'd barely closed her eyes. He might be snoring and unconscious, but she had been supremely conscious of the heat of his body pressed hard against hers. She had shifted slightly to see if he would wake—or if he'd been merely faking it—but he hadn't moved, except to breathe more deeply and settle more firmly against her. His arm snugged her closer. His breath tickled the hair against her ear.

How was she supposed to sleep like that?

She didn't think any woman would be able to sleep tucked hard against Flynn Murray, with him holding her tight.

She couldn't. Her mind spun. Her body hummed with awareness. She wanted—Dear God, she didn't know what she wanted!

She knew what she *shouldn't* want!

She had no doubt at all about that. But as she lay there in Flynn's arms, traitorous thoughts kept creeping in. They were foolish silly thoughts. Airy-fairy, happy-ending thoughts. Idealistic thoughts—ones that the young innocent Sara McMaster had once entertained.

But not this Sara, she reminded herself. This Sara knew better. This Sara was a realist. And dreams—even waking ones—about a happy ending with Flynn Murray were not realistic.

Even less realistic now than before, she reminded herself, because now he wasn't simply a peripatetic young journalist out to write a name for himself.

Now he was an earl.

She was sleeping with an earl.

Well, not exactly sleeping—though he was—but she was in bed with an earl. How unlikely was that?

She felt as if her whole world had been turned upside down. She'd finally psyched herself up to date Adam—to move out of limbo, to forget the past.

And now here she was, wrapped in the past's embrace.

He was asleep, though.

She could have slipped away then.

But she'd been cold and he was warm. And it was true what he'd said, there had been no place to go except the too-short sofa, and what if Liam woke up again and looked for her?

All manner of arguments had arisen in her mind—and every

one of them, damn it, had offered reasons for her to stay right where she was. It was foolish to do so.

But it was only one night, she told herself. One night to confront the past and get over it. She might as well be comfortable and warm while she did it.

She had shifted in his arms then, half-expecting that he would wake up. But he was deeply asleep, and she was able to roll onto her back and then turn further so that she lay facing him, her knee sliding between his, his leg trapping her right where she'd turned.

But here she could study him in the light reflected off the snow outside the windows. Could drink him in, looking her fill. In sleep he looked younger, more like he had when she'd met him. The lines bracketing his mouth had softened, his lips were parted, curved in a slight smile.

She wanted to touch them. Maybe if she did, she would learn to resist the effect they had on her. Because she was going to have to. They weren't going to spend however many nights he was here visiting in her bed. This was a one-off.

Yes, he would be part of Liam's life now and, peripherally, she supposed, part of hers. But just as they had six years ago, now too they inhabited two different worlds.

He was the earl of Dunmorey—the ninth earl of Dunmorey. He lived in a castle in Ireland, for heaven's sake! And she lived in the small story-and-a-half bungalow in Elmer, Montana, that her great-grandfather, Artie, had bequeathed her. "It's yours," he'd told her the day before he died. "So you can always do what you want to and know you've got a roof over your head."

Definitely two different worlds, Sara thought, closing her eyes and trying not to think about who was holding her.

Maybe that was when she'd slept.

It was just past 5 a.m. when she jerked away. Jerked away

because though Flynn was still fast asleep, he had rolled onto his back and hauled her with him!

Now she was lying on top of him, her cheek against his chest, while his arm was draped loosely across her back.

Just like last time.

Just like the night they'd made love. The very last time he had taken her, Flynn had drawn her on top of him and had encouraged her to take the lead. "Your turn," he'd said, in that soft sexy voice. "Do what you want, Sar'."

And she had. She had explored his body, had touched and tasted, had learned what made him grip the sheets in his fists, what made him arch his back, what made him grit his teeth and say, "Damn it, Sara, you're killing me," before she slowly eased her body around his, before she took him in.

He had shattered then—and she had shattered with him. And had fallen asleep on his chest, cradled in the warmth of his arms.

And she remembered it all now so vividly that she felt as if her heart would burst through her chest. She remembered how wonderful it had been. And how cold and empty she'd felt after he had gone.

There was enormous temptation to stay there now, to recapture the joy of those brief moments, to rest her head against his chest, to listen to the steady thump of his heart.

But she didn't—because even in the darkness before the light of day she was a realist now. And Sara knew better than to stay with temptation too long.

So, quietly, she'd slipped out of the warm bed into the cold room. She was glad it was cold, she told herself, grabbing her clothes from the hook on the closet door and hurrying into the bathroom to get dressed. It made reality easier to bear. And as long as she didn't pause to look at Flynn still sleeping soundly, she'd cope.

Of course she would.

By the time she had to wake up Liam at seven-thirty, she had finished the bookwork for the hardware store she'd had to leave undone yesterday. She'd made his lunch. She'd done a load of laundry, fed the cat, done all the things she normally did.

She had her life back under control.

And if she'd assiduously avoided even glancing at the bedroom door she'd shut behind her when she crept out after waking Liam, what difference did it make? She knew Flynn was there.

It wasn't as if she were pretending otherwise.

Unfortunately, Liam knew it, too. And he wanted to dash in first thing and wake Flynn up.

Sara wouldn't let him. She'd shooed him past the door, threatened dire things if he woke Flynn up, and tried to keep him busy downstairs until it was time for school. But when she'd gone to the basement to put the washing into the dryer, she forgot to say, "Do *not* go upstairs."

And so, of course, Liam had.

And when she came back up and discovered his absence from the kitchen, there had been no question about where to look. She'd just hoped she wasn't too late.

Of course she had been.

And so she'd come face-to-face with Flynn, grinning and stretching and far too handsome for his own good. Or her good, more to the point. Sara felt all her hard-won resolution to resist him threaten to desert her then and there.

Fortunately, she wasn't quite the ninny she'd been at nineteen. She'd behaved—if not with quite the sangfroid she would have wished—at least with polite dismissive behavior. So what if she had lain in his arms all night?

Nothing had happened.

And nothing would.

And if she'd hustled Liam downstairs quickly, it wasn't because she was afraid of her feelings. It was because Liam needed to get his jacket and boots on and put his truck in his backpack for show-and-tell. It was nearly time to go to school.

"I'm not takin' my truck," Liam protested. "I'm takin' my dad."

"Don't be silly, Liam. He's still in bed. Besides, your truck is a wonderful thing to take. And you made it yourself."

"A dad's better," Liam said stubbornly, and clutched his backpack against his chest.

Sara would have argued with him, but she heard the thud of footsteps coming quickly down the stairs. Abruptly she turned and began scrubbing out the oatmeal bowls.

"All set." Flynn's voice was cheerful and upbeat. Turning, she saw that he was dressed in the same jeans and shirt and sweater he'd worn yesterday. Since he hadn't brought his luggage in, he'd had no choice. But his unruly hair was damp and combed, though his jaw was still dark with whiskery stubble, which made him look both piratical and sexy as all get-out.

Sara grimaced.

Flynn rubbed a hand over his jaw, misunderstanding—thank God—her expression. "I know. I found the razors. But I didn't have time. I'll shave when I get back. The kids won't care."

And the teacher will drool on your shoe tops, Sara thought, clenching the dish-washing sponge in her fingers. And just wait they found out he was an earl! "You don't have to go with him."

But Flynn was grinning and looked as if he relished the whole idea. "Of course I do. How many kids get to bring their long-lost dads to show-and-tell?"

He probably would relish it, Sara thought. He never minded the spotlight. Not even if it brought renewed focus on her youthful indiscretion with him. After all, he didn't have to live here.

Now he shrugged into his jacket as Liam hopped from one

foot to the other in gleeful anticipation. "I'll be back in a while." He opened the door.

Liam, pausing only to give her a smacking kiss, scampered out ahead of him. "Bye, Mom!"

"Bye."

"Bye, Sar'. *Slán leat*." "Goodbye" in Irish. He'd taught her that six years ago. But foolishly she hadn't thought he'd meant it then. Now she wished he did.

"Goodbye," she said gruffly, turning back to the dishes, willing him out the door.

But instead of leaving, he crossed the room and spun her away from the sink and into his arms, wrapped them around her.

"Flynn!" she protested.

"Sara," he murmured, a wicked grin on his face. And then his mouth swooped down and he kissed her with as much enthusiasm and far more effect than Liam had.

Her brain buzzed. Her body melted. Her sanity scattered. She tasted toothpaste and warm hungry male—one particular male. She felt the rasp of his whiskers against her cheek. She clung to him, all her control shattered. No fair! No fair!

What was he trying to do to her?

"Dad! C'mon!" Liam's voice drifted back from outside, impatient now. And when the kiss still went on, the door banged open.

Sara's eyes flew open to see Liam staring at them in amazement from the door. His eyes were like dinner plates. His mouth like an *O*. And then a grin split his face. "Wow," he breathed. "Oh, wow."

Oh, whoa, Sara thought. Oh, no!

She squirmed and finally twisted out of Flynn's embrace. Her heart was pounding. Her face was flaming. She was furious, and Flynn was grinning from ear to ear.

"I've missed you, Sara," he said.

Resolutely she shook her head. "Well, I haven't missed you! And I do not want you giving Liam ideas," she added through her teeth.

Although one look at their son told her it was far too late for that. She could almost see the wheels spinning in Liam's head.

And when Flynn followed him out, she heard Liam say, "Does that mean you're gonna marry my mom?"

Great minds, Flynn decided, thought alike.

Marrying Sara was the best idea he'd had in ages. And the fact that Liam had it too, and was obviously in favor of it—they'd discussed it on the way up the hill to school—made it a definite winner.

Not that he told Liam that. He just said it was definitely something to think about. And he asked what Liam thought.

Liam said he could use a father. Someone to build snow castles with and make forts with. And someone to keep his mom from being lonely.

"Is she lonely?" Flynn asked.

"Not when I'm home," Liam said. "But I can't be home all the time. Sometimes I play with my friends. And I go on sleepovers. She's lonely then. She says Sid's enough, but I don't think so."

"Sid?" There was another man in her life besides the cowboy?

"The cat."

"Oh, right." Flynn was surprised how relieved he was to discover that the main man in Sara's life had four paws and purred. He wanted to make Sara purr.

"If you got married, you could stay home with her," Liam said as they climbed the steps into the school building. "And," he added hopefully, "maybe we could visit Dunmorey."

It sounded like a good idea to Flynn.

Staying home at night with Sara would certainly be no hardship. Nor would building forts and snow castles with his son. He'd relished the time he'd spent with Liam so far.

And Sara? Well, they hadn't had much time—but then, they never had. Still, they could start. She was the mother of his son. And despite her resistance, despite her edginess and her prickly behavior, he was sure she was still Sara underneath. She sure as hell kissed like Sara!

It was a good thing Liam had come back in the door or he'd have forgotten all about being in show-and-tell at kindergarten.

"We'll discuss it," he promised Liam and followed his son into the school building.

Sara had the accounts from Taggart Jones's and Noah Tanner's bull-and-bronc-riding school all over the kitchen table. She'd spread them out as soon as the door had banged behind Liam and Flynn.

She refused to think about the kiss Flynn had given her. Refused to even acknowledge Liam's tactless question to his father as they went out the door. This was her work time. She had things to do, accounts to finish. Yesterday had been a lost day. She needed to get her act together.

But she hadn't managed much in the hour and a half she had between when Flynn and Liam left and when she heard the back doors rattle open and Flynn appeared in the room.

He was, of course, grinning broadly, looking inordinately pleased with himself.

"Sure an' I'm the hit of the Elmer kindergarten class," he announced in his best stereotypical heavy Irish brogue.

"Sure you are," Sara muttered, determined to ignore him. If she did, she had decided, he would leave her in peace, go back home. Go away!

So she spared him only a brief glance before going back to the column of figures she was clicking her way through on her calculator. She knew she would have to do it over later. Her brain around Flynn was far too irresponsible.

"It was fun. I got to show 'em Ireland on the map and point out where Dunmorey was," he went on cheerfully. "They were impressed by the castle."

"I can't imagine why," Sara said dryly.

He laughed. "Nor can I. It's a moldering pile of rocks. A demanding moldering pile of rocks."

Sara doubted that. She shrugged. "I'm working," she informed him, in case it wasn't completely clear.

"I can see that you are." His voice was solemn. His tone was not. She shot him a quick look to see a twinkle of amusement in his eyes.

"You're bothering me," she said.

"Am I? Good." And instead of apologizing and leaving, he took off his jacket and leaned back against the counter, smiling at her.

"It isn't good," she said in clipped tones. "I have work to do."

"I can wait. I'll go out to my car and get my laptop."

"No!"

"Well, if you're busy—"

"All right, fine," she said. "I won't be able to get any work done with you here."

"Fine. Let's talk," Flynn said.

"About what? Liam?"

"Liam," he agreed. "And other things." He started to grab one of the kitchen chairs, but then grabbed her hand instead, pulling her to her feet.

Sara tried to tug her hand out of his, but he wouldn't let go. He drew her with him towards the living room. "What other things?" she demanded.

"Us." He slipped his arms around her.

Her stomach clenched. She tried to pull away, but he held her close. "There is no us!" she protested.

"Is there not, Sara, *a stór*?" His eyes bored down into hers. His lips were a fraction from hers. Instinctively she wetted her own.

But he didn't kiss her. He steered her to the sofa where they'd sat last night. He didn't expect her to sit there with him again, did he? And *talk*?

As he turned, she took advantage of his bad leg and momentary imbalance to duck around him to get to her grandfather's old rocking chair.

But he was faster on his feet than she'd thought and he snagged her back, tumbling them both onto the sofa where she landed on top of him, looking straight into those mesmerizing eyes. They regarded her slumberously and far too sexily. How *did* he do that?

She scrambled to sit up, but he had hold of her hand. If there was no retreating to the rocking chair, at least she got to her back-against-the-sofa position she'd held last night. And then she answered his question. "No," she said fiercely. "There is not an 'us'!"

"And the kisses?" he probed, cocking his head, watching her, his fingers still laced with hers.

She pulled them out of his and hunched her shoulders, looking away. "No big deal."

"Liar." His voice was soft, but definitely challenging. "They are a very big deal. Need me to prove it?"

She glared at him furiously. "No, I don't need you to prove it. What do you want me to say? That you can turn me to putty? That I melt in your arms?" Even now, being this close to him— her knee touching the hard warmth of his thigh—her body wanted things her brain resisted.

His mouth quirked into a grin. "Well, I wouldn't mind hearing it."

"Consider it said." She bit the words out. "But it doesn't make any difference, Flynn. It doesn't matter. It was brief. It was meaningless. It's over."

"It's not over." The smile was gone. "Why are you fighting

it, Sar'?" he demanded, leaning closer. His voice had a rough edge to it. "Why are you fighting *me*?"

"Because I don't trust you! I don't know you. I thought I did— I thought you were the one person in the world who understood me, who would be there for me, who loved me—and I was wrong!"

There. He'd asked. She'd told him.

She couldn't get much clearer than that. She knotted her fingers together and turned her head, stared unseeing out the window. But out of the corner of her eye she could see his own hands. Saw him crack his knuckles. Heard him let out a harsh breath.

Then, "Maybe I'm the one who was wrong," he said quietly.

His words made her look over at him. Maybe he was wrong? About what? She couldn't ask. She waited for him to explain.

He didn't say anything for a moment. Then he did, speaking quickly. "I did what I thought was best, Sar'. Maybe I was wrong. Obviously, you thought I was. I can't change it. But I can do something now."

She tilted her head. "What do you mean?"

"You're upset because I wasn't there for you then. Fair enough. Now I can be. Now I will be," he amended.

She just stared at him.

He nodded, as if he'd made up his mind, then smiled at her, confident now. "We can tie the knot."

"What?"

"Get married."

"Don't be ridiculous. You don't want to marry me."

"I do." It sounded so like a vow she wanted to put her hands over her ears.

"No, you don't! You want Liam. And Liam thinks you should marry me."

"He does, in fact," Flynn said, and grinned as if Liam's suggestion made it all perfectly reasonable.

"He's *five,* Flynn! You don't let a five-year-old tell you who to marry!" She jumped up and slapped her hands on her hips, looking at him indignantly.

"I'm not doing it only for him," he protested, standing, too.

"I suppose you imagine that you're doing me a favor, too?" Sara spat.

"I'd be doing us all a favor. We're not indifferent to each other, Sara!"

They certainly weren't. She wanted to kill him.

She took a breath, tried for calm. Tried for some "indifference." And when she had got as close as she could, she slowly shook her head.

"No," she said. "Thank you," she added, though the words were dry and bitter in her mouth and she hardly felt thanks were in order. "Thank you for your very eloquent proposal. But I will not marry you."

Because, by God, lack of indifference on his part, complete hormonal meltdown on hers, and a five-year-old's blessing were not sufficient reasons to, as Flynn had so eloquently put it, "tie the knot."

For a man who made his living with words, Flynn thought, he had sure as hell made a mess of the ones he'd used to propose marriage.

But hearts-and-flowers were hard to come by between here and Elmer Elementary School, he thought as he stood out in the snow, trying to come to terms with his colossal screwup. Trying to figure out how to get it right.

He could hardly proclaim undying love, could he, when he'd only been back a day?

But, damn it, there was something—besides Liam— between them.

He'd felt it six years ago when Sara had knocked the breath

out of him. He felt it again now. Then he'd been too stupid to recognize it.

Maybe, let's be honest, he'd been afraid of it. Maybe he'd grabbed Sara's determined goals as a reason for leaving. But even if he'd wanted to marry her then, the truth was, he hadn't had much to offer her—a fledgling journalism career about to take a turn for the dangerous. A life of traveling wherever his stories took him. He had been a man on the move with no place to call home.

And Sara had been all about home. She might not have known it then, and he might not have been able to verbalize it—God, he really was bad with words when they mattered!—but it was true.

As different as she'd been from her family—her amazing mother, her tough, caring grandmother, her crazy siblings—she was still a part of the whole warm welcoming household. They sustained and supported her. She might live in contrast to them sometimes, but they had made her who she was.

Just as Dunmorey had made him who he was—a man on the move, a man who'd begun by rejecting expectations he couldn't live with, and now a man determined to prove his father wrong.

But he was more than that, too. He was a man with a son he wanted to be a father to.

And a man who'd just botched a marriage proposal to the woman who had stolen her way into his heart.

What heart?

A lot of people had asked that question over the years. And it was a fair one, Flynn had to admit.

He was well-known in journalistic circles for getting deep inside his subjects—and personally keeping everyone at arm's length. But why wouldn't he? After all, when the first experiences you could remember were of your father telling you that you didn't measure up, you learned not to care.

"Can't you get anything right?" his father had said furiously more often than Flynn wanted to remember. It had been the mantra of his youth. He could almost hear the old man saying it again now.

"I can get it right," he said fiercely to the old man, to himself and to anyone else who happened to be passing Sara's snow-covered garden. He hadn't wanted to get married. He'd dismissed his mother's determined attempts to get him a suitable wife—not that it had stopped her.

"I'm not interested," he'd told her.

"You will be," she'd said, "when the right one comes along."

Well, the right one had. Sara had.

And he wasn't going to walk away again from the one good thing that had ever happened to him.

That should have been the end of it.

But though Sara had made her dramatic exit, Flynn didn't leave. Oh, he went outside, and she dared hope. But, as she peeked through the kitchen curtains, he stood in the garden, kicked at the snow, then paced around, jammed his hands in his pockets and still looked, heaven help her, like the sexiest man on earth.

She was hopeless. Absolutely hopeless.

"Go away," she told him though she knew he couldn't hear her. Sid came up and head butted her shin. "He wanted to marry me," she told the cat. "Because we're not indifferent to each other."

She didn't know whether to laugh or cry. So she did what her mother would have suggested had Polly been here—she got to work.

He came back when Liam came home from school. She didn't know where he'd gone in the meantime. She didn't care.

She wished he'd already left, but she supposed it made sense to wait until Liam came home. He'd need to explain to Liam that he had to go.

But when Liam came in to sling his backpack on the chair and give her a hug, it wasn't to look crestfallen about his father's departure, it was to say he wanted to take Flynn to grandma and grandpa's to see his colt.

"What?" Sara still had her arms around him, but she looked over his head at Flynn who was standing inside the door. "You're leaving," she said.

"Just to Grandma's," Liam said pulling back and correcting her assumption. "To see Blaze. Dad says his brother is gettin' a horse. A stud." Liam turned to look at his father to make sure he'd got the right word.

Flynn nodded. "A stallion." He lounged against the counter, seeming perfectly at ease now. He certainly didn't look as if he had just proposed marriage to her—and been turned down. So apparently, despite his eloquent words, he was reasonably indifferent.

"I know what a stud is," she said. "I thought you'd be leaving."

"Just to Grandma's," Liam persisted, as if he couldn't believe his mother was so obtuse.

"I'm not leaving," Flynn said, and his eyes met hers, clear and direct and determined.

Which meant what?

Nothing, Sara assured herself, beyond the fact that he was staying to spend some time with Liam. Absolutely nothing to do with her.

"Fine," she said dismissively. "Go. But don't—" she looked at Liam "—eat so much you spoil your dinner."

She didn't want Flynn out there. Didn't want him establishing any sort of connection with her family. But she didn't see any way to prevent it with Liam having made the request. So she did the next best thing when they'd left. She rang her grandmother and told her they were coming.

"He's back?" Joyce said.

"Just to see Liam," Sara insisted. She had no intention of mentioning his proposal. "He wants to be a father to his son."

Joyce made a harumphing sound. "About time."

"Yes, well, apparently he didn't know." Sara repeated the saga of the letter following him all over the world.

"If you say so," Joyce said when she had finished.

"It's true." Sara didn't doubt that. "And, I think he's good for Liam."

"He'd better be," Joyce said fiercely, "or he'll be sorry he ever came back. And what about you, Sara? Is he good for you?"

"I'm fine," Sara lied.

If she said it often enough, though, she was determined it would be the truth.

"What can I do for you, baby?" Her grandmother obviously wasn't fooled.

"Just be polite," Sara said. "And, for Liam's sake, you probably shouldn't let Walt shoot him."

For her own sake, it might have been a blessing, because it seemed as if, far from making his excuses and leaving, Flynn was determined to stick around.

She succeeded in—mostly—putting him out of her mind while he and Liam were at the ranch.

But her grandmother rang after they'd left and said, "I'd forgotten what a charmer that man can be."

It wasn't what Sara wanted to hear. "Don't tell me he proposed to you," she said lightly.

"I'm married," her grandmother reminded her, then asked suspiciously, "did he propose to you?"

Sara didn't answer that.

"Did he see Blaze? What did he think?"

Her grandmother took the bait. "Oh, yes. Blaze was on his

best behavior. Flynn was impressed. He's impressed with that boy of his, too."

"Liam's mine."

"Of course he is, darling," Joyce said. "And he knows that. Says you've done a marvelous job with him. Had only good things to say about you."

"How nice of him." Sara clenched her teeth.

Her grandmother laughed. "I think he's a little bit smitten."

Sara didn't. She thought he was "not exactly indifferent." It was not the same thing.

"He was just being polite," she said. "I've got work to finish up before they get back," she told Joyce. "I'd better get going. Oh, by the way, did he mention when he was leaving?"

"No. Is he?"

"Of course he is."

Dear God, she hoped so.

But he certainly gave no sign of it. He came in with Liam when they got back. He took off his jacket and his boots and when she grudgingly offered a cup of coffee, he accepted.

"Is the Busy Bee still the only place to eat in town?" he asked. She nodded.

"Then let's go there for dinner."

"Yea, let's!" Liam was all for it.

"You and Liam can—"

"All of us," Flynn said firmly.

She glared at him. He looked back impassively, waiting for her answer.

She shrugged irritably. "Whatever. But go away now. I've still got work to do."

He and Liam went upstairs. She could hear Liam chattering away, could hear Flynn's occasional more-measured tones.

She tried to work. By saying the figures out loud as she stabbed them in, she managed to keep on task. But it was almost a relief when, an hour later, Liam clattered down the stairs and came into the kitchen.

"Me an' Dad are starvin'."

They went to the Busy Bee. It was, as always, full of locals—cowboys and shopkeepers, Carol from the grocery, Loney from the welding shop, the elder Joneses back from Bozeman.

If everyone in Elmer didn't already know that Flynn Murray was back before the meal—which thanks to Liam almost everyone did—by the end of it, Sara was sure his presence in town was common knowledge. And apparently they all remembered him from when he'd come to report on the cowboy auction. Though really she knew they remembered that he'd left a child in their midst.

Everyone dropped by their table to say hello, to check him out, to be told by Liam, "This is my dad."

And Flynn, damn him, charmed them all. He shook their hands, asked about their families, their cattle, the weather, chatting easily, his hand on Liam's shoulder all the while and his knee pressed against hers under the table.

"Glad you're back," everyone said one way or another. "A boy needs his father."

"He does," Flynn agreed. "And I need my son."

"And Sara needs—" several began.

Sara, fortunately, always managed to cut off those suggestions before they left anyone's mouth. She'd never interrupted so many people in her life.

"It's been lovely to see you again," she said determinedly and looked towards the door hopefully.

"Ah, right." They nodded and nudged each other, and she realized she was giving the completely wrong impression.

By the time they got to dessert, Sara thought Flynn could have run for mayor—and won.

When they got home, she was hot, even in the frigid air, was frazzled and had had enough.

"I don't know what you think you're doing." She rounded on him the minute she'd sent Liam up to take a shower.

"You don't?" He sounded surprised. "I'm courting you."

She stared. "What?"

"Courting. Don't they use that term in America? It's when I come around and woo you, ask you out, bring you flowers and—"

"I know what the term means! Stop it!"

He shook his head, slowly and deliberately. "I blew it this afternoon, Sara. I'm not blowing it again."

"There is no again!"

He just looked at her and she knew he didn't believe a word she said.

"You are not spending the night here," she informed him.

He lifted a brow, as if assessing how serious she was. She was very serious indeed. She didn't need any determined-to-seduce Flynn Murray in her house—in her bed—another night.

"You can stay and say good-night to Liam. Then you leave. Promise me."

He studied her for a long moment, as if weighing her seriousness. Apparently he figured that she was very serious indeed, because after a long minute he nodded. "If that's what you think you need, Sara."

She didn't think it, she knew it.

"It's the way it is," she said sharply, and she turned and hurried upstairs to make sure Liam was getting on with his bath.

When he was finished and in bed, Flynn sat beside him and told him a story about Dunmorey castle and an earl who got stabbed defending it against the bad guys.

"He won, didn't he?" Liam's eyes shone eagerly. "He didn't die, did he?"

Flynn shook his head. "Of course he won. That's why we've still got the castle. And he lived to a ripe old age. Died in his bed with his boots on."

Liam giggled. "How come he wore his boots to bed?"

Flynn shrugged, a wry expression on his face. "Probably because the place was knee-deep in water."

"Really?" Liam's eyes got wide. "But I thought you said there wasn't a moat."

"There isn't. The roof leaks. Although, to be fair, it probably didn't in his day."

Liam settled back against the pillows and gave a little wriggle of contentment. "It sounds so cool. I wanta see it."

"Liam!" Sara said sharply. "It's time to go to sleep." And it was not time to talk about going to see any castles.

"But—"

"In time," Flynn promised. His eyes met Sara's, though, not Liam's. And while she read challenge in them, to her dismay she read *promise,* too. "Your mother's right. Time to go to sleep." He got off the bed and leaned down awkwardly to give his son a kiss. "Go to sleep now."

"But—"

"Sleep," Flynn said firmly before Sara could, which annoyed her further, because Liam would have argued with her, but he settled in without another word when Flynn told him to.

She glared wordlessly at Flynn who gave her a bland look in return. So finally she simply bent and kissed Liam good-night, then waited for Flynn to precede her out the door.

"You need to go now," she said when they got downstairs. "I have work to do."

He drummed his fingers on the countertop for a moment, as if deciding whether to argue with her or not.

"You promised." There was a look in his eyes—a determined-to-seduce look that made her hold her ground and meet his gaze with a steely no-nonsense one of her own. Though she knew if he walked into the living room and sat down, she couldn't throw him out.

Finally he shrugged lightly. "Whatever you say, Sar'." He snagged his jacket off the hook by the door and slipped it on. "See you in the morning."

She shook her head. "No, you won't. I have work to do. Liam's in school."

"We can both work."

She snorted. "Doing what?"

"My book. Estate business." He shrugged. "I've got plenty to do. I'm not one of the idle rich, believe me."

"You have a castle."

He laughed humorlessly. "Not exactly a money-making proposition. More of an albatross. A responsibility."

"Like Liam."

"Not at all like Liam." He moved closer, his eyes boring into hers. Her own went to his mouth, remembering the last time he'd looked at her that way.

Quickly Sara took a step back. But it was too late. Flynn reached for her, slid his arms around her and drew her hard against him.

"Flynn!"

"I'll go," he said. "But not yet. I'm courting." And he bent his head and touched his lips to hers.

Sara went still. Resisted. She fought his touch, his taste with every bit of determination that she could muster.

It didn't work. There was a gentle persuasiveness to his kiss. It didn't demand or assert. It asked. It promised.

He kissed her with hunger, with passion, and yet with the assurance that she could take as long as she wanted to come around. He would still be here, kissing her, as if he had all the time in the world.

And damn it, she tried. She tried so hard to remain indifferent. To tune him out, turn him off. And she couldn't do it.

The kiss went on. And on. He touched her lips, stroked them lightly with his tongue. Pressed butterfly kisses to her cheeks, her eyelids, her jaw. His breath caressed her, made her weak, fed her hunger, shattered her resolve.

She could fight him. She couldn't fight herself. She couldn't turn her back on the surge of passions and emotions that for six years she had tried to pretend didn't exist.

She kissed him back. She couldn't help it.

She was her own worst enemy.

She opened her lips under the teasing temptation of his. She welcomed the nibble of his teeth, the flick of his tongue. She sighed and heard him groan, felt the heat of his body as it pressed against hers. Trapped between him and the door, she should have pushed him away. But nothing in her wanted to do it.

She needed to stop this. Call a halt. Push him away. Everything rational in her told her that. And the traitorous hungry Sara who had missed him and loved him wouldn't let her. It said, "Later. Just a few more seconds. Just a taste. Just a touch. Just a little longer."

Until at last it was Flynn who stepped back, who pulled away.

He dragged his mouth from hers and set her away from him, breathing hard, his voice ragged as he said, "We do still have it, Sara." His mouth twisted. "If you see what I mean."

She stared at him, stunned and shaken, her tender mouth a silent *O*, her heart slamming against her chest. Would she have stopped if he hadn't?

Would she?

He opened the door, his gaze never leaving hers. "I'll be back in the morning, Sar'. *Coladh sámh*."

Sara blinked. "*Coladh sámh?*" she repeated dazedly.

Flynn's mouth twisted wryly. "Sweet dreams."

CHAPTER SEVEN

SWEET dreams?

He ought to have his head examined. His own were highly charged, erotic, and frustrating as hell, which probably served him right.

What kind of idiot broke off a kiss when the woman he was wooing had finally started kissing him back?

This one. Flynn Murray.

Because it had seemed like a smart idea at the time. And because he'd given her his word.

As much has he would have loved to have swept her off her feet and up to her bedroom to make love to her, he couldn't. The time wasn't right. Not now. Now yet.

It would be marvelous and sexy and he was certain he could make it good for her. It would also blow up in his face.

Sara valued promises. Integrity. Keeping your word. And while he might have been able to subvert her resolve in the short run, there would be recriminations, angst and remorse after.

If he had taken her up to her room and made love to her, she would have hated him more in the morning than she was already trying to hate him now—and with far better reason.

So, he'd left. He'd kept his word.

The mistake might have been kissing her goodbye to make

sure she thought of him after he left. He hoped she had, because he had certainly suffered the plight of the terminally frustrated thereafter.

Flynn wasn't used to thinking in terms of the *L* word, but he sure as hell didn't know what else you would call the sort of martyrdom that had had him stopping the car and throwing himself into a snow bank instead of throwing Sara onto a bed and giving them both what they really wanted.

So he dreamed of her—and of fulfillment.

And he awoke denied, and more frustrated—and determined—than ever.

He was up and at the grocery store at six. He hit the florist shop as soon as he saw the light on. And he showed up on Sara's doorstep at eight-thirty, bearing his laptop, groceries, a book and flowers.

"For you," he said, handing her the bouquet. They were daffodils, bright and sunny yellow, shouting of spring in the midst of a Montana winter. "When I saw them, I thought of you." She always looked like spring to him.

Even this morning with her eyes slightly bloodshot, her hair tousled, and her face pale—from lack of sleep, he dared hope—she was the bright spot in his life.

Her eyes widened when he thrust the flowers into her hands. But she didn't speak. She just stood there, holding the damn daffodils in nerveless finger, staring at him.

"I'm not kidding," he said irritably, when no enthusiastic thanks, no smiles, no gushing were forthcoming. "They remind me of sunshine. So do you."

At her startled blink, he grimaced. "More eloquence," he muttered. "God help me."

But then she grinned—and it was such a delighted, delightful grin that the sun really did seem to come out. "Thank you," she said. "They're lovely."

And the brightness in her eyes told him she meant it.

"Dad! You're back!" Another bit of brightness—albeit a moving one—as Liam hurtled down the stairs and flung himself at Flynn. His son was still wearing a pajama top with his jeans, he had only socks on his feet, and his hair wasn't combed. "Guess what Mom did! She slept through her alarm!"

"Did she?" Flynn couldn't help grinning at that. Had her night been as bad as his had been? He hoped so.

"It didn't go off," Sara mumbled, her back to him as she put the flowers in a bright-red glazed water pitcher and set them on the table.

"That happens," Flynn agreed happily.

She shot him a look. He shrugged, grinned again. She made a tiny irritated huffing sound, then turned to Liam. "Go put a shirt on. And your boots. You can't go to school in your pajamas!"

"I'm going. I'm going." Liam rolled his eyes, then grinned at Flynn, yanked his pajama top over his head and, waving it like a banner, raced back upstairs to get a shirt for school.

"And hurry!" Sara yelled after him. "What *is* this?" She demanded again as Flynn began unloading the bags onto the table.

"Amazingly enough, it's food." Which she could see if she looked. "I can't expect you to feed me without contributing."

"Who said I was going to feed you?"

He smiled. "Don't be churlish, Sara, *a stór*. It doesn't become you."

She narrowed her eyes at him, then raked a hand through her hair, mussing it the way he wished he could have mussed it last night. "I worked very late last night," she told him. "I'm tired. I have a lot to do today."

"Well, I won't bother you today. I'll be silent as a mouse."

"You're gonna stay?" Liam demanded, reappearing with his shirt on, though buttoned wrong. He was hastily redoing it as he looked to Flynn for an answer.

"Hoping to. Unless your mother kicks me out."

Both of them turned their gazes on Sara. The look she gave Flynn said, *You will be sorry.* But she sighed and told Liam, "He can stay."

"So you'll be here when I get home?" Liam pressed.

"I'll be here," Flynn promised.

"I don't know what you're going to do here all day," Sara grumbled after Liam finally left.

"Work, same as you." He unloaded the groceries, and though she muttered, she put them away. When he finished, he opened his briefcase and got out his laptop, then picked up something else, weighed it in his hand a moment, then turned and held it out.

"This is for you, too."

She shut the cupboard where she'd been putting the groceries and turned, putting out her hand. "What is—your book," she said staring at the hardback book in her hands and then at him.

Flynn felt far more nervous than he'd expected, giving it to her. He didn't care what anyone else thought of it. But Sara's opinion mattered.

"It's the third one I've written. They've all come out in Europe, but this is the first one to be published over here."

She was turning it over in her hands, studying the cover, the title, the picture of him on the back.

"It's not out yet, officially. Comes out in a couple of weeks. You're the first on your block to have one." He grinned, feeling oddly self-conscious, wondering if it had been a mistake. It had always been a mistake to show his father anything he'd done.

Sara opened it. Found the inscription on the title page where he'd signed it for her. He'd debated about what to say. Had finally scrawled the words in it this morning right before he'd left the motel. He didn't know if he'd done the right thing. Maybe he'd just made things worse.

"Sara," he'd written, "this is what I was doing when I should have been with you. I will be from now on. Love, Flynn."

She read his words in silence. Stared at them for far too long. Then she lifted her gaze and met his, hers was steady and serious.

"Thank you for the book." Her tone was quiet, almost formal, giving nothing away. Making no promises.

But he took heart. At least she didn't throw it at him.

Sara felt like she was under siege.

A very tempting sort of siege—complete with flowers and groceries one day, dark chocolate and darjeeling tea the next.

When Flynn Murray set out to get something—or in this case, someone—he obviously left no holds barred.

He was there every morning. He was there all day long. He worked hard. He paused to talk. He told her about places he'd been, people he'd met.

He told her about his book. She hadn't been able to resist reading it. She might have been more capable of resisting him, if she'd tried.

But she wanted to know about the places he'd been, the people he'd interviewed, the men who had shot him…

The night she read that part, she cried.

"It's a wonderful book," she told him. "You make these people so vivid. So real."

"They are real," he'd said. "I just wrote what I learned."

But he had written it so clearly, so descriptively, so well.

Which was why it seemed so strange when he talked about Dunmorey and his natural eloquence deserted him. Then he was left with stark silence, long pauses, and the barest words to manage what he wanted to say.

The castle's history, he could manage easily enough. The

tales of politics and perils, of feisty ladies and fierce earls came easily enough off his tongue.

But when he talked about recent times—about his childhood there, about his brothers—the flow of words nearly dried up.

He did talk a little about Will.

"He was a bloody hero," he'd told her raggedly one day. "Always did the right thing. Was always there for everybody. He'd have been a hell of a better earl than I'm being."

Sara doubted that was true.

She saw how hard he worked. He got a fair number of calls from his agent and his editor, from someone in publicity who was trying to set up a book tour for him, but mostly he had calls about Dunmorey.

He might be half a world away, but he was never far out of touch with what was happening with the tenants, the land, the farm, the new stable. Everything that was being done he had a hand in.

She caught only snatches of conversation, but she was impressed by how diligent he was, how committed, how much it mattered to him.

And when she commented on it, he shrugged. "Who else is going to do it? I'm the earl."

He was the earl.

Something else to think about.

But as the days went by and they worked on their respective jobs, she learned that he was still the Flynn she'd fallen for. And though she did her best to keep him at arm's length, he could stay at arm's length and still tease her, cajole her, charm her.

And the sneakiest part was that he did so in a way that was not overtly romantic. He never resorted to a big-time seduction. There were shared confidences, teasing grins, light touches. But there were no more deep passionate kisses. A look was all he needed to set her on fire. And the looks were still there.

He could smoulder for Ireland, she thought.

But it was as if he knew she had her guard up, that she could resist him if he tried to seduce her in the usual way.

So he didn't do it the usual way.

Instead he fixed her toaster. He changed her fuse. He shoveled the snow off her porch roof.

"You shouldn't be driving out in the middle of nowhere in the middle of winter by yourself," he'd objected when she'd told him that morning she was going out. He'd wanted to go with her.

But she had dismissed his concern. "I grew up in Montana. I'll be fine."

And she was, though it started to snow before she got back. The roads got bad, and going over the pass, she had to stop and put on her chains. So she was later than she expected.

Flynn and Liam were waiting at the door.

"We were worried," Liam told her. One look told her it wasn't Liam who'd been doing most of the worrying.

"You shouldn't have been." She shrugged off her jacket and bent to give him a hug. He wrapped his arms around her neck and gave her a fierce one in return. "I have a cell phone," she reassured him. "I'd have called if I'd had a problem."

"And we certainly could have done something about it from here," Flynn said sarcastically.

Sara looked up in surprise to see him glowering down at her. His dark hair was tousled, as though he'd run his hands through it. His voice was angry. A muscle in his jaw ticked.

She stood up again. "I would have called," she said again. "Really, I'm fine." She went so far as to reach out and give him a reassuring pat on the arm.

But the pat disappeared as he hauled her hard against him and held her tight.

He kissed her hard. Desperately, almost. The first kiss he'd given her since that night. She could feel his heart pounding against her chest.

"You'd better be fine," he said roughly. "You aren't doing that again."

"Of course I am. It's my job."

"Then I'm going with you."

She didn't argue with him. There was no point. He wasn't going to be here forever. They both knew that. He had a book tour coming up starting next Monday. His publicist was always calling with new strategies, new possibilities. And when those dried up, he had duties—plenty of them—back in Ireland.

They hadn't talked about it, but they both knew it was only a matter of time until he would be leaving. His visit here was just that—a visit—and it was drawing to a close.

When he was gone, she would do what she had always done.

"You scared me to death. Don't ever do that to me again," he said fiercely, his eyes alight with green fire.

"I was fine," she said for the third time.

"You might have been," he said heavily, shaking his head. "I wasn't."

She was going to be the death of him.

If not of frustration, then of worry. His reward, he guessed, was the way she began gradually to relax around him. She smiled more, was defensive less. She talked more, too—told him about Liam's babyhood, about her work, about the rest of her family. And she began to ask about his.

Flynn didn't mind telling her about his work. The writing was his joy. Though for Sara, he did gloss over some of the more gruesome things he'd seen and some of the grittier bits of his experience.

He was all right when he told her about Dunmorey, too—at

least the history and geography of it. He could tell her about the mad earl and the bad earl and all their various lascivious ladies. He did so with relish. And he went on and on about the gardens and the woods and the lake. It had, after all, been the Eden of his boyhood. Remembering that part of Dunmorey was a pleasure, even if it did lead him to talking about Will.

He told her about Will, about what a good brother he was.

"A saint, really," he said, his throat tight. "He could get along with everyone. Do everything." It was still hard to believe he was gone. Not that he didn't have constant reminders.

Every day—even in Montana—Flynn got phone calls about the estate, from Mrs. Upham and from Dooley, the farm manager. He dealt with them. But when the contractor for the stables and the bank financing the stables got into the act, "Direct your questions to my brother," he told them firmly.

Sometimes, like this afternoon, he found her looking up from her accounts and watching him, smiling when he got off the phone from the latest crisis.

"What?" he said as he hung up. "Something funny?"

Sara shook her head. "You really are the earl," she marveled.

"Yes," he said a little stiffly. It was all too reminiscent of his father's doubt. "Is that a problem?"

"Just a reflection. When you talk to your editor or agent or those publicity people—you're quick and witty and conversational. But when you do earl stuff, you use a completely different voice. Your Earl's Voice."

Flynn frowned. "My what?"

"Your voice. It goes all clipped and formal and authoritarian. Very 'not suffering fools gladly.' You stand up straighter, too. And you look down your nose." She slanted a grin at him. "Very impressive."

He gave her a mock scowl. "Is that so?"

She widened her eyes and nodded impishly. "And a little scary."

"Scary? We don't want that." He set his phone on the counter and came around the side of table. "We'd rather have you laughing than scared."

And then, because he couldn't help himself, because it had been far too long since he'd touched her and he wanted to every minute of every day, he hauled her to her feet and began tickling her.

She did laugh then, wriggling in his arms, making him hotter and hungrier for her than ever. His own laughter dried up in the heat of his desire. And it was a small step to sliding his arms around her, pulling her hard against him, and finally hungrily kissing her.

And almost at once he felt her response, felt her arms come around him, felt her lips open under his, her tongue touching his.

Neither of them were laughing now. They were all hands and mouths and bodies pressed tightly together. He tugged up her sweater to let his hands roam over the soft silken skin of her back. He felt his own shirttails dragged out of his jeans, knew the feel of her fingers as they slid up his spine, the simple touch making him quiver with need for her.

"Sara." He trailed kisses along her jaw and when her head dropped back, he trickled them lightly down to the base of her throat. His hands slid down her back and dipped beneath the waistband of her jeans, traced the edge of her panties, then slipped lower still, to knead the soft globes of her buttocks, to feel her press close against him. His heart pounded. His breathing quickened. He needed her now, needed to take her up to her room and get rid of all these restricting clothes and—

The door banged open. "I'm home!" Liam sang out. "Oh!"

"Liam!" His name was a gasp on Sara's lips.

She jerked her hands away from Flynn's back and stumbled out of his embrace. Her face flamed and her fingers fumbled as she frantically adjusted her sweater, trying to catch her breath and smile a welcome at their son over Flynn's shoulder at the same time.

Flynn didn't see Liam's reaction. Sara had been the one facing the door, not him. And even now he didn't turn around. Didn't dare. Left his shirttails out. Discretion and all that, though he doubted Liam would notice anything amiss.

Liam was five, not fifteen. He'd seen them kissing. Big deal. Well, not to a five-year-old.

But Flynn needed a minute. Hell, he needed a lifetime. His body was trembling. His breathing was coming in short shallow gulps. And he barely even had it under control when his phone rang for the twentieth time that day.

Sara grabbed it off the counter and thrust it into his hand. "Why don't you take the call in the living room," she suggested crisply, then turned to Liam. "So, how was school?"

Flynn expected Sara would freeze him out after that. He anticipated a return of the arctic chill she'd treated him to when he'd first arrived. But while she seemed to step back a little that evening, she didn't try to bite his head off or withdraw completely.

She was a bit quieter at dinner, contemplative almost. Distracted, perhaps.

While they were sitting in the living room after eating and Flynn built a fire in the fireplace, she just took up some mending and didn't say a word. It was, of course, barely noticeable because Liam never met a conversational lull that he couldn't fill.

Still, Flynn was aware of it. And worried about it, too.

After Liam went to bed, they came back downstairs. He considered apologizing. But he had nothing to apologize for, damn it—except for possibly scandalizing their son. There had been two people involved in that kiss. Two people who wanted it to happen. Not just him!

And he wasn't sorry he'd done it.

"Sara—"

"I'm a little tired tonight," she said, moving around the living room, straightening things up, instead of sitting down and picking up the jeans she had been patching. "I think I might go to bed early."

"Are you brushing me off?"

"No! I— No," she said more moderately. "I…just need a good night's sleep." She didn't look at him when she spoke. She was focused on lining up the magazines on the coffee table with military precision.

"Are you okay?" He wasn't apologizing, but he was concerned.

She nodded, her back still to him. "Of course. I have to be up early. It's getting closer to tax time. I have a lot of people coming in. The Joneses will be here in the morning." She turned long enough to give him a fleeting smile.

"All right," he said. "I'll shove off then."

He was tempted to go back and kiss her, to prove it wasn't a fluke what had happened between them.

He didn't, because somewhere in his life he really had learned patience. He would overcome. He would survive.

Eireoidh Linn.

His lips quirked at the appropriateness of the sentiment. Apparently he did have something in common with the earls of Dunmorey after all.

It wasn't a good night's sleep she needed, Sara thought, lying in her bed and staring at the ceiling.

It was Flynn.

The minute he walked out, she wished she'd called him back. She'd fought with herself all afternoon, all evening—ever since Liam had walked in the door and interrupted their kiss. She'd tried to understand what had happened, tried to think, to analyze, to rationalize.

But try what she would, there was only one conclusion. And there was no sense in lying to herself anymore.

She loved Flynn.

She supposed she always had. Her body was simply more honest than her brain. Braver, too. More willing to risk.

And after that kiss today—a kiss which she had wanted and had participated in every bit as much as he had—there was no way she could go on pretending she didn't care. If Liam hadn't come in just then, she knew exactly where they would have ended up. Right here in her bed.

They would have come upstairs together and followed their desire to its natural conclusion—and it would have been her choice as much as Flynn's.

Tomorrow they could. The thought danced through her mind, teasing her, tempting her. Daring her.

Yes, tomorrow they could!

She fell back onto her bed, hugging her pillow tight.

The bedside phone rang. She grabbed it. "Hello?"

"Hi. It's Flynn."

Of course it was. Her breath caught in her throat at the unexpected joy of hearing his voice. "I was just…thinking about you."

"I'm on my way to the airport."

"What?"

"All those phone calls today about the book tour… It was supposed to start Monday. My publisher just called. They got a slot open tomorrow on *US This Morning*. I'm it."

"But where is he?" Liam asked the next morning when he came down to find his mother alone in the kitchen.

"He had to go," she said, proud of herself for the cool dispassionate tone of her voice. "You knew he was leaving."

"But Monday!" Liam protested. "He said Monday!"

"Things change." Didn't they just? And wasn't she glad she hadn't made a fool of herself last night.

"When's he comin' back?"

Was he coming back?

Sara had thought he was six years ago. Would have bet her life on it. This time, of course, he'd insisted he would. He'd sworn up and down.

"It's not like last time, Sara," he'd said. "I've got the bloody tour, then I'll be there."

But she still felt as if she'd had the rug—or perhaps her whole world—pulled out from under her. Her own fault no doubt. But she couldn't help the feeling.

"Why'd he go?" Liam demanded. "Why didn't he say good-bye?"

Sara explained about the sudden open slot on a national television program, about him needing to take advantage of it, about barely being able to catch the last plane out.

And wasn't it lucky she'd wanted an early night? she thought humorlessly.

"Can I watch?" Liam demanded, already heading for the television.

Sara wanted to say no. She wanted to crawl back into bed and pull the covers over her head.

"Go ahead," she mumbled.

And because she was a masochist, she even went and watched with him. She stood there behind Liam, gripping the back of his chair, and watched as Flynn, bright-eyed even after what had to have been a sleepless night, and drop-dead gorgeous as always, charmed them all.

The interviewers, the audience, millions of viewers at home, no doubt, lapped up his wit, his humor, his smashing grin, twinkling eyes, unstoppable charm. He was the Flynn she'd fallen for all those years ago, flirting with the world the way he had once flirted with her.

"Is that all?" Liam demanded when the segment was over.

It was enough, Sara thought. "Yes," she said.

"But—"

"They only do short clips to give people a taste," she told Liam. "To whet their appetite."

She was sure the viewing public's appetite had been well and truly whetted. She personally didn't think she'd ever feel like eating again.

"What'd you think?"

"I—" She sounded shocked. As if she didn't expect his call. As if she thought she'd never hear from him again.

Think again, sweetheart, Flynn thought. He'd called her the minute he'd been able to get two minutes to himself. Had jammed himself into the only reasonably quiet space he could find after he left the studio. He'd only been off the air an hour. Less. But it seemed like forever since he'd talked to her on his way to the airport last night.

He hadn't wanted to leave. "Tomorrow?" He'd been aghast last night when the publicist had to tell him about the interview slot.

He'd just got back to motel, feeling edgy and worried about leaving Sara to have her "early night"—hoping it didn't mean she'd be mustering all her defenses—and when his mobile rang, he'd grabbed it, hoping against hope it would be her.

In his wildest dreams she'd be saying, "Come back. Let's finish what we started."

But it had been his publicist, Gary, saying, "I have great news!"

From a publicity standpoint, of course, it was. It was a coup to get him on the show. "Absolutely fantastic," Gary had said. "You can't buy exposure like this!"

Flynn had suggested alternative days. Next week.

"Tomorrow morning," Gary had said. "The only slot we'll ever see. Be there."

So he was here. But his heart was back in Elmer with Sara.

"Or didn't you watch?" he said now. Not that he wanted her answer to that. He thought he probably already knew it. And he was delighted when his fears weren't confirmed.

"I…we…watched."

So she'd told Liam. Maybe it was going to be okay. "Good. I was afraid you wouldn't. Figured you'd be ticked. You have a right to be," he said honestly.

"No."

A swift protest, which meant, he supposed, that she still didn't think she had any rights where he was concerned.

"Yes, you do," he said firmly. "I didn't want to come. But frankly, I didn't have a choice. There's a lot riding on this book. I need it to be a success. Not just for me—but for Dunmorey."

"Dunmorey?"

He'd told her a lot about Dunmorey, but not about how much money it took to keep it going. But that was his problem, no one else's. "There are a lot of things that need to be done," he said stiffly.

"Of course." Her voice was fading. Was it a bad connection or…?

"I'm only trying to explain why I needed to do this. I didn't want to go so suddenly. It shouldn't have been like that."

"You do what you need to do."

He was losing her. He could hear it in her voice. "Sara!"

"You were great," she said. "I have to go. The Joneses will be here any minute."

"I'll call you this afternoon. I'll talk to Liam. And you."

But she was already gone.

* * *

She didn't know what to think.

He called them every day. To talk to Liam, of course. But sometimes he called when Liam wasn't even there.

"He's at school," she always said impatiently. "You know that."

"I do," he replied unrepentantly, a smile in his voice. "I must have called to talk to you."

Of course they talked about Liam. Flynn wanted to know everything. And then he asked about Sid, about Celie and Jace, the rest of her family. And then he asked about her.

"I'm fine," she always said. "Busy, very busy." It was March now, tax season. It was absolutely true.

"I miss you," he told her.

"I—" But the words stuck in her throat. She'd had too many years of denying what she felt for him to find them easy to say. Her one night of honesty—cut out from under her almost immediately by his departure—didn't seem to extend very far.

"You can do it," he said.

"Can do what?"

"Say the words. Miss. You. They aren't hard. Come on. Try it." He was laughing.

She wanted to laugh. She wanted to cry. "Go away, Flynn Murray," she said. "I have work to do."

They kept him sane.

Liam, of course. But mostly Sara.

He never knew what city he was in, what show he was on, forgot almost at once who he was talking to because, though he did everything his publisher asked him to, his real focus was on Montana.

On a little boy in Montana that he couldn't imagine living without now.

And on the little boy's mother whom he wanted more than he wanted food or sleep or a *New York Times* bestseller—though it turned out he had one of those on his hands.

It was nice. More than nice. He was glad. But he was thinking more about Sara.

He missed her desperately. Told her so every time he called.

She didn't say she missed him. She usually said, "I'll get Liam." Sometimes, though, he managed to call during the day when Liam was at school.

She acted impatient, but she didn't hang up. That was a plus. And if he asked about Liam, she usually began to talk to him. Of course she told him about Liam's activities first of all. But when he pressed a bit, asked the right questions, she told him what she'd been doing that day, too.

She told him about Sid's trip to the vet because he had a bad tooth. She told him about the truck that overturned on the highway to White Sulphur Springs. She told him that Sloan was in Rome and Polly, Daisy and Jack were going to go visit him.

He hung on every word. It made him feel as if he were there. With her.

To keep her on the phone, not because he gave a damn about any of it, Flynn told her about what he'd seen in San Francisco and Dallas and New Orleans and Chicago. He told her funny stories about things he'd seen and people he'd met just to hear her laugh. He missed her so damn much.

"I'll be back in four weeks," he said, and thought it sounded like forever. But then it was three weeks. Two weeks. And then, at last, it was one.

He began counting the days, the hours until he could get back. Began making plans.

His editor said the book had done so well they were doing yet another printing and wasn't that great. And it was, of course. But the best thing was that he was going to be back in Elmer in twenty-seven hours.

With Liam. And Sara.

And then his brother Dev called from Ireland.

"The bank is balking at the loan on the stables. They want more collateral. They want to see business plans."

"So show them," Flynn said. He'd been blessedly free of most Dunmorey worries while on tour. But now it felt like the other shoe, about to fall. "You've got everything we did." The plan had been Dev's primarily. Flynn's part had been to put up the castle as collateral.

"I have," Dev said. "But to go any further, they need to see more assets. They say there's too much debt. Dunmorey needs more revenue production. More avenues for income."

"Tell me something I don't know."

"They want to talk to you."

"So tell them to call me."

"In person," Dev said. "Friday."

"Like hell!"

"It won't go through otherwise," Dev said. There was more than a little desperation in his voice. "Doesn't matter that the earl of Dunmorey is backing me. They only want to talk about money, Flynn. We can make it back with this horse. I know we can. We've just got to get up and running. And that means talking to the bank again. Friday."

Flynn had planned on being in Elmer on Friday at long last, settling in for a spell, enjoying his son, courting Sara, convincing Sara.

"Friday," Dev said. "Or we're done without ever having a chance."

Flynn knew the feeling all too well.

* * *

"I have to go to Ireland."

They were in the airport, still collecting his bags, Liam hanging on his arm, Sara standing there, dazed at how her heart had leapt at the sight of him, then plummeted at his new revelation.

"But you just got here," Liam said, climbing up Flynn as if he were a tree.

"And I want you to come with me." He said it to both of them, but he was looking straight at her.

"Yea!" Liam cheered and threw his arms around his father's neck.

"What!" Sara was appalled, shaking her head. "When? No!"

"Yes. I have to go. Tomorrow. On Dunmorey business. And I don't want to go without you."

"Well, you're going to have to."

"Can we see the castle?" Liam was squirming in his arms between the two of them. "Can we?"

"We can," Flynn said.

"No," Sara said. "We cannot. It's tax season. I have commitments."

"But, Ma—"

Flynn set Liam down and pointed him in the direction of the luggage carousel. "Go see if my bag's there yet."

Liam opened his mouth to protest, then, seeing the look on his father's face, bobbed his head and scampered off to look for Flynn's baggage. Sara stayed where she was.

"I have to do this, Sara."

"Do it." She folded her arms across her chest. "Doesn't matter to me."

"It matters to me! You and Liam matter to me. I've been waiting all month to be with you again."

She just looked at him.

"They have phones in Ireland. Faxes. The Internet. You can talk to your clients, do their taxes."

"I don't want—"

"You're being selfish, Sara."

"I?" She stared at him, furious at the accusation.

"Do you remember what you told me the hardest part of your life was?" Flynn asked, making her blink in surprise.

Her eyes narrowed suspiciously. "What are you talking about?"

"Six years ago," he went on. "You took me up to see the ranch house where you'd lived when you were little. You showed me the swing your dad had hung in the tree. You showed me the tree house he built for you. Remember?"

Sara's throat tightened. She nodded.

"I remember, too. And you said the hardest part of your life was when your dad died and you couldn't have him there anymore. Do you remember that?"

The noise and bustle of the airport swirled around her, but she didn't hear or see it because yes, damn it, she remembered that, too.

She could still get a prickling feeling behind her eyes every time she thought about that swing, about the way she'd laughed when her dad had pushed her, about the tree house he'd built for her and her sisters. About how she'd carried the lumber for him and brought him the hammer and the nails when he'd asked. About how she'd followed him around and he'd called her "the best kid in the world."

She blinked rapidly, clenched her jaw tight, finally bit out the words, "Of course I remember. So what?"

"All you wanted was a chance to be with your dad. And you couldn't have it because he'd died. I'm not dead, Sara. I want to do those things with my son. Why do you want to deny Liam what you wanted yourself? Give us a chance. Come with me, both of you."

CHAPTER EIGHT

It was no time to be having second thoughts.

The plane was just landing. Liam, who had slept for a good chunk of the flight over the pond, was now wide awake, peering out the window, asking questions a mile a minute. Sara was answering them with less than her customary briskness. She didn't look as if she'd slept much at all.

Flynn knew she'd tried because he had never shut his eyes. He'd sat there the whole flight, trying to imagine what was going through her head, what she thought of his heavy-handed emotional manipulation that had got her to agree to come to Ireland, what she was going to think of Dunmorey—what was going to happen next.

He would have preferred to play it cool, to go back to Montana and let her come to the gradual realization that she and Liam belonged with him.

He knew from years of working with reluctant, nervous, highly volatile people that the best results occurred when they thought the story he was doing was their own idea; when they thought it was in their best interest to give him what he wanted; when they trusted him.

He'd given Sara little reason to trust him over the years.

Now she had even less.

But he couldn't leave them behind, couldn't just walk away from what they'd begun to find in Elmer. He loved them. Both of them. Liam as his son, of course. But Sara—Sara was his heart. He couldn't live without her.

He'd thought he had a fair chance of convincing her in Montana. Now he felt like he was starting all over again—from the worst vantage point possible.

Oh, he had no doubt Liam would be delighted. Getting to visit the ancestral castle was draw enough for any little boy, especially one as predisposed to be thrilled as Liam was.

But there was little about Dunmorey to enchant a reluctant woman at the best of times. These were hardly the best. The place was downtrodden and damp.

And, of course, as usual, it was raining.

"Doesn't it ever stop?" he growled into his mobile phone at Dev while they were waiting to board a short commuter flight to Cork. Liam had Sara by the hand and had dragged her over to look out the window at all the planes. He was chattering eagerly as usual. Sara still was barely saying a word.

Flynn didn't like it. He wanted back the passionate devoted Sara of old or the occasionally prickly but generally expansive and good-natured Sara he'd got used to in Elmer. The one who had kissed him so passionately in the kitchen the afternoon he'd ended up leaving wouldn't have been bad either. Or even the slightly remote one of later that evening.

But this one? This one was so quiet she scared him.

It was making him crazy.

But there was damn all he could do about it now.

And he feared that with the rain bucketing down, when she saw Dunmorey things were just going to get worse.

"Clean up around the place as best you can," he told Dev. "I'm bringing company."

"Company? Now?" Dev wasn't pleased. "We aren't exactly in shape for entertaining, if you know what I mean. Ma's not here. I'm up to my eyeballs in horse stuff. And you're going to be, too. Who the hell is this company?"

He hadn't said. Hadn't ever told Dev about Sara—or even about Liam.

Announcing he had a five-year-old son was not something he had wanted to do over the phone. And Dev had been in Dubai when he'd left. He'd just sent his brother an e-mail saying he was heading for the States. Dev knew his book was coming out there soon. And if that was what he thought Flynn had gone to deal with, so be it.

There would be plenty of time to reveal his son's existence, he'd assured himself, once he'd met the boy.

But meeting Sara again had made him put all discussion of his son and the boy's mother on hold. He knew he couldn't talk to his brother about Liam without mentioning his mother. And things had been too tenuous with Sara.

He didn't want to talk about either until he had them both where he wanted them—in his life forever.

At least, that had been the plan before Dev's phone call three days ago.

Now all bets were off.

"Not company, really," Flynn said now. "My son."

There was a dead silence on the other end of the line. Then Dev said, "Bad connection, this. What did you really say? I thought you said your son."

"I did."

"Son?" Dev repeated, stunned.

"That's right. He's five. His name is Liam. He looks…like Will." Flynn started out fine, finished badly. But it was all he could manage.

"Like Will?" Dev was incredulous now.

"You'll see."

"But who is he? When—?"

"I'll explain later. He and his mother are with me. So straighten things up. Put on a clean shirt. Pick up the buckets. We can't do much about the rest of it, but I don't want them tripping over buckets first thing they step inside the door."

Dev made a noise that sounded like a dazed half laugh. "Whatever you say, my lord."

"Stuff it," Flynn said and hung up. Then he mustered up his "everything's under control" face and prayed that it was.

"They're callin' our flight, Dad!" Liam broke away from his mother and came running towards him. "We're almost there!"

And Flynn, catching him up in his arms before Liam could plow into his leg and knock him right over, hoped everything went as smoothly as Liam seemed to believe it would.

"Sorry about the rain," he said to Sara with an apologetic shrug. "It's Ireland."

"No problem. Better for my skin than Montana's wind and cold." Very contained. Very polite. She'd worked on someone's taxes all the way over. But at least she wasn't fighting with him. He hoped that was good.

"We're off to see the castle!" Liam sang out, causing passengers to turn and look, then smile in their direction.

Sara's cheeks reddened as she shushed him.

"He's excited," Flynn said. And as they boarded the plane he knew he was, too.

Personally he'd never been much for fairy tales and castles growing up. The castle part had been all too real, but the fairy-tale endings simply weren't. His father had often seemed more ogre than lord of the realm. And happiness had always been in short supply.

But he'd known happiness—or come close—with Sara and Liam the weeks before the book tour.

And now? Well, he'd asked for this. He'd insisted upon it.

And now they were here. "Be careful what you wish for," his mother had always said. "Take it easy. Take it slow. Be cautious. Be smart."

But he'd jumped in. Apparently he hadn't learned as much patience as he'd thought.

It wasn't your average fairy-tale castle.

It was so much better. So much more...real.

Not that Sara wanted to fall in love with Dunmorey, mind you. It was the last thing she wanted—to get emotionally engaged to a place she was determined to resist.

But how could she resist this?

She hadn't known what to expect. But she'd certainly never expected it to sit on the rise of the hill, dark-gray granite, square and boxy, hunkered down like a petrified stone frog, squatting and scowling as the rain coursed down its face.

A petrified stone frog with a turret that stuck up like an off-center top hat, giving it a slightly rakish, not-quite-put-together air to go with what looked like long-standing endurance. It also looked a little ragged around the edges.

Sara loved it on sight. But at the same time, she began to understand some of the reasons for multitude of phone calls Flynn had dealt with. Being lord of Dunmorey might not be all house parties and riding to the hounds. The sheer weight of it looked as if it could oppress all but the most determined and driven of men. And the farm they'd passed and the stretch of river they'd crossed and the houses they saw were all part of the estate holdings.

All of them were his responsibilities.

"It does, too, have a moat!" Liam exclaimed, craning his neck, pointing at the water they crossed going over the cattle guard onto Dunmorey land. "You said it didn't!" he accused his father.

"Is that what it is?" Flynn looked surprised. "I always thought it was a drainage ditch."

His wry tone made Sara smile. "Perhaps it's all in the mind of the beholder."

He shot her a look of surprise.

"It's beautiful," she said, and meant it. The green rolling hills, the hedges and fences and huge arching trees—it was so lush and green and alive. Montana was just coming into the early days of spring—still spare and often icy.

"You think?" He sounded doubtful. He'd grown quieter and edgier since they'd landed in Cork, she noticed. And the closer they'd got to Dunmorey, the less he'd said.

Was he regretting that he'd brought them?

Certainly he had reason to. Liam was a lovely little boy, and she didn't think so just because he was her son. But he was also a ball of energy, a demand on one's time, a perennial distraction. From the snatches of the phone calls she'd heard between him and his brother over the past two days, Flynn didn't sound as if he needed any distraction.

Of course that was probably why she was here—to keep Liam in check. If she weren't, he'd have to find a nanny.

No, that wasn't fair. He'd made it clear that this invitation wasn't just for Liam. He'd been at pains to be sure she knew he wanted her here, too.

"Besides," he'd added grimly, cracking his knuckles, "you have to see it sometime." Whatever he meant by that.

So she'd come. She'd agreed to his emotional manipulation. But only partly because what he said was true and she knew she didn't have the right to deprive Liam of his father's love just to protect herself.

There was no protection. She came because she wanted to know more about the man whom, against her will, her wish and her better judgment, she loved.

She dared—in her bravest moments—to believe there was something real and honest and true between them. Something that went beyond the physical desire that he relished and even she could no longer deny.

But she wasn't sure. She didn't know.

Coming here she hoped to find out—to learn who Flynn Murray really was beyond the man she knew in Elmer, beyond the charmer she'd long ago fallen in love with.

"I'd like to say it's not as bad as it looks," he said now, jerking her back to the moment at hand as he drove up the lane toward sthe castle. "But that wouldn't be true. The inside is worse than the outside. The upside, however, is, I might not have it much longer."

His tone was light, but there was a painful undercurrent in his tone that made her look at him sharply.

Sara frowned. "Not have it? Why not?" she asked as he rounded the last curve of the gravel drive and parked by the massive double front doors.

Liam had his seat belt off and the door open almost as soon as the car stopped. He got out and stared straight up at the massive structure that loomed above him. His jaw dropped. "Wow," he said. "Oh, wow."

And then he was off running, trying to see it all. The rain was coming down in earnest. He was getting drenched.

"We can take him in," Flynn said.

But Sara shook her head. "Let him run. He's been in cars and planes too long. He'll dry."

"Don't count on it," Flynn muttered.

"What?"

He just shook his head wryly. "Nothing." He got out, and Sara followed suit, meeting him at the trunk of the car while he got out the luggage. "Why might you not have the castle much longer?"

"The long story or the short one?" Flynn began hauling out their bags. "I could give you a long complicated answer to do with revenues and farm prices and restoration costs. But the short one is, frankly, it can't support itself. Hasn't for a lot of years. It's been cut back, cut back, cut back. Try to reinvest where it will make the most sense and turn the best profit. But it's not entailed any longer. The old man and my grandfather saw to that. They wanted to be able to sell it off if worse came to worst."

"But it's been in your family for three hundred years!"

"And I could be the one to lose it." His jaw tightened and he kneaded the muscles at the back of his neck. "I didn't say I liked the thought," he said gruffly, "but the farm can only do what the farm can do. And the stud is costing plenty of money to get up and going. It will work in the long run. I believe that. But by then I might already have had to sell. It's like trying to keep alive some extinct dinosaur."

"A giant frog," Sara murmured.

Flynn blinked. "What?"

"Never mind." She shouldn't have said a word. "I just…" She shook her head. "I'd hate to see you have to do that."

"So would I," Flynn said fiercely.

She glanced over to where Liam was already trying to scale one of the rough granite walls. "It's a great place for children."

"The gardens are," Flynn agreed. "It's when you're grown-up that it gives you problems."

"I can see where it might," Sara agreed. "But it has definite charm."

Flynn snorted. "Charm? Hardly. Wait'll you see it."

It sounded more like a threat than a promise. But before Sara could reply to that, the door to the house opened and a reasonable facsimile of Flynn came out, grinning.

"Dev," Flynn said. "My younger brother. Dev, this is Sara. She's, um—" he hesitated "—Liam's mother." He jerked his head towards the little boy halfway down the lane.

Dev looked, did a double take. "He is like Will."

Flynn nodded. "Wait'll you meet him."

But Dev was already looking again at Sara. "Liam has a very beautiful mother." His grin widened and he gave her an appreciative look. Then he shook Sara's hand and, by virtue of not letting go, drew her into the entry hall, leaving Flynn to shut the car doors and, glaring at him, carry in the bags.

"It's…nice to meet you," Sara began, then stopped. She'd come through the first entry with its mundane collection of boots and croquet mallets, bows and arrows, walking sticks and umbrellas. It could have been anybody's mud room, albeit bigger and a bit more grand.

But then he steered her through the next set of doors into an entry parlor with gilt and tapestries, marble pillars and a mirror the size of a small lake. She could only stare—at everything else and at her small, insignificant damp bedraggled self.

Dev saw the direction of her gaze. "Huge, isn't it? They put it there to make the room look bigger."

Bigger? It was the size of half her house.

"I should take off my shoes."

"Nah, don't. Your feet will get wet."

She paused, halfway to bending down to take them off. "What?"

"Roof leaks. Not here," Dev said, "but all over upstairs. In the kitchens. Windows let the rain in, too. Carpets are soggy. Floors gets wet. Keep your shoes on," he advised.

"Oh. Right. I, um, will."

"This way," he said and started to lead her past doors that dwarfed her. "I've got a fire in the blue parlor."

As opposed to the red one? she thought a little desperately, a little wildy as she followed him. For if Dunmorey Castle had looked like a squat granite frog from the outside, it was clearly beyond elegant within.

Shabbily elegant, yes. Possibly threadbare in spots. But definitely formal, imposing and historic. As Dev led her to the blue parlor, portraits of men and women with decidedly Murray features stared down their noses at her from both sides of the hallway. They looked austere and remote and judgmental.

A part of her wanted to turn tail and run.

"I'm seeing why Flynn spent so much time in America." Dev pulled open a heavy oak door, and held it for her.

"Yes, the book tour was long and—" Sara began.

"And he had a couple of other things to keep him occupied," Dev finished smoothly. He was smiling, but Sara felt guilty, understanding that she and Liam were those other things.

"I know you needed him here—"

"He's the earl," Dev said simply. "But he is entitled to a life."

"I guess," Sara said. She looked around the blue parlor. The walls were blue, the furniture was leather and oak and on the wall there were more silk tapestries.

"Sit down." Dev gestured to one of the chairs. "I'll yell for Daisy to rustle up some tea."

She didn't imagine he meant literally, but he went out into the hall and bellowed down it.

A young woman's voice bellowed back, "Get it yourself!"

Dev laughed. "That's Daisy. Our right-hand girl. She cooks and cleans, keeps us out of mischief, and apparently thinks she's busy. Probably getting your rooms ready," he reflected.

Sara felt more of an imposition than ever. "She doesn't need—"

"It's her job," Dev said. "She doesn't mind. And she does way more than we have a right to expect. So I'll make the tea. You can stay here or come down to the kitchen with me."

"I…I should help Flynn. Or get Liam," she said, wishing she could do something to help.

"Flynn's fine. And he'll watch your boy. He does look like our Will." He shook his head. "Coming? Hope you don't mind dogs," he said, leading her out into the hallway once more to be surrounded by a pack of three young spaniels and the most enormous Irish wolfhound Sara had ever seen. "Out of the way, you lot." Dev pushed past them. "Go bother Daisy."

With the dog entourage milling around them, Sara followed him down yet another long hallway, trying to keep up and take it all in at the same time.

This hallway was less formal. The formal portraits had given way to paintings and photos of rural landscapes, mounted stags' heads and stuffed salmon. At the far end it got positively mundane with a rack for fishing gear and hooks for dog leashes.

"Here we are," Dev said and led her into a kitchen about the size of her entire downstairs.

You could have roasted an ox in the fireplace at one end of it. And probably once upon a time, people had. Now an Aga was tucked into the opening and actually looked small. A large modern stainless-steel refrigerator hummed alongside it. On the other side she saw a microwave on the countertop.

The sink had both taps and a pump handle. Dev was using the former now, filling the kettle. On the other side of the sink the countertop contained a series of dog dishes, a bright blue baby bath and, beside it, a plastic high chair.

Sara took it all in, but her gaze stopped on the baby bath and the high chair which were even more out of place than the microwave.

Dev plugged in the kettle, then followed her gaze. "Those are Eamon's," he said. "He belongs to Daisy."

"I see. I feel terrible, putting you out this way. Obviously you weren't expecting us."

"Didn't even know about you."

She stared. "Didn't…know?"

He'd been gone almost two months. He'd known about Liam all that time. And he hadn't ever said?

"Sorry. Shouldn't have said that," Dev apologized. "None of our business really. It's what I said, Flynn's entitled to his life. It's just…surprising. I was gone when he left. In Dubai getting our stud. Got an e-mail. He only said business in the States. I had no idea. But it's grand news," he added cheerfully and gave her a long appreciative once-over that would have made her blush if she weren't so confused.

"You didn't even know about Liam?"

"Not till he rang this morning."

Sara didn't know what to think about that.

But Dev had an opinion. "He's always gone his own way, done his own thing, our Flynn. It's what's made this so difficult, him having to take over. Ma reckons he needs a wife to show him the way things ought to be done."

"Really?" Sara said faintly.

"But I'm thinking you're the best thing that's happened to him since…forever, I'd say."

Sara flushed. "That's ridiculous. You don't know me."

"I know Flynn. He isn't known for sharing what's nearest and dearest to him. But if he brought you back here, you matter. And I like the look of him. And sounds better than he has in ages."

Did he? How had he sounded before? And why?

A hundred inappropriate questions begged to be asked. But as "our Flynn's" footsteps were fast approaching with Liam in tow—she could hear the constant barrage of questions—she didn't ask.

"I saw a fish, Ma!" Liam informed her. "A big fish! And a gee-normous dog!" His eyes were wide, his arms stretched out as far as he could reach. "Did you see him? His name is O'Mally. He's just a puppy, seven months old. Dad said he can sleep with me!"

"He did, did he?"

Flynn shrugged. "Why not? He sleeps with Sid."

"There's only the matter of about a hundred pounds difference."

"I just thought he'd make Liam good company. Make him feel at home."

He was probably right. They'd had a dog, Flash, when Liam was born. But Flash had died last year. She'd told Liam they would get another dog before Sid forgot what it was like to have to share his house. They just needed to find the right one to fill the hole in their lives.

O'Mally looked as if he'd fill almost any hole imaginable.

"Cool, huh?" Liam said. "An' did you see the buckets?"

"Buckets?"

"Upstairs. We took the bags up an' I met Daisy an' her baby an' Dad says there are lots of buckets for the rain."

"We're getting a new roof." Flynn was looking more and more uncomfortable as the revelations continued. Dev, however, was grinning all over his face. He poured the tea into mugs, added milk and passed them around, then added a plate of biscuits—"Cookies," Flynn explained to Liam who looked worried until he saw them—then said, "So tell me where you come from."

Sara let Flynn tell Dev what he wanted him to know. And, of course, Liam chipped in. She didn't say much at all. She just looked around, let the conversation wash over her. As much as she'd liked Dunmorey on sight, she was still having trouble thinking of Flynn as master of it all.

It was huge, magisterial, daunting. The kitchen—despite its great size—was the only place she really felt at home. Probably, she thought stifling a yawn, it was because the kitchen was where she belonged—with the staff.

"You need some rest," Flynn said abruptly. "Let me show you your room. You can take a nap."

"Not me!" Liam protested. "I don't want a nap!"

"By heaven, no. Not you," Dev laughed. "I'll take Mr. Energy with me to the stables."

Liam's eyes got rounder. "You got horses, too?"

"We have a couple. One of them is a brand-new stallion. Come see," Dev invited, then turned to Sara. "I'll keep an eye on him."

Liam hopped from one foot to the other. "Can O'Mally come, too?"

"Liam," Sara admonished.

But Dev just laughed. "Can ducks swim?"

"Yes! C'mon, O'Mally!" And Liam looped his arm high over the dog's back—they were pretty much the same height, Sara noticed—and they trooped out the door after Dev.

In the quiet after their departure, Sara realized that for the first time since Flynn had come back, they were alone.

Flynn seemed to realize it, too, and for once was absolutely silent.

"It's…lovely," Sara said at last. She stopped before she said it was also immense and overwhelming.

"Not lovely," Flynn replied, cracking his knuckles. Then he dipped his hands in his pockets and began to pace. "It's a disaster, in fact. You can see how much needs to be done." He gave a sweep of his hand that seemed to encompass the entire castle.

"Probably should just torch the whole thing," he said bitterly, "but it's so wet, I doubt it would burn!"

"And you don't want it to burn." Sara knew that instinctively.

He hunched his shoulders, then opened the door and gestured for her to follow. "No, I don't want it to burn," he said leading her back down the hall. "And I'd like to show you around more now, but I need to get together the stuff we have to take to the bank tomorrow. So I'll show you to your room so you can rest."

The spaniels followed in their wake. Sara patted their heads and tried to keep up, still gawking. "If there's anything I can do to help—"

Flynn shook his head. "Thank you, but this is our problem. My problem," he corrected himself. He stopped at the foot of the stairs and turned to the spaniels. "No," he said to them in his lord-of-the-manor voice. It was the same voice he'd used to decline her offer of help.

He tried to imagine what the place looked like through her eyes.

The prospect made him wince. All those dour old ancestors with their beady green eyes glaring down at her. Faded rugs. Peeling paint. The dogs milling around. The buckets everywhere.

He was used to it and he still found it appalling. Not the trappings. He could care less about the trappings. But the castle seemed so damn soulless. Not exactly home sweet home.

No, when he thought of home—of warmth and comfort and welcome—he thought of Sara's.

He saw her to her room. Fortunately one with only two buckets—and those empty at the moment. There was a fire in the fireplace, too, warming its usual cold-as-cockles air. Bless you, Daisy, he thought, sending her a silent thank-you.

Sara stood in the middle of the room, looking around in silence, unmoving.

"It's…not exactly what you're used to," he said awkwardly. No warmth. No heart.

Sara turned. "Well, I'll do my best not to muss it up or break anything."

"No," he said quickly, "that's not what I meant. It's just…" But somehow he couldn't express how inadequate it felt—he felt! "I hope you'll be very comfortable here," he said finally. "I'll… see you later."

She nodded. "Thank you."

He turned to go when she said his name. "Flynn?"

Hopefully, he turned back. "Yes?"

"You look tired, too. You should try to get a nap, too." Her face was suddenly flushed and she looked as awkward as he felt.

He sighed wearily. "Nice idea. No time."

Nothing on earth sounded better. He would have loved a nap. With Sara in his arms.

But he couldn't even let himself think about it. He had to come up with a reasonable plan—on paper at least—for Dunmorey's financial future. He shut himself in his study and set to work.

Two hours later he stared bleakly out the window at the coursing rain and faced the fact that he was wasting his time. All his hopes and dreams were clearly fantasies.

Back in the autumn, the plan for the stud had seemed reasonable. Back in February, when he'd left for Elmer, he'd believed in the possibility that they could do this—could have the stud and Dunmorey, too, and it wasn't simply a pipe dream.

And once he'd met Sara again, he'd even dared dream that he could marry her and live happily ever after.

Today in his dripping, crumbling pile of stone, he had no choice but to stare reality in the face. It was going to be one or the other—the castle or the stud. And the future was not in a five-hundred-year-old pile of damp rocks. They would have to sell Dunmorey.

Eight earls before him had done the job. He would be the earl who bit the dust.

And Sara? Well, for all that she said polite things, she looked appalled most of the time. Coercing her into coming with him had been a mistake.

It had seemed like a good idea at the time. Of course he hadn't seen her in a month, and he'd have done anything—said anything— to guarantee that he didn't have to leave her behind again.

But now, despite Liam's enthusiasm for the castle, the stables, even the drainage ditch, for God's sake, and despite Sara's own polite tolerance so far, he knew he'd jumped the gun.

He might be able to impress a five-year-old with the family castle, but Sara was, above all, a realist. She would see Dunmorey for what it was—a mouldering pile of stones that echoed the past and had nothing to offer the future.

As a CPA, she would see the way the bank saw, even if he and Dev had tried to pretend otherwise. They'd been blinded by having grown up here. They saw it no more clearly than Liam did.

Pity little boys didn't run banks, he thought grimly.

Even their mother seemed to have seen it more clearly than they had, perhaps because she'd only married into the disastrous mess.

After his father's death, the duchess had told Flynn time and again that if he wanted to keep Dunmorey he'd have to marry money.

"It's what your father did," she'd reminded him bluntly. His mother, too, was a realist. She'd even laughed and promised to bring him home a rich wife when she'd left to visit her sister in Australia after Christmas.

"Yeah," Flynn had said, "you do that."

But he didn't need her to find him a wife. He'd already found the wife he wanted—Sara.

He didn't want anyone but Sara.

And now he'd invited her to watch him fail.

Sara saw a note had been shoved under her door when she got up.

When she'd opened her eyes to the amazing four-poster bed and the heavy dark ornate bureau and chairs beside the fireplace, she had for an instant thought she was still asleep, caught in some very vivid dream.

And then she realized where she was. She scrambled out of bed, switched on a light, then riffled through her suitcase for a pair of jeans and a sweater. She pulled them on quickly because the fire had gone out and the room was cold.

Exhausted, a little bit dazed and a lot uncertain, she had taken refuge in slumber. And for once her body had cooperated, and she'd fallen asleep the instant her head had hit the pillow.

And now it was—she glanced at her watch—nearly 6 p.m.? Good grief! And she had left Liam in Dev's care all afternoon.

She stuffed her feet into her shoes, then picked up the note.

In Flynn's spiky handwriting, she read, "Liam's asleep in the room next to yours. I've left a light on and a string trail downstairs for when he wakes. Check on him if you want."

She felt a bit less guilty, breathed a little easier then. She took time to wash her face, comb her hair, then straighten the covers on the amazing, opulent four-poster bed. Then she opened the door and tried to decide which of the rooms on either side of hers was Liam's. The line of string leading from under one of the doors was the clue.

She eased open the door. There was a low light on in the room, making it easy for her to see Liam all but buried beneath a thick duvet in the midst of a gigantic bed.

Beside him, four times as big, lay O'Mally. He opened one eye and watched Sara approach. She hoped he was as friendly when he was sleeping with Liam as he had been earlier. Apparently he decided she was safe because he thumped his tail twice, then laid his head back down and closed his eyes even as Sara approached the bed.

Liam was sprawled on his stomach, very little of him visible beyond his face, his tousled hair and part of one arm, which was crooked around Curious George. His back was snug against O'Mally's. Clearly they were a pair.

Sara smiled, then leaned over and pressed a light kiss to Liam's temple. His lips moved in a smile. His father's smile. His father's mouth. The mouth, she now knew, that had belonged to generations of his Murray forebears, not to mention his uncle Dev. For him she was glad they had come.

For herself…well, it was certainly an experience.

She settled the duvet around him more closely, then scratched O'Mally behind the ear and was rewarded with another tail thump on the bed. Fearing that it would wake Liam, she turned to leave. Taped on the inside door handle she saw another note: "Liam, follow the string and find me. Love, Dad."

At least there was no doubt that Flynn loved his son. She was happy for Liam.

She didn't have to follow the string.

When she finally came downstairs after stopping to look her fill this time at the portrait in the hall and down the stairwell, the sound of raised voices arguing in one of the rooms drew her.

She heard the words: "Dunmorey" and "sell" and "don't add up." That was Flynn. Then she heard Dev's more Irish inflections arguing about paddocks and stalls and future earnings.

And then she heard Flynn roar, "There won't be any earnings unless we sell, damn it! That's what I'm trying to tell you!"

The voices lowered again, but Sara hurried away, not wanting to eavesdrop, much less walk in on a family quarrel.

She hurried down the hallway past the disapproving ancestors and ducked into what turned out to be the formal dining room. Her mother's dining room table was big. But it didn't come close to the size of this one. Her mother didn't have two pairs of three-foot-tall silver candelabras on hers. Sara had no trouble imagining them lit and elegant lords and ladies—generations of them—taking meals here.

Because the voices continued, she did, too. She found a billiards room and a room she thought of as the yellow parlor because of its color. She found a music room and a small office that looked, from the delicate feminine furniture, as if it must belong to Flynn's mother, the countess.

She tried to imagine what a countess would be like. She was glad the countess wasn't here. She was quite certain Flynn's mother would not be as approving as Dev was.

Because Sara knew had no business in the countess's office—could you get arrested for it? she wondered—she hurried back out.

There was lots else to see. It was not the sort of house she was normally invited to. Every piece of furniture, every knickknack, every doily and painting doubtless had a memorable history.

She could see where it would be hugely demanding. But at the same time it was a shame no one paid any attention to it—because clearly no one did.

Most of the rooms were dusty and neglected. If just one girl was in charge of the cleaning—Daisy of the baby and the biscuits—if she got to each room once a month, Sara thought she would be doing well.

She was just heading down the hallway towards the kitchen to see if she could make a cup of tea, when she heard Dev's voice.

"Be damned if I'm askin' you to sell!" A door banged furiously down the hall.

Quickly Sara ducked into the kitchen and was putting on the kettle when Dev shoved open the door and stopped in surprise at the sight of her.

"Ah, and you're awake, then." He was breathing hard and made a conscious effort to slow himself down. "Did we wake you, yellin' like that?"

"No. I—were you yelling?"

He grinned. "Tactful of you."

Sara smiled. "Would you like some tea?"

"I would. Or something a damn sight stronger. He's a pain in the arse, your man."

"Not mine," Sara said quickly.

But Dev didn't seem to notice. "As if I'd expect him to sell the damn castle to fund the stables!"

"Is he?" She knew he'd mentioned it, but couldn't believe he'd decided so quickly.

"Trying not to. It will kill him to have to do it. There has to be another way!" Dev looked like he wanted to kick something.

"He's not doing it lightly," she said. "I'm sure."

"Hell, no, he's not doing it lightly. He's got a streak of responsibility as wide as the feckin' Nile, does our Flynn. Blatting on about 'the future!' But it will gut him to do it on account of the old man."

"Old man?"

"Our dearly departed father," Dev said bitterly. There was apparently no love lost between the old earl and his youngest son, either. "Never gave Flynn the respect he deserved. Blamed him for Will dying."

Sara gasped.

Dev gritted his teeth. "Like he'd got shot and come home on purpose just for that." He stalked across the room and stood with his hands braced on the kitchen sink, staring blindly out into the darkness. "The old man should've blamed Will, damn it. Stupid helpful bugger, always trying to do the right thing," he said in a choked voice.

Flynn had called Will a saint. But she had no idea what happened. He hadn't told her that.

Dev did. Then, "Left Flynn holding the bag. And the old man telling him he was useless, that he was never going to measure up."

"How could he possibly think that?" Sara was outraged. She couldn't imagine any father believing, much less saying such a thing.

Dev shrugged. "It's the way he was. Now Flynn's earl, he's doing his best to prove the old bugger wrong. I figured I could help if we got the stud going. It would help. I just didn't think it would cost this much."

"How much?"

He told her. It was a substantial sum.

"Only way he thinks we can do it is to sell," Dev said glumly.

Sara made the tea, though she thought something stronger might definitely be in order. Since she didn't know where the whiskey was, she filled three mugs.

"Brave soul you are, if you're going to take it to him." Dev raised his brows. "Of course he might not act like such an eejit around you."

Sara hoped that was true. But even if he did, she understood more now. Appreciated the pressures on Flynn—from within and without. She admired the amount of time he'd spent with them in Elmer. The flurries of phone calls made a lot more sense.

She carried the tray down the hall and tapped on the door where she'd heard them arguing earlier. For a long moment there wasn't any reply, and she thought he might have left.

But then she heard a chair squeak and Flynn's gruff voice. "Scared to come back in?"

Balancing the tray with one hand, she opened the door. "No. I just brought you some tea."

He leapt out of his chair and raked a hand through his hair. It looked as if he'd done that already a time or two. Quickly he crossed the room to take the tray from her. "I thought you were Dev. Sorry."

Sara shut the door and followed him back across the room. "I'm glad I'm not."

Flynn grimaced. "You heard?"

"Some. Not all of it. When I came downstairs you were, um, talking. So I went along the hall. I was making a cup of tea when Dev came in. He's upset."

"Why? He's getting what he wants!"

"But he thinks it's coming at too great a cost."

"He told you?" Flynn scowled furiously.

"He's worried about you."

Flynn snorted. "Doesn't need to be. I'll survive. *Eireoidh Linn*. It's the bloody family motto!" He prowled the room with exactly the same ferocity that Dev had displayed in the kitchen.

Sara watched him, then sat down on one of the chairs by the fire. "Yes, but it doesn't sound as if he wants it at the expense of Dunmorey."

"Well, how the hell else is he going to get his horses? They're a potential moneymaker. The castle isn't! It's—"

"A potential moneymaker, too."

He stared at her. "What?"

"I said, the castle certainly can earn you some money."

Flynn gave a disbelieving laugh. "Yeah, right. Did you trip over a bucket and hit your head? It's a money pit, not the other way around! And the new roof—which I promise you it will be getting sooner rather than later—is only one of its problems."

"But it has so many possibilities, too!"

"Try telling the bank that."

"If you want me to, I will."

Their gazes met, locked. She knew she'd overstepped, put her foot in family business where it had no business being. But what she said was absolutely true.

Flynn just stared at her a long moment, then raked his hand through his hair again. "Look, Sara, I know you mean well. You're kind to be thinking anything good about this place. But even my father, who lived and breathed Dunmorey, knew it was just a matter of time until we'd have to let it go."

"Then your father was exceedingly shortsighted."

Flynn's brows arched in surprise. And from the look on his face, Sara wondered if anyone had ever dared dispute the old earl's wisdom regarding the ancestral pile. Or anything else for that matter.

Taking advantage of his look of astonishment, she pressed on. "You're so used to it that you don't see what you've got here."

"On the contrary, I know exactly what we've got here. We've got a pile of rubble and mildew, going from bad to worse."

"Only if you give up on it." She jumped up, needing to move, as well. "You have this amazing history. Hundreds of years of it. I've heard you tell Liam bits of it. And this gorgeous place—no, truly, it is gorgeous." She forestalled his protest. "The woods, the meadows…the moat—" she grinned "—and the castle, too. It's just run-down. But it must have seen bad times now and then. Every place does. But truly, Flynn, it's magical. Didn't Liam think it was magical? It just needs work, care. Love."

"Money," Flynn stuck in.

"Well, who's making the bestseller lists these days?"

"Banks aren't impressed by bestseller lists."

"Have you asked them?"

"I wasn't on it when I last talked to the bank. But—"

"Then you don't know. They'll think you're a hot commodity now. And if you refurbished some of the rooms, you could turn them into a conference or retreat center. You have this huge amazing dining room—" she stopped, embarrassed "—I snooped while you and Dev were…discussing. But truly, it would be great for meetings, for banquets. Have you ever tried any of that?"

"My father would have died first."

"Well, your father has died first. Now it's your turn." She warmed to her topic even as he raised his brows. "You could make part of it a bed-and-breakfast. Think how many people would love to have tea and kippers with the lord of the manor!"

Flynn groaned. "Sara, we don't eat kippers."

Sara ignored him. She was on a roll. "Corned beef and cabbage then. Whatever. When you get the stud going, you can have guests who come to see the horses. You can do history weekends and have experts talk to people who come to learn about life on the manor. There are tons of possibilities. This castle is your greatest resource, Flynn. You can't sell it!"

"I can't afford it."

Sara flopped back down in her chair again and stared up at him. "Or," she said airily, "I guess you could just give up."

"Damn it, Sara!" His jaw tightened.

She shrugged lightly. "Do whatever you want. Liam's seen it now. We could go home tomorrow."

Their gazes clashed again—hers challenging, his a hard furious glare. The silence went on…and on.

She knew he was fighting himself even more than he was fighting her.

"You used to be a sweet young thing," Flynn said gruffly when he'd unclenched his jaw enough to get the words out. "What the hell happened?"

Sara smiled. "I met you. I had Liam. I grew up."

CHAPTER NINE

"So what do you suggest?" Flynn leaned against the bookcase, hoping he looked calmer and more in control than he felt.

It was bad enough to finally come to the realization that he was going to have to sell to support the start-up of the stud, and then have Dev yell and carry on and storm out the door like he'd been insulted.

It was beyond infuriating to have Sara in here now, taking his brother's part.

Most of all, he didn't understand why she was coming up with all these ideas out of nowhere. She didn't even like the place!

"I suggest you don't do anything drastic, like even thinking about selling Dunmorey, until you've tried some of the things I've told you."

"And I'm going to do this how?" he demanded impatiently. "I know you're trying to help, Sara. But I've told you, we're going to the bank tomorrow. If we want anything from them, we have to show them a new business plan illustrating how we intend to maximize our assets."

"So do that. Show them plans for a retreat center, guest accommodations, manor house tours, the whole kit and kaboodle."

It was tempting. God, it was tempting.

So was she. Sara in a fit of enthusiasm was a sight to behold, her cheeks flushed, her eyes bright, her whole body quivering.

He saw the same drive in her now that he'd seen six years ago when she'd been focused on med school.

And in spite of himself, he felt her kindle the same enthusiasm in him. But still he hesitated, afraid to hope, to believe.

"Why?" he asked.

"What?" She frowned.

"Why do you care?"

She opened her mouth. Then she hesitated, too, and he thought she might just shrug, blow him off, change the subject. But she didn't.

She looked him straight in the eye. "Because you do."

It was the truth.

She'd been going to give him the truth back in Elmer, the morning he'd ended up in New York. She would have dared to tell him then—but was glad she hadn't after he left her.

But this leaving had not been like the first one. He had called every day. He had come back, and not just for Liam. For her as well.

He'd brought them to Ireland for reasons she wasn't clear on yet. Well, no, that wasn't accurate. The Liam reasons she understood very well. He wanted his son. He loved his son.

And the reasons he'd brought her? Those she desperately hoped she knew. But she couldn't ask. She could only guess.

And because she understood now how much Dunmorey and all that it entailed mattered to him, she would do whatever was necessary to help him save the castle.

"Look," she said when he didn't speak, "I think I can help. I don't just do taxes, I do business plans, as well. Ranchers are always going in for loans. It's the story of their lives. And I've worked with a lot of them. I know ranches aren't castles, but they cost a lot to run. You have to be creative, to think outside the box. I can do that. And I can write it up—if you want."

He didn't answer. He just stared at her.

And Sara knew she had misread everything.

"Or not," she said hastily. "I should keep my mouth shut. Not interfere. It's your castle, your brother. It's none of my business."

But Flynn just shook his head. "I think you just made it your business," he said, never taking his eyes off her. "Dear God, Sara. I hope you're right. Let's get Dev back in here and talk."

They talked most of the night. Sara was in intense mode, tossing out ideas right and left. He would happily have just sat there and watched her, but her enthusiasm was catching. And a surprising number of her ideas tickled his fancy—from the pony rides for children to getting restoration experts to come and teach their skills using Dunmorey as their canvas.

"Like painting workshops," she said. "Only, you'd get a lot of work done that way."

Flynn could see the potential, could feel the energy growing. The only idea he balked at was her suggestion of writers' weeks.

She grinned at him. "They could come and sit at your feet."

"Don't be daft," Flynn said.

But Dev said, "Write it down."

Sometime in the middle of the night, Liam woke up once, followed the string down, O'Mally at his side, and found them in Flynn's study. He blinked at them sleepily. "Whatcha doin'? Why's it dark?"

"Because it's three in the morning, boyo," Dev told him.

Liam wrinkled his nose. "How come I'm hungry?"

"Because you slept through dinner," Sara said. She looked at Flynn. "Can I get him something to eat?"

He stood up. "You stay here and work on this horse stuff with Dev. Liam and I will make tea."

"Tea?" Liam's nose wrinkled again.

"Food," Flynn promised. He took his son's hand and led him towards the door, glancing back to give Sara a nod of encouragement.

Truth be told, he was the one who was encouraged.

Encouraged? Hell, it was all he could do not to dance down the hallway, bad leg and all. Sara was interested! Sara was involved!

Sara didn't hate Dunmorey!

He and Liam made tea and sandwiches and piled biscuits on a plate, then carried it all back down the hallway to his office. Sara and Dev were sitting on the floor. They both looked up when he and Liam came in, and Sara gave him a smile that nearly stopped his heart.

"I think it will work," she said. Her voice had a thread of exhaustion in it, but there was elation, too. "Let me type it up and you can take it in tomorrow. It will certainly give them something else to chew over. I don't think, looking at it, that they will turn you down flat."

Flynn set down the tray and reached down to haul her to her feet. "You don't, huh?"

"No, I—" She started to explain.

But Flynn had all the explanation that he needed. He kissed her.

He'd kissed her in the airport when he'd got back from the tour. But it had been a chaste kiss, a kiss capable of being witnessed by their five-year-old.

He had been all too aware of having nearly scandalized Liam in the kitchen the day he left.

This kiss was spontaneous, not calculated. Spur-of-the-moment like that one had been. But he'd intended it to say thank you, to say how glad he was she'd come, that she was involved, sharing Dunmorey, sharing his life.

He certainly hadn't intended the heat of it to deepen, to catch fire, to become so much more—to want so much more.

Tell his body that!

It was as if the weeks of frustration, of need, of desire had finally taken their toll, as if all the willpower he'd used to bide his time, to court, to woo, to wait, was gone. The dam burst.

The mere taste of Sara's lips made him weak-kneed with longing and hard with desire. It was like touching a match to a pile of dry shavings. Sparks shot. Flames soared. Her lips parted. Their tongues tasted, teased, tangled.

"Please, not in front of the children," Dev said with loud good cheer. Then "Pass me a sandwich," he said to Liam.

Sara jumped back. Flynn flung himself down on the sofa and tried to get a grip. He didn't want a grip. He wanted Sara upstairs in bed naked.

"Have a sandwich," Dev said and passed him one.

"I don't see why you want me to come along."

It wasn't the first time Sara had said this as Flynn took her by the hand and kept a firm grip on it as they walked towards the bank. "I don't belong here."

"You absolutely belong here." Flynn held the door for her. "You wrote the plan."

"But it's your castle. Your future."

"Your plan."

"But it's just speculative at this point."

"So you can tell him that as well. Sit." He pointed her to a chair, then, when she sat, loomed over her making sure she didn't bolt. At least that was what it felt like.

It was insane, dragging her to their business meeting. She didn't know how such things were done in Ireland, she said. She knew more than he did about business plans in any country, he countered. He'd write anything she wanted forever for her if she'd do this for him, he added.

She wondered if he'd write "I love you, Sara," if she asked him to. It was so much the only thing she wanted—had ever wanted from him. But how could she ask that?

She had his kiss. It had been a wonderful kiss. A reminder of the kiss in Elmer. But somehow even better.

More intense? More emotional? More from the heart?

Or was she kidding herself?

"Mr. Monaghan will see you now."

Mr. Monaghan was weedy, slender, with a too-big suit and a too-small moustache. He wore half-glasses that slipped down his nose. He shook hands with them all, but his gaze skated right over Sara.

He was all attentive to Flynn, though, "my lording" him so often it made Sara's teeth hurt. But even while he was doing so, he nattered on about grave concerns, serious doubts and ended by saying, "I really don't think we can offer much help."

His unhappy, yet almost obsequious negativism, made her want to strangle him. She didn't blame Flynn when he shoved her business plan across the desk and said in his Earl's Voice, "Read this."

Mr. Monaghan sat back and blinked, but took the proffered papers and began to read.

They waited in silence. The clock ticked. Outside, cars puttered past on the street. Inside, Dev drummed his fingers on his thigh. Flynn didn't move a muscle or make a sound. Sara held her breath instinctively and had to force herself to breathe.

As he read, Mr. Monaghan's brows lifted a little. And then a little more. And then he cocked his head and pushed his glasses up. Sara glanced at Dev. He was leaning forward a little. Flynn was looking intent.

"Hmm," murmured Mr. Monaghan. Then, "Mmm." He went on more rapidly to the next page and the next.

"What did you have in mind with using the castle as a site of training historical restorationists?" he asked.

Dev and Flynn looked at Sara.

She took a breath and jumped in.

The questions came fast and furious after that. Mr. Monaghan moved back and forth through the business plan asking for clarifications, making notes, nodding, pushing his glasses up, and murmuring, "Yes, I see. Yes, that could do very well. Yes, an interesting notion."

And then set the papers in a neat stack on his desk and sat back and smiled at Flynn for the first time. "Well, my lord, this looks quite promising. I will, of course, have to take it to the board. But I see no impediments now. Let us hope that Dunmorey lives up to its potential. I feel confident it can. I'm sure we'll enjoy doing business together."

In an ancestral sense, Flynn had always known Dunmorey was *home*. But even though he'd grown up loving its grounds and its walls and its stolid granite self, he'd never felt at home there.

Until now.

"It's amazing what a bit of money can do for a place, isn't it?" Dev said three weeks after the loan was approved. And yes, there was a new roof and new paint and new linens and cleaned draperies.

But it wasn't any of those that made the real difference.

The difference was Sara.

It was the vases of fresh flowers she put in every room. It was the music she played. It was the warmth of sunlight—was it his imagination or could Sara actually make the sun come out?— splashing across the warm dark-walnut dining room table.

It was the way she left windows open and doors ajar so that breezes and boys and dogs could wander freely in and out. It was the smell of baking—of breads and biscuits, tarts and cakes—as she and Daisy spurred each other on to greater accomplishments.

It was the miles of wooden railway that she allowed Liam and the boys from the manor farm, Joe and Frank, to run in and through the yellow parlor. It was the bucket of Legos, the Star Wars guys, it was the comfortable way she encouraged Liam and O'Mally to sprawl on the rug while Liam drew pictures.

There was joy in Dunmorey for the first time in Flynn's memory. There was the sound of laughter, of little boys' feet pounding down the hallway.

He didn't remember ever laughing here before Sara came.

He didn't ever remember family meals around the big oak table in the kitchen. He and Dev had eaten there occasionally when it was just the two of them. But now they always ate there—not just he and Dev and Sara and Liam, but often, too, Daisy and little Eamon. One afternoon, to his astonishment, they'd even been joined by Mrs. Upham.

He'd expected Mrs. Upham to criticize Sara's familiarity and had been ready to defend it. But even Mrs. Upham had been charmed.

"Hard worker, that girl," Mrs. Upham said. "Gives her all." It was her highest accolade.

"She does," Flynn agreed.

She had—ever since she'd got here. Had worked almost nonstop on whatever needed to be done. And when she took a break, it wasn't to actually rest, but to turn to doing her Elmer clients' taxes.

He worried that she was working too hard. He wanted to tell her to stop. He wanted to care for her and cosset her and take her to bed and ask her to marry him. But he was afraid to rock the boat.

He'd jumped the gun once before. He'd made her angry, scared her away. So as much as he desperately wanted her in his bed, wanted her to be his forever, he held his peace. He didn't want to scare Sara away.

As wonderful a home as she was turning Dunmorey into, he sensed that she wasn't ready yet.

She still hurried past the stern, formal portraits in the hallway. She only went into the formal dining room to polish the silver. And she stayed away from the rose parlor—the most formal one—where his mother always entertained guests.

"You can do what you like with it," he told her. "Change it if you want."

"No." She shook her head. "Some people prefer that."

"You mean Rawsby's wife?" A few days earlier an old school friend and his new bride had stopped for a visit. Jack had been happy enough to get down on the floor and play with Liam and his trains. But Charlotte, his wife, had sat by primly and looked as if she could hardly wait to escape.

It was only when Sara had suggested they take tea in the rose parlor that Charlotte had deigned to smile. But she hadn't had much to say to Sara even then. Her conversation had been with her husband or Flynn.

"She was rude," he told Sara after. "Don't pay any attention to her."

After all, the rest of the castle and its inhabitants and its tenants responded to Sara's warmth, to her cheer, to her unfailing hard work.

She showed them possibilities that they barely believed existed.

Dev had laughed that first night when she'd suggested giving pony rides to the children of tourists who would be coming to view the house.

But when she pressed the issue, he found some ponies in the neighborhood and offered them board if he could use them for rides. He hired two teenage girls who, when they weren't drooling over Flynn and Dev, actually helped with the children. They were a great success.

"How do you think of these things?" Flynn asked her one night when they went for a walk down by the lake. It was another habit they'd fallen into most evenings. They walked and talked and shared their days.

Sara shrugged. "I just look around and think, What would I like to do? Chances are pretty good if I'd like it, someone else will too."

And it was how Flynn came to build the tree house.

He didn't tell Sara what he was doing. And he swore Liam to secrecy. He didn't know if she would think it was foolish and that he'd be better spending his time on something else, or if she would say he was ruining a fine old tree—which his father had once said when at twelve Flynn had suggested it—or if he would regret having done it once he had.

But as a child he'd wanted a tree house more than anything. He'd wanted a place to go to get away from the castle, from its demands and confines. He'd wanted a place—a home—of his own.

So he took a page out of Sara's book and decided that if he'd once wanted it, maybe someone else would, too. Like Liam.

Or Sara herself.

So every afternoon after he'd worked on estate business, he and Liam disappeared down into the woods. The tree he picked was the tree he'd climbed as a boy. It was the tree that had been his haven even without a house.

It was an ancient ash with low spreading branches that made it perfect for what he had in mind. He brought the lumber down one evening when Sara was busy with a bunch of guests who were being shown around the stables. She and Dev had to be there. He and Liam did not. The timing was perfect.

The work was harder than he'd thought. His leg made climbing difficult. But Liam was as agile as a monkey and as fearless as Flynn had always been.

"Hand it to me, Dad! I can do it, Dad!" He was thrilled with the idea of their secret hideaway. He never stopped grinning.

"What are you up to?" Sara asked him more than once when Liam would giggle.

"Can't tell. Me 'n' Dad got a secret."

And they had a bond—a sense of joy and accomplishment and connection—that he'd never shared with his own father.

But that had been the earl's choice, Flynn realized, not his.

They weren't telling her something.

They went off together every afternoon, Flynn and Liam, and she had no idea where they were or what they were doing.

It made her nervous, edgy. It worried her.

Everything had been going so well with the castle, with the stables, with all their ideas. Sometimes she found it hard to believe what some paint and paper, spit and polish, and a whole lot of elbow grease could accomplish.

She felt good about it. Good about everything.

Almost.

There was something wrong between her and Flynn—and she didn't know what it was.

He loved what they were doing in the castle. She could see it in his body language, in his eyes, in his face. He threw himself into all of it. Worked on his new book in the morning, but in the afternoons he got involved in working on the restoration. Or he had until recently.

Two weeks ago he'd disappeared one afternoon. She hadn't thought anything of it at first. He often had meetings with his tenants or local tradesmen that she knew nothing about.

But then he began to take Liam. They didn't say where they were going. And if she asked, Liam would only say, "Can't tell. It's a secret." And he'd grin.

She didn't imagine it could be too terrible if Liam was grinning about it. But she didn't like him having secrets from her. Didn't like him having secrets with his father. Didn't like being left out.

She felt just a little left out. Because of that—and because after having pushed and cajoled and manipulated her until she'd actually come to Ireland, now he had backed off.

They'd had one passionate inappropriate kiss which she put down to jet lag—and thanked God Dev had interrupted—and that was it. Well, besides some hand holding when they walked down by the lake.

Maybe he was getting cold feet. Maybe seeing her here was making him realize they didn't belong together. It was possible, goodness knew. Every time she walked past that damn mirror in the entry hall she felt small and out of place.

Maybe Flynn felt the same way. Maybe he just didn't know how to tell her.

It was possible.

And it was particularly possible to think so today. Having just endured her first formal tea with a dozen society dames—in the rose parlor no less—she was feeling out of sorts and out of place.

She didn't need to finally get rid of them all and come out into the garden for a breath of fresh air and a bit of equilibrium to spot Flynn and Liam coming up the path from the woods together. They were talking, laughing—and then they saw her and Liam said, "Shhh!"

"We missed you at tea," Sara said, annoyed. Not Liam, of course. But every one of the women had hoped Flynn would drop in. They'd been polite enough to her, but they were obviously a little uncertain about her status. As was she, to be honest. "Mother of the earl's love child" was not exactly a preferred role in their society.

"We were busy," Flynn said. "Down in the woods," he added. He hesitated, looking nervous, wary.

And Sara felt suddenly even more nervous and wary, too.

"In the woods?" She frowned. "Clearing trails?" It was the only sensible thing she could think of that they'd have been doing down there. And even that, given Flynn's leg, didn't seem sensible for him.

"No." Liam grabbed her hand. "C'mon. Come see."

She dug in her heels until she looked at Flynn.

He shrugged. "Why not?"

Liam was pulling her down the path now. She walked this way with Flynn most evenings. "Where are we going?"

"To see what we been doin'."

Still mystified, still a little wary, Sara allowed herself to be towed. It was a warm evening for midspring. The flowers on the garden paths were dancing in the breeze. They turned away from the lake and went deeper into the woods until they reached the far edge overlooking the fields and the river.

Liam stopped abruptly. "There!" He pointed up.

"What?' Sara's gaze followed his finger. "Where?"

At first she didn't see what he was pointing at. But then, about thirty feet up, amid the boughs, she thought she saw sawn planks. Her eyes widened and she turned to look at them. "Is that a tree house?"

Liam bobbed his head. "Me 'n' Dad built it! It's a-mazing! You gotta come see!" He pulled on her hand again until they reached the tree. Then he let go and began scrambling up through the branches. "Follow me."

But before she did, Sara turned to look at Flynn. "This is what you were doing? Building a tree house? The two of you?"

He gave a small nod. "I thought about…what you said…" He looked away, then back at her. "What you said about…if you wanted something, maybe someone else would want it too…."

"You mean, like Liam?"

"Like Liam," he agreed, then met her gaze. "And you."

* * *

And that was how she knew.

Flynn had brought them to Dunmorey for the castle—to show his son his heritage, his history, all those stones piled upon stones. It was impressive. It was, in its way, beautiful. Certainly it was memorable.

But in building the tree house—with his own hands, with his own heart—he had made them a home.

And that was why, after they put Liam to bed that night, she laced her fingers through Flynn's and looked up into his eyes. "I love you," she murmured.

It was a truth she had held in her heart too long.

Now she offered it to him.

She didn't know which of them moved first. Didn't know whether she wrapped her arms around him or if he swept her up into his embrace and bore her away to his bedroom.

It was not a "lord of the manor" room. Even after the recent refurbishment, he had insisted on keeping his own boyhood room and refused to move into the old earl's chambers. Everything was simple, neat, functional.

It was fine with Sara. The trappings didn't matter, only the man.

She didn't want any other man. Never had.

If she belonged with any man, Flynn Murray was the one.

He laid her on his bed and came down beside her. And even fully clothed she could feel the heat of his body next to her. His hands slid under her sweater, stroking her skin. And against her softness, she could feel the calluses on his fingers. Workman's hands, she thought with a smile.

He made his living with words. They were a tool. He used them easily, smoothly, cleverly. But his hands had built the tiny hidden house, the home he'd made for the three of them.

She sought his hands and drew them away from her skin,

touched her lips to them. Kissed his fingers. Nibbled on each in turn. Sucked them.

"Sar'," he murmured. "You are askin' for it."

She smiled. "I know."

Her words seemed to galvanize him. He pushed up to kneel awkwardly on the bed and strip her sweater over her head. She wriggled out of it, then reached up to do the same to him. Then, with his chest bared, she ran her hands over his hair-roughened skin, drew light circles around his nipples, made him catch his breath.

His fingers made quick work of the button and zip of her jeans, then he tugged them down her legs and ran warm, roughened fingers back up them from her instep to the juncture of her thighs.

It was Sara's turn to gasp as he slipped a finger inside the leg opening of her panties and skimmed the part of her that pulsed for his touch. She raised up and fumbled with the fastener of Flynn's jeans. But her fingers trembled and he groaned and said, "Let me."

He had them undone in seconds. But then it was her turn to tug them down over his hips and down to his knees. He shifted awkwardly on his bad leg to let her slip them past, but it was difficult and he cursed.

"No," Sara said, and she gave him a push, toppling him over, then she sat up to pull them off him.

"It's ugly," he said. "You don't want to look."

"It's you," she said. "I want to see every inch of you. Please." She met his gaze then in the half-light. "Please," she repeated.

He sighed and swallowed, then lay back and let her look her fill. Six years ago she'd been too innocent, too circumspect to dare to do what she did tonight. Six years ago she'd been caught up in a fantasy. This was reality. This Flynn was a flesh-and-blood man, not a dream of her youth.

He had wounds and imperfections. So did she. She bent her head and kissed his chest, his hard flat belly, his thighs, the scarred and puckered flesh above his knee. And when she did, her hair brushed lightly against him. Made him tense. Made him quiver. Made him reach for her.

"I want you, Sar'. Now." His voice was ragged, desperate, urgent.

But no more than her need was. And when he reached for her, drew her up against him and rolled her over beneath him, she was all too willing to accommodate, to mould her body to his, to reach between them and take him in.

His breath hissed through his teeth. "Yess. Sar', it's been so long. Too long. Don't ever—never—" He couldn't finish, could only move. And Sara moved with him, filled with him.

It was everything it had been six years ago and more. And this time he took her with him over the edge. And when he groaned her name, she whispered his.

And later when he slept, she kissed his hair, his cheek, his jaw. And smiled through her tears with the joy of believing her youthful dream was even better than a dream.

It was real.

CHAPTER TEN

THE sun in her face woke her.

Sara blinked, feeling fuzzy, warm and boneless. Also momentarily disoriented. And then delighted as she remembered where she was—in Flynn's bed.

If loving Flynn six years ago had been the stuff of dreams, this loving had been far better.

Six years ago they'd spent a night of desperate beauty, stolen from the real world.

But last night had been a night of joy, of tenderness, of passion, the culmination of the sharing of their lives built on weeks—months—of getting to know each other for real.

It had been perfect.

The only thing better would be if he were still here. The pillow where he'd laid his head still bore the indentation. She reached out a hand and stroked the soft cotton and felt it was cool to the touch, so he had been gone awhile.

She didn't remember him leaving. She did remember his kiss. Or had she only dreamed it?

No matter. There would be more.

A lifetime's more.

Of course they would go back to Elmer eventually. Maybe they would marry there? Or here? It didn't matter.

She only needed him.

He'd asked her once in the middle of the night, while they were lying wrapped in each other's arms, what had happened. What was different? Why now?

"Not that I'm not glad," he'd said with a shaky laugh. "I'd just like to know so in case I annoy you, I can do it again."

"The tree house," she'd told him. "You have all this and yet you made that for us. A home."

It could still cause her heart to skip, her eyes to prick, her throat to tighten. And the thought always made her smile.

She didn't suppose they could get married in the tree house. Earls, even unstuffy ones like Flynn, probably drew the line at that.

They'd have to talk about it though. He'd ask her to marry him again. Maybe he'd ask her there.

Or maybe this time she'd ask him. A man didn't have to do all the asking. He'd done it once. Maybe this time it was her turn.

If he were here now, she'd ask him. Where was he?

She rolled over and checked the clock. Ten o'clock? Good heavens!

Instantly she leapt out of bed, dragged on yesterday's clothes and dashed to her own room, hoping Liam wouldn't see her.

But no one saw her. Everyone else had doubtless arisen long ago. She supposed Flynn had made Liam breakfast already. She pulled a brush through her hair. It was in one of its uncooperative moods. She should have taken time for a shower, but she'd need a shower later.

This morning, she had told Flynn yesterday, she and Liam were going to clean out the old chicken house.

"Fresh organic eggs for our guests," she'd said.

And he'd shaken his head. "More projects."

"Yes."

Besides, it was fun to do some hard physical labor, especially when you could see how much better things looked when you were done. So she'd need a shower after the chicken house when she and her clothes would be far grubbier.

She stuffed her feet into her shoes and hurried downstairs. She even waggled her fingers at the generations of dead Murrays who looked down their aristocratic noses at her as she went.

They were harmless, she decided. They might even approve of what she was doing. They, like Flynn, seemed to have been all about preserving the castle and the lands.

The kitchen was empty. The dishes were, surprisingly, already done. Daisy usually left the breakfast dishes in the sink while she cleaned in one wing of the house or another. Today the kitchen was spotless. Even Eamon's toys, usually scattered about, were neatly put away.

Sara frowned. Dishes done? Daisy gone? Dev would be at the stables. But what about Flynn and Liam?

The tree house? It was a possibility. Sara hurried back down the hall to go out into the gardens. And that was when she heard Liam's voice from the rose parlor.

The rose parlor?

He was talking in his excited voice, too—a mile a minute—but she couldn't hear what he was saying. Nor could she imagine who he was talking to.

Not Flynn, surely, unless he had decided to begin giving Liam lessons in family history. She'd never taken him in there before. The stuffiest most breakable room in the entire castle, it was reserved for state occasions—and people like Charlotte Rawsby.

Surely Flynn hadn't let Liam go in there by himself! No, of course he hadn't. Liam had to be talking to someone.

She turned the knob and pushed open the door.

And found the parlor full of people. All of them turned to stare

at her. Dev looked delighted. Liam looked happy. Flynn looked…
uncomfortable.

And the other two people—both women—looked at her as if
she'd already cleaned the chicken house before she'd come in.

The elder, an elegant woman of about sixty, had a *Town and
Country* look—all sculpted cheekbones and arched brows with
frosted graying hair in a casual cut that had no doubt cost enough
to feed a small third-world country for a week. She might as well
have had the word *countess* stamped on her forehead.

The other woman was younger and gentler looking, with a sweet
bow mouth and wavy blonde curls. She wore a twin set, tailored
slacks and pearls. She looked like a Charlotte Rawsby clone.

Oh, Lord.

Sara cringed at the thought of meeting her future mother-in-
law for the first time while she was dressed to clean the chicken
house. But at the same time she knew exactly what her own
mother would say.

"Buck up," she could hear Polly's determined tone in her ear
as if her mother were actually sitting next to her eardrum. "Unless
you've done something wrong, you have nothing to apologize for."

So she did what Polly would do. She said, "Good morning,"
as easily and cheerfully as she could.

Flynn set down his tea cup and was on his feet at once, smiling
at her. "Ah, good morning!" He took a step towards her, but
stopped abruptly, his progress halted by a tea table, his mother's
chair and that of the twin set woman.

Neither looked inclined to move.

He hesitated, then turned his attention to the countess,
"Mother, I'd like to introduce Sara—"

And Sara prepared her best meeting-mother-in-law smile.

But then Flynn stopped. She was Sara—and his mouth was
open, as if he would finish, if only he could think of what to say.

Liam, thank God, said it for him. He leapt up from where he was playing with a truck on the floor and ran across the room to throw his arms around her hips.

"My mom!" he announced proudly.

And Sara felt his solid little body with a relief that swamped her, and found herself clutching his thin shoulders as if he were her anchor in a storm.

"Ah, yes, your mother," the countess murmured. She regarded Sara over the top of her teacup. It was as effective as the Murray nose, Sara thought.

"I see," the countess said.

And Sara had no doubt that what Flynn's mother saw didn't make her happy at all.

The part of her that had squirmed yesterday when dealing with the biddies who had muttered about her being "mother of the earl's love child" wanted more than ever to turn and run today.

The part that was Polly and Lew McMaster's daughter dug in her heels and stayed right where she was.

Flynn found his voice—his earl's voice, even—at last and managed to finish his sentence. "This is Sara McMaster," he said. "My mother, the Countess of Dunmorey."

But where was his support? His declaration? His love?

Was this the same man who had made love to her so tenderly and ardently last night? The man who had built her a tree house? Who had made them a home?

Right now he looked as if he were searching for an escape route. He looked annoyed and embarrassed and out of sorts.

Welcome to the club, Sara thought irritably.

"Miss McMaster." The countess inclined her head and gave Sara a flinty smile like something you'd see on the head on an old postage stamp. It was an acknowledgment. It wasn't a welcome.

Sara smiled, too, hoping it looked more genuine. But she

was damned if she was going to curtsy. Though she did say with all the politeness she could muster, "It's a pleasure to meet you, my lady."

Was it "my lady?" Or was it "your grace?" She had no idea, and Flynn had never bothered to school her in all the aristocratic protocol.

"Don't worry," he'd said, dismissing her concerns. "You're an American. No one expects you to know that stuff."

Her lady-grace-ship certainly seemed to.

"Sara's the one who had the idea about the retreat center I was telling you about," Flynn said now and shot her a smile, though he was still trapped on the far side of the room. The countess wasn't giving an inch. "And the garden tours," he added. "And she's been helping redo the rooms."

"Came up with pony rides, too," Dev put in. He gave Sara a conspiratorial wink. "She's got a ton of good ideas."

"The restorationist." Flynn continued. "And she's been doing a lot of the manual work. The painting and wallpapering. Well you can see that, can't you?" He waved a hand around as if Sara had redone this room. She hadn't.

But the countess didn't look so sure. She let her gaze examine every inch of the parlor before it finally came to rest again on Sara.

"Did she?" Pause. "She's been very busy. She's certainly effected a great many changes around here."

Sara wasn't expecting approval by now, but she did wish that the countess would stop talking about her as if she wasn't even here.

But then, so was Flynn. "She wrote the business plan we took to the bank. Monaghan was impressed. Last time I was in he said we should make her our new business manager." The grin he gave Sara invited her to share the triumph.

Sara wasn't feeling quite so triumphant. She stared at him. Business manager?

"It's unbelievable how much she's contributed," Flynn finished. "We couldn't have done it without her."

Past tense. As if her work was done.

"Goodness," the countess said. Then at last spoke directly to Sara. "You seem to have been quite an asset to the manor."

"I've enjoyed the opportunity," Sara said politely and got for her trouble a wintery smile.

"I do hope Flynn remembered to put you on the payroll."

"Sara isn't the hired help, Mother," Flynn said sharply.

The countess looked momentarily taken aback at his vehemence. But then she simply nodded and gave him a thin smile. "Of course not, dear. She's the mother of your…child."

The pause allowed each of them their adjective of choice.

Sara began to steam. She waited for Flynn to say something— anything!—that would make her position clear.

But he only nodded curtly. "She is the mother of my child," he said firmly.

He never said she was the woman he'd spent the night with, never told his mother she was the woman he was in love with, the woman he hoped to marry.

Because, Sara realized, maybe he didn't.

He'd never even said it to her. Not since they'd been back at Dunmorey.

A deep well of cold seemed to be spreading in the pit of her stomach. She felt disoriented, dazed. Doubting now everything she'd got up this morning believing.

Maybe she was good enough to be his business manager, his bed partner, the mother of his love child, but now that Dunmorey was beginning to thrive again, perhaps he'd realized that for the rest—the society part—she didn't measure up.

God knew it was true.

She'd been completely out of her depth with the ladies at the tea yesterday. And she'd never felt so uncomfortable as she had when entertaining Charlotte Rawsby—unless you counted right this very minute.

"I hope you'll share your business plan with Abigail," the countess said now.

"Abigail?"

The countess turned a much warmer smile on the young woman seated in the rose-colored chair. "Abigail just finished a master's degree in finance. I'm sure it will be a great help."

For what?

Dear God, did the countess mean what it sounded like she meant? Was she planning on installing Abigail as lady of the manor?

As Flynn's wife?

What did Flynn think about that?

He might, she realized now, think it was a good thing. Abigail was certainly better suited than Sara was to dealing with all the pomp and circumstance that went with being the countess of Dunmorey.

If he was going to make a success of Dunmorey now—and prove once and for all that he was up to the challenge—a wife like Abigail was exactly what he would need.

"Tea?" the countess offered.

Sara nodded jerkily and took it, though a stiff shot of whiskey might have done better. It was all so "civilized."

Except it wasn't.

"I was quite surprised to meet Liam when I arrived this morning."

"Were you?" Sara said. Because Flynn hadn't told her any more than he'd told Dev about his son? She fixed Flynn with a hard accusing look.

He met it without apology.

"I've been visiting my sister in Australia," the countess said.

"Gloria and I live so far apart that we rarely get to see each other. Every few years I go out for several months or she comes here."

"How nice," Sara murmured.

"It was. I had a lovely visit. Of course I had no idea what was going on—" the countess looked around and stopped abruptly.

She didn't need to finish. Sara could fill in the blanks. Flynn's mother had had no idea what was going on here and was obviously displeased with what she found.

"Of course it was a serendipitous trip in another way," the countess went on. "I had the great good fortune to meet up with an old school chum. And Letty has lent me her most wonderful daughter." Another fond smile in the younger woman's direction. "Abigail reminds me of myself at her age."

Sara managed a polite smile. Dev seemed to choke behind his hand. Was it a laugh? Somehow, to Sara, it didn't seem especially funny.

"Abigail is an even more accomplished pianist than I was, though," the older woman went on.

"I just enjoy it," Abigail said with a self-conscious shrug and a genuine smile.

"Do you play, Miss McMaster?" the countess inquired.

It was amazing, Sara thought, how a woman could be so rude while simultaneously being perfectly polite. Polly would be laughing her head off with Dev. And Sara felt some of her mother's determined toughness settle in and take root.

"I don't," she said cheerfully. "No musical talent at all."

"Sara does a lot of other things," Flynn began in her defense, but Sara had had enough.

She wasn't going to let him waste his time trying to impress his mother any further. It was already clear what his mother's opinion was. And if all Flynn could do was defend Sara by reciting lists of things she could do, then it was clear that she didn't belong here at all.

"But my brother Jack plays the kazoo," she went on brightly. "And my sister Lizzie plays the washboard. And my other sister Daisy plays the spoons."

"Washboard? Spoons?" echoed the countess.

Even Flynn blinked at this recitation. Dev snorted. The countess, while taken aback, looked as if she felt more justified by the second.

"How…entertaining. I'm sure you're longing to see them again."

"Yes," Sara said, and the longing was growing by the minute.

"I'm sure. From what Liam tells me, you've been here awhile. How long are you planning to stay?"

"Forever," Flynn answered flatly at the same time Sara said, "We're leaving in the morning."

This time it was Flynn's teacup that rattled. He banged it down on the mantel. *"What?"*

He stared at her, stunned. But Sara knew the moment she said the words that they were the right ones. She'd been living in a fantasy if she'd thought she could live with attitudes like Flynn's mother.

"Our tickets are round trip," she said flatly. "We've been here six weeks. That's long enough."

Indeed it was, said the look on the countess's face.

The look on Flynn's face was one of fury. "No," he said.

"Flynn, you can't control everyone," his mother chided.

He shot her a furious glare. But Sara was more concerned that Liam was looking at her, stricken.

"We're going home? Tomorrow?"

Oh, God. Don't let him start to cry! "We've been on a vacation, Liam," she began in her best soothing mother tone. "We came to visit your dad, not to move in with him."

"But—"

"When we go home, you'll see Annie and Braden again. And Aunt Celie and Uncle Jace. And Grandma and Grandpa." She would have recited the whole population of Elmer or the whole state of Montana if it would make Liam remember the wonderful people he'd be going home to. "You'll like that. You can tell them all about the castle."

"And the tree house?"

The words were like a stab of pain. "And the tree house."

Liam's lip quivered. "But we just made it! I wanta stay in it. I wanta—"

"Tree house?" The countess's eyes widened. She looked from Liam to Flynn. "You built a tree house? The earl doesn't allow—"

"Mother," Flynn said, "I am the earl."

And in the shocked silence that followed, Sara picked up Liam's truck. "Come on," she said. "We'll do the chicken house. Then we have to pack."

"But—"

"It's been a pleasure to meet you," she said politely, her gaze going from Abigail to the countess. Not to mention enlightening. "Good day."

She backed out of the room, towing Liam with her, shut the door and headed for the garden. She didn't look back.

The door to her room was shut.

Flynn didn't let it stop him. If he knocked he knew she'd say, "Go away."

He shoved it open. She said it anyway.

"No, I'm not going away," he said. "And you're not, either."

But it looked like Sara thought she was. She had two suitcases open on the bed and she was pulling clothes out of the drawers of the bureau and flinging them in.

"I certainly am." She didn't turn around, didn't even glance his way. She kept moving with the economy of controlled fury.

"Don't be so stubborn. It's all a misunderstanding," he said. "My mother didn't understand about us."

"Because you didn't bother to tell her!" More clothes came out, were flung into one of the cases.

Flynn snatched them out again and tossed them back into the drawer. "I didn't know she was coming! She showed up in the middle of breakfast. She and that…that…"

"Bridal candidate?" Sara suggested sweetly.

Flynn felt hot blood course up his neck. "Not my idea. She thought she was helping."

"Maybe she is."

"Don't be stupid. She's not."

"Perhaps she wouldn't have bothered if you'd told her you were…involved."

"But I wasn't, was I? You said no."

"Well, I shouldn't have changed my mind! And I'm changing it back again right now."

"Sara—"

"No. I made a mistake. I've made a lot of them where you're concerned, it seems. But I should have known better than to make this one. I thought it would work—"

"Damn it, it will work! My mother knows the truth now. She knows I love you. She knows you and I—"

"—are just too different." She spun around and glared at him. "She knew that very well. I didn't even know what to call her!"

Flynn frowned. "What?"

"Your mother! The countess. Or maybe she's a duchess. I don't even know! And I didn't know what to call her, either. Is she *my lady?* Is she *your grace?* I didn't have a clue! I still don't. I don't belong here!"

"Of course you belong here." He grabbed the latest armful of clothes away from her before she could put them in the suitcase. "Who brought the damned old pile to life again? Who got the bank on our side? Who got the stables finished? Who organized the nature walks? Who put the flowers in the vases?"

"I'm sure Abigail can put flowers in vases better than I can!"

"I don't want bloody Abigail! I want you!"

"Well, you can't have me."

And she grabbed the armful of clothes right back, flung them in the case, jerked down the lid and snapped it shut.

"Sara—"

She shook her head, her eyes flashing fire at him. She folded her arms across her chest. "I won't stop you having Liam. We can work out some sort of visitation. He can come for summers or something. And—" she shrugged "—we'll figure it out."

"Marry me, Sara, and we won't have to 'figure it out.'"

"No."

"You love me."

"Maybe I did. All right, maybe I do. But I'm not putting up with this. I'm not going to live in a place where I always come up short."

"What? Who said—?"

"No one had to say. I felt it. Just like you felt it. You should understand that. You and your father…you didn't want to always come up short, did you?"

She went for the jugular, he'd give her that. His mouth tightened into a firm line. He tried for his patience and clung to it. Just.

"No," he said. "I didn't."

It was suddenly quiet. So quiet he could hear his heart beat, hear her quick, shallow breathing.

She shrugged. "Well, there you are then. You want to prove

him wrong. And I don't blame you. And your mother is right. You don't need me. You need someone who can fit in. Someone who belongs. Abigail."

"I don't want Abigail, damn it! I want you."

But she only shook her head. "I'm leaving in the morning, Flynn. And there's nothing you can do or say to stop me."

"Sara—"

"You can take us to the airport if you want. If you don't, I'll call a taxi."

"You're not calling a damn taxi!"

To say that Liam wasn't happy was putting it mildly. He was stubborn, grumpy and out of sorts. He didn't want to say goodbye to Dev. He didn't want to leave the horses. He was tearful over leaving O'Mally.

"Why can't he come, then?" he asked Sara over and over.

"Because we have no room. Sid would have a fit."

Liam stuck out his lower lip. "Sid would like him. And we'd have plenty of room if we stayed. Sid could come here."

There was no arguing with him, and no reasoning with him. And Sara wasn't doing too well with reason, anyway. For a basically sane and sensible woman who valued logic and rational thought, she was a quivering jelly of emotions.

And it was all Flynn Murray's fault.

Well, maybe not all. Maybe more than a little of it was her own.

She'd just been swept up in the moment, in the challenge of saving Dunmorey, in the dream of happily ever after with the love of her life.

But just because you could refurbish a castle, make it homey and comfortable, didn't mean you ought to marry the prince.

Or the earl.

She ate dinner in her room, letting Flynn have Liam by himself for the evening. But then he had some work to do, and so she took a reluctant feet-dragging Liam around to say his goodbyes.

"Why should I?" he muttered. "It's not my idea."

"You'll be glad you did," Sara said, and knew she sounded exactly like her mother.

They went to the manor farm and said goodbye to Frank and Joe. The three boys kicked rocks and muttered at each other, then socked each other on the arm. She took him to the stables to say goodbye to the horses.

"Dev was gonna let me ride Tip Top," Liam muttered.

"You can ride Tip Top when you come to visit."

"I don't wanta visit. I wanta live here."

So did she, but it would never work. "We don't always get what we want," she said in her Polly voice.

Liam gave her a baleful look and kicked more rocks all the way home. She suggested they stop by the tree house. But he wouldn't do it.

"Why not?" She wanted to. Wanted to climb up once more and sit there and wallow in her misery. That was how much of a masochist she was.

Liam folded his arms across his chest. "Don't want to."

So Sara shrugged. "All right. It's up to you."

"If it was up to me," Liam said blackly, "we'd stay here."

As even her mother wouldn't have had a good comeback for that, Sara kept her mouth shut, too.

When they got back, the manor house was silent. Usually they all met in the yellow parlor in the evenings and talked and laughed and played with Liam and went over the projects for the next day.

Tonight the parlor was quiet when they went past. There was a light on in Flynn's study, but not a sound came out.

"I wanta see Dad," Liam said, and ran to the door.

"He might be busy," Sara warned.

But Liam pushed open the door. And Flynn, who was sitting at his desk with papers in front of him, turned, and his face lit up at the sight of his son.

"Dad!"

And Flynn opened his arms and Liam ran into them. In the hallway, Sara didn't move. But her gaze met Flynn's over the top of their son's head. Her throat was so tight she could barely swallow. His jaw worked.

"Sara—"

She turned away. "You have this time with him. Put him to bed. We need to leave at nine. I'll see you then."

And she bolted up the stairs without looking back.

At five minutes to nine she and Liam were standing in the entry hall with their luggage. O'Mally was there, looking worried. Liam was looking miserable. Dev had come through and given them both hugs.

"You'll be back," he told Liam and gave him a hard squeeze. "Or maybe I'll come and see you."

For the first time Liam looked a tiny bit eager. "When?"

Dev clearly hadn't expected to be put on the spot, but he thought a moment and said, "I could come in August."

"How long's that?" Liam asked.

"Two months."

Liam sighed at how long that was, but suggested, "And maybe you can bring O'Mally."

"Maybe," Dev agreed. He shifted awkwardly from one foot to the other, as if he wanted to leave but didn't know how.

"I'm sure you've got things to do," Sara said. "Get ready for those afternoon pony rides?" It hurt to say the words because those had been her idea.

He nodded.

She checked her watch. "Or maybe you can take us to the airport. If Flynn doesn't hurry up."

She hadn't seen him since she'd left Liam in his study last night. He wasn't there this morning. She'd seen no one at breakfast but Daisy and Eamon. She supposed the countess breakfasted in her room. Probably Abigail did, too. Flynn wasn't there, and his car wasn't out front as it usually was.

It was threatening rain. Dark clouds were pushing in. It would take them longer to get to the airport in the rain.

"He'll be here," Dev said.

But it was nine now and still no Flynn.

"How long will it take to get a taxi?" Sara asked.

"He'll come," Dev said again.

Sara tapped her foot, glanced at her watch. He wouldn't make her miss her plane, would he?

Would he?

And then, coming up the drive, she saw his car. He pulled in near where they all stood and got out. He looked resolute and grave. He wasn't smiling.

"Finally," Sara said. She wasn't smiling either. She thought she might never smile again.

"*Slan leat,*" Dev said. "So long."

Sara knew there was an appropriate Irish response, but she couldn't think of it. Couldn't think of anything now except keeping her composure and her resolution. "Bye, Dev." Then she turned to her son. "Get in the car, Liam."

He flung himself on O'Mally and hugged the dog fiercely.

Sara couldn't watch. "Our suitcases are in the entry," she said to Flynn. "I'll get them."

But he opened the trunk of the car, then turned on his heel and disappeared into the castle. Seconds later he returned with Liam's cases and stuck them in the trunk.

"Liam. Into the car. Now."

Another fierce hug of O'Mally. Sara hoped to God she didn't have to drag Liam off him. It didn't bear thinking about.

Flynn came back with her bags and stowed them alongside Liam's. He went back into the house.

"Liam!"

His face crumpled silently, but at last he dragged himself away from the dog and climbed into the backseat. There was a child's booster seat there so he could see out. But he didn't look. He just put his hands over his face.

Flynn came out with two more suitcases and shoved them into the trunk, then turned and headed into the castle again.

Sara frowned. She looked in the trunk, then glanced at her watch, then waited until he came out with two more suitcases. "These aren't mine." She gestured towards the last two he'd put in the trunk. "And those certainly aren't." She nodded at the two he carried.

"I know that." He brushed past her and wedged them into the trunk as well, then slammed the lid. "They're mine."

She stared. Birds sang. In the meadow one of Dev's horses whinnied. Far off she could hear some farm machinery chugging away. "I— What?"

She hadn't heard him. Or if she had, didn't understand him.

"I said they're mine. I'm coming with you."

"What!" She must have shouted because all of a sudden Liam was peering at them through the backseat window.

"I said, I'm coming with you. To Montana. To Elmer. Hell, I don't care where."

Sara felt faint. Now she truly didn't understand him. "You can't."

"Of course I can. I can do what I damn well please." It was his earl's voice again. But then he said, "I threw it over. Wrote a letter. Abdicated. Resigned. Whatever the hell you want to call it. You don't want me because of the earldom, then I don't want the bloody earldom."

"Don't be ridiculous! Of course you want it. You want to prove—"

"I'm done proving. I don't have to live my life trying to prove my old man wrong. I know he's wrong. I know I'm good enough. And I don't need to be earl to prove it. I just need to be the best man I can be." He paused, met her gaze squarely with his heart in his eyes. "And I'm the best man I can be when I'm with you."

And then it was raining. Or were those tears running down her cheeks? She didn't know. Didn't care. Only cared about him.

He was standing so still, rigid almost. So rigid that she nearly knocked him right over when she threw herself at him.

"Oh, Flynn!"

And his arms went around her, clasped her hard against him, held her as if she were his lifeline—the only thing that could save him.

"Sara," he said, his voice broken, then hopeful. "Sara?"

"I'm here," she whispered, and told the truth when she said, "I'm not going anywhere."

He kissed her then—and she kissed him back. She clung to him and they held each other and rocked each other and cried and it did rain then. A few drops at first and then harder and harder.

They didn't care. They didn't notice.

They didn't notice anything until a small hopeful voice asked, "Does this mean we aren't leavin'?"

Flynn's mother was in the entry when they came back into the house. She looked at her sopping-wet son and at Sara, their arms around each other's waists, and she actually smiled.

Sara blinked at the countess, then stared at her own reflection in the mirror. It was, as usual, wet and bedraggled and small. But it was standing in the embrace of the man she loved—who loved her. Together she knew they were big enough.

"A mother's duty is to look out for her son's future and his happiness," the countess said. "You, as Liam's mother, surely understand that."

Sara nodded. That was true.

"I didn't know you at all. My son—" she shot a despairing look at Flynn "—believes face-to-face conversations are essential for imparting important news. And he did not believe he should do so in front of an outsider. Abigail," she elucidated. "Who is a lovely girl, but obviously not for him."

"There is only one woman for me," Flynn said firmly.

"So I see," his mother said, and with a real smile this time, held out a hand to Sara. "He took Abigail to the airport this morning early. It's why he was late getting back."

Sara stared, still stunned by the turn of events. But she took the countess's hand and found it warm and soft, but with calluses on her fingers. Flynn's mother smiled at Sara's surprise.

"I can get my hands dirty, too," she said. "I garden. Perhaps I can help with some of your tours—if Flynn has persuaded you to stay."

"I'm not staying," Flynn said firmly. "I told you. If they won't let Dev take the title, then the hell with it—"

"Don't say that!" Sara interrupted fiercely. "Don't. And you can't give it up."

"I have. Or I will. I—"

"No. I don't want you to."

He stared at her and shook his head. "But you didn't want—"

"I didn't want to marry a man who thought I was only Liam's mother and a good business manager. I wanted to matter."

"You always mattered! My God, Sara. What do I call you? *A stór.* My heart. I'm not alive without you. The bloody earldom—"

"Is part of who you are. And I love the man you are. And we can go back to Elmer sometimes. I love Elmer. But I love you more."

"Me, too!" Liam said. He was grinning from ear to ear, his face streaked with tears and rain, too, his arm looped over an equally grinning O'Mally.

They were married in Elmer in August. The countess—"call me Minnie" she told the wedding guests—was an enormous hit.

"Better even than when Sloan married my mom," Sara said. She was lying in bed with the man of her dreams. The wedding reception was still going on in the village hall. When they'd left, the countess was doing a square dance with Loney Bates from the welding shop. "Because everybody knew Sloan already. No mystique. Your mother has mystique."

"Not as much as you," Flynn said. He couldn't believe he'd finally got his ring on her finger. It seemed like it had taken bloody years. Well, in a sense it had. Liam was nearly six.

"She's charming them all." She giggled.

"Sara," Flynn said in his Earl's Voice.

She stopped giggling. "What?"

"I refuse to spend my honeymoon discussing my mother."

Sara pretended to consider that. "Well," she said eventually, running her bare foot up his bare leg and nuzzling his shoulder at the same time (it was wonderful to be able to multitask), "do you have any better ideas?"

He groaned. "I imagine I can think of one or two." He rolled her onto her back and began to press kisses all over her. She wiggled and giggled and then, as his mouth began to work real magic on her, she arched her back and clutched at his shoulders.

"Flynn!"

"Mmm?" He kept kissing. Teasing. Tempting. Tasting.

"Ahhh." She reached for him, drew him in, felt the completeness she only knew with Flynn.

"Mmmm." And he began to move.

"You do have good ideas," she whispered as the rhythm quickened. She moved, too, caught up with him, savored him, sheltered him, shattered him. And together, the two became one. "Very good ideas," she murmured when she could finally speak.

"I'm glad you think so." Flynn's voice was a smile against her lips. "I'll love you forever, *a stór*. And I promise I've got lots more ideas where that came from."

THE FRENCH
ARISTOCRAT'S BABY

BY
CHRISTINA HOLLIS

Christina Hollis was born in Somerset and now lives in the idyllic Wye valley. She was born reading and her childhood dream was to become a writer. This was realised when she became a successful journalist and lecturer in organic horticulture. Then she gave it all up to become a full-time mother of two and run half an acre of productive country garden.

Writing Mills & Boon® romances is another ambition realised. It fills most of her time, in between complicated rural school runs. The rest of her life is divided between garden and kitchen, either growing fruit and vegetables or cooking with them. Her daughter's cat always closely supervises everything she does around the home, from typing to picking strawberries!

You can learn more about Christina and her writing at www.christinahollis.com.

CHAPTER ONE

AN awful racket bounced Gwen out of bed before she was fully awake. Stumbling around her bedroom in the afternoon heat, she tried to find her clock. When she did, it was silent. The ringing was coming from somewhere else. It must be her mobile. In horror, Gwen realised she had fallen onto the bed too exhausted to switch on her alarm. She had overslept, and was already at least an hour behind schedule. Now it sounded as if one of her few remaining members of staff was phoning about the evening shift. With growing dread, she searched frantically for her phone. Finally she tracked it down. It was in the pocket of her apron, at the bottom of her washing basket.

'Gwenno! What took you so long to answer the phone, love?'

For once, Gwen was glad her mother rang every day.

'Mam! It's great to hear from you, but this time I *really* can't stop—I've got my hands full, getting ready for this big flash party tonight. I was terrified you were one of the kitchen staff, calling in sick!' She gasped, and then made a face. Blurting out the truth to her mother like that was a big mistake. Everyone back at home had

to go on thinking she was making a success of her new
life. They *had* to... 'That is—I mean...I've got more
than enough people working for me, but each of them
has their own speciality. I can't afford to lose a single
person!' She finished in a rush, her fingers crossed. In
reality, Gwen was desperate to cut costs. Rather than
employ enough staff, she was currently doing the work
of at least three people. Trying to save money was costing her a lot. She was so exhausted, there had been a real
danger she might have dozed off during the party preparations. That was why she had dashed home to snatch
a twenty-minute nap in the middle of the day. She
checked her watch, and discovered with horror she had
been asleep for nearly an hour and a half.

'My God, I should be at the restaurant! We'll never
open in time! I've got so much to do!'

Dashing around the room, she tried to gather together
her clothes for the evening with one hand, while the
other clamped the mobile to her ear.

Gwen's mother had an answer for everything. This
disaster was no exception.

'You've told us all about your dozens of staff, Gwenno.
Let them start earning all that money you pay them!'

'Dozens of staff? Er...yes, yes, of course I have...it's
just that I like to do as much as I can myself. It's my
own fault for loving the job so much. I'm still not used
to being sole owner of the restaurant, and sometimes it
gets a bit much,' Gwen said quickly, the reply sounding
horribly false to her own ears. Was that a tinge of suspicion she heard in her mother's voice?

'We didn't lend you all that money to run yourself

into the ground, Gwenno. It was supposed to help you become Le Rossignol's chef-patron.' Mrs Williams said each foreign word carefully. 'See? We're all practising for when we come over to visit you!'

Gwen's heart hit the floor, but she managed to manufacture a careless laugh.

'Great! I can't wait to see you all again. It's been months!'

'It's been four months, three weeks and five days since you finally managed to buy the restaurant,' Mrs Williams said. She sounded almost as proud as Gwen felt, when she had the energy. 'And there was me and your dad worried to death you'd given up a good steady future with us in the shop to chase some silly dream!'

Gwen wanted to cry, but didn't dare. The thought of her family discovering the truth behind her supposedly successful new life in Malotte was more than her pride could stand. She was adamant she could make a success of the business, but times were hard. Every booking had to be treated with great care. Much to Gwen's disgust, that included tonight's reception for a hideous countess. The horrible woman only wanted to make a good impression on her rich stepson. She wasn't interested in Gwen's skill or the restaurant, merely in her own reputation.

Gwen could only hope the man in question would be more appreciative.

Etienne Moreau's day was equally busy, but his timetable ran according to his own schedule. That was exactly as he liked it. Even his social life now ran like clockwork, but he was increasingly finding socialising to be a sick joke these days. People considered his name a big attraction on a charity invitation list, so he sometimes felt obliged to give them what they wanted. *If only I weren't always surrounded by apple-polishers,* he thought, scrubbing long, strong fingers irritably through his thatch of dark hair. A proper conversation wasn't so much to ask, was it? He disliked having to be constantly on the lookout for lame-duck projects, or women on the make.

The country's grandest money men had invited Etienne onto their board of directors. Their idea had been to simply use his title to impress their shareholders, nothing more. Within days they had discovered their mistake. Etienne had been born into privilege, but that had never been enough for him. His late father had considered work undignified, but Etienne had never been satisfied to be simply a name on some headed notepaper.

He sighed. In exactly ninety minutes' time, a servant would be ready to step forward as Etienne descended the main staircase of his chateau. The man would insert a freshly picked carnation into his master's buttonhole before opening the front door. It had been the same in his late father's time, and for as far back as anyone could remember, so Etienne, albeit reluctantly, humoured his faithful staff. In one brief, heart-stopping moment a couple of years ago, he had imagined his own son and heir taking over, in his turn.

But that was before Etienne had learned the truth about a lot of things, including human nature. Now he focused only on his work, and his ruthless single-minded approach had resulted in endless successes. In fact, for a man with nothing to prove, Etienne was proving un-stoppable. A shame that even this was beginning to pall.

I need to find a new challenge, he thought. He had been brought up to slip smoothly into the role of Count of Malotte. Now he was actually in charge, the largely ceremonial role gave him too much time to brood. He wanted distraction. Perhaps this evening's engagement might offer something different?

Gwen showered and dressed in a flash. Unable to face the pile of unopened letters on her dressing table, she stuffed them into a drawer. Lately, they contained nothing but bad news. Her new life was turning out to have some hard, horrible moments, but she was determined not to give up. Opening her wardrobe, she took out the dress she would change into before the guests arrived at Le Rossignol that evening. Gwen's clients at her restaurant expected a total dining experience. That included ex-changing small talk with a calm and assured chef-patron. It was the only part of her job Gwen wasn't keen on, but it was turning out to be a very important source of new business. She had to persevere, and it was tough.

Gwen had always dreamed of becoming the chef in a top-class restaurant. She had managed it in record time by going into partnership with her best friend from catering college. Carys had supplied the glamour and business sense. Gwen had done the cooking, and kept her head down. Their system had worked perfectly, until her partner's romantic adventures had thrown the busi-ness into chaos. Carys had vanished, leaving Gwen high and dry. Unable to find another partner, Gwen had been faced with a stark choice. She could sell up and go home. That would mean admitting to her parents that 'The Le Rossignol affair', as they called it, was a big mistake. Or she could mortgage herself to the hilt and make her new life work, alone. One path led back to the safety of the village shop where she had been born. The other route disappeared into an unknown future, but at least it was her own. She would be independent, without the need to rely on other people.

Gwen had found it no real choice at all. She had spent sleepless nights trying to talk herself out of the mad idea, but in the end her dream had won. Instead of selling up, she had bought the balance of the business. Her family was convinced she was throwing good money after bad. Gwen had a horrible feeling they were right, but would never have admitted that in a million years. Besides, if she managed to pull it off she would have the satisfaction of saying, *I did it all myself.* She had always known it would be hard but now, all alone in a foreign country, there were times when she ached for a shoulder to cry on. One frantically busy day dissolved into another. Time was passing her by so fast. She sighed. Her greatest pleasure came from cooking the food, but she spent more time nowadays pandering to the people who ate it.

Carrying her dress downstairs, she laid it reverently on the back seat of her car. One eye on the time, she hopped into the driving seat and got another nasty shock. When she switched on the ignition, the car's petrol gauge barely moved out of the red zone. She groaned in horror. Not today, of all days! She didn't have time to stop off at the garage. She looked up at the bright cloudless sky, then down the winding country road towards town. It was downhill all the way to Le Rossignol. Maybe it was hot enough for the engine to run on fumes and good luck until she got there.

Five hours later, Gwen poured herself into her stunning dress. It was the only formal gown she had, and it was perfect for an aristocratic party. Cut from midnight-blue velvet, it clung to her generous curves in all the right places. She watched herself in the full-length mirror she had hung in her office to check her appearance at moments like this. Her soft blonde hair coiled like liquid gold over her bare shoulders. The effect was stunning, but Gwen wasn't impressed. All she saw was a girl from the Welsh valleys done up like a dog's dinner in a totally impractical dress that would show every mark.

That was exactly what the snooty countess of Malotte expected to see. With a long-suffering smile, Gwen went out to give her public what they demanded.

The restaurant's bar and lounge area was soon crowded. Girls hired for the evening moved among the glittering guests with trays of tempting titbits. Gwen's eyes darted around the room, looking for her client, the countess. Then her attention was grabbed by something far more interesting. A new arrival stood in the restaurant's entrance. Everything about him made her stop and stare. He surveyed the restaurant's crowded lounge bar with the haughty look of a general inspecting foot soldiers. It was an imposing sight. The newcomer was one of the

tallest there, and his austere good looks singled him out
in other ways, too. Everyone—absolutely everyone—
turned to watch as the mystery man walked in.

To Gwen's astonishment he headed straight for her.
Clusters of people standing around in the reception bar
parted to let him through.

'*Bonsoir*. You must be Gwyneth Williams.'

He dipped his head in greeting. The fact he knew her
name surprised her, and that wasn't all. She could feel
him penetrating her polite disguise. His gaze seemed to
recognise the social misfit within, and it made her nervous. She disguised her true feelings with a professional
smile and stepped forward to greet him.

'*Bonsoir, monsieur.* Yes, I'm chef-patron here. I'm
usually shut away in the kitchens, but tonight is a
special occasion.'

His dark eyes glittered like jet. 'Indeed. I had no idea
how special until a moment ago.' Charm flowed from
him as he caught her hand and lifted it to his lips. 'My
name is Etienne Moreau. I'm a frequent visitor to this
restaurant. I'm sorry we've never met before.'

Gwen was enchanted. Despite the dozens of people
surrounding them, he had the ability to make her feel
as though they were totally alone. After weeks of work
and worry, it felt as though all her Christmases had
arrived at once.

'Thank you! Would you care for a drink, Monsieur
Moreau?'

One of the waitresses moved forward, but Gwen
waved her away. For the first time, socialising was giving her something to enjoy. She swung around to the

other side of the bar, glad to have something to do. The
sight of a man like Etienne Moreau with his soft dark
hair and golden skin was enough to stun anyone into
silence. The countess Sophie, who was throwing this reception, had dropped some heavy hints about her
stepson's dislike of idle chit-chat. She had warned Gwen
to give him a wide berth. If there hadn't been a big
balance still outstanding on the party bill, Gwen would
have delighted in ignoring the instruction. Now there
was only the black marble bar between her and this
gorgeous man. It didn't feel like much in the way of protection when Etienne's dark eyes could cut through the
crowd like lasers. Gwen swallowed hard, reached for the
ice bucket and gripped it tightly. No wonder the countess Sophie was so protective of her stepson. All the
women within sight were drooling openly. The object
of their desires barely acknowledged them. Gwen tried
to behave in an equally offhand manner. She smiled
pleasantly at her stellar guest. No one could complain
if she was only serving the man. It was her job, after all.

'Excuse me, *monsieur,* what would you like?'

Etienne Moreau had paused to question a nearby
guest about a recent business deal. His attention instantly swung back to Gwen. He focused his gaze on her
as though she was the very last thing he expected to find
at a family party. With warm concentration, his pensive
brown eyes took in every detail from her tumble of
honey-blonde hair to the curves sculpted by her beautiful blue evening dress. After due deliberation, his in-
spection returned to her eyes. Then he smiled, and
Gwen's world stood still.

'I'd like something you could not possibly offer me over a crowded bar.'

The gentle lilt of his accent should have been relaxing. It had quite the opposite effect on Gwen. The wicked smile lighting his face turned her insides to jelly. She was used to fending off all kinds of trouble from men, but for the first time in her life she felt like meeting it head-on. The sensation made her smile right back at him. Her professional approach might hide the effect he was having on her, but it couldn't steady her voice.

'I—I mean, what would you like to drink, *monsieur*? Le Rossignol has a large selection of fine wines and spirits,' she said, trying to disguise her uncertainty by casually leaning forward against her side of the bar. His dark eyebrows rose in appreciation. Gwen's unspoken reply was to lean back again. He smiled.

'I'll have a *léger Colombien, s'il vous plaît*.'

Coffee was the very last thing Gwen served the sort of people who partied at Le Rossignol, not the first. Despite that, she was ready for anything. At one end of the bar was the best hot drink console she could afford. While she busied herself creating Etienne's coffee, Gwen was aware of him chatting idly with others at the bar, but she didn't hear a word. She was too busy enjoying the sensation of his interest running over her. Although she had her back to him, it was as tangible as a touch. When she turned around, his eyes were warm with possibilities. As she passed him the cup his glance flicked down to her left hand.

'*Merci, mademoiselle.* Won't you have one with me?'

'No, *monsieur.* I'm working.'

His beautiful white teeth flashed in a wicked smile. 'I suppose that means Sophie got to you first. She must have threatened to lay a curse on you, if you distracted me for too long.'

One look and those few words almost made Gwen forget everything she had ever known. Only thoughts of her overdraft stopped her melting into a quivering heap, right there in front of him.

'Not at all, *monsieur.* I'm on duty. To linger with one guest, however charming, would be unprofessional,' she said with an ease that felt anything but natural. 'And now, if you would excuse me, I must circulate.'

The smile Gwen gave him faltered as she saw the warmth in his eyes. Unable to meet the silent laughter dancing there, she left him with as much slow dignity as she could muster.

Etienne sipped his coffee. Darkening with thought, his eyes glittered as he watched her walk away. His companions at the bar were still talking, but he took only a polite interest.

'It didn't take you long to get over Angela, did it, Etienne?' One of the guests laughed, tracking his gaze.

The question brought Etienne back to the present with a jolt. His lip curled with a sneer of disdain. 'Sentiment is for women and children. I don't waste time on it.' Shrugging his shoulder nonchalantly, he pushed the empty coffee cup aside. 'Excuse me. I should go and have a word with the countess Sophie.'

Leaving the bar, Etienne strode away through the reception area without a backward glance. He wished the past could be ignored as easily as he could sideline people. Work sometimes dulled the edge of his pain, but never for long. It was so much easier to skim over the surface of life, moving on to the next sensation before he had too much time to think about it. He spent his days crowding his troubled mind with other people's money worries. When he was able to use his power and influence to help them, it gave him a sense of satisfaction but left his body restless. For hundreds of years the Moreau family had been warriors. Intellectually gifted, Etienne found balance sheets and bank reports easier to read than people—and far more honest. He preferred to use his mind for work and keep his body for more civilised things than warfare.

Right now he was wondering how quickly Miss Gwyneth Williams would surrender to his charm.

As usual, everyone wanted to talk to Etienne. It took him quite a while to track Gwen across the room. A little glance over her shoulder and a half-smile told him she knew he was watching her. That pleased him. It made up for the fact that his stepmother's niece Emilie was in attendance tonight. A plump, pretty girl dressed in a tight sheath of pink satin, she was standing a respectful distance behind the countess. As Sophie Moreau realised Etienne was on his way over, she eased Gwen aside and jostled the astonished Emilie forward. Etienne didn't need to wonder why. He shot a conspiratorial look at Gwen. There was a little crease between her brows as she spoke to the countess, but it disappeared as he caught her eye. Her beautiful face lit up with a mischievous smile, but she was playing hard to get. As he drew closer she disappeared into the kitchens. Etienne was left to corner his stepmother alone.

'Are you having trouble with the staff, Sophie? Would you like me to hunt that woman down and have a word with her?' he offered innocently.

The countess scowled. 'Certainly not. You aren't here to work, Etienne. You're here to tell your cousin Emilie what you think of her. Hasn't she grown?'

There were only two things in Sophie Moreau's favour: Etienne could read her like a book, and she always came straight to the point. Arching one dark eyebrow, he hid his distaste behind a pleasant smile. Lifting the young girl's hand to his lips, he gave it a formal kiss.

'You have, Emilie. How old are you now? It must be all of—sixteen, is it?'

'Eighteen! That's why you've agreed to be guest of honour at her birthday party, next month!' his stepmother hissed.

'I would never let a step-relative down.' Etienne inclined his head graciously at Emilie. The girl simpered, the restaurant's discreet lighting bouncing off her orthodontic scaffolding.

'Emilie will be leaving her boarding school at the end of next term. Unless you can think of a good reason to free her from the dreadful place before then, Etienne?' Sophie leered at him.

Feigning ignorance, Etienne waited.

'Unless…' The countess leaned forward, prompting him. Tiny beads of perspiration were visible on her faint moustache. She stopped squinting and started frowning.

'Oh, for goodness' sake, don't be difficult, Etienne! You need a son and heir to carry on the Moreau family line, and inherit all those beautiful houses of yours!'

Etienne sliced off Sophie's words with a fearsome glare. After a moment's alarm, she surged back with added venom. 'It must be two years since you got your fingers burned by that awful woman—you must think of the future, Etienne.'

'Why? You seem to be doing enough of that for both of us, *step*mother.' Etienne answered with crushing emphasis.

Out in Le Rossignol*'s* kitchens, preparations for dinner were running exactly on time. Everything was ready to go. It all looked immaculate. Gwen had lost count of the compliments her staff and the restaurant had been given as she moved among the guests. Even so, her nerves were in shreds. It didn't help to have the waitresses chattering like magpies with all the gossip they picked up as they circulated with drinks and canapés. As Gwen checked the silver salvers before they were carried out one of the regular waitresses passed on a particularly juicy titbit.

'*Madame* wants to make sure she carries on getting a share of Etienne's fortune after he marries. That's why she's trying to pair him off with her niece.'

'I've told you before, you mustn't pass on anything you hear, Clemence!' Gwen rebuked her, wiping a drop of champagne from one of the glasses. 'It would be horrible for a nice young girl like Emilie to find out people were talking about her.' However, Clemence's words sent evil thoughts flooding into her heart. Secretly, she turned green with envy at the idea.

'Don't worry, Chef, it'll never happen! You only have to read what they say about Etienne Moreau in the papers to know that—'

The doors leading into the restaurant opened, bringing another collection of empty trays for refilling and cutting off Clemence's shameful but undeniably interesting gossip. Beyond the traffic of waiters and waitresses, Gwen glimpsed the countess Sophie and her niece backing away from the impressive count. Clemence saw it too.

'Look—he's given them the brush-off. Now's your chance, Chef! Count Etienne is worth a fortune. He spends a lot in here, and he's our best tipper. Be nice to him!' Clemence said with a wink.

With alarm, Gwen found her heart thumping at the simple mention of his name. She found it hard enough to talk to clients at the best of times. To walk up to this gorgeous man would be impossible for her, unless she had an excuse, and something to hide behind. She found both at the bar. Keen to get opinions on a new Bordeaux she was thinking of putting on the wine list, she poured him a glass. As she carried it over she tried to distract herself from the warm, liquid feeling suffusing her body. It was no good. The magnetism of the count's slumberous dark eyes demanded her full attention. His expression made her forget any worries she might have had about her only formal dress. He liked it, she could tell. The classic cast of his features and the resolute line of his jaw marked him out as something really special. As she drew closer to him Gwen's body responded with an urgency she had never known before. She fought against a tide of desire that threatened to escape in a moan of longing. That scared her. This man was a total stranger, and she was a hard-working, down to earth woman. How could anyone sway her with such strong emotions at first sight? That thought alone was a powerful aphrodisiac.

A tingle of excitement ran along every nerve in her body. Nice girls like her weren't supposed to have irresistible physical yearnings like this. Nice girls stayed at home, minding the village shop. They didn't dress in midnight-blue velvet and gallivant about in front of foreign aristocracy. Gwen knew her family would be speechless at the mere thought of it. They had made enough fuss when her eldest brother Glyn married a girl from Bristol and moved across the river. Mrs Williams' sisters had always warned that Gwen had a wayward streak, and, with an unusual surge of devilment, Gwen wondered if they might be right…

Etienne's day had been totally predictable, but his evening was improving by the minute. He had given his stepmother something to think about, and now he was enjoying the sight of Gwyneth Williams bringing him a second drink. Although he visited Le Rossignol often, he'd never been lucky enough to meet her before. He had heard whispers about her, and they were all true. She really was worth watching. Her voluptuous charms were enhanced by the cut of an evening dress so beautiful, no other woman in the room was worthy of it. Its pacific-blue colouring and glorious texture made him want to reach out, to touch and possess. The sinuous way this woman moved through the crowds towards him made Etienne wish they were the only two people in the place…

He brought himself up short for even considering it. That disastrous liaison with Angela Webbington should have put him off ill-considered flings for life. But who wouldn't be tempted by the charms of a woman like this Gwyneth Williams? It was no wonder the gaze of every man in the place followed her. She had the perfect hour-glass figure—full, soft breasts and a beautifully defined waist emphasising the smooth curve of her derriere. When she reached him and lifted those long dark lashes to reveal the clear beauty of her azure eyes, Etienne re-discovered the full physical meaning of the words 'sexual chemistry'.

'You've been very generous to my staff in the past, *monsieur*. Allow me to offer you this, with the compliments of Le Rossignol.'

Her words lilted like music. They had an immediate effect on Etienne. A powerful chain reaction coursed through his muscular body, coiling in his groin ready for action. She passed him the glass. Their fingers touched for an instant, but before they could exchange any words Gwen was called away. Etienne watched her go, his unwanted drink forgotten. As she passed by a gaggle of male guests one of them said something to her. Etienne was too far away to hear what it was, but saw her round on the man with icy disdain. Roses flared in her otherwise pale cheeks. Etienne instantly began moving forward. Although Gwen looked to be coping, he knew you could never be sure in situations like this.

Gwen counted to ten silently, thinking of the final demand notices she had at home. She had to pander to these awful people. Their word of mouth recommendations were vital if her business was to survive.

'You're wasted in the kitchen!' The groper smirked. 'You look like you're sitting on a fortune, *bonbon*. How about it?'

In one swift movement he stuffed a five-hundred-Euro note into her cleavage.

Gwen's brittle smile was for public consumption only. She pulled out the banknote and dropped it onto the floor.

'I've got plenty more where that came from,' the man scoffed.

'I'm so glad, *monsieur*,' Gwen managed with dignity. Turning her back on the group, she walked back into the safety of her kitchens. Her head was held high. When she looked like that, the staff went quiet.

'Ask Eloise to check the guest list,' she announced into the relative silence. 'She can put a marker on the names of those men sitting beside the aquarium. In future we're going to be fully booked whenever they ring for a reservation. I won't have men who behave like that at Le Rossignol—we don't need them,' she stated, with more conviction than she felt. Right now her business was balanced on such a knife-edge she couldn't afford to turn anyone down. She had to take so much care not to upset her rich clientele. They all knew each other, and word travelled around their clique at the speed of light. The rich stuck together in their own little world. People like her were expected to fetch and carry, and take all the flak. It was so unfair.

It was a relief for Gwen to retreat from the social whirl into the organised chaos backstage. This was the world she knew, and a place where she was in total control. Outside in the restaurant she was expected to be constantly charming and beautiful—something ornamental rather than useful. Here in the noise and movement of the kitchens, she could be herself. She could concentrate on producing the best and most beautiful meals her customers would ever experience. Until that evening, the satisfaction of a job well done had been enough for her. But now something threatened to come between Gwen and her work.

She had been introduced to something—or rather, *someone*—far more potent. Etienne Moreau was already affecting her behaviour. As she'd confronted that drunk she had known the handsome count was watching her. A situation that made her feel like running for the hills had had to be faced in a way she knew would impress him. She needed him to see her in action as the perfect hostess, and totally in control.

Because whenever she glanced in his direction, control was the last thing on her mind.

Etienne saw Gwen's confrontation with her guests, and how she handled it. It was quite obvious Le Rossignol's chef-patron was a woman who knew her own mind. He admired the cool way she managed to defuse the situation herself. *Defuse but not disarm*, he thought, making a mental note to mention the bad behaviour he had seen to some of his more influential friends. He recognised the villains, and they would find themselves excluded from society's more discerning events from here on in. *Not that it's any of my business,* he warned himself, annoyed that the little drama should have unsettled him so much.

For once, when his stepmother begged to parade him in front of a few more of her friends, he was glad of the distraction. While she was busy showing him off, she couldn't return to her favourite subject of what a superb wife and countess her niece would make. That alone would have been a good enough reason to submit to a tour of the gathering, but Etienne had a darker motive. He wanted to keep an eye on the lovely Gwyneth Williams. A natural at moving through polite society, Etienne could appear perfectly charming while his mind was occupied with something else. Tonight, there was only one thing concerning him. Covertly, he watched Gwen as she went about her work. When the rowdy group of men summoned her again he stiffened, noticing a subtle change in her attitude. Her beautiful, heart-shaped face was a carefully managed mask of indifference, but tension was obvious in her rigid bearing and hesitant footsteps. The second she got close enough, one of the group reached out as though ready to paw the smooth curve of her rump. Gwen leapt away with a cry but before she could say anything more Etienne was there, confronting her attacker.

'Leave her alone,' he commanded.

'Says who?' The young man lumbered to his feet. It was obvious he had been drinking before he arrived at the restaurant, and was now well beyond the stage of either good manners or good sense.

'I do.' Etienne's voice was as cold as a blade, and he felt no need to identify himself by the age-old title of

Count of Malotte. Tonight, everyone who was anyone knew who he was.

'Like I care about that!' The drunk swayed, then without warning took a swing at Etienne. Gwen shouted a warning, desperate to save the handsome stranger who had stepped in on her behalf. It was the worst thing she could have done. Distracted by her cry, Etienne was a split second too slow to avoid catching a glancing blow to the side of his jaw.

The party erupted in a flurry. In one smooth movement Etienne seized the drunk and pinioned his arms behind his back.

'Let this be a warning to anyone else with a taste for trouble,' he announced to the crowd as he frogmarched his attacker out of the building. Everyone stared after him. Gwen could not move. If she took one step she knew she would fly straight to the door, desperate to know what was happening. That would make a bad situation worse for her sophisticated guests. Instead, she had to wait along with everyone else. Minutes passed in silence. Then suddenly Etienne was there among them again. Breathing quickly, his dark curls tousled, he acknowledged the spontaneous applause with a diffident smile.

'Your cheek is bleeding,' Gwen said faintly, transfixed by the sight of a thin seam of blood trickling over the otherwise perfect surface of his sun-bronzed skin.

He stopped adjusting his clothes and looked at her.

'There's no need to sound so worried, *mademoiselle*,' he murmured, as though not quite able to believe what she had said.

The strange way he spoke made Gwen think this man

wasn't used to being worried about—not on a personal level, at least. People might bow and scrape before him, but she had a shrewd suspicion they were only out for what they could get, like the countess. A surge of empathy kicked her into action. She knew what it was like to put on a brave show, and she might never get a chance to see such a gorgeous guy at close quarters again.

'Of course there is, *monsieur*. Health and safety would never forgive me for standing by while one of my clients bled all over the place!' she rallied. With a smile, she gestured towards the back of the restaurant. 'Would you mind stepping into my office?'

Her heart was thundering loudly as she spoke. She was amazed he couldn't hear it, and still more amazed at the devastating way he smiled and said, 'Nothing would give me greater pleasure, *mademoiselle*.'

And with that he headed straight for the door marked 'Mlle G Williams—Private.'

CHAPTER TWO

GWEN was busy wondering what she was going to do, now she had persuaded one hundred and eighty pounds of handsome hunk into her office.

The sight of Etienne standing outside on the balcony almost robbed her of the courage to go in. Silhouetted against the setting sun, his broad shoulders and tall, erect frame looked magnificent.

'*Entrez,*' he commanded.

Etienne Moreau was unlike any man Gwen had encountered before, but hearing him speak to her like that came as a shock. Her reply was instant and instinctive. 'I was going to, *monsieur*. It's my name on the door, isn't it?'

He whipped around, as fast as her retort. Gwen didn't have time to be alarmed. Astonishment became amusement as he focused on her face, and laughed.

'Of course. What was I thinking of?' he said with a winning smile.

Gwen had no idea. He was filling her mind with so many disturbing thoughts. It was all she could do to stop her legs trembling as she walked through the room towards him.

'I've retrieved your wine, *monsieur*. And can I thank you for dealing with that drunk? It was so brave. You didn't deserve to get hurt,' Gwen said as she stepped through the French doors and joined him on the balcony.

'Ordinarily I wouldn't have done. He was wearing one of those cameo rings idiot boys have taken to wearing. That's what did the damage.'

As he took the glass of Bordeaux from her the town below exhaled a warm breath into the evening air. It lifted the curtains behind her. Light flooding out from the office illuminated the ragged cut to his cheek. Gwen was transfixed.

'*Merci,*' he said softly.

'What about that cut?' she managed eventually, her mind whirling with the tiniest details of it. 'I'll fetch the first-aid kit—'

'That won't be necessary.'

The same commanding tone that had summoned her into her own office drew her hand up to his face.

'Oh, but you must at least let me clean it up for you—' Unable to resist, she touched the spot lightly. Her fingers came away dark with blood. With a little gasp of dismay she swayed, accidentally brushing against him. 'I'm sorry, *monsieur*,' she muttered.

Etienne Moreau knew an advantage when he saw one. A smile spread across his face with all the promise of a new day dawning.

'Are you, *mademoiselle?* I'm not. It's brought us together.'

'H-has it?'

Her eyes were wide and very blue, he noticed. It occurred to him that shock must have thrown the sophisticated chef-patron off her stride. The delicate fragrance of roses shimmering around her aroused something primitive in him. There was only one thing to be done. He decided to make everything all right for her, in the way he knew best. After months of growing discontent, this evening was turning into something memorable for him. He glanced at the wine in his hand. The last thing he needed now was alcohol. It might bring him back to earth.

He put the glass down.

A furious tide had engulfed him when he saw that lecherous drunk hassling her. Seeing such a man getting so close to this lovely girl was an outrage. She deserved much better. And now he was alone with her. Desire flamed within his body, fuelled by the purity of her clear blue eyes and those soft, slightly glossed lips. He hungered for her with a raw, naked need that would not and could not be denied.

'Is there anything else you need, *monsieur*?'

Her voice was a whisper, her eyes full of anticipation.

'Yes,' he breathed. 'You.'

She gazed up at him. Her eyes were large and full of questions Etienne could not wait to answer. His body took control, pulling her into his arms and holding her tightly against him. Gwen was in the grip of feelings so powerful that she simply melted against him. His hands went to her hair, his fingers digging through its thick tumble of soft, caramel-coloured curls. Tipping her head back, he feasted his eyes on her face. Uncertainly, she mirrored his movements, raising her hands to the lush darkness of his hair. It was short and silky, tempting her fingers to explore him with the same overpowering need that fuelled his desire. When his beautiful mouth took possession of hers it was with a passion that powered straight through her body.

Gwen had never experienced anything like it. Etienne Moreau overwhelmed her with such fire and urgency that she felt like a leaf in a hurricane. Her heart pounded, while her mind became a perfect storm of images—his tongue penetrating her mouth, his hands luring her onwards until he withdrew, teasing her. Gwen was left quivering from head to foot, at the mercy of so many sensations her brain could hardly cope. Hungry for his kisses, she rose on tiptoe, desperate not to lose contact with his body for an instant. Teased into peaks of excitement, her nipples thrust against the lacy restraint of her bra until it hurt. He was filling her senses so totally she barely noticed. She no longer knew or cared what was right or wrong.

Suddenly the wail of a police siren tore through the streets below, startling them both, and they jerked apart. Once she was deprived of the hard temptation of him, arousal flooded Gwen's brain until speech was almost beyond her.

She looked up at him, still dazed, as he allowed his hands to drop lightly onto her shoulders and gently eased her away from him. Then he stepped back and looked down at her. His lips were slightly parted. She could see from the quick rise and fall of his chest that he was breathing fast. The arms that had held her so tightly now hung loosely by his sides, his hands and their long, strong fingers slightly curved. Her eyes took in every detail of him, from his hawk-like profile and the glint of perfect white teeth against the pale gold of his skin, to his easy stance. Here was a man who took women in his stride. As she slowly returned to earth after their paradise of a kiss a sudden increase in the clatter of silver and china from inside the restaurant dealt the final blow to her dreams. Dinner was being served. She had abandoned her staff when they needed her most. Kissing a man when she should have been supervising them was bad enough. When that man was also a guest and probably a friend of her landlord, her guilt became a real wall of worries.

Gwen had brothers. She knew what men were like. The thought that this aloof man with the smouldering eyes might tell Nick, her landlord, about their kiss made her feel sick. Nick and his family had been good to her, letting her buy out the business for a good price. They had taken a loss on the deal, but it had still cost Gwen everything she'd had and hefty loans from her parents and the bank. Nick was still owner of the little *gite* in the hills where she was staying. His rich, influential friends were Le Rossignol's best customers, so she needed to stay on the right side of them. This was not the way to do it.

A breeze sighed over the balcony, but this time it was chill. It reminded Gwen of the groans of 'I told you so' waiting for her back at home if her dream of running a top-class restaurant in France failed.

Etienne's face was expressionless; he seemed to have

retreated from her. 'This was an accident. Accidents happen,' he said in a low voice.

Gwen tried to catch her breath. It wouldn't be held, and escaped as a sigh. His attitude should have come as a relief to her. Instead it left an aching void. She wanted this man to want her, in exactly the same hot, heady way she wanted him. It nearly sent her over a precipice of temptation. Colour flared in her normally pale cheeks. What had possessed her to do a thing like that? With his relentless masculinity close enough to touch, that was an easy question to answer. Etienne's body was a powerful incentive for Gwen to behave in a way she would never have dreamed possible. He roused her to fever pitch, but now he was leaving behind a burning ache for him, deep within her body.

'Tension expresses itself in many ways,' he added. A tiny muscle flinched in his jaw as he spoke.

The tilt of his chin and that macho dismissal told Gwen all she needed to know. Now she understood why Clemence had warned her about this man. He was the sort who took what he wanted, without offering anything in return. He would never feel the need to feign interest in her as a thinking, feeling human being.

'I discovered long ago that money and manners don't often go together, *monsieur*,' she said icily. 'I'm certainly not proud of this little interlude either, I can assure you.'

Picking up his forgotten glass, she started towards the French doors.

'But I am.' Etienne's voice was low with amusement and he seemed to have recovered his wicked smile, as if the odd tension that had covered him a moment ago had been shrugged away. 'It's in my blood, *cherie*. You are irresistible. I succumbed to your charms. What better reason for pride could there be?' he finished in a throaty whisper.

Gwen gave a huff of disapproval at that, but she was hiding a blush as she hurried away. Those words of his would echo in her head for the rest of her life. *He called me irresistible!* she marvelled. No one had thought to give her such a compliment before. Five feet three with a tumble of unruly honey-blonde waves, she felt too short and shapely to turn heads. Her bright blue eyes with their long dark lashes were a good feature, there was no denying it. *But irresistible? Me?* she wondered, wishing she could believe him. There was no doubt she had preened before her bedroom mirror when she had first tried on this stunning dress, but that had been behind a securely locked door. Now the delectable Etienne Moreau had kissed her, and complimented her. Much more of his talk and she might—just *might*—start believing it!

There was no time for Gwen to try out her budding self-confidence. As she left her office the countess Sophie steamed towards her with an evil glint in her eyes.

'I hope you aren't annoying my stepson,' she warned, a purplish stain flushing through her thick layers of face powder and blusher. 'He doesn't take kindly to being manhandled by the lower orders.'

If only you knew! Gwen thought. The lovely Etienne hadn't been showing any signs of prejudice a few moments earlier.

'I took the count a drink, showed him where the first-aid kit was and thanked him for saving me from unwanted attention. That's all, *madame*,' Gwen said boldly.

The fat, bejewelled countess looked down her fleshy nose at Gwen. 'Good. I hope this sort of thing doesn't happen often. I expect better from a place that charges so much.'

With that, she swept away to the sympathetic company of her grand friends. Gwen felt her eyes filling with furious tears. She pressed her lips together tightly, to stop a vicious retort bursting out. Her bills couldn't be paid until she had banked the balance of this awful woman's invoice. All the loathsome countess had to do in her pampered life was sign cheques and authorise payments. Gwen earned every cent of her money. To get it, she had to smile politely all evening while being bullied and generally treated like dirt by her so-called 'betters'. One of her mother's favourite sayings came back to haunt her: *'The rich get all the pleasure, the poor get all the pain'*.

She bolted into the kitchens. For the rest of the evening she worked behind the scenes, unless it was absolutely vital for her to emerge as the glamorous hostess. She understood cooking and loved it. Socialising was a part of her life she was really beginning to hate.

For the past two years, Etienne had been living under a heavy cloud of memories. His relentless lifestyle of work and partying was a reaction to it. He had been dead to pleasure for so long, something as simple as that reckless moment with Gwen should never have been able to lighten his mood. Yet somehow it had. There was something about her so unlike the others; it made him smile to think about it. He knew he should be wary, but it was difficult to forget the girl's proud assurance that she wouldn't be boasting of the experience. Etienne had been burned by kiss-and-tell merchants in the past. He knew the way they worked. That, and the fact she kept to her kitchen for most of the rest of the evening, made this little *mademoiselle very* unusual. As he circulated and made polite noises to his friends and acquaintances Etienne kept half an eye on the kitchen doors. Whenever she came out, she would scan the party, but when she made eye contact with him she always blushed and looked away. He wasn't about to put her on the spot by approaching her again. That would only encourage Sophie to get up on her hind legs. He was content to appreciate the divine Mademoiselle Williams from a distance. Her rare appearances made an otherwise dull evening worthwhile. To his surprise he found himself totally unable to take his eyes off her.

It was a long time since any woman had done *that*.

Eventually, the happy racket out in the restaurant died down. Chauffeured limousines queued up outside to collect their glamorous owners. Gwen pasted on her sociable smile, and went out to wish each and every one of them a good night. She looked forward to gazing up at Etienne one last time, but she was to be disappointed. The whisper around the kitchens was that he had left earlier with a few friends. Gwen was quick to stop her staff gossiping, but that didn't prevent her listening to what they said. Apparently the more restless spirits had gone on to an exclusive casino in town.

A long time later, Gwen said goodbye to the last of her staff. Then she locked the door with a thankful sigh. As usual, she was the last to leave. Checking that everything was spotless after the party and ready for the next opening took a long time. With no money to pay more than a skeleton staff, Gwen always tried to make life as easy as possible for them all. Once she was sure the whole place was perfect, she checked again. Her upbringing had convinced her that you couldn't be too careful when profits were being squeezed like a ripe Jaffa orange. Work absorbed so much of her time that her high standards were allowed to slip a bit once she locked the restaurant door behind her. There was never enough energy left after work for perfection in her everyday life. It didn't usually matter, but tonight it was destined to come back and haunt her.

The downward spiral began when she put the key into the ignition of her little car. The engine had to be coaxed into life, and the reason was easy to remember from earlier that afternoon. The petrol gauge was now well into the danger zone. Gwen dropped her head onto the steering wheel and groaned. She had meant to pop out before the garage closed and fill up, but there hadn't been time. Now it was far too late to try. She wondered briefly about going back into her office and trying to sleep on the floor. Her nice comfy bed called too loudly, so she abandoned that idea. All she wanted to do was get home. She pointed her tiny Citroen in the right direction and hoped for the best.

It was a bad idea. The car spluttered to a halt halfway up the twisting mountain road leading to her rented cottage. With a sigh, she nosed it up onto the verge. Unlocking its boot, she grabbed the petrol can. There was barely an eggcup full of fuel inside it. A couple of weeks earlier she had given the contents to one of the waiters to top up his moped. She had totally forgotten to refill the can.

Gwen was faced with a long, dark walk home. Locking the Citroen, she started off. With no one to blame for the situation but herself, she tried to make the best of it. During the day, the views from this road over the Mediterranean were spectacular. At night the uphill journey was breath-robbing rather than breath-taking, although there were compensations. A million stars speckled the sky from one horizon to the other. If that wasn't enough to take Gwen's mind off her blistered toes, the nightingales that gave her restaurant its name were in full song. It was the perfect opportunity to let her mind wander back to that breathtaking kiss with the man who had called her irresistible.

Her head was so full of romance she was only dimly aware of a wholly man-made sound attacking the peace and quiet of the hillside. It took the blazing spotlights of a fast car to bring her to her senses. She jumped off the road in panic, but the vehicle slowed dramatically. Drawing level with her, it paused. The driver opened his door and hailed her.

'Ah, *c'est le chef anglais*! Where are you going on such a dark and lonely night?'

It was him. Etienne Moreau. Gwen was hardly able to believe it. He was behind the wheel of a sleek, low, sports car and with relief she saw he was alone. To have met the gorgeous Etienne with another woman so soon after that wonderful kiss would have been unbearable.

'I'm on my way home. My car broke down.' Gwen smiled ruefully, hoping he wouldn't want details. This was the man who called her irresistible. She didn't want her fantasy wrecked by hearing him call her an airhead for running out of petrol.

'The red Citroen C1 with the parking scrapes and missing offside wing mirror, parked half a kilometre back?'

Gwen nodded, trying not to look pained. That was all she needed. A fantasy man so perfect he knew enough about cars to recognise an idiot when he saw one.

'Get in. I'll give you a lift.'

Gwen looked over his impressive car as it purred contentedly beside her. And then the look in his eyes. They mirrored his words, after that brief moment of passion… *You are irresistible…*

Panic overwhelmed her. It was one thing to fantasise about a man. With her dream threatening to come true, she felt totally inadequate.

'N-no—it's OK. I'm fine. Totally. I'm nearly home. I couldn't possibly…'

The wider he smiled, the faster her voice dwindled.

'Nonsense. Get in. How could I let you walk any further on those stilettos, and still call myself a gentleman?' he added with perfect logic, casting an appreciative glance at Gwen's small, shapely feet. They were peeping out from beneath the hem of her dress as she held it up, away from the long grasses of the verge. She let her hands fall, freeing the folds of material to hide her painfully impractical shoes.

'So—will you accept a lift from me now?'

Gwen sighed. Her feet did hurt, the road was long and dark and Etienne's warm car, not to mention the man himself, looked wonderfully appealing.

'Thank you. That's very kind.' It was tricky keeping the apprehension out of her voice.

Without a word, Etienne took the magnum of champagne that was propped up on the passenger seat. 'You'll be a much more interesting companion than this, *ma chef anglais*. I won it in a charity auction! Perhaps I will donate it as a prize somewhere else.' He laughed as he got out of the car and walked around to where Gwen stood. Filling her arms with the heavy foil-wrapped bottle, he opened the car door for her. Gwen thanked him with a smile.

Getting into the confined space of the passenger seat was another trial. It sharpened her nerves to the point where she had to say something to cover her embarrassment. 'Although I should tell you, *monsieur*, I'm Welsh, not English.'

'Ah, that explains it.' Etienne nodded sagely, slipping into the driver's seat beside her. He paused, one hand on top of the steering wheel.

'Before we start, give me your keys. I'll arrange for someone to collect your car, and get it fixed.'

'Thank you, that's really kind,' Gwen muttered, glad he would never see the tell-tale bill. When she was safely belted in, he pushed his sports car into gear and powered on up the hill.

She watched him, her eyes narrowed.

'Why should the fact that I'm Welsh explain anything, Count?'

Etienne gave her a lazily superior smile. 'That rebellious streak of yours…the way you chose to try and walk home in those ridiculous little shoes instead of phoning someone for help… I should have guessed. And don't bother using my title,' he added casually. 'In my experience, people who call me by it are only looking to gain some advantage.'

Gwen felt slightly affronted, having never tried to gain anything from anyone in her life. 'OK, Monsieur Moreau.'

'It's Etienne.' His voice crackled, then softened as he asked, 'Where do you live?'

'I'm staying in Nick's *gite*, right at the top of the hill. You can drop me anywhere that's convenient for you.'

'And you are his fiancée's best friend, Gwyneth.' Etienne's accent turned her name into something beautiful and exotic, but his words were an accusation.

Gwen stiffened. No matter how gorgeous he was, she couldn't stop herself reacting angrily.

'I was his *ex*-fiancée's *ex*-best friend. And, please call me Gwen!'

'*Dommage*!' He inhaled sharply. 'That's some reaction. What caused the split between you?'

Gwen wondered where to start. She felt like blaming Carys for all her problems, but that wasn't entirely fair. Nobody had held a gun to Gwen's head and made her buy out Nick and Carys' share of the business. 'Well, she upset Nick *and* eighteen months' worth of arrangements by running off with another man on the very day of their wedding. She's cost me a fortune by abandoning our partnership, and I'm so shattered I hardly know what day it is any more.'

She hadn't meant to sound so resentful, but it was impossible not to warm to her theme. Etienne glanced at her. Despite the darkness, he was clearly shocked.

'What happened to the unbreakable bonds of sisterhood? All for one, one for all, and take the man for everything he's got?'

'I'm old-fashioned,' Gwen said primly. 'I expected our business partnership to be like marriage—forever. And an engagement is almost as binding—certainly when it gets all the way to the big day.'

'Are you saying you would rather see your best friend trapped in marriage to a worthy, predictable man like Nick, rather than let her follow her heart?'

'I'd rather things were exactly as they were, with Carys still my partner. She knew what Nick was like before she agreed to marry him. Why did she have to take off like that, all of a sudden? She left me right in the lurch,' Gwen grumbled, heaving another huge sigh. 'I thought she was resigned to life with Nick. I'd always told her not to expect carnivals when he was in town, but she wouldn't listen!'

'That isn't what I told Nick when he asked me to be his best man,' Etienne growled. He was staring straight ahead at the road and gripped the steering wheel with both hands for once.

Gwen was amazed. 'I never saw you at the supposed wedding?' she ventured.

That day, she had hardly seen anyone beyond her crew of catering staff. She had been determined to put on the perfect reception as well as acting as bridesmaid, but one thing was certain. However busy, she could never have missed seeing Etienne. He would have stood head and shoulders over the rest of the guests in every meaning of the phrase.

'Like Carys, I cancelled at the last moment. My father's funeral was held on the same day.'

'Then I'm sorry,' Gwen said quietly.

Etienne made a small gesture of acceptance, but added, 'Thank you, but my father the late count was nearly ninety. He died peacefully, in his sleep.'

'All the same, it must have been a horrible experience for you.' Gwen fell silent. For once, she was wishing her own family weren't so far away.

'And?' He prompted, when she had been lost in thought for some time.

Puzzled by the questioning note in his voice, she looked at him. He pierced the shadowy interior of the car with a sly grin. In reply she frowned and shook her head in a silent appeal for more details.

'This is where you ask me what he left.'

'Do I? Why?' Genuinely confused, Gwen picked up her handbag as Etienne turned his car into the narrow driveway leading to her home.

'Because that's what single women always do when they meet me.'

Gwen paused as the cold, hard meaning of his words sank in. They were weighed down by the resignation in his voice. Here was a man who had everything— looks, style, a title, the money to back it all up—and no doubt all the hangers-on that came with such privileges.

'Oh, dear. You're almost making me feel sorry for you a second time!' She chuckled self-consciously. 'And there was me about to invite you in for coffee, to thank you for running me home. I'll bet your fan club all do *that*, too!' She tried to laugh off the confession. To her surprise, he joined in.

'Yes. Until tonight, I've always refused—but for one night only, I might allow myself to be tempted by a chef-prepared *café noisette*—and perhaps a little something to go with it?' he added in a wicked whisper.

The intimacy in his voice stroked a finger of desire all the way down Gwen's spine. Accepting a lift from a strange man was right out of character for her. Inviting him into her home was something else again.

It must be the season for taking risks.

She drew in a long, slow breath. The sophisticated tang of his aftershave bolstered her courage until she was able to speak with hardly a tremble in her voice.

'If you're sure an invitation wouldn't be too predictable?'

'You're doing the inviting. It's your call, Gwen.'

Her mouth went dry. He was putting her in the driving seat, but she had never felt so close to losing control. When she spoke, she could only manage a faint whisper.

'I wanted to thank you for saving me tonight, not only from that…' she had to choose her words carefully, in case the drunk was one of Etienne's friends or relatives '…guest, but from a long walk home, as well. That's two rescue missions in one evening. It seems only fair to offer you coffee.'

'Then the least I can do is to accept.' He smiled, and the starlight seemed to dance in his eyes. Gwen was overwhelmed. It took a lot of concentration to get out of the car, find her house key and open the door. She was trembling with sheer amazement at what was happening. Etienne Moreau could stop her heart simply by looking at her. She had thought she would never see him again after the party—but here he was, coming into her house to drink coffee!

She groped for the light switch and pressed. Nothing happened. Etienne was following her closely. Although the thought of him so close behind her was wickedly tempting, she kept moving. The bulb in the hall must have blown, and she had to reach the wall lights before either of them stumbled in the dark. She clicked the second set of switches. There was still nothing. A little breeze followed them into the house and sent a sheet of paper flickering off the telephone table. Gwen clapped a hand to her face in horror as she remembered what it was. The electricity bill. How long had she been promising herself she would get around to paying it? Too long, as far as the electricity company was concerned.

Etienne bent down and picked it up.

'Is this important?' It was too dark for him to read inside the house, so he stepped back outside. Gwen darted after him, but she was too slow.

Glancing at the bill, he made sympathetic noises. 'So this means we'll be drinking chilled champagne rather than hot coffee!' He shrugged. 'I can live with that.'

'No—I'm sorry, I can't possibly invite you in when I've got no power!' Gwen peered around helplessly in the gloom for inspiration. 'But if you were desperate for a drink, I could light a fire in the old range and boil a pan of water on that—'

She stumbled to a halt in the face of his devastating smile. This had been the perfect chance to spend a little while longer basking in it. She had blown it. He wouldn't want to sit in a dark house. Every second in his company was worth losing a whole night's sleep, but it was slipping away through her fingers. Gwen cursed herself silently.

'I'm such a fool—first the car, and now this!' she announced, already moving towards the front door again. 'I'm so sorry I can't offer you anything, Etienne.'

She was getting ready to close the door behind him when he left, but he stayed where he was.

'Let me be the judge of that, Gwen. Why don't we talk about it over champagne at my place instead?'

His voice was as soft as a breeze moving through the pine trees outside.

Gwen had been busily covering her disappointment by fussing with the door. At his words she stopped. Maybe there was a God in heaven after all! She was getting a second chance. For a heartbeat she allowed herself to experience the fierce thrill of anticipation. Then reality supplied a quick cold shower.

'You don't know how much I'd really love to, Etienne, but I shouldn't…'

'I know,' he crooned, his voice warm with understanding. 'So let's go.'

Reaching out, he caught hold of her hand. His palm was as smooth and warm as his seduction technique.

Gwen's body tried to follow him, but her mind was weighed down with responsibilities.

'Oh, Etienne, I *can't*…maybe we should just say goodnight and leave it at that…' She managed to hang back, but disappointment trailed from her every word. 'I'm so sorry, but I need to be up early. It's another really busy day tomorrow and I have to be on top form…'

He let go of her hand. Looking down, he directed his expression of burning intensity straight into her soul. But when he spoke, his words were directed more to himself.

'I've stumbled on a woman who would put an early night before coffee with me?' he said slowly.

He seemed taken aback, musing over what had obviously never happened before. Gwen smiled.

'Believe me, Etienne, it's a tough call. But don't worry. Your reputation as a ladies' man is completely intact. Nothing would have persuaded me to miss out on coffee with you—apart from a seven a.m. delivery to Le Rossignol.'

His roguish smile completely overwhelmed her, and he took her hand a second time. 'I'll have someone deal with the delivery. After all, you must admit that coffee and conversation would round off the evening perfectly?' Leaning forward, he whispered softly in her ear. 'Very few people refuse me.'

His dark eyes were teasing her and his beautiful mouth tempted her even more than his words. He was good—*very* good. Gwen felt herself waver. Would it be so bad? Just for one night—to be a little irresponsible?

Her hesitation was all it took to make Etienne smile again and Gwen melted. She forgot all her money

worries—some things were beyond price and she gave
a slow nod of assent.

Releasing her hand, Etienne flipped the car keys out
of his pocket and began to walk away from the house.
When Gwen didn't follow him instantly, he stopped
and faced her.

Watching him warily, Gwen ran her hand up and
down the edge of the door. He raised a mocking brow.

'What's the hold-up? Why are you looking at me
like that?'

She moved uncomfortably inside her seductively
sleek velvet dress.

'I'm still not quite sure…this is all so sudden…'

'Shh!' Laughing, Etienne put a finger to his lips.
Then he reached out and caught her by the hand again.
'You talk too much, Gwen. Don't build obstacles where
there aren't any. Merely accept what I'm offering.'

Oh, if only…she thought.

CHAPTER THREE

WITHIN seconds, Gwen locked up and bounced into the passenger seat of his car. She was breathing fast, and he noticed.

'Do I make you nervous, Gwen?' His smile flashed very white in the darkness as he nosed his car along the narrow drive. When they reached the lane he turned back down the hill.

Gwen put a hand to her chest. She could feel her heart fluttering like a butterfly in a box.

'No! Well—a little—it's just that I'm not in the habit of going back to the house of someone I've only just met. We've only really exchanged a few words.'

'I seem to remember we exchanged a *little* more than words,' Etienne said, his beautiful French accent giving the words a cadence that spoke straight to the soft, malleable centre of her being.

Gwen looked away, blushing furiously. He was waiting for her to respond, she could tell. His presence was so overwhelming she felt his gaze linger over her like a caress. Then, just as noticeably, its power flicked away from her as he turned his car in at a pair of huge, wrought-iron gates. As Gwen looked up at them her eyes widened.

'My goodness!'

He was unimpressed by her reaction. 'You have never seen these gates before?'

'It's not that. I pass them every day on my way to and from work. I just never dreamed I'd actually get to see who lives here, or what's on the other side of them. That's all.' She gazed around, wondering what on earth she was letting herself in for.

'Not many people do,' Etienne said firmly as a security guard let his car pass. 'Everyone needs a place where they can get away from the glare of publicity. Somewhere they can be themselves. This chateau is mine. It's not my ancestral home—that's on the Loire, *naturellement*.'

There was a long, wide approach road to his hillside home. The chateau looked like a fairy castle cut from black velvet and pinned against the star-speckled sky.

'It's beautiful,' Gwen breathed as Etienne brought his sports car to a halt in front of the South front.

'Wait until you see it in daylight.'

The car's interior light flared as he opened his door. Gwen glimpsed something close to a smile on his face. It had vanished by the time he opened the passenger door to let her out. With one hand he relieved her of the huge champagne bottle. As she stood up his other hand hovered so close to her body she tensed with the expectancy of his touch. When it came, he brushed his palm lightly against the small of her back. The sensation made her gasp, but he intended only to guide her towards his house. His touch fell away at the sound. When they reached the front door he stood aside to let her enter the grand, marble hall first.

'I'll swap this for a more convenient size.' He indicated the bottle in his hand, its foil glittering like gold beneath the security lights. 'Make yourself at home, Gwen. I keep very irregular hours, so my staff do not wait up for me,' he said as she looked up in awe of the large, high-ceilinged room lined with family portraits. Then he disappeared into his warren of a house.

Gwen gazed at the splendour, wondering how anyone could call a lofty old place like this home. It glittered with more gilt and antiques than a museum. The wide open spaces of it made her feel small and uncomfortable. Uneasy at Etienne's absence, she lowered herself onto the very edge of a chair set beside the doorway. She wanted to know what he was doing while he was out of sight. The urge to go and look for him only faded when she heard his sure, steady footsteps again. They were growing closer at a leisurely pace. She tensed, wary of his return but at the same time desperate to see him again.

He didn't disappoint her. As he strolled into the room she fancied he was taller, darker and more imposing than she remembered. She took in every detail of his strong profile and smooth, flawless brow. He accepted her scrutiny with a smile that made her blush.

'Supper has been laid out in the summer drawing room. Join me. We will have champagne later.'

'Are you sure there is enough for two?' Even as she spoke Gwen knew it was a silly question.

'My kitchens always provide plenty,' he said amiably.

'Well…if you're sure they won't mind…'

In the low light, his eyes became intense dark pools. 'You shouldn't worry too much about what other people may think or say, Gwen. This is your life, to live as you want.' He levelled a gaze at her that flickered with intent. Gwen wished she had that sort of courage. From the moment she'd first spotted Etienne entering the party, her head had been filled with thoughts of him. His presence had drawn her attention time and time again. The first time they'd been alone together, she had been powerless to resist his attraction. Now she looked up at him in the certain knowledge he could easily rob her of her last strands of self-control. He was on his home ground, the ideal place to prove how strong his hold over her was.

'I can't do this,' she said faintly. This was unknown territory for Gwen. Her fingers went to the watch strap she always fiddled with when she was nervous.

'I've arranged for your restaurant delivery to be dealt with. You've got absolutely nothing to worry about. It's not that late,' he intoned gently.

'Not for you, maybe, but…I'm beginning to think this is another mistake, Etienne. I should never have come here. I should go…' She sprang to her feet, desperately trying to prove to them both that she was still her own woman. It was hopeless.

'No, you shouldn't. Do you *honestly* think I would let you go back to a house with no power or light?' Etienne's voice was reassuringly hypnotic. 'I can't let you suffer in darkness. Stay here, Gwen. Nothing will happen that you do not want to happen.'

When he said it like that, there was no question of

her going anywhere else. They both knew why she was really here. The only connection it had with electricity was the sizzle of arousal whenever she looked at him.

After all, Gwen thought defiantly, she had been working flat out for months. She was long overdue some pleasure. And she was here in France to live out her dreams—surely that allowed for a little adventure as well? Looking up into Etienne's heart-stopping expression, she knew there would never be a better time to indulge herself.

The second she softened, Etienne moved forward and held out his hand for her. She tentatively placed her palm in his, in a gesture of trust, and he led her through the cool, echoing shadows of his chateau to a small, intimate dining area. Delectable-looking food was laid out on a table along one side of the room. He walked past it, and poured them both a shot of strong coffee. Gwen looked at its colour uncertainly.

'That looks so strong. I'll never sleep tonight,' she murmured.

A leonine smile widened Etienne's generous mouth. 'Good.'

His voice was as silken as the touch he laid on her arm. It slid over the thin fabric of her light jacket until it reached her shoulder. Gwen was transfixed. Her eyes were fastened to his every movement. Then she made the fatal mistake of transferring her attention to his eyes. From that moment on she was totally lost. She had spent her whole life playing by the rules. Now she was staring rebellion straight in the face, and it was wonderful.

'I—I don't know what to do, Etienne.'

'Stay with me tonight.' His voice was husky. 'I haven't felt like this in a long time. Far too long.'

Gwen's mouth went dry. Etienne Moreau must be a very lucky man. She had never felt as good as this in her entire life. A tiny voice whispered warnings in her ear, but it was drowned out by her thundering pulse. The man of her dreams was already moving on from entrancing her mind to working his magic on her body. He took her in his arms, and a sultry heat warmed a secret place between her thighs. It sent waves of desire rolling through her body. She felt her nipples peak as his irises expanded with desire for her. When he bent to plunder another kiss from her lips, Gwen was quick to respond. She mirrored his demands in a way that made him purr with pleasure.

She clutched at him. The unexpected strength of her physical reaction was almost frightening. She felt his hands slip inside her jacket, easing it off her shoulders. He held her tightly, her breasts compressed against the hard masculine plane of his chest. Her body craved more of this new experience. This felt so wild and free, so right. It was such a wonderful release from work and worry. She surrendered herself to pleasure. Her lips parted, eagerly enjoying the expert touch of his. In response he slid his hands over her inviting, velvet-clad body and held her close to him.

'Do you still want that coffee?' He chuckled softly into her hair.

Gwen shook her head. 'I want to go on doing this.' Her breathy whisper escaped into the night. She raised her hands to ruffle eager fingers through the midnight darkness of his hair. Her responses felt so natural, so good, she couldn't have stopped if she'd wanted to.

His kisses sought out all the delicate places on her throat, turning Gwen weak with longing. The more she responded to his touch, the more obvious his need for her became.

'I want you. Stay here with me tonight,' he repeated, nuzzling into her neck.

Despite the delicious lassitude flooding her body, Gwen retained enough sense to realise this was a turning point. She had been careful and sensible all her life. There had been boyfriends, but she had never been tempted like this before. Etienne's touch stroked away all her preoccupation with study and work. The idea of pushing him away made her ache with unfulfilled longing. She wanted him, whatever that meant. The alternative was to leave right now and never look back. Gwen knew she could not do that. The memory of what might have been would surely haunt her for ever. It was impossible to believe that any other man could ever make her feel like this. To turn her back on Etienne would condemn her to a lifetime of wondering.

'But I'm nothing to you…' Gwen knew that was how it worked. She slaved to put on glittering parties; Etienne moved through them like a comet in the night sky.

He silenced her with another incredible kiss. 'Tonight we are everything to one another. Let tomorrow take care of itself,' he murmured, searing her with the raw heat of passion.

Then his smile reached right down into the depths of her soul and rocked it to its foundations.

He wants me, she thought in wonder. Suddenly, that

made him the most important thing in her life. Right now she was the centre of his universe. That thought alone was enough to make her stretch out and experience life. She had spent months sacrificing everything. This was surely a moment to indulge herself for once.

'Yes…' she murmured.

Her reply unleashed the full power of his kisses. As he held her against his body she felt the ridge of his erection, pressing proud and hard against her. It was tangible proof that he needed her, and acted on Gwen like the finest aphrodisiac.

He carried her up wide stone stairs and through hallways sketched in moonlight. When they reached a room warm with the fragrance of cedar wood he closed the door behind him and laid her down on a wide, soft bed scattered with pillows and cushions. Not sure what she should do or say, Gwen raised herself on her elbows. His magnificent silhouette hovered over her, and she was unable to take her eyes off it. He bent down and began kissing her again with an urgency that made her dizzy.

'I've been looking forward to this all evening,' he murmured.

Gwen's breasts strained within the tightly boned bodice of her evening dress. Excitement defined the peaks of her nipples through its sumptuous fabric. Etienne's hands were drawn to explore her. He brushed the thick mane of her luxuriant hair back over her shoulders so that his touch could run unhindered over her sensuous curves. He took his time, relishing the narrowness of her waist and the full, tempting flare of her hips.

'Your body is so beautiful, *chérie.*'

'Really?' Gwen was so astonished she could hardly speak.

He nodded. 'You are exactly what I need. The moment our eyes met I knew you would breathe life into my existence.'

His voice was as soft as a summer breeze across the maquis. The warmth of his words sent a shiver of anticipation along her spine. In her innocence she reached for him, looking for reassurance. As her hands met at the back of his neck the silkiness of his hair and the smooth warmth of his skin inspired her. She could not stop exploring him, moving her touch over his skin and hair and clothes. Catching the end of his formal black tie, she was surprised at how easily it came undone, slithering free from the collar of his shirt.

His perfect white teeth flashed a smile. His eyes were dark pools of temptation, waiting to engulf her.

'I hope I'm not being too reckless,' she breathed.

Shrugging off his jacket, he lay down beside her, kissing and caressing her with a skill that made all rational thought slip away. Whenever Gwen tried to think beyond the moment, his fingertips brushed off her thoughts. They ran over her with such skill that the future became something that happened to other people, not to her. She was suspended in wonder. Etienne wanted her, so nothing should be allowed to stop him.

Her pulse sang to the rhythm of his body as it moved against hers. In one slow, smooth movement he unzipped her beautiful velvet dress all the way down the back. Then he peeled away its dark blue velvet, revealing her pale, pure body within. Gwen felt a tingle of apprehension. Etienne didn't notice her slight hesitation. He was totally absorbed by the sight of her full breasts, beautifully contoured by the white lace of her bra. Lowering his head, he kissed the darkness of each nipple through its crisp white covering. A cascade of new sensations rippled through Gwen, escaping in a moan of pleasure. A light dew of excitement bloomed over her entire body. She warmed beneath his hands, but he pulled away from her. An ache of longing low down in her belly twisted like a knife. She reached out to stop him leaving her. Then she realised he had only let her go so he could strip off his own clothes.

His body was a revelation to her, but she felt a first frisson of fear. The phrase 'an innocent abroad' rose up to taunt her. What would an experienced man like Etienne make of her? Then he moved in close to her again and the need to reach out and touch him drove every other thought from her mind.

He was built like an athlete. The taut muscles of his broad chest and sleek long limbs rippled. Lit by pale light from his bedroom windows, they gleamed like liquid gold beneath his smooth skin.

'I'm all yours,' he said thickly.

Her hands slid over the smooth glory of his pectorals until they reached the crisp dark curls of his chest hair. Tracing the narrow band of it down until it widened across his belly, her fingers hesitated, and then reached for his proud manhood. At the brush of her fingers he let out a long moan of pleasure. With that encouragement, Gwen couldn't resist going further.

Encircling him, she felt skin as delicate as an eyelid slide beneath her touch.

'Slowly, *chérie*! You go too fast!' His laughter was soft and low in the dusky light. Pulling her up into his embrace, he kissed her again, long and hard as he freed her from the restriction of her bra. As it fell away he moved his attention from her mouth to her breasts. Rolling her onto her back, he teased one nipple with the tip of his tongue while rolling the other between the pads of his thumb and forefinger. Gwen was seized by a fever of excitement. It tossed her around on the bed until she was nearly senseless. When his hand slipped down to explore the curve of her bottom, she arched her back, thrusting against his touch. In response his fingers slipped beneath the flimsy fabric of her panties, pulling them away in his eagerness to explore the warm secrets of her femininity. She shuddered with pleasure as his fingertips found her little bud and teased it into life. Her breath came in staccato sobs, the foreign language of sensual delight. She writhed beneath his touch, the sheer cascades of pleasure almost too much to bear.

'Watching you is the most erotic thing I have ever seen,' he whispered, gathering her up in his arms and covering her with his body. As he slid between her thighs Gwen sobbed with a purely sexual need that could no longer be denied.

Etienne looked down at the beautiful creature lying beneath him on his bed. This was a moment to be savoured. He had never in his life experienced desire like this. Gwen had brought him to such a peak, his entire being sang with it. Gazing at her fragile beauty, he saw his red-hot desire reflected in her eyes. As he plunged into her warm welcoming body she cried out, clutching at him as he filled her with one ravishing, potent thrust.

'Did I hurt you?' He gasped, looking down at her.

'No—I'm all right,' Gwen exclaimed. The pain was already a memory as her body moulded to his in growing excitement. She felt as though she were born to be one with him, and it was unbelievably good. 'Please…don't stop…' she implored.

Etienne's gaze cleared. Her voice and smile were urging him on, and yet her body had resisted.

'Are you a virgin?'

'I was,' she murmured, struggling to open her eyes in the face of another rising tide of passion.

'Why didn't you tell me, *mon amour*?'

Gwen tried to think, but his body was too much of a distraction. 'I thought it would stop you wanting me,' she said eventually.

He shook his head. 'I should have been the judge of that, *ma chérie*.' Then he placed a single reverent kiss on her lips.

When he moved his hips again she felt the whole hot, hard insistence of him willing her to respond. She reacted to his proud dominance instantly, an unquenchable fire running all over her body. She cried out, not in pain, but for release from a desperate search for satisfaction. At last he slid his hands into the small of her back and pulled her tight against his body, catapulting her to orgasm. She flew among the stars as time stood still. Her body gripped him in spasms of exquisite pleasure, drawing him on to the point of no return. With a guttural cry he shuddered to a climax and she was there, her body one with his.

Gwen relaxed into his embrace with a sigh of absolute contentment. She had never felt so close to any other human being in her entire life. Etienne had coaxed her body to heights she had never imagined. A delicious lassitude washed over her, until a dark cloud crept over her horizon. She would have liked nothing better than to talk with him now, but found she couldn't. His rejection when they had kissed in the office dragged her back to earth like a lead weight. If she tried to build on this heaven by breaking the comfortable silence that lay between them now, he might be struck by second thoughts this time, too. What if he came to his senses and dumped her?

'I must go,' she mumbled, determined to jump before he could push her. Quicker than summer lightning Etienne's arm snaked out. His hand closed around her arm, preventing her escape.

'Stay,' he murmured in an echo of his command to her earlier that night.

Pulling her back against his body, Etienne buried his face in her soft, flower-scented hair. He smiled to himself as he drifted between waking and sleeping. This woman really was one of a kind. She was the first who had ever volunteered to leave his bed. He normally had trouble in evicting one-night stands. He was a proud man, and was mildly surprised to find he hadn't taken Gwen's escape bid as a snub. Instead he found it refreshing—especially as she snuggled back into the curve of his body with an ease that felt totally natural.

A girl like Gwen Williams was exactly what he needed. His stepmother was always trying to marry him off. What would *her* reaction be if she heard about this? His mouth twitched in a smile. Gwen certainly wasn't countess material, but that didn't matter to Etienne. Although bitter experience had put him off marriage for life, he was an honourable man. And what red-blooded male could resist taking a mistress as gorgeous as Gwen? It was an opportunity made in heaven. This was the first time in years he had felt free to give his powerful libido its head. Gwen was sex appeal and innocence in one irresistible combination. She was the perfect antidote to his working life, his grasping stepmother and her hoard of needy relatives. Gwen was as willing and eager to please him as he was to indulge her.

The thing that most appealed to Etienne was that she hadn't once asked about the size and number of his estates, or his bank balances. In his wide experience of women, that was a miracle in itself. Unlike the rest of his acquaintances, Gwen spoke to him as though he were an ordinary person and that, Etienne knew, was exactly what he needed. With her as his mistress, he knew he would never be bored again.

Gwen opened her eyes and squinted towards a patch of daylight beyond the window. It must be very early. Dawn was barely brushing the Eastern sky. There was a sweet fragrance in the air she couldn't quite identify. And then she remembered…it was Etienne. She blushed. His arm was still around her. Memories of the hours they had shared came flooding back. She listened to the slow, steady breathing of the man who had taken her body and soul time and again during the hours of darkness. A man who, despite his vast wealth and status, had encouraged her to throw off every one of her inhibitions. If that weren't incredible enough, Gwen knew she would do it again and again, as long as it was with him.

And yet she couldn't stay. He wouldn't want her any more—and in any case, she had to get to work. It wasn't only a thirsty car and an impatient electricity company that worried her. Bankruptcy was staring her in the face. Now she was the sole owner of Le Rossignol, she had to make it pay. Physical need for Etienne fought with her fear of financial ruin. She had left her home in the Welsh valleys so that any mistakes could be made well away from her pessimistic friends and family. Despite their warnings, she had been almost sure this venture would be a success. The only uncertainty had been her business partner, Carys. Now her feather-brained 'friend' was out of the picture, Gwen was doubly determined to make a go of things. But from now on, in those few moments when she wasn't worrying about her fledgling business, she knew she would dream of Etienne.

His breathing was slow and steady. Trying to harden her heart, Gwen began inching herself across the cold expanse of bed, away from him. Her foot had barely been touched by the morning air when Etienne stirred and enveloped her in a firm embrace again.

'Don't tell me you're thinking of getting up so early?'

he murmured. The kiss of his stubble rasped over her skin as he nestled against her shoulder.

'It's light enough for me to walk home and start trying to sort things out.'

'Wait…I'll ring for breakfast,' he said, surfacing fully. 'We have things to discuss.'

'We do?' Gwen asked nervously. Waves of panic uncovered a sense of shame that she had totally cast aside until that moment. She clutched a handful of the thin sheet and buried her face into it. What had she done? What madness had possessed her to surrender everything to a man she had met only a few hours before? Pulling her knees up to her chest, she contracted into a tiny ball of guilt. Mistaking her movement, Etienne released her from his grasp.

'Of course—you'll want to freshen up. There should be everything you need in my bathroom, but if you want anything else, use the bell to call one of my staff.'

'No!' Gwen couldn't bear the thought of total strangers getting the idea she was nothing more than another notch on this man's ego. 'No—thank you. I'll manage.'

He was reaching for his phone, but paused long enough to grab and kiss her before she could scuttle off to the bathroom.

In that instant Gwen knew why she had fallen into his arms so readily. Etienne Moreau was a force of nature, and one she never wanted to resist.

'It's a rare woman who offers to merely "manage" when she could have all my staff running around for her,' he murmured into her hair.

'I've been brought up to take care of myself,' she

said, forcing herself to pull away from his embrace.
She kept hold of the sheet as she did so, wrapping it
around herself for the journey to the bathroom.
Considering the number of times they had made love
during the night, there was no point in trying to be
modest in front of him, but Gwen needed to make the
gesture. Head down, she bolted.

The en-suite was as well stocked as Etienne had said
it would be. Gwen found every variety of shower gel
from revitalising to relaxing, toothbrushes, a selection
of toothpastes and a small but elegant collection of cosmetics. Everything was shrink-wrapped and sealed, as
though Etienne's room was in a hotel rather than a
private house. The thought that a million other women
could have passed this way did nothing for Gwen's self-
esteem. When she heard the distant clatter of staff
arriving with a breakfast trolley, she hid inside the
bathroom until everything went quiet again. She gave
it a couple of minutes, and then emerged.

Etienne's bedroom was deserted. Venturing into the
lounge, she saw a pair of French doors standing open
on the other side of the room. They were draped with
curtains of the finest lace and, beyond them, Gwen
saw a breakfast table set on a wide balcony. Enough
food for two was laid out as a spectacular buffet,
complete with starched linen napkins and solid silver
cutlery. It was a display Gwen would have studied for
ideas if her mind hadn't been full of a more pressing
problem—the tall, broad and totally unmistakeable
figure pacing back and forth beside it. Etienne was
oblivious of the stunning view over the hillside as he

spoke into a mobile phone. Even at this distance, he was magnificent. Gwen felt totally out of her depth. She wouldn't have needed the hundreds of family portraits on show downstairs to know he was a born aristocrat. Poise and confidence were obvious in his every word and movement. Despite the intimacy of their night together, at first she could not bear to meet his keen ebony gaze. She concentrated on the only thing she was qualified to do. When he closed his call she took a deep breath and stepped out onto the balcony to join him.

'What would you like for breakfast, *monsieur?*'

As she took a plate from a heated trolley she heard the soft click of his leather-soled shoes on the ancient stones. Then his hand covered hers and he took the plate from her unresisting fingers.

'What happened to "Etienne"? And you aren't one of my staff.' He raised one fine, dark eyebrow in subtle amusement. 'Concentrate on serving yourself, Gwen. I have something very different in mind for you.'

Dragging his gaze away from her, he let it fall onto the breakfast display. As he did so he frowned, as though it was a chore diverting him from something much more pleasurable.

'Try the crêpes. They're the best you'll ever taste.' Lifting a warm croissant onto his own plate, he looked straight back at her.

Gwen took one of the almost transparent pancakes onto her plate. Breakfast with Etienne in his suite was a once-in-a-lifetime experience, but the business part of her brain refused to let go. She felt it was her duty to find out what her customers enjoyed.

'I'll get my chefs to give you their recipe.'

For the first time that morning Gwen's smile was as confident as her reply.

'Thank you. That's very kind, but I'm quite happy with the one I use already. Everyone has their favourites.'

Etienne looked at her carefully. Then he smiled. 'Yes, and I'm no exception. I enjoyed last night, Gwen, as you may have noticed—several times.' His afterthought was a wicked drawl.

Until that moment she had been stealing little glances at him. Now she gave a nervous chuckle and stared resolutely at the breakfast display. Pretending that the choice between berries and syrup was almost as important as his comment, she tried to look cool, calm and composed. It was impossible. Etienne was standing so tall and serene beneath his native sun. She could hardly believe she had spent the night with him.

'In fact, I'd like to make this a more regular arrangement,' he continued.

Gwen had been about to lift a spoonful of fresh fruit salad from a crystal dish. At his words she froze. A droplet of juice trickled down the bowl of the solid silver serving spoon, trembled at its lowest point for a second, and then dropped onto the snowy white tablecloth.

'You want to *what*?' she said faintly.

'I have a lot of things on my mind, Gwen. I need distraction—something to take my mind off it all and restore my faith in human nature. Last night I found the perfect solution, in you. We would make a good team. I'm sure of it. With my support you would be released from all your obligations. There would be no need for you to slave away in a kitchen. You would be free to enjoy life as it should be lived, with no worries.'

She gazed at him, so clearly puzzled that he laughed. When he did that it made her smile, although she still shook her head in bewilderment.

'What do you mean, Etienne?'

'Exactly what I say. I'm so delighted to have found you, *chérie*, it would be my pleasure to provide for you, financially. I don't want you waiting on other people. I want to keep you all to myself, and support you in the way you deserve.'

He was seducing her all over again, simply by using his deliciously accented voice and the promise in those beautiful dark eyes.

Gwen had thought it was impossible for her to be any more nervous. Now the butterflies in her stomach were under attack by a snake of suspicion. She might have been physically innocent when she met Etienne, but growing up with older brothers had given her a basic understanding of the male mind. Preparing for the worst, she hoped for the best and asked slowly,

'Why would you offer me money when we only met last night?'

Taking her free hand, Etienne raised it to his lips and placed a delicate kiss on each of her fingers in turn. Then he looked deep into her eyes and delivered his reply with all the relish of a professional seducer.

'I would have thought that was obvious, *chérie*.'

CHAPTER FOUR

'I want to keep you in my life, Gwen. As my mistress,' Etienne added, since she was looking at him with something close to suspicion. 'Think of the advantages. I could set you up with a restaurant—in Monte Carlo, maybe, where your Michelin-starred menus could dazzle the clientele downstairs while your body delights me in the apartment above…'

His voice was a silken thread, drawing her into his plans. A furious blush began to rise from Gwen's breasts. It was slow to kindle but flared in painful intensity as it reached her cheeks. Dropping the serving spoon with a clatter, she confronted him with eyes as hard as sapphires.

'How dare you? You said our first kiss was an accident. You were right. Anyone can make a mistake, *monsieur*, but it takes a first-class philanderer to build on one and then dress it up with an offer like that!'

He stared at her, totally unable to understand her reaction. 'Gwen? You're upset?'

She glared back at him. 'That's an understatement!'

Still mystified, he gave a particularly Gallic shrug. Acquiring a mistress had never been a problem for him before. Until now, his only difficulty had been tact when ending relationships. Gwen was introducing him to a whole new range of experiences. So far they had all been stellar. This was the first irritation. 'But why should you take offence? It's a perfectly natural arrangement. What's your problem?'

She glared at him. This was unbelievable. She'd just had the most sensuous night of her life and now it was all coming down to money! She felt her fairy tale quickly slipping out of her grasp. 'I don't want anyone controlling me! I ran away from home to escape all that. Now I'm making my own future.'

'You ran away from home?' He looked concerned. 'How long ago was that?'

'Last year.'

That was when Etienne made his next mistake. He smiled. It was a miscalculation, because it did nothing to calm her down and everything to inflame her.

'And *don't* look at me like that! It's not funny. I'm mad at you!'

'You're a grown woman, Gwen. You're too old to run away! Why didn't you simply say you left home?'

'That's not how my family see it,' she said bitterly.

Etienne was on her wavelength immediately. 'Ah… trouble with the relatives?' he said with all the weight of personal experience.

'No—not at all. And that's the problem. My family have always been far too protective for my liking. They've never wanted me to fail, so they've never wanted me to do anything. They want my life to be like them—far too good.'

'That's all I want, too,' Etienne said in a silky voice, reaching for the cafetiere. 'Let's take a seat and discuss this over a coffee.'

'If you're only asking me to be your mistress, then there's nothing to discuss,' Gwen rallied, putting down her plate of crêpes untouched.

'Why not? It's the perfect solution.'

'For you, maybe. You'll have everything you want whenever you want it, with no strings attached.' She could hardly believe what she was saying. All she wanted to do was step back into his arms but, amazed at her own courage and glad of her self-discipline, she was finally finding the courage to stand up for herself.

'How can you say that, *mon amour*?' He looked puzzled. 'As my mistress, you'll benefit from my generosity. You'll have anything and everything you want, too. You can have expense accounts at all the stores you like. I could treat you to a nice little love nest in Paris, *par exemple*. We can live together there whenever I'm in the city. What is your heart's desire? Name it and it's yours. There's no limit.'

Gwen was aghast. 'Well, there's certainly no limit to your nerve! Is there nothing you won't try? Unless it's the idea of making an honest woman of me, as they call it back home.'

He laughed. 'Marriage, you mean? No, I'm afraid that will never be on offer. And there's no need to look so shocked! You've found my Achilles' heel, so the least I can do is to be honest with you. I was nearly caught in that honey trap once before, *chérie*. No woman is going to hold me hostage like that again. You can have absolutely anything you like, except my signature on a marriage certificate.' He chuckled. 'Apart from that one small detail, my generosity knows no limit. Try me. Name your price.'

Reaching for a napkin, Gwen wiped her hands and dropped it onto the table in a symbolic gesture.

'It's nothing you could buy, no matter how much money you've got, *monsieur*. I want my independence, and the chance to make my own way in the world. I don't want to go through life being carried by anyone else.'

Taking a step back, she took one last look at the temptation of him. It was almost impossible to make a stand, he made her body quiver just looking at her, but her principles were at stake. She had to harden her heart.

'I escaped from one gilded cage. I'm not going to let myself be tempted into another. *Au revoir, monsieur.*'

In a swirl of midnight-blue velvet, she was gone.

Etienne never normally wasted time on breakfast. As far as he was concerned, it was something to restore his energy levels after a late night and before an early meeting. That was all. This morning there was a different reason most of his food went untouched. He moved to pour himself a second cup of coffee as Gwen stalked away through his suite. When the door slammed shut behind her, he turned his attention to the beautiful array of food laid out on the table. He didn't normally linger over his selection, but today he had some time to fill. It wouldn't be polite to start eating before Gwen returned. She would come fluttering back to him at any minute in a flurry of tears and apologies. Etienne was quite confident about that. It was what women did.

He had a long wait. When he finally saw Gwen again, she was down in the courtyard. He caught sight of her briefly, storming away from his house with her beautiful dress billowing. She didn't give him a backward glance. Marching down the drive, she disappeared from his sight.

Etienne lowered his eyebrows in silent disapproval. Miss Gwyneth Williams really was one of a kind. This made her the first woman to abandon him of her own accord. *He* was always the one who made the decision to leave. *He* made the first move. *Always.* This was not going to plan. Gwen hadn't even looked back so that he could give her a casual wave, dismissing her from his life for ever. *She didn't give me the satisfaction*, he thought irritably, but his indignation was short-lived. Gwen Williams had satisfied him in quite another way. It was one that would live far longer in his memory. Her mind was her own, but her body must surely be his. He had seen it, and taken her, exactly as he had possessed so many other lovely things that caught his eye.

She couldn't be allowed to snatch it away.

Etienne took his breakfast over to the dining table and sat down in solitary splendour to consider this. As always, the financial press lay beside his place. He usually read it from cover to cover. Today, for the first time in two years, it remained untouched. Instead, he worked his way through far more pastry, crêpes and fruit than he would normally eat.

It was an attempt to distract himself from the enigma

that was Gwen. In her anger, she had revealed something that only made him want her more. Until he'd met her, he had been confident he knew exactly what sort of woman could abandon a happy family. Angela Webbington had shown him how it was done. Yesterday, he had seduced Gwen in the delicious belief she was totally different from his ex-fiancée. Now he didn't know what to make of his little Welsh wonder. Last night she had held him spellbound. This morning, his sweet and tender stranger had shown him a core of iron. He now knew she had the determination to walk away from blood relatives—*family!*—because they cared about her too much.

Etienne shook his head in silent disbelief. If he could continue humouring his stepmother simply because it was his father's dying wish, why couldn't Gwen see how lucky she was? He wondered how it felt to be part of a normal family. The appalling woman who styled herself 'Countess Sophie' continued to dictate shopping lists onto his dead father's exclusive headed notepaper, yet Etienne let her get away with it. That woman was so far beneath his contempt he didn't bother registering his annoyance. Gwen Williams, on the other hand, had run away from something he envied. Etienne's idea of family was people who liked you because they wanted to, not because it was their duty or because they hoped you'd remember them in your will. Why had Gwen run away? From people who wanted her with them? Did she need saving from herself—to be shown how important it was to have people who cared? If she did, he was certainly the man to do just that. It was just a shame she hadn't realised it yet.

She soon would. Etienne was completely confident of that.

Gwen was so furious, she forgot all about her blisters until she reached her front door. There she kicked off her shoes and stood on the still-cool stones while she rummaged for her key. Etienne Moreau was the absolute limit. It had been so perfect last night and then he thought his money could buy everything, including her. She felt insulted. Stamping upstairs, she threw off her beautiful gown. She intended to shrug off that infuriating man in the same movement. It wasn't quite as easy as she hoped. As she pulled on her working clothes it was impossible not to notice how soft and supple his expensive shower gel had left her skin. She lifted her arm and inhaled its heavy, floral perfume again. From that moment on, she would never be able to smell the fragrance of jasmine without being wafted straight back to the luxury of Etienne's suite. And the memory of the night they had shared…

Gwen caught sight of her reflection in her bedroom mirror and it shocked her. Overnight, the vigorous businesswoman who was always so quick to rebuke her from the glass had been replaced. A misty-eyed stranger gazed back at her now.

She jumped straight back to life as a loud knock echoed up from downstairs. There was someone at the door.

'Just a minute!' she called, scrabbling around to collect the unpaid electricity bill, her house keys and bag before flying down to throw open the front door.

It was Etienne. Dressed in another beautifully crafted suit, he pulled off a pair of slick black shades. They flickered in the morning sunlight as he closed the arms and posted them into the top pocket of his jacket. Stunned into silence, Gwen stared at the face she had seen transformed by pleasure such a short, painful time before. He was as unrecognisable as her reflection had been in the mirror upstairs. His eyes showed none of the soft sensuality she remembered so well. They now watched her acutely. The early stubble that had rasped against her naked skin was gone, but his freshly shaved face had lost none of its attraction for her. It made her want to stroke him. If ever a man's body demanded a woman's fingers to peel away his smart façade, it was Etienne's. Despite her fury, Gwen could not help staring. She had an almost overwhelming desire to reach out to him. He had assumed she was dying to become his mistress. He was wrong, but she still wanted to experience the passionate animal lurking beneath his civilised exterior—just not quite so formally…

'You've come to apologise?' she ventured.

That wiped the smile off his face. He grazed his lower lip with his teeth.

'No…what for?' he questioned, mystified.

Gwen was already crimson, but could at least give the appearance of being in control. She hardened her features. He mustn't guess she was thinking about the way his muscles bunched beneath the fine gold skin of his chest. Fidgeting with embarrassment, she blew a stray curl of hair back from her brow with a gust of hot breath.

'You know very well what for, Etienne Moreau.'

He gazed at her, shaking his head. 'No, I don't.'

She stared back. His ebony eyes looked so steady and honest she found it impossible to believe he was goading her. And yet she was being forced into saying words that made her blood boil with embarrassment.

She glared up at him malevolently. 'You tried to buy me. You reduced me to the level of a bowl of bouillabaisse! *You asked me to be your mistress!*' she hissed.

To her total amazement, his response was a confiding chuckle.

'What's the matter with that? As far as I'm concerned, that is one of the greatest compliments a man can pay a woman.'

'Well, it comes pretty low on *my* agenda, I can tell you!' Gwen snapped. The day was already warm, and she was getting hotter by the second.

Etienne managed to stop smiling, but could not hide the relish in his eyes. 'That isn't how it felt to me, last night,' he murmured.

Gwen struggled to hang onto the remains of her self-control. If only he weren't looking at her like that, all flashing dark eyes and lupine grin. It was all she could do not to cave in and smile back.

That would be disastrous. She had principles at stake. They had forced her to walk away from him once. To run back into his arms now would show him how vulnerable she was. She hadn't escaped from the claustrophobia of home to get locked into a relationship that would die with the speed of his enthusiasm.

'Fine—we've established that you're totally unrepentant. So what makes you think you can hunt me down in my own home? I've told you, I'm not interested in your shabby little offer. If you're not here to deliver an apology, would you mind telling me why you *are* here?' she snapped.

As she spoke she caught sight of her car. It was standing on the terrace, in the shade of the gnarled old golden rain tree. She stopped. Her glance flicked from Etienne's face to the Citroen, and back again. There was absolutely no trace of amusement in his expression now. Annoyance spoke loudly in his every movement as he pulled her keys from his pocket and thrust them towards her.

'I came to return your car.'

His voice was full of contempt. It was nothing compared to the awful crawling shame that slithered over Gwen in an agony of embarrassment.

'Oh...er, yes...of course!' Desperately she looked down at her bag, rifling through tissues, receipts, lipstick, foreign coins and parking permits. 'How much do I owe you?' she muttered.

'Stop!' he said in a voice that instantly commanded her full attention. Looking up, she winced as his eyes inflicted points of pure pain.

'I wouldn't dream of insulting you again with talk of money, Gwyneth. Consider it my pleasure,' he said through a smile that showed all his teeth, but not in a good way.

Gwen opened her mouth to reply, but he was already on his way, shaking off her wordless outrage. She watched him storm away in total silence, fighting the urge to call him back. Maybe this was for the best. It was hard to know which was worse. A man who couldn't admit he was in the wrong—or a debt that he wouldn't let her repay.

She knew both would work on her like grit in an oyster.

Fury propelled Etienne down the hill in silence. Two rebuffs in as many hours were unknown. What on earth had he been thinking about, laying himself open to such an attack? As he strode through the great gates of his chateau he wondered what had come over him. This wasn't how it was supposed to work. The thought of never seeing Gwen again worked on him like a headache. If he picked up a girl, they had a good time and when the evening was over, so was the liaison.

The only exception to that rule had been Angela. They had fitted together so perfectly it would have been a sin not to take it further. Old money and new ideas, 'tellystocracy' and the real thing combined in the most beautiful couple in the public eye. They had been so perfectly matched, it had been a nightmare. One word had kept coming back to haunt him. Duty. Celebrity anchorwoman Angela could not understand why she should respect the Moreau family and its traditions. That had spawned a million arguments, but the final crowbar forcing Etienne and Angela apart had been far smaller, and totally innocent…

The memory of the day he discovered Angela's worst deception still had the power to pierce Etienne like a barb. Gwen Williams was obsessed by her career. In that respect she was exactly like Angela Webbington. Why should he be surprised if both women were cut from the same fabric? With a snort he decided it was madness to have considered making Gwen his mistress. A short affair was one thing. Offering to restrict himself to one woman for an unspecified length of time was quite another. They always put themselves first and others nowhere. One tragic error of judgement in his life was surely enough of a warning.

It had taken Etienne a long time to start getting over that.

And now there was Gwen.

He marched on. The sun was rising higher in the sky by the moment, but Etienne would have been at boiling point if it had been January. He had never lacked for anything in his life, and he wasn't about to start denying himself now. Whatever happened, he was going to have Miss Gwyneth Williams.

He stopped—why was she playing on his mind so much? Was it simply because he couldn't have her, or because she was something special—? No, he baulked at using that word. It was too loaded with meaning. She was *totally unlike* any other woman he had ever met. That made her...

He gazed along the drive towards his impressive chateau, trying to think of a description.

Unique. Yes, that was it. He smiled. She had shown no signs of fawning around his money. Quite the opposite. She had stood up for herself. He couldn't help contrasting her behaviour with Angela. His ex-fiancée had made a career out of defying him for the hell of it, and the headlines.

He continued on towards his home, but this time more slowly. Maybe there were faults on both sides. If he had given Gwen time to cool off properly, they might have laughed about their argument. It would have been forgiven in an instant. The making up would have been a lot slower, and supremely enjoyable. He liked that idea. Gwen had a lovely laugh. That wasn't the only thing he enjoyed about her. She pleased his body in a way more experienced women had never managed. Gwen, in all her innocence, was a superbly generous lover. He remembered how responsive his body had been to her touch, and her delight in it. The simple act of thinking about her made him want her, right here and now. He turned in a crunch of gravel and took two long strides back towards her house. Then he stopped. Striking while her anger was hot had made her reject his offer a few minutes before. It obviously wasn't the way to tame her. A woman like Gwen deserved careful handling.

For once, Etienne would have to make haste slowly.

With a smile, he strolled back home to plan his next move.

Gwen's embarrassment was so total she thought she would never recover. She could have cooked crêpes on her cheeks. Etienne had been doing her a favour, but she had yelled first without even bothering to ask questions. She had wrecked any hope of seeing him ever again. It was the worst disappointment she had ever suffered—and when her staff clocked into work at the restaurant, it got a whole lot worse.

'And don't forget, the Count of Malotte is booked in for lunch today!' Clemence the waitress nudged Gwen archly.

'I had no idea, but I doubt if he'll turn up,' Gwen said grimly. 'He's probably had enough of my kind of hospitality to last him a lifetime.'

She was wrong on both counts. Etienne was determined to taste it again—but on his own terms. The first volley of his attack on her will power arrived shortly before lunch that morning. Gwen was busy in the kitchen. Suddenly there was a commotion out in the restaurant. Wiping her hands on a cloth, she rushed out in time to see three large, flat cardboard boxes being unloaded from a florists' van. The delivery man handed her an expensive, tissue-lined envelope and—more importantly as far as Gwen was concerned—an invoice with the word 'paid' stamped across it in large, comforting letters.

She tore open the envelope. It contained a short note written in real ink on handmade paper. She knew who it was from without needing to see the bold, flowing signature at the bottom. The faintest trace of Etienne's sophisticated aftershave had been enough to get her pulses racing.

Dear Gwen,
It would be pointless to send flowers to you at home. You obviously spend all your time at Le Rossignol, so I've arranged to have regular deliveries of fresh flowers sent to the restaurant from now on. That way you can appreciate them. There will be a bouquet for each table, and a complimentary corsage of miniature orchids for each female diner—

'So? What do you think?'

Gwen jumped at the interruption. It was a deliciously familiar voice. She looked up, and found herself gazing straight into the beautiful brown eyes of Etienne Moreau.

'I think you're full of surprises.' She folded the letter and carefully replaced it in its envelope. Then she slid it into her apron pocket. 'Thank you, Etienne. It's far more than I deserve. I can't tell you how sorry I am for the misunderstanding earlier,' she muttered, after checking none of her staff were close enough to hear.

He waved away her apology. 'Oh, this is inconsequential. It's a simple gesture, nothing more.'

He couldn't have been more wrong as far as Gwen was concerned. It meant all the world to her. No man had ever sent her flowers before. She looked up at him with shining eyes, but he hadn't finished.

'I knew a hard-headed businesswoman like you wouldn't want money wasted.' He went on, before she could interrupt. 'This way my honour is satisfied, and you get a unique selling point for your restaurant.'

With that simple phrase, her newly revived dreams melted like candyfloss in a heatwave. The ulterior motive behind his gift robbed it of all romance. Gwen put on a brave face and tried not to care. She only had her own temper to blame, after all. It was too late for regrets.

'Ah, so they aren't a sign of your affection. They're for the good of your conscience and my restaurant!' She tried to chuckle, but it was difficult while she was so busy trying to swallow her disappointment.

'Yes, and I can do Le Rossignol another good turn too,' he said with satisfaction. 'I have a business proposition to put to you, Gwen. When I've finished lunching here, you can come back to my yacht with me and we'll discuss it.'

'Today?' she enquired, leading him to his table.

'Of course. Good ideas won't wait.'

'But it will have to…we've got another big party here tonight. I've got to supervise everything!'

Etienne was unfazed. He sat down and watched with interest as Gwen's staff began unpacking the flowers and putting them out on display. 'That's not a problem— I'll send a couple of my chefs down from the chateau. They can cover for you.'

Gwen gaped at him. 'No—I don't think so! This restaurant is my life. I can't abandon it on a whim!'

Etienne clicked his tongue in disgust. 'If this place is so important to you, you can spare a couple of hours to consider its future.'

'It wouldn't have a future if I hadn't mortgaged myself to the hilt. I can't let my guard down for a minute, much less go gallivanting off on a private yacht for the afternoon! And me on a yacht? What on earth would my old mam and dad say?'

'If they had any sense, they'd tell you to do as I say,' Etienne said mildly.

Gwen was aghast. She couldn't possibly leave it at that. Hands on hips, she regarded him, her head on one side.

'I thought you were issuing me with an invitation, not an order?'

He raised a mocking brow. 'I was. You don't have to come, but you would be crazy not to hear what I have to say.'

'In your opinion,' she said caustically, but her suspicion had no effect on Etienne. He was far too sure of himself.

'You'll be of the same opinion, when you've listened to me.'

Gwen pulled out the chair beside him and sat down. 'All right—if your idea is so good, tell me about it now.'

He shook his head. 'All the relevant paperwork is set out in my conference room aboard *The Windflower*. You'll see it this afternoon.'

'No, I won't, because I shan't be there. I'll be here,' she explained patiently. 'I've told you. I must supervise arrangements for the party.'

A small wrinkle appeared between Etienne's brows. He took a sip of mineral water, which gave him time to iron out his frown. 'I'm giving you the opportunity of several lifetimes, and you want to delay things? I thought you couldn't wait?' He looked at her narrowly.

'I *can't* wait, but I *must*,' she stated.

He turned slightly in his seat, studying her for some time before replying.

'A good manager knows how to delegate,' he said eventually.

Gwen was glad he sounded reasonable rather than irritated, but it still took courage to state her case.

'Maybe: but I'm not just a manager. I'm the owner, head cook and bottle-washer. There is no fallback position. It's me. Although,' she added quickly, raising her hand to stop him objecting, 'I *might* be able to get away tomorrow. Le Rossignol is closed for our half-day. I usually spend the time stocktaking and going through the accounts. If your offer of some temporary help right now still stands…' she ventured, looking up at him from beneath her long, dark lashes. He gave a brief nod.

'I *could* try and get everything done today, so I've got tomorrow afternoon free.'

'Then I suppose that will have to do.' He returned her look with interest. 'I'll send a car to pick you up, then, after lunch. It wouldn't do to have you run out of petrol again, would it?'

She flushed in embarrassment. Until that moment she had been totally unable to tear her gaze away from him. Now her eyes were glad to have an excuse to escape.

'Tell me—did you drive my car back to the *gite* yourself this morning?' she said in a low voice.

'Of course.' He shrugged as though the gesture was nothing. But to Gwen, secretly, it meant a lot—that he'd gone out of his way for her. Then he checked his watch with a deftness of touch she remembered so well, and Gwen signalled for his menu to be brought. As he studied it her mind was a jangle of possibilities. After the way she had spoken to him earlier, seduction must be the very last thing on his mind. His businesslike attitude just seemed to confirm this. Still, he was here and she could at least try to make amends. Wistfully, she realised he would be highly unlikely to pull her in out of her depth, ever again.

He looked so calm now, Gwen began to doubt her sanity. They had tumbled through the night, she had snubbed him, stormed off and then snubbed him a second time, yet there was absolutely no trace of their history on his face or in his manners. Both were as perfect as ever.

'Thank you for sorting out my car. It's fine now,' she said uncomfortably, hoping his staff hadn't told him of her simple stupidity in letting it run dry.

'As good as any old vehicle can be,' he allowed. 'My mechanics gave it a full service. Then I filled it up with petrol. She'll be good for a while longer.'

Gwen gasped. 'Oh, I must owe you a fortune!' She couldn't believe he'd had to take her car to the filling station for her—it was all so embarrassing.

He looked equally shocked. 'Of course not. It was all done on site at my chateau. There's no charge. Once the problem had been identified, my people did a few little repairs and a spot of touching up. After that, I said I'd test-drive it for them.'

'And did you?'

'Only as far as your *gite*, as it turned out. I was intending to drive you down to Le Rossignol.'

That revived something of Gwen's fighting spirit. '*You* were going to drive me in *my* car?' she asked pointedly.

Etienne struggled visibly to bite back a smile at her indignation.

'You are a remarkable woman, Gwen,' he drawled. 'Last night was a unique experience. I feel privileged to have been part of your life, if only for a few hours.'

Watching him skate on a veneer of perfect manners made her feel totally inadequate. If he was struggling to ignore the bad feeling that had passed between them, then perhaps she should, too. Gripping the edge of her chair, she wondered what to say. Surely if he really considered her mistress material he would have bundled her straight back to bed first thing that morning. Staring across the table at him now, she saw no trace of the wild beast who had ravished her time and again through the hours of darkness. Now he was reduced to the status of a normal executive, lunching at his favourite restaurant. *Reduced*? Gwen almost laughed out loud at that idea. Etienne Moreau was unique, to use his own word. His effect could never be lessened in any way. Beneath those beautiful clothes he had the body of a god and the bearing of a count. Turning down his offer had been close to impossible. It was only her self-esteem that had made her do it. Now she wasn't sure how much restraint she had left.

'You're right. Last night was wonderful.' She passed the tip of her tongue nervously over her lips, remembering. He noticed, and relented slightly. She saw it in his smile. Almost immediately, his expression was shadowed with regret. Gwen found she had to look away. She took refuge behind a sharp, businesslike tone.

'But this is today, Etienne. Now, if you would excuse me, you're quite right. I must get back to work. Sex and business don't mix.'

CHAPTER FIVE

She had meant to walk straight out of the door in a businesslike manner, but made the mistake of looking back at him. She was immediately caught in Etienne's gaze. His velvety brown eyes had softened dangerously and were sparkling with mischief. 'How would you know, Gwen? I was your first—and if you let me have my way, I'll be the only man you'll ever need.'

His smile was slow, seductive and totally irresistible.

'You're awfully sure of yourself, Etienne.' And with good reason, she thought with a sigh. She turned to leave, unable to bear the infuriating temptation of him any more. Etienne raised his dark brows in a warning gesture.

'Experience can't be denied.' His voice had all the depth and intensity of crushed cacao, but it brought Gwen no comfort at all.

'That's what worries me. You have a track record, I have none—or at least I didn't until I met you,' she said, feeling a flush run over her cheeks and wishing she didn't blush quite so easily. Etienne was far too self-confident to need any encouragement. 'I'd like to keep it that way, thanks, until I find a man who thinks the same way as I do.'

'I thought I did. Until we met, I lived in the present and looked to the future. The past was no good to me. Haven't you said as much yourself, in abandoning your family to come here to Malotte?'

His innocent smile made her suspicious. 'Are you suggesting that meeting me has changed your outlook on life?' she said warily. Etienne's smile spoke for him. He was lulling her into a false sense of security with warm brown eyes and a knowing expression. He was charming, he was delightful, and she wished with all her heart that he could be hers.

Her heart in her mouth, she waited. Etienne stayed silent.

Eventually, her nerve broke.

'Well, I can't hang around here all day—'

'No other woman could have—'

They had started to speak at exactly the same time. Gwen stared at him. What on earth had he been about to say?

'Go on,' she said faintly.

'No…I interrupted you. You're right, Gwen. I should let you get back to work. Carry on and I'll see you tomorrow,' he said with graceful insistence.

Gwen let her eyes rest on his face. He was lovely, but she had to pack up all her fantasies in a cast-iron trunk and head back to real life. This wasn't the time to feel angry, embarrassed or ashamed. It was an opportunity to imprint every nuance of Etienne upon her mind, for from this moment on their relationship had to stay on a purely business footing.

'Why are you staring at me like that?' he said, without looking up.

'Because I'm waiting to take your order, of course,' Gwen improvised quickly, pulling the pantry notebook from the pocket of her apron.

'I'd rather you left your staff to deal with that side of things. As I said, I've got something far more interesting on offer for you, Gwen.' He paused. 'I was going to wait till tomorrow, so that I could have all the financial documents for you to look at, but I want to offer you a business proposition—nothing more. I have visited Le Rossignol often enough to know that your restaurant would benefit from serious investment, and I have been thoroughly impressed by what this place has to offer.'

Gwen's mouth fell open. 'Are you offering me money again?' she said faintly.

'Not in that way!' He laughed. 'This would be a strictly business arrangement, binding on both sides. I don't waste money, Gwen. You have made your feelings clear earlier, and now I'm making mine clear. I'd like to invest in Le Rossignol.'

If anyone needed financial help, it was Gwen. Etienne Moreau was clearly more than just sex on legs. He knew how to use all his attributes to the best effect, and not simply his body. She was tempted instantly. How could she not be? This might be a solution to all her problems. Her first reaction was to reach out and hug him. She stopped herself just in time. This was *just* business! Any kind of physical contact with him might push her over that precipice of temptation again. Instead, she pressed her hands to her cheeks in delight.

'Etienne…are you really sure you want to do this?'

'I've told you—when it comes to my best interests I look to the future, rather than dwelling on the past.'

Gwen let her breath go in a great gasp.

'Wait until you see my offer before you commit yourself,' he warned, but his smile had a playful twinkle she had never noticed before.

Gwen's world was spinning. A few bittersweet hours ago this man had stripped her of all her inhibitions. She wasn't going to show him how he could still affect every fibre of her being.

Gwen set off early for work next morning. Her car's interior was already baking. She was so distracted by thoughts of her meeting with Etienne, she started fiddling with its air-conditioning straight away. It hadn't worked for months, but within seconds a cool breeze was rippling around the car. Etienne had worked a miracle. But then her core temperature began to rise. It looked as if she would have to fight on several fronts to stop him filling her mind completely, but he was proving to be as useful as he was charming. She smiled. Lounging around on a yacht while he talked business sounded close to heaven. She would have to keep her professional hat jammed well down over her eyes to stop the seductive Monsieur Moreau feeding her emotional candyfloss. She was going to make this work! He'd respected her decision not to become his mistress, and now he was treating her like a professional.

She impressed on everyone that she was determined to take the afternoon off, for once. It worked like magic. Lunch was cleared away in record time. After that, all she had to do was wait for the car Etienne had promised. That was the worst part. Each time she checked the time, the hands of her watch had hardly moved. Desperate that no one should see who was picking her up from work, Gwen let her staff leave early. Only minutes after she let the last one out the back door, a chauffeur arrived at the front.

Suddenly her whole body was alight with fear. What would happen when she was alone with Etienne again—on a yacht?

Slinging her bag over her shoulder, she strode out into the sunlight. She wasn't carrying much, but it gave her something to do with her hands. It was hard to look confident when her nerves were stretched to breaking point. The chauffeur swung the car door open for her. She was faintly alarmed to find Etienne seated inside. This was a test, but it wasn't as worrying as it might have been. She had been scared of making a fool of herself by trying the wrong door, or failing to get it open. Now she could step inside with confidence.

'You were ready and waiting?' He sounded impressed.

Gwen relaxed a little more. *This might not be such an ordeal after all,* she thought, trying to forget the last of her fears. She settled back in the expensively fragrant seat.

'Of course. How long is this meeting likely to take?' she said briskly. Out of the corner of her eye she saw Etienne raise his eyebrows.

'That depends—although as you've already broken

my rule about answering back, the prospects don't look good.' He shot a sideways glance at her—full of mischief.

Gwen steeled her resolve and ignored his teasing. 'Why don't you outline your idea to me now? That would save time. It's a shame we didn't discuss it fully yesterday in my office, as I suggested.'

'No, it isn't. That's your workplace. People are in and out all the time, asking questions and dragging you away at irregular intervals. If I took you to a rival establishment for lunch you'd spend more time dissecting their menu than listening to me. Also, I have the yacht—why not mix business with pleasure and take you out to sea?'

Gwen gave him a calculating look. 'As long as you aren't taking me for a ride as well.'

A familiar wicked smile spread over his face. 'Oh, no,' he said, adding after a suggestive pause, 'Not *this* time.'

There was hardly any time to enjoy the sensation of riding in Etienne's luxurious car. In only a few minutes it drew to a halt outside the Hotel Splendide and the chauffeur leapt out to help her from the car.

'You've changed your plans already, Etienne? I didn't think you'd really take me onto your yacht, but this makes up for it!' She gazed up at the magnificent building, trying to take in every aspect of the luxurious hotel and its hordes of uniformed staff.

'Make the most of it. We're not staying here. There's a helicopter waiting for us on the roof.'

Gwen was horrified. 'Etienne! You can't just walk

through a place like this and expect to use their helicopter!'

He was dismissive. 'Of course I can. It's my hotel, and my helicopter. *The Windflower* is moored offshore, well away from prying eyes and long lenses.'

They were wafted up to the roof in an elevator that was as silent as it was smooth. Etienne escorted her out onto the roof. Gwen was nervous as the pilot helped her into her seat and fastened the seat belt. Nothing like this had ever happened to her before. However, after a moment of fear as they lifted off, she slowly began to relax. The bustle of the world below faded away as they zoomed towards the sea. She had no sooner decided she liked the sensation of flying in a helicopter than they began circling in to land on the deck of an enormous ocean-going yacht, moored far out in the bay.

'I didn't think it was possible for your eyes to get any bigger, Gwen!' Etienne smiled. He moved as though he was about to lay his hand on her shoulder, but pulled it away at the last moment.

'It's enormous—and so beautiful!' She sighed, gazing down into the perfect blue of the on-board pool. 'However much must it have cost?'

It would have been an obvious comment to make to any of her friends from the valley back at home, but the worst sort of social gaffe in the circumstances. Her hands flew to her mouth.

'Oh, Etienne, how rude was *that!* I'm so sorry!'

He chuckled indulgently. 'Don't be. Your honesty sends a real breath of fresh air through my life, Gwen. Any other woman would have pretended to be gazing into my eyes while her mind calculated my net worth. Business associates would assume it was leased. The truth is *The Windflower* is all mine. But when it comes to how much she costs—well…' he gave another of his characteristic shrugs '…it would be rude to discuss it. As I've told you before, I value my privacy highly. When I discovered that there are a thousand tiny, uninhabited tropical islands scattered around the world, it was a challenge I couldn't resist. I contacted a designer and asked him to build me a vessel that provided seven-star accommodation. He did the work, all I did was sign the cheques. Whatever she cost, she's worth every cent. Whenever I get some free time, I head out to sea. For those occasions when my companion doesn't feel like sharing a hammock slung between two palm trees, I can whisk them back to my ship on the launch or by helicopter, depending how far out she's moored. As a floating pleasure palace, she's invaluable.'

As he spoke he leaned across her, so close she could feel the warmth of his face next to hers. A mad impulse made her want to kiss his cheek, but she resisted. He kept his eyes resolutely fixed on his beautiful yacht, but Gwen guessed he was waiting for her to make a move. He was so sure of himself, it made her even more determined not to let herself be swept away by the rip tide of her desire. The half-smile sculpting his beautiful mouth dared her to go back on her word and give in to his every temptation. After stalking out of his house in such fury, she couldn't possibly back down. She drew in one long, slow, lingering breath. It was filled with the high notes of his cedar-fragranced aftershave. That was delicious enough, but beneath it simmered the warmer, darker temptations of vital maleness.

'I'll bet your lifetime list of islands has a column for women, too,' she murmured, finding it hard to sound sarcastic when he was so very close.

'It's a hobby,' he said with a mischievous grin.

The helicopter drifted into land exactly on the target painted in the middle of its upper deck. As the rotors slowed to a halt a long procession of Etienne's domestic staff emerged. They greeted her with smiles as he introduced each of them by name. Gwen had been nervous. Now she felt much more relaxed as Etienne showed her down from the deck. The contrast between hot bright sunshine and the cool silence of the luxurious living conditions was like chilled champagne.

'This is lovely,' she sighed. Her sleeveless T-shirt was no protection against the midday sun. She was glad of the cold kiss of air-conditioning on the tender pink skin of her shoulders. 'It's even better than your hotel.'

'I should hope so. And this is only the offices and boardrooms. The suites are situated where they get the best views.'

Everything had a brand-new sheen about it. Gwen wanted to run her fingers over the polished, turned wood of handrails or the sleek chrome and glass fittings. Each time they passed an open door, she couldn't resist peeking in. Etienne clearly did a lot of entertaining. There were several lounges and public areas, all decorated with restrained good taste. Everything had the look of money well spent—a lot of money. The only thing the place lacked was people.

'Where is everyone? You've got dozens of staff on here—I've seen them. Where are they now?'

'In a ship this size it is easy to disappear. That's why I like it so much.' He ran his hand along a polished rosewood rail. Gwen saw real pride in his movements, and satisfaction in his smile. 'I can slip away from the largest party, and everyone will assume I'm merely circulating in some other part of the yacht.'

'It sounds like you enjoy socialising about as much as I do,' she joked.

'No, I hate it.'

He was deadly serious. So was Gwen.

'Snap.'

'I can't believe that.' His expression eased, as though the ice had been broken and he was glad neither of them had fallen through. 'You were born to entertain, Gwen, if anyone ever was.'

His voice was like satin now. With blinding insight, Gwen knew he was calling to mind the way she had pleased him in bed. Her mind filled with unforgettable images, too, but she wasn't going to fall under his spell again. Her first experience had given him the impression she was his mistress for the asking, and that made her wary. She wasn't going to let him take advantage of her so easily this time. Her self-esteem depended on it.

'Your staff didn't turn a hair when you introduced me. I suppose they're used to you bringing an endless procession of women on board,' she said, reminding herself that spectacular skills like his weren't honed over one night, or even a thousand.

Etienne had an easy answer. 'The reason for that is simple. They know you're here on business.'

Gwen laughed. 'When their boss has your taste for the ladies? The staff here must have seen a thousand different ones. I'll bet they're all discussing exactly what sort of "business" we're up to right now!'

'Gwen!' Etienne looked shocked as he showed her into a boardroom and flipped the sign outside to 'In Conference'. 'They wouldn't dream of it, if they wanted to keep their jobs. I hope you don't allow that sort of gossip in your kitchens at Le Rossignol!'

'Of course I don't. My staff don't have time to look up from their work. Nattering about anything is right out of the question.'

Trying to forget all the gossip she had heard about the Countess Sophie's plans for Etienne, she followed close behind him. He led the way into a light, airy room furnished with high-tech screens and projectors. A long, highly polished table stood in the centre, surrounded by chairs. A crystal carafe of iced water and two glasses stood beside a blotting pad placed at the head of the table. Gwen also noticed a small collection of official-looking documents. Etienne strode towards his place and pulled out the grand carved chair nearest it. He gestured for her to sit down. As she did he poured a glass of water and placed it on a coaster beside her.

'I thought you would be too sensible to allow chit-chat to distract your staff. It's another sign of a good businesswoman. The other night I saw how much you hate to disappoint your customers.'

That wicked smile was dancing around his handsome

mouth again. Gwen stared at him, willing herself not to blush. It didn't work.

Taking his seat at the head of the table, he opened the file that lay on top of the pile before him. She watched his eyes scan the first page, wishing he would look at her. When he did, she was unprepared for the effect it would have. Her blush returned with increasing heat. The urge to move in her seat with the memory of squirming beneath his hands fired her with a desire she knew she could never risk tasting again.

'It's true: any visitor to Le Rossignol can be sure their privacy will be respected,' Gwen said, trying to settle herself. Despite everything, the amusement in his eyes was infectious. Her façade of disapproval cracked with a smile, but she was determined to keep this business meeting on track. 'Any secret is totally safe with me.'

'I knew it would be. That's good. I'd prefer our discussions here today to remain confidential,' he said, and then dropped his voice to a seductive whisper. Leaning forward, he smiled at her with a warmth that threatened to melt the core of her resistance.

'The fact is, I'm hoping to make you an offer you can't refuse, Gwen Williams.'

Her eyes widened with alarm. If he was making a move on her, she would be powerless to resist. They were miles out to sea. There could be no escape this time. Terrified he would trample all over her feelings again, Gwen knew she must resist. She also knew it would be far too great a test of her will power. Her body was urging her to stay, and melt into his arms again. It was left to her mind to try and save her self-respect.

Dropping her hands flat on the boardroom table, she tried to spring to her feet. Quickly, Etienne dropped his hand over hers. It was a heavy, decisive movement with no trace of seduction or romance. She froze, and looked into his eyes. They were glowing, but with nothing more than cold reason.

'Relax! I've told you before. It isn't that sort of offer, Gwen.'

Slowly, she sank back into her seat. His message was received and understood. She looked down at her reflection in the mirror-like sheen of the boardroom table. For some time Etienne didn't move a muscle. Then slowly he withdrew his hand, dragging his slightly roughened palm across the smooth, delicate skin of her fingers. Picking up his pen, he switched his attention to a report on his blotter. While Gwen waited in silence, he made some notes. The sound of his gold nib inscribed the silence. When it seemed he had forgotten her, she lifted her palms slowly from the table, ready to put them in her lap. She was mortified to see they left prints behind on the polished surface. They lasted only as long as the pressure of his hand had done on her skin. *His memory of our night together must have vanished in the same way,* she thought.

Etienne continued to study the open file before him. When he sensed she had settled again, he looked up from his notes. His expression had all the integrity of jet. It combined beauty and inescapable darkness in one irresistible look.

'I'll come straight to the point, Gwen. I need to broaden my investment portfolio. The hospitality industry is exactly the type of diversification I need. Le

Rossignol has been my favourite restaurant from the moment Nick bought it. I've since discovered its success is entirely due to your flair in the kitchen. I'd hate to see it close through lack of working capital. That's why I want to inject some money into your business.' He paused minutely as Gwen opened her mouth to interrupt. The look on his face dared her to disagree. Taking her cue from his expression, she said nothing, but smiled instead.

Etienne looked back at his notes and reconsidered. Clearing his throat, he rephrased his last words. 'I want to ensure I can dine there whenever I like, safe in the knowledge that you are going to be the hostess and head of the kitchen. In short, Le Rossignol needs money, and I have plenty of it. Funds would be the only thing on offer—it's no good expecting me to lend a hand with the washing-up,' he coaxed her with a smile.

Gwen tried to respond, but she could barely form a reply. 'If you know so much about the money side, I'm amazed you aren't ready to employ someone for little details like that,' she said faintly.

'Talking about the work is the extent of my skill in the kitchen,' he replied with dry humour. 'That's why you will remain in complete control. I've had my experts draw up a legal document—this is your copy.' He closed the file he had been working on and slid it across the table to her. 'Where they've been too pompous I've added a few foot-notes so that you and I both know exactly what they mean.'

Gwen stared at the orange file as though it were a snake ready to strike. How could anyone put money into a business without wanting to control it?

'Th-thank you, Etienne. That's very kind of you,'

she said slowly, hoping she really could believe that. She had been brought up by hard-nosed business people. She knew what business life did to people, and couldn't bear to think of Etienne being similarly underhand. 'But I have to ask—what's in this for you?'

'I've told you: it is part of my wider strategy to spread my investments. In addition, I get to eat and entertain at the finest venue in this part of France.'

'And that's all?' She watched him carefully. He showed no outward signs of tension whatsoever. Leaning forward, he clasped his hands loosely on the desk before him. He was the perfect businessman, ready for the next topic on his agenda.

'What happens if I say no?'

He stared at her, taking some time to compute what she had said. Then without warning he broke eye contact, poured himself a glass of water and took a long, slow drink. When he put down his glass, he stretched the silence further until eventually he announced: 'If you do, you will prove yourself to be as sadly misguided as the last woman who refused to take my advice. I'm sure you know what happened to her.'

Gwen felt her stomach turn a somersault. In a couple of days, Etienne had flipped her life upside down to devastating effect. When she looked at him now, her eyelids fluttered with apprehension. In contrast, his gaze was rock steady. Penetrating her puny defences, his single-minded power alarmed her. She passed the tip of her tongue nervously over her parched lips.

'I hardly like to ask,' she said faintly. Etienne looked surprised, and suspicious.

'You must have seen the press coverage at the time?'

Gwen shook her head, confused. His laughter subsided into a bitter smile.

'It was front-page news. The glossies had a field day.'

Gwen, who couldn't remember when she last had the time to read anything beyond a recipe book, stared at him bleakly.

'Thank you for your discretion, Gwen, but don't worry about hurting my feelings. I no longer have any. They were burned away long ago. Angela Webbington's deceit made sure of that. And with your links to Nick, I'm sure he's told you all the repulsive details the media missed.'

'No…I hardly know the man.' She shook her head, bewildered. 'He's my landlord, that's all. Since Carys jilted him and I bought out their share of the business, we've rarely had time to chat.'

Etienne stared at her for a long time. Gwen felt under intense pressure, but she could do nothing about it. She had never heard of this Angela Webbington in her life, but she was certain of one thing. The moment she next got her hands on a computer, search engines would be humming with the name.

'There's no point in expecting me to crack and change my story, Etienne. I can only tell you the truth. I have no idea what went on in your past. And I'm not sure I want you to tell me, right now,' she said uneasily. 'I'd rather feel free to come to my own decision over your plan. I don't want the shadow of some other woman's mistake hanging over me.'

His expression changed, but she found it impossible to tell what was going on in his mind.

'Then you're very wise,' he said quietly. 'Let's concentrate on my plans to become your business partner, instead. What do you think, Miss Williams?' he said, gently mocking her earnest expression.

Gwen took a deep breath. She felt on safer ground when the talk turned to Le Rossignol, but had to speak her mind. The chances were Etienne wouldn't like that, and she didn't relish the thought of provoking him.

'I—I shall have to think about it,' she ventured, too afraid of what she might see to lift her eyes from the smart, customised file in front of her. Then she thought of a way to escape from this confrontation with her dignity intact. 'Can I take this away with me and study it? I could give you my answer tomorrow.'

He was silent for so long, Gwen couldn't stand it. Finally she let her eyes work their way across the table until she reached his blotting pad. His hands were there, as smooth and golden as ever. They cradled the barrel of his fountain pen as lightly as they had once danced over her body. Now they were still. Her gaze was drawn inexorably upwards, over the body she craved to his resolute stare. It was softer now, but still warned her to keep at arm's length.

'Is that all right? Can I have some time to consider your offer?' she repeated nervously. He pressed his lips together. It was a gesture of exclusion, concealing every trace of their naturally sensuous shape.

'I can't deny I'm surprised, Gwen. I thought you'd jump at the chance. But you can certainly take time to read over the contract—of that I insist.'

'I didn't come this far to sign away everything I'm

fighting for in a moment of desperation— I mean, *to sign away all my rights without studying what my responsibilities will be,*' she corrected herself quickly.

Etienne raised a brow at the word she had been swift to cover up. 'Desperate, Gwen?'

There was no point in denying it. This man knew all about her unpaid electricity bill. He probably suspected lack of money was the reason her car ran out of petrol. That stung, because it wasn't true. Gwen raised her chin and looked him straight in the eye. 'I always pay my debts. It's finding the time to do it that's the problem.'

He nodded. 'That's why my idea is your perfect solution.' Looking closely at her face, he ran his gaze over her again and again as he catalogued all the details. 'I can see how heavily the responsibility weighs on you. When was the last time you had a decent night's sleep?'

Gwen blushed. Etienne's eyes, which until then had been riveted on her, flicked away. It was his turn to make a correction. '*Uninterrupted* sleep, that is?'

'I can't remember. There's always something that needs attention. Or somebody,' she finished lightly.

'Then why don't you look upon my offer as a way to buy yourself some time? My investment in Le Rossignol would fund extra staff, new equipment, IT training and anything else you need to make your business run more smoothly. Notice how I used the term investment. I didn't call it my *money*. I know how you feel about offers of personal generosity.' He looked at her acutely from beneath his fine dark brows.

Gwen did not share his quiet amusement. She winced

at the memory of what had happened over breakfast the previous day. Etienne didn't let that stop him for a minute. He was already moving on.

'Under this scheme, you'll be free to concentrate on the things you do best—catering and entertaining. I'd be your sleeping partner, an arrangement that will benefit us both. A *business* arrangement, that's it,' he stressed again.

Gwen hardly needed his emphasis. The perfectly produced business plan in front of her and his quiet formality would have been reassurance enough. The fact she was indeed desperate added another good hard shove in the direction of accepting his offer.

She sat on her hands. Every instinct told her to play it cool; this just seemed too good to be true. Could anyone be so kind without an ulterior motive? She organised her face into an expression of deep scepticism. It was either that, or throw herself across the desk, showering him with grateful kisses while she searched for his chequebook. She let her dangerously dishonest expression slide across the table and onto her lap. There she studied her hands with their crossed fingers, and hoped.

'I still don't know…' She squeezed the words out as though they were taxable. 'I need to think about it.'

Well—I never knew I could lie like that! she thought, astonished. In a few short hours Etienne had introduced her to all sorts of new experiences. She despised dishonesty, both in herself and others. The only way she managed to get the words out was by telling herself she wasn't actually altering the truth. She was only backing away from it.

To her surprise, the reply pleased him.

'Good—I'm glad you want to give it such careful consideration. That shows sound business sense. Study the papers, and the draft contract, too.' With a small smile, he nodded and handed her a second file from his pile of paperwork. 'And now, you have a choice. I have an appointment on the mainland, so I'm flying straight back. You can either travel with me, when you can spend a few hours wandering around the shops until I'm ready to return. Alternatively, you can stay here and enjoy what *The Windflower* has to offer while you study the paperwork at your leisure. Then, if you have any questions, we can discuss it over dinner.'

CHAPTER SIX

ETIENNE might have proved he had the selective memory of a gentleman, but Gwen was still uncertain.

'Dinner? Where? Le Rossignol isn't open tonight, and I was only going to have salad at home—'

Etienne shook his head with a smile.

'It will be served here on *The Windflower.*'

Gwen looked around, almost breathless with delight. Dinner on his private yacht sounded like heaven. It only took her a few seconds to discover the flaw in his plan.

'What happens if I haven't come to a decision by this evening?'

'It doesn't matter. I expect you'll get a certain amount of pleasure from a gourmet meal you haven't had to plan and organise yourself?' He grinned. 'I don't employ a huge staff purely for my own benefit. When I entertain a prospective business partner, I *entertain.*' He stressed his final words as though the phrase should be inscribed in block capitals over the entrance to every room. Gwen smiled, recognising again their mutual desire to put on a good show for the benefit of others. All the fight flowed out of her in an instant.

'I'd be delighted to stay here,' she said with real feeling. 'Although I'm afraid I don't have anything to wear.'

He laughed. 'If that troubles you so much, I could send someone to the *gite* to collect something for you?'

Gwen bit her lip. Her only formal dress he had already seen. Not, she reminded herself sternly, that this mattered. Her aim was to dress appropriately, not to impress him... *Yeah, right*, said the annoyingly honest voice in her head. She *could* take up his offer of a lift back to the mainland and hit the shops instead, but she didn't want to. For one thing, she couldn't afford to splash out on a new dress. For another, she was itching to sample what life on *The Windflower* had to offer. While Etienne was on shore, she could indulge her fantasies in safety. She swallowed her pride.

'My blue dress is in the wardrobe at home...'

Etienne held out his hand for her keys and Gwen handed them over in silent amazement at this man who seemed able to solve any problem and persuade her into anything. As she told him where to find all the things she would need to get ready for dinner that evening she marvelled at how helpful he was being. His reaction when he'd mentioned the name 'Angela Webbington' had disturbed her. He had presented himself then as some sort of hollow, disappointed man. Right now, nothing could look less like the truth. Etienne was his usual, charming, irritatingly compelling self. Her curiosity was well and truly aroused. What sort of grim secret could such a man be hiding? She had noticed that laptop computers were available for use in all the public areas of the ship. The temptation to find out the worst about him began to dangle before her. If Etienne assumed his past was common knowledge, he wasn't likely to care if one more person found out about it. *And putting a couple of names into a search engine hardly amounts to snooping, does it?* she reassured herself.

After pocketing her keys, Etienne reached out and patted her unexpectedly on the arm.

'My people will be very careful. You don't need to worry about a thing,' he said as his touch dropped away from her.

Gwen thought of the moment she had tried to slip out of bed and he had drawn her back into his body with those same, strong hands. Memory snatched the breath from her throat. She looked up quickly to see if he had noticed. He was looking at her, but his expression was as impassive as it had been when he was annotating his business proposition. With an awful pang she realised their moments together had passed. Any fear she might have felt at being alone with him dissolved. He wanted her business as a project now, not her body for his plaything. She had lost her chance. The only thing she had left was her dignity, and she wasn't going to let that go without a struggle. She tried to make it sound as though she were still in two minds about accepting his invitation.

'OK, thanks. What time is dinner, and where will it be served?'

'I haven't decided on either yet,' he said affably. 'Don't worry. When it's ready, I'll send a steward to find you.'

'I'm sorry I misjudged you, Etienne. You really did invite me here for business, after all!' Gwen said, trying to keep her voice light and casual.

'How could you ever doubt me?' He gave her a particularly winning smile as he escorted her to the door. 'You made it quite clear yesterday that you don't want to become my mistress. Nothing else was on offer. I'm a straight-talking man. Unlike some people, I don't make promises I can't keep.'

'I'm glad to hear it.' Gwen tried to leave it at that, but some devilish impulse forced her to add, 'It doesn't stop you keeping plenty of company, though! I lost count of how many women I saw you talking to at the reception.'

'None of them matter.' He sliced the remark at her sharply.

Taken aback by his bitter tone, she thought of his bathroom back at the chateau, stocked with cosmetics for every taste and occasion. Evidently, plenty of women passed through his hands, but none made much of an impression on him. That made his mention of the shadowy figure of Angela Webbington all the more interesting. She had mattered. Gwen's curiosity increased until she could hardly stand it.

'You're looking thoughtful, Gwen?'

She jumped guiltily, and said the first thing that came into her head. 'Do your staff treat all your female visitors the same?'

'Gwen, you are very worried about the staff. They are not here to judge you, they are here because they have jobs to do.'

He started walking away and then stopped a little short of the boardroom door. 'And of course,' he continued with a hint of mischief in his eyes, 'there's all the difference in the world between the way I introduced you as "Miss Gwen Williams" today—' standing a little apart from her, he extended his palm to an imaginary member of staff exactly as he had done earlier, up on deck '—and this…'

Before Gwen realised what was happening he had closed the gap between them and slid his arm around her waist. It enclosed her with a memory of those sublime moments they had shared as he lowered his voice to say, 'Meet Gwen, everybody…'

Instinctively, she relaxed against the delicious pressure of his arm. Almost at once it slipped away from her, like a dream. It was a painful reawakening. Gwen blinked quickly, trying to dismiss the sinful feelings that kept creeping up on her. When Etienne leaned across her in the helicopter, and now as he demonstrated his technique with conquests, the urge to take matters on her own lips and kiss him almost made a fool of her. Gwen knew she must forget their night of passion. Etienne certainly had. From the way he casually left her side and opened the boardroom door to usher her out now, he couldn't have meant anything by it. All his little gestures, like those smiles that made her feel like the only girl in the world, must be totally unconscious.

He summoned a steward to show Gwen to her suite. She swept past Etienne with what she hoped was an air of professional detachment and followed the man to her temporary home. Only then, behind locked doors, could she allow herself to grieve for what might have been.

* * *

Etienne could not watch her walk away. He went back into the boardroom, locked the door and leaned back against it. Anyone would have to break through four inches of solid mahogany and his iron determination to get in. This whole situation was bizarre. Gwen Williams was a real challenge. She confronted him with both the easiest and the most difficult situations. Here was a woman who didn't want to become his mistress. If that wasn't unbelievable enough, it really mattered to him! She was so totally unlike any other woman he had bedded. He couldn't let the memory go. They talked together then, and they were still talking now. She said things he found worth listening to. He found he wanted to know what she was going to say next. Whenever he closed a door on her, it could never quite shut her out of his mind.

It had to be because she had resisted him. That was surely the top and bottom of it. He wanted her to want him, body and soul. Anything less was unnatural. Gwen's body language kept saying yes. Yet she had refused him twice, and nothing on earth would persuade him to risk asking her again. Instead, he had changed tack and was offering her the only thing more powerful than his attraction for the opposite sex—money. It was incomprehensible that any woman would take advantage of that before his body, but Etienne had to give her the chance. Once again, she flew in the face of reason. She hadn't accepted straight away. He tried to persuade himself this was a good thing. Gwen was the first girl who had touched his heart since Angela. And, if he put her on a similar pedestal he would expect her to fall to earth with an equally leaden thud, but it hadn't happened yet, despite her circumstances.

Until he took her home and found the place was condemned to darkness, Etienne had had no idea that she was in such financial difficulty. It didn't take much imagination to realise other parts of Gwen's lifestyle would be under threat. She was obviously desperate for money, but she still held out against him. She refused to take the easy way out. He had never before known a woman with such an independent streak.

Smiling to himself, he moved away from the door. He strolled back to the boardroom table. His personal copy of her file lay on top of his pile of paperwork. Placing one long golden finger on her name, he traced over the letters.

This girl was one in a million. She fully deserved to succeed.

A steward showed Gwen to her suite. It was magnificent, with a view across gentle blue waters to the coastline beyond. He gave her an amazing guided tour of the staterooms and their private spa, but Gwen couldn't take in much detail after the first few seconds. She was more interested in the laptop on the table in her reception room. Once she was alone, she locked the door. It only took seconds to enter the name 'Angela Webbington' into a search engine.

What she discovered about Etienne's past made her wish she hadn't been in such a hurry to pry. There were pages of photographs of his ex-fiancée. Angela Webbington turned out to be a tall, whippet-thin blonde.

Gwen was built for comfort rather than speed, and cringed. Each time she looked at Etienne, she thought of sex. When he looked at her, she had a horrible feeling all he now thought was 'chef'. If this Angela was his ideal woman, then Gwen's fantasies of being leapt on again with a cry of undying lust were sadly misplaced.

She sighed. It had been a mistake to ever emerge from her kitchens. She was at her best when she was being brilliant behind the scenes. Angela Webbington was a force in front of Stateside TV cameras. *I'm fooling myself to think the other night was anything more than an accident of lust,* she thought. *I happened to be in the right place at the right time, that's all.*

She scrolled down the web page sadly, but things suddenly got a whole lot worse. A terrifying headline screamed: *'Baby or Bastard?'*, adding in only slightly smaller letters: *'"I'll disown you both!" vows future count.'* It was accompanied by a photograph of a gaunt Angela. She had been snapped leaving what the report identified as an abortion clinic. Gwen switched off the screen.

For a long time, she sat staring into space. The blank computer mirrored her thoughts. The report was simple and straightforward, but her reaction to it was complex. Etienne had been a spectacular lover, but she could not imagine him as a father. He was too much like her own dad. They were both totally absorbed by their own lives. Gwen had decided very early in life that real fathers should have a life outside work. In primary school, she had listened to her classmates' stories of holidays in foreign countries. The Williams family had been restricted to half-day trips. Her parents never travelled further than they could help. Everything revolved around the opening hours of their shop.

Gwen looked around her luxurious on-board suite. She could understand a rich man like Etienne not wanting to be tied down. There was something of that in her own character. Everything she did was a reaction against the restrictions of her earlier home life. Her move to France had scandalised her extended family, who all lived within a few miles of each other. That was bad enough, but the ultimatum Etienne had given to Angela Webbington went even further. A man who could abandon his fiancée and unborn child was surely capable of anything.

Although the room was warm, Gwen shivered.

She had known the charming Etienne had a ruthless streak, but she had not thought him capable of such coldness. She picked up his proposal and began to read it. At first, she could not concentrate. Haunted by that one incident in his life, she wanted to know more. Yet she was scared about what she might unearth. Her worries meant she only skimmed through the paperwork to begin with. Then a wicked idea took root in her mind, and began to grow. It was so terrible she could hardly bear to think it—but it was a truth that couldn't be denied.

Anyone cold-hearted enough to abandon their fiancée on the mere suspicion of infidelity was bound to succeed in business. When it came to the cut and thrust of business life, Gwen knew her limitations. She was hopeless. She let paperwork pile up. Dealing with bad payers and unreliable tradesmen kept her awake at night. When it came to cooking, she was a star performer. Anything else was a case of damage limitation. A ruthless man like Etienne Moreau would never stand for that. His money and network of advisors would be invaluable.

With him on her side, she could not fail.

She settled down to read the paperwork more carefully. It wasn't long before she realised what a good scheme Etienne was actually putting forward. Any worries she had about accepting his investment began to recede. He would provide a large sum of money up front, and the services of his marketing team would be available for free. That alone would have persuaded Gwen to sign up. The prospect of handing over the restaurant's promotion and website updating made her feel weak with relief. All she wanted to do was create dishes and cook. In return, Etienne was offering her an eighty-twenty split of the profits. She felt that was worth haggling over, so left the contract unsigned. Then she pushed it aside and tried to enjoy her spell aboard *The Windflower*.

That was easy, although it took some getting used to. At first she crept around like a mouse, half afraid she might wake and find it was all a dream. The suite she had been given was large and luxurious. There were lush arrangements of flowers on every horizontal surface, and all the rooms were cushioned with the exclusive silence that only thick, wall-to-wall carpeting could bring. The cupboards were packed with delights, in the same way Etienne's bathroom back at the chateau had been. Nothing was left to chance. She even found a cupboard filled with brand-new robes and swimming things in every size, for guests to use in the private spa.

Worrying about Le Rossignol was such a major part of Gwen's life it was hard to stop, but within an hour *The Windflower* had almost caressed it from her mind. The place was a delight from top to bottom. She had never enjoyed such a leisurely afternoon. *Actually,* she thought as she floated on her back in one of the shimmering, soft water pools, *I can't remember enjoying an afternoon off at all!*

She had spent her childhood studying, and her adulthood gaining skills. For the first time in her life she had the perfect excuse to do nothing for a few hours. She felt like a hamster released from its wheel. It was lovely. Every so often she stretched and sighed, simply because she had the space and time to do so. The sky had never seemed quite such an irresistible shade of blue as she enjoyed doing nothing, for once. The only thoughts in her head revolved around Etienne. She kept mulling over the things she had seen on the Internet. Newspaper coverage at the time had called him 'ruthless' over his handling of the Angela Webbington saga. There was no doubting his financial flair when she looked over his partnership proposal. But could she trust him? His smile made her feel like marshmallow. But the look on his face as he had stood on her doorstep, refusing to apologise, had hinted at something far darker beneath.

Despite the heat of the Mediterranean sun, she felt her skin go cold.

* * *

Etienne didn't intend wasting any time on the mainland. He sent his driver to collect the list of things Gwen wanted, while he called into his office. Working steadily, he soon emptied his in-tray, despite being distracted by a particularly tricky puzzle. Whenever he sealed a deal, he always presented the other party with a bottle of something sophisticated. So far, he had only dealt with business*men*. He knew Gwen would sign his agreement in the end, and wanted to make a similar gesture. The trouble was, he couldn't decide what it should be. Her furious reaction when he'd wanted to make her his mistress meant a bottle of vintage champagne was right out of the question. She would probably think he was just trying to get her drunk. His gift needed to be subtle, yet irresistible—like Gwen herself. He liked the perfume she wore already, and was in no hurry to change a winning formula. Without knowing its name, he was not about to risk buying the wrong brand.

He spent a long time with his brow ridged in thought. This task was outside the scope of a PA. Etienne wanted to do it alone, because Gwen deserved his personal touch. That was where his problem lay. Other women were easy to spoil. He had accounts with the finest chocolatiers and florists all over the world for exactly that reason. But he had dined at Le Rossignol often enough to know nothing could compete with Gwen's handmade luxuries. As she was currently staying on board *The Windflower,* the very last thing she needed right now was a bouquet of flowers. His staff always ensured there were armfuls of the things in every room. Any more, and the place would look like a funeral parlour. As Etienne walked out of his office he pulled out his mobile. Much as he hated to delegate in this case, it was time to enlist some help.

And then he glanced up, and saw the perfect solution to his problem.

It was displayed in a shop window on the other side of the road. Until that moment, he had been confident Gwen was totally unlike any other woman he had ever met. That was what made it impossible to get inside her guard. Now with a grin of triumph he remembered she *did* have one, single weakness. It hadn't registered with him at the time, but thinking back he recalled that she had let something slip only a few hours earlier.

Putting away his phone, he strode through the traffic to buy Gwen the present of her dreams.

While the deliciously feral shape of Etienne was away, mousy little Gwen was transformed. She was free to make the most of her chance to play. The longer she lingered aboard *The Windflower,* the bolder she got. Wistfully, she realised that if she hadn't snubbed his first offer, she might be swanning about this ship as Etienne's mistress. That illicit thought excited her. It coloured the rest of her afternoon. She swept along corridors, danced around the ballroom in solitary splendour and tried to imagine life as his *belle de jour*. She went up on deck and looked out towards the coast as though it were her own private kingdom. Somewhere out there, Etienne was busy with balance sheets and dry-as-dust documents. She thought back to their session in the boardroom. Smiling, she imagined his head bent over some tricky calculation. That endearing little crease would appear now and then between his brows as he applied his mind to some problem or another. Gwen had seen it so often over the past few days, but this afternoon there was a painful difference.

She was certain that, right now, she was the very *last* thing on his mind.

Gwen had just emerged from a long, luxurious shower when there was a knock at the door of her suite. Pulling on a silken robe, she hurried to open it. A steward stood outside in full uniform. He was delivering the things she had asked to be fetched from her house, but that wasn't what caught her eye. The man was also carrying a large white cardboard box, tied up with wide pink ribbon. Thanking him, she took the parcel inside her suite, wondering what on earth it could be. There was an envelope tucked inside, lying on layers of pink tissue paper. It was a card written in Etienne's distinctive handwriting. All it said was:

I saw this, and thought of you.

Gwen peeled back whisper-thin sheets of pastel paper like the petals of a rose. At their heart lay the most beautiful dress she had ever seen.

It was the full magnolia—a soft profusion of raw silk, simple, clinging and unutterably stunning. Spellbound, she lifted it up. The low-cut, subtly embroidered bodice would accentuate her voluptuous shape perfectly. The skirt fell in sensuous rustling folds to the floor. She inhaled the fragrance of luxury, long and lovingly.

And then she let slip a little moan of dismay. This was every woman's fantasy brought to life, but she couldn't possibly let it be hers. After she spent the afternoon strutting around *The Windflower* imagining life as Etienne's mistress, he presented her with this. This dress was exactly the sort of thing a man would buy his mistress. In an instant, she realised what had happened. Etienne hadn't taken her first two refusals seriously. A gift like this was a very obvious sign that he was choosing to ignore them. He assumed that because she was considering his business proposal, she would cave in to all his other demands, too. And as she imagined the silk of that dress against her skin she couldn't be at all certain that he wasn't right.

She dropped the dress as though it were suddenly red-hot. Putting her hands to her mouth, she stared around her sumptuous suite. *Appearance is everything here,* she thought. *If I wear this dress tonight, I'll fit in perfectly. And Etienne will know he's won...*

It took her a long time to get ready for dinner. As she added a dash of perfume behind her ears another knock came at the door. It might as well have been a hammer blow.

'Come in!' she called, expecting a steward who would escort her to dinner.

'I can't. I don't have a key.'

Etienne's voice came as a shock. Jumping up from her seat at the dressing table, Gwen crossed her changing room, but couldn't quite make it all the way. Memories of his ruthless treatment of Angela Webbington stopped her. She already knew sparks would fly tonight, but nothing had prepared her for the way she would feel as the showdown began.

'The door isn't locked,' she told him, in as reasonable a voice as she could manage.

When he didn't enter straight away, she walked hesitantly through her suite. Assuming the catch must have stuck, she intended to help. When the door popped open as she reached it, she jumped back in alarm.

Etienne was looking magnificent in full evening dress. His stark white cuffs were enlivened by gold studs, which he was twisting between his fingers.

'I didn't mean to startle you—' He began with a smile, and then stopped. Looking her up and down appreciatively, he studied every facet of her appearance. Then he widened his smile. 'You look lovely, Gwen. I'll get one of the seamstresses to alter the new dress for you. I'm sorry it didn't fit.'

Gwen had been primed to expect instant fury when he saw her in the blue velvet gown of their first meeting. His actual reaction completely foxed her. She reacted in the only way she knew.

'It didn't fit with my lifestyle—or the image I have of myself,' she said smartly. Picking up her handbag from a side table, she headed out into the corridor. 'Thank you for the gift, Etienne, but I've told you before. I'm here to consider your business proposal, and nothing more.'

'I know. That's why I bought you that dress. It was simply a present to celebrate our business partnership,' he said with a faint air of puzzlement. 'Whenever I enter into a new working relationship, I like to make a significant gesture. A dress seemed more your style than a gold fountain pen. Especially as you seemed sad about not having something to wear.'

Gwen hesitated, one hand lingering on the door of her suite. When he put it like that, he sounded almost convincing.

'It is a truly beautiful dress...' she agreed.

It would have been the easiest thing in the world to go back and change. But when she looked into the depths of Etienne's eyes they were dark with significance, and she knew she had been right. 'But a pen *would* have been more practical,' she added.

He lowered his head in grave acknowledgement. 'Yes, it would. I know—but I'm afraid I wasn't feeling very practical when I spotted that dress in the designer's window. Not that it matters.' He brightened, gallantly offering her his arm. 'You look absolutely wonderful.'

It was hardly the response Gwen expected, and she blushed. 'I was afraid you'd hit the roof. I thought you'd be furious,' she murmured.

'I've told you, Gwen. I don't waste words—or emotions.'

He smiled, and his expression backed him up. Gwen tried to take his arm in the spirit in which he offered it. The feel of his sleeve beneath her fingers was wonderfully provocative. She could only wonder how much more responsive she would have felt in that beautiful new gown.

Etienne looked every inch the suave, sophisticated aristocrat. Gwen had thought it was impossible for him to look better than he did the moment she first laid eyes on him. She was wrong. His perfect tuxedo, brilliant white shirt and black tie were perfectly set off by a small white rosebud in his buttonhole. His appearance almost made her forget the Internet coverage of his ill-fated affair with Angela Webbington. The tabloids had hacked out a flinty picture, but tonight there was no trace of the short-tempered, humourless man they described. Gwen hoped that pitiless nature had been exaggerated. After all, tabloids were hardly famed for being overly concerned with factual detail and as long as he confined his bad temper to her business enemies, it could be turned to her advantage. All she had to do was make sure she didn't get her own fingers burned. Or her heart.

She tried to laugh. *Chance would be a fine thing!* she thought.

Etienne frowned.

'This is a serious occasion, Gwen. It's a special dinner in honour of our new business venture.'

'Of course,' she responded quietly, thinking, *It's no wonder poor Angela disappointed him. Who could live up to standards like his?* 'You look wonderful, by the way.'

'And you look as spectacular as the moment I first saw you,' Etienne replied.

Seared by his gaze, Gwen paused. 'That's a matter of opinion!' She suddenly didn't feel very glamorous in her old dress. So she pushed on, refusing to let her feelings show. 'I should warn you that flattery is even less likely to cloud my judgement than buying me things. In any case, what makes you so sure I've decide to let you buy into Le Rossignol?' she added impishly.

He looked at her as though he could hardly believe what he was hearing.

'Only a fool would refuse such an offer, and you're very far from that,' he said, in a voice that would have cut diamond.

Gwen shot back, 'Or the size of your ego has over-shadowed any thoughts of failure.'

He treated her to a smile filled with feline satisfaction. 'I've never met a woman who's complained.'

As he spoke his eyes travelled from the crown of her head down to the tips of her toes. Then his scrutiny moved slowly back up again. 'You don't need designer dresses to make you look wonderful,' he murmured. 'You have a natural beauty beyond fashion.'

'I'll bet you say that to all the girls.' Gwen chuckled, before his gaze silenced her. It was filled with the predatory tension that had thrilled her from their first meeting.

'I mean it, Gwen. Any man would be proud to escort you into dinner. I'm glad that honour falls to me this evening.' He gave a little bow. Gwen felt herself grow several inches in stature.

'The honour is all mine,' she breathed with a sparkling smile.

This was rapidly turning back into the dream to end all dreams. Etienne was so darkly handsome, and he was standing so close her heart bounced with anticipation. It took a huge effort to remember what had happened to his ex-fiancée. She had been the media's idea of a trophy partner, yet it had ended in disaster.

'Although that's as far as it's going to go tonight, Etienne,' Gwen warned quickly.

'I rather got that impression. Although it's early yet,' he added, a half-smile dancing around his lips. 'Who knows what might happen?'

Summoning up all her will power, Gwen regarded him boldly. 'I do—and it's going to be absolutely *nothing*.' She gave him a meaningfully honest smile. 'So, to get me into the mood and you out of it, how about telling me what happens to your conquests who *aren't* entirely satisfied, Etienne?'

'There haven't been any,' he said innocently as they strolled along the wide, thickly carpeted corridor towards the state dining room. Gwen hesitated. He was lying. He must be. She had seen the coverage of his broken romance, Angela the wronged fiancée and his hideous ultimatum.

'I'll prove it to you again, if you like.' He turned a slow, devastating smile on her. She pulled her hand from the crook of his arm, mostly to stop herself from leaning into him. In response he stopped and narrowed his eyes in disapproval. 'Any time, Gwen.'

CHAPTER SEVEN

LOOKING him directly in the eyes, Gwen laid her hand on his arm again. He smiled as her fingertips connected with his. It was the worst thing he could have done. Her body began to betray her with a long slow-burning blush of anticipation.

'That's better. You may not know how to accept a compliment about your appearance gracefully, but you can't possibly object to taking my arm.'

'I'm sorry,' Gwen said, and then decided to draw another line in the sand straight away. 'The truth is, I'm not used to getting praise for the way I look. It's what I do that has always mattered, to me and to others.'

'OK,' he allowed as they reached their destination. 'But I wish you had felt able to accept my gift in the innocent spirit in which it was offered. I always like to make a little gesture to my new business associates. That dress was yours.'

He stood aside to let her enter the dining room. Gwen gasped. Its walls were mirrored from floor to ceiling. They reflected a beautiful table, set with silverware and fresh flowers, a handsome man in a tuxedo—and a beautiful woman with a glow in her eyes that Gwen didn't recognise. It was a seductive picture and for the second time that day Gwen let out a little moan of dismay. Etienne strolled past her and picked something up from a place setting on the grand dining table.

'As far as I'm concerned, all you need now is this single finishing touch.'

He turned, his hands moving towards her breast. She jumped back before noticing the corsage of miniature orchid blossoms held in his fingers.

'May I?'

'Of course,' Gwen said, breathless and annoyed at herself for being so. When his warm fingers slipped between her skin and the fabric of her dress, she had a different reason to feel embarrassed. Etienne's deft movements as he secured the flowers sent a torrent of hormones surging through her body. The nearness of him and his touch was enough to turn her legs to jelly. Her discomposure was so obvious, she waited for him to comment on the effect he was having on her. There could be no denying it. Any concern she might feel for Angela Webbington now was overwhelmed by a fierce flush of arousal. She raised her eyes to Etienne's face. It was impassive.

He finished fastening her corsage and took a step back, but did not look down to admire the finished effect.

'There. That looks almost as beautiful as the wearer.'

'How can you tell? You aren't looking at it.'

'I've seen enough.'

He sauntered off to pull out her chair. When she was seated, he took the delicate linen and lace napkin from her plate. Shaking it out, he draped it over her lap. As he did so his fingers trailed across her thighs. Gwen looked up, but he was already heading for his seat on the other side of the table.

With silent efficiency, uniformed staff delivered soup and crisp rolls, warm from the oven.

'So—what is your verdict?'

Gwen was lifting a pure white curl of butter from a crystal dish set in crushed ice. Leaning forward, his dinner forgotten, Etienne looked as driven as he had done earlier in the day when he was talking business.

'It's delicious, Etienne. My compliments to your chefs. This consommé is as good as anything we serve at Le Rossignol.'

'I'm talking about my business proposition.'

That explained the tension obvious in every inch of his body. Gwen smiled and took her time coaxing the chilled butter onto her bread.

'I think it's an absolutely brilliant idea,' she said, when she thought he had waited long enough. 'My only reservation is the division of profits.'

With a sigh of relief he sat back and picked up his soup spoon.

'Knowing how independent you are, I thought you would kick if I refused to take anything at all.'

'That's right—which is why I want you to reverse the order. You're putting up the money and taking the risk, so it's only right you should get the higher amount.'

She heard his spoon click against the fine china of his soup dish. He had stopped moving. She looked up, and found him staring at her, shocked.

'You don't mean that?'

'Of course I do. I'd cook for nothing, me. Well, enough to cover my costs, anyway,' she conceded. 'I'm not interested in making a fortune. I'd rather work on my reputation as a chef.'

'You're joking,' he said quietly.

Gwen mirrored his expression of disbelief. 'No. Why would I joke about a thing like that? I'm happy enough in my work. As long as I've got enough to cover my bills, I'll reckon myself lucky beyond the dreams of millions.'

'You're saying you don't want my money?'

His voice was indistinct, as though the words were having difficulty making themselves heard through the stone wall of his disbelief.

'No, not at all. I need your investment to keep my business afloat. In return, I want you to be fairly rewarded for the risk you're taking by investing such a huge sum of money.'

His laughter was incredulous. 'It's no wonder you were too proud to wear your new dress. I might have guessed we have differing views with regard to money. That amount is nothing, believe me. It's a mere drop in the Med!'

Gwen paused, and fixed him with a knowing look. 'You know your trouble? You want a taste of real life— a visit to my family home back in Wales would soon knock a few home truths into you!'

She had meant it as a joke. Etienne didn't laugh. Her own smile died as she saw the generous line of his lips struggle to rise in response.

'I don't doubt that. I've never had a home, only houses.'

'But you've got a family that goes back centuries!'

Gwen countered, thinking of his portrait gallery back at the chateau. 'It's a family that makes a home, and you've got more of that than most.'

He shook his head. 'I don't have any blood relatives left at all. My father was the last Moreau of his line. He was already an old man when I was born. He never made any attempt to hide the fact that if it wasn't for the family name, he would have remained childless until the day he died.'

Gwen almost dropped her spoon in horror. 'He told you that?'

Etienne shook his head. 'He didn't need to. After thirty years of being a widower, he married his house-keeper. I've never got on with Sophie, but my father knew I would consider it my duty to provide for her, as his widow. Watching them no doubt helped to give me rather a jaundiced view of relationships.'

This was getting heavy. Gwen tried to lighten the atmosphere and said brightly, 'Well, as long as you remember the "strictly business" rule, you'll have no problem with *our* relationship.' Her words had the desired effect. He laughed out loud.

'Gwen, I've never ridden a bicycle, but it must be exactly like dealing with you—a constant search for balance!'

She stared at him, unable to believe her ears. 'You've never been on a bike? How did you get around when you were a kid?'

'By car, of course. With a chauffeur,' he added quickly.

Gwen shook her head in amazement. 'That would have gone down a storm at Cwmbach Primary, I tell you.

Anyone turning up at the gates with a man to carry their satchel would've been dunked straight in the mud.'

'They tried that at my school. I floored them,' Etienne said succinctly. 'It wasn't as if I didn't want a bike, like all the other boys. My father finally relented when I was twelve. He presented me with the best bike money could buy, costing hundreds of thousands of francs. It came complete with more safety equipment than anyone could ever need—*including stabilisers*.' He finished in a way that told Gwen the horror of that moment had never entirely left him.

'I suppose your chateau on the Loire has plenty of private roads and tracks where you could have used them out of sight, to begin with?'

Etienne grimaced. 'That was too far beneath my dignity. If I couldn't have what I wanted on my terms, I wouldn't have it at all. I made them take it back to the shop.'

Gwen stared at him. He had been a wilful little monster in need of a good talking-to even then.

'That was a bit childish, wasn't it? Denying yourself something you really wanted, for the silliest little reason?'

'I was a child at the time. I'd never do a thing like that now,' he assured her.

'Nor me. If anybody gave me a fantastic present like that, I'd be falling all over them,' Gwen said, then fell suddenly silent. If that were true, she would be sitting there in her brand-new dress. She was as ungrateful and quick to condemn as the young Etienne had been. She looked up, expecting to feel the heat of his superiority. If he was aware of the irony of the situation, he hid it well. After checking to see that she had finished her soup, he summoned his staff. As they materialised to clear the first course Gwen came to a decision. Standing up, she cleared her throat uncomfortably.

'Would you excuse me, Etienne? There's something I have to do. I won't be a moment.'

Taking advantage of the short delay while the staff served the main course, she walked with great dignity as far as the corridor. Once out of sight, she sprinted to her suite. In seconds, she tore off her blue gown and wriggled into the spectacular silk dress. Retrieving the corsage Etienne had given her so carefully, she got back to the dining room as fast as she could. Pausing to collect herself outside the door, she took a deep breath.

The enormous dining room was echoing to the quiet efficiency of Etienne's staff. They were still plating the *Assiette de cochon de lait rôti,* but as Gwen entered everything stopped. For a fraction of a second she had the full attention of every single person in the room. Everyone stared. Then Etienne cleared his throat, and the waiters and waitresses remembered their manners. Heads down, they hurried back to work. Gwen blushed. Her shy smile was repeated on every mirrored surface, trapping her in embarrassment.

Quietly, Etienne got to his feet. Ignoring his staff, he walked straight to her side and took her arm again.

'I knew this dress was the perfect choice for you. It looks every bit as spectacular as I imagined,' he murmured warmly, gazing down at her for long moments before escorting her back to her seat.

'It feels absolutely wonderful,' Gwen agreed, twirling the orchid corsage between her fingers.

'Would you like me to fasten it for you again?' He smiled.

Her insides turned to cream and honey. This time she didn't flinch as he moved in close to her. Instead, she was disappointed when he slipped his fingers inside the shoulder of her dress to fix the flowers in a totally uncontroversial position.

From that moment on, something changed between them. Etienne relaxed in her company in a way he had not done before. They discussed the small print of the partnership contract. He called for champagne to toast their new enterprise, and Gwen's spirits bubbled like the wine. The thought of having the freedom to concentrate on her cooking while specialists did all the jobs she hated set her spirits free. Etienne was such good company, the end of their meal came far too soon. His stiff formality had given way several times, prompting Gwen to make a spontaneous offer as they finished the last mouthfuls of *Soufflé aux framboise*.

'Why don't we take coffee in my suite instead of here, Etienne? We can alter both copies of our contract at the same time,' she suggested as the waiter brought them a trolley loaded with silverware and petits fours. He considered this, then checked his watch and shook his head.

'I'm sorry. Once I've seen you safely back to the mainland, I have another appointment.'

'Oh.' She could not keep the disappointment from her voice, and he laughed.

'You're trying to knock me off balance again,

Gwen! You were so keen to stop me propositioning you earlier on! How can you have the nerve to sound disappointed now?'

'This evening has been one of the best times I've had in my life,' she said with a smile that could only hint at the strength of her true feelings. Etienne stood up. Strolling around the table, he waited while she got up from her chair. This time he did not offer her his arm.

'Surely the best time was when we were in bed together, in my chateau,' he said softly.

She held her breath, but the moment did not last. He rebounded with a chuckle. 'But that was in the past! Now we are partners in business, not crime, Gwen.'

Leaning forward, he kissed her softly on the forehead.

It was the closest she would get to his heart.

For several weeks, Gwen managed to keep up her relentless approach to work. She spent practically every waking moment at the restaurant. The pressure on her should have eased, but she was still convinced that the place couldn't function without her. Then she began to see Etienne's investment paying dividends. Instead of employing just anyone, she could afford to advertise in trade magazines for top graduates. With Etienne's advisors taking the routine work off her hands, she could spend more time in the kitchens. She experimented with new dishes to complement established favourites on the menu. Life was looking up, especially as she now had a glamorous receptionist to take over the front-of-house work she hated. There were only two tiny clouds on her horizon. One involved Etienne. He entertained at Le

Rossignol often. His fellow financiers were always men, but Gwen didn't like the way her new receptionist fawned over him. It needed a will of iron to ignore it, but her second problem had no solution at all.

Gwen now had plenty of free time, and most of it was stress-free. But no matter how much extra sleep she got, she felt permanently exhausted. That was bad enough. When she started to feel sick as well, the challenge of getting out of bed each morning became harder by the day. She hadn't taken a day off for illness since her college days, and wasn't about to start now. Some days were easier than others. As long as she kept busy, Gwen could hide the way she was feeling.

And then her period didn't arrive. That was unusual, but she managed to put it to the back of her mind. After all, she had lost weight. Telling herself that the time to worry was when the weight started piling on did not work for long. She began to worry. Etienne had taken precautions. She was sure of that. In fact, she was absolutely positive, which only made her worry more. Perhaps she was ill, not pregnant. That thought really scared her, so she worked ten times harder at the restaurant. Her bouts of sickness got worse. She could not face going anywhere near the food-preparation areas. Soon the restaurant itself began having a bad effect on her. She could not stand the smell of the flowers Etienne had delivered each week. Shortly after that, she began to feel strange all the time. Grasping at straws, she wondered if it could be put down to the Mediterranean sun. That seemed unlikely. She spent so much time at work, she was practically nocturnal. For some time, no one guessed she wasn't feeling her best. But she was fooling herself, as well as everyone else.

Gwen was piping meringue one day when she noticed her expensive new receptionist was getting agitated. The poor girl had the telephone to her ear, but wasn't able to get a word in edgeways. From the way she kept jerking it away from her head, it was a roasting, too. Putting on her best professional smile, Gwen swept out into the restaurant and lifted the receiver from the girl's hand.

'Good morning!' she announced briskly, before recognising the furious voice on the other end of the line. 'Etienne?'

He stopped in mid-rant. All trace of anger evaporated from his voice and she heard that deep, irresistible drawl.

'*Bonjour,* Gwen!'

There was genuine pleasure in her smile at the sound of his voice, and her voice reflected it. 'What can I do for you that my receptionist can't?'

'I rang to book my usual table. I will be arriving in ten minutes.'

Gwen looked around the crowded restaurant. 'I'm sorry. Absolutely every seat is taken.'

'Including the one you always keep in reserve?'

She laughed. 'Including that one! The Duke of Prestatyn brought along a couple of extra guests, so we had to do some quick rearrangements.'

Etienne chuckled indulgently. 'Archie? Don't worry about him. He's some sort of relative on my mother's side. That'll be fine. He won't mind sharing a table with me.'

'I'm sorry, Etienne, His Grace already has six people

seated around a table designed to take four. They're taking turns to breathe.'

'That's what I like to hear.' She could almost feel the warmth of his satisfaction. 'Business is booming!'

'Thanks to you. I would never have survived without your help, Etienne,' she admitted quietly.

'Yes, you would. You have all the qualities needed for success, Gwen. I merely developed your potential— in all sorts of areas.'

Gwen felt herself blushing.

'You'll never know how grateful I am, Etienne.'

'I'm sure something can be arranged!'

There was that slight chuckle in the back of his throat again. It still affected Gwen as easily and completely as ever. Heat rushed through her. She was glad this conversation was going on over the telephone. One pass of Etienne's rapier glance over her body would have told him all he needed to know. The slight flush to her cheeks and her dilated pupils would only encourage him. If he got close enough, he might just be able to hear the pounding of her heart.

She gave a little cough and tried to shake her thoughts back into some sort of order. 'Yes, I'm sure it can, but I'm afraid it won't include a table here today, Etienne. We're fully booked all the way through until closing time tonight.'

He clicked his tongue. 'I enjoy solitude, but I eat here alone at the chateau too often for it to be any sort of treat. Send me up a selection of the dishes you have on offer. Bring them yourself, and we can talk while we eat.'

Gwen's laughter diluted his heavy hint of seduction.

'I can't take time off from the kitchens when we're so busy! I'll have something ready by the time you've sent a car down from the chateau. But don't tell your friends. This isn't a takeaway. It's a special service for my very own business angel.'

'You're too kind,' he said in honeyed tones. 'But I can imagine what my chefs would say if I allowed you to do that. For you to bring me some titbits made with your own beautiful hands would be one thing. To send out for them would be disastrous. My staff would think I was heading down the trail leading to dial-a-pizza and popcorn in front of the flat screen. I would have a riot on my hands. They would abandon me. I'd be forced to exist on fast food and fizzy soft drinks.'

Gwen gave up and laughed. 'Fine, then. Even I can't condemn you to such a fate.'

'Good. Then I shall see you for lunch at the restaurant in a few minutes.'

'You'll have to sit at the table in my office, mind. It's the only place I can fit you in!' For a few seconds Gwen laughed with an ease she hadn't felt for weeks. Talking with Etienne always made everything all right again.

'That doesn't worry me at all. The satisfaction of walking through a packed restaurant will make up for having to eat in the office!' He joked so warmly it almost took Gwen's mind off her sudden, unexpected swell of nausea…

Etienne was still smiling as he reached the restaurant, a few minutes later. He had been furious at the news that there would be no table waiting for him. Then Gwen had

come on the line and he remembered switching into seduction mode automatically when he first heard her.
But, for the first time in his life, it had not worked immediately. Gwen had laughed and humoured him, but
she hadn't giggled like a schoolgirl. She had kept a firm
grip on the situation. In Etienne's experience, women
rarely objected to charm and the chance to stop what
they were doing to talk to him. Gwen certainly did make
him work a little harder and, to his surprise, he thoroughly enjoyed it! She was playing hard to get and he'd
heard it mentioned that a pleasure postponed was always
sweeter. This was going to be a lunch to remember.

It was just as well he didn't realise exactly how memorable it would turn out to be.

As Etienne strode into the restaurant his smile soon
faded. Greetings and waves were ignored as he scanned
the packed tables. Gwen was nowhere to be seen. It
was one of her inflexible rules that no guest was left to
linger in the reception area. Within seconds the new receptionist appeared and directed him towards the bar.

'Where is *Mademoiselle le chef*?'

'I'm afraid she's indisposed at the moment,
monsieur. Can I help you?'

'Gwen is arranging a table for me in her office,' he said
smoothly, as the girl looked in need of an explanation.

'That might be rather difficult, *monsieur*. Her office
is in use at the moment. I'll get you a drink.'

Etienne ordered a martini he didn't want. He scanned
the crowd, looking for Gwen's beautiful face and listening for her laughter. He was getting impatient but when

he looked at his watch it was to see that barely ten minutes had gone by since he arrived. It felt like several lifetimes. What was going on? She was always a professional to her fingertips, but there was no sign of her anywhere today. He took his drink over to a seat in the corner of the bar area. It gave him a good view of the whole restaurant, but not the one thing he really wanted. Running a finger idly around the rim of his glass, he waited. Time passed, but she did not appear. Unused to waiting for anything, Etienne became restless. Something must have happened. It was unthinkable for his arrangements to be delayed like this. She knew he was coming. Where was she?

He was about to walk over and rap on her office door when it was flung open wide. Gwen emerged with a smile and a quip for the nearest diners, but Etienne was not fooled for a second. Pausing only briefly to give a distracted greeting to his cousin the duke, he moved quickly across the room to her side.

'Gwen? What is it?'

'Etienne! I hope we haven't kept you waiting!'

'That doesn't matter. It's you I'm worried about. You look terrible.' His gaze sharpened. 'What's the matter?'

'Nothing. I'm fine. It's all perfectly under control.'

She turned to walk away. He grabbed her arm to stop her, but used a little too much force. She yelped, causing him to release his hold but it was too late. Everyone within earshot looked up.

'I'm sorry, I trod on *mademoiselle's* toe,' Etienne explained, smoothly bundling Gwen back into her office. There he slammed the door and leaned back against it.

'There's no escape until you tell me what is going on.'

'You wanted lunch here.'

She hesitated, and her features moved in a way that worried him. When she spoke again it was with an obvious effort.

'I was getting the room ready. After all, I can't expect a French count to eat off a tray, can I?' She tried to laugh, but it was no use. Looking around the office with its neatly ordered files of paperwork and pot plants, Etienne knew she had been doing nothing of the sort. There was a cold compress, a glass of iced water and a large bowl on the coffee table.

'I'm not buying that excuse. You're too pale, Gwen. And you've got such dark circles under your eyes.' Stretching out one finger, he touched her cheek experimentally. Gwen shrank away from his touch.

'You're sick, aren't you?' he persisted.

Her eyes popped in horror. 'No! Don't say that word in here! If the customers hear, they'll think it's food poisoning. I'll be closed down!'

'It isn't, is it?'

Gwen was horrified by his suggestion. 'Of course not, no! I'm scrupulous about hygiene. I eat exactly the same thing as all the rest of the staff, and no one else has suffered so much as a headache for weeks.'

Etienne watched her closely. Now he came to study her with a financier's mentality rather than the eye of lust he noticed that the curves he remembered so fondly were not quite as generous as before.

'When you can keep it down,' he suggested. 'You've lost weight, Gwen.'

'Everyone does in summer. It's the heat and all the salads. I'm fine, Etienne, really.'

He made a noise in his throat, hinting at his deep scepticism.

'OK…as long as you're sure.'

Gwen had hardly finished nodding before the most awful feeling washed over her again. She lurched for the bowl and was heartily sick. Etienne was there with words of encouragement, but his attitude changed the moment she tried to tell him it was nothing.

'It's far from nothing, Gwen. You're too ill to work. I'm going to call my doctor, and then I'm taking you home. You're not setting one foot inside this restaurant again until we've found out what this is all about.'

The fact she was too weak to argue gave him no pleasure at all. Hustling her out the back way with a quick word to the receptionist, he drove to her cottage at top speed. She was still wobbly as she got out of the car. When he tried to carry her upstairs she was well enough to put up a spirited defence.

'I don't need your help, Etienne. I'm fine and I certainly don't need you carrying me up any more stairs!'

He was affronted. 'If I wasn't a gentleman I would laugh at the suggestion that something might happen today. I would never take advantage of a sick woman.'

'I keep telling you, I'm not sick! It's nothing. It'll pass off. It always does.'

'You mean this has happened before?'

'Once or twice, maybe.' She shrugged like an insolent child.

'Really? So exactly how long has this been going on?'

'I don't know!' She pushed her curls back irritably from her forehead. 'A couple of weeks? Maybe longer. I haven't been taking notes. I'm too busy working. As I've told you before, I don't have the time to be ill.'

Etienne's personal doctor was there within minutes. He took one look at Gwen and frowned.

'We have not met before?'

'No, I'm Etienne's business partner.'

Gwen waited for the man to laugh or make some suggestive comment. Instead he smiled quite innocently before asking if there was a Mr Williams. For the first time, Gwen felt fear. She looked at Etienne with terrified eyes.

'Next of kin, you mean? Oh, my God! It's *that* serious?'

'Not necessarily.' The doctor was quick to smile. 'If it was anyone but you who had called me in, Etienne, I'd start by asking Mademoiselle Williams the obvious question.'

'Which is?' Gwen looked from one man to the other. She was really scared now.

'I'd merely enquire if there's any way you could be pregnant, Mademoiselle Williams,' the doctor said in a matter-of-fact way. Gwen stared at him. He smiled back, his expression gently prompting.

It was the one cause Gwen flatly refused to acknowledge. She had made a million excuses to herself and tried to ignore all the signs, but this was the showdown. She felt like the *SS Titanic*, steaming towards a giant iceberg labelled disaster.

'I—I don't know.' Shocked, Gwen appealed to the doctor with her eyes. But he had turned away, preparing to take a blood sample.

'It's a question I ask all young women as a matter of

course, that's all. When they present with bouts of sickness but are otherwise fit and healthy, it's the most natural thing in the world to suspect pregnancy.'

She blinked at him, lost for words. Etienne was equally staggered.

'*What?* But I can't see how you could possibly be pregnant,' he said faintly.

'That's staff for you, Etienne.' The doctor grunted.

Gwen was appalled at his bedside manner and in other circumstances would have called him on it, but she was too shocked by the possibility of pregnancy to say anything. She looked away quickly as the blood started to flow from her arm and into the vacuum container. There was silence in the room. It was broken only by the warble of birdsong outside, floating in from the garden. The doctor wrote Gwen's name on the phial of her blood, his pen scratching through the tension. Finally Etienne walked over to the window. Hands on hips, he stared out across the valley. His voice, when it came, was as parched as the landscape.

'It's impossible. We only spent one night together.'

It was the doctor's turn to stop and stare.

'You mean you and Mademoiselle Williams…' Frowning, he turned his full attention on Gwen, aghast.

Gwen sprang up to defend herself, but Etienne was already there. Whirling away from the window, he caught her by the shoulders. The look in his sloe-dark eyes was enough to silence her.

'It can only be me. That's right, isn't it, Gwyneth?'

He called her by her full name. Gwen shuddered. She had thought she was in trouble. This confirmed it.

The doctor looked distinctly uneasy. 'That's ridiculous.'

'But why should you automatically think Etienne wasn't the father of this…' her nerve almost failed her, and she took several attempts to force the word out '…baby?'

It wasn't the doctor who answered, but Etienne himself. 'The doctor knows my views. I think a child should have two responsible parents,' he said stiffly.

It was an answer. Whether it was the whole truth, Gwen wasn't sure. She couldn't help but think about the baby Angela Webbington had aborted. Which part of that unhappy couple had been the irresponsible one?

'What can I say?' The doctor shrugged, addressing his gesture of exasperation to Etienne.

'Nothing. Don't say a thing, Doctor. If Gwyneth is pregnant, then she and I will sort this out together, between us.'

His smooth reply sounded almost practised. The icy calm was certainly enough to freeze Gwen's blood. Alerted to the possibility she might be carrying Etienne's child, the doctor carried out the rest of his examination with that in mind. All the signs were there, he told them, but official confirmation would have to wait.

'That's fine. You have the number of my mobile. Ring the moment you know. I'll deal with everything here,' Etienne said, hustling the doctor out of the room.

A cold knot of dread tightened inside Gwen. She had a horrible suspicion she knew exactly what he meant.

She sat on the edge of her bed, staring at the floor. Her hands were clasped so tightly together the knuckles ached. She heard Etienne and the doctor muttering outside her window. She couldn't hear what they were saying, and didn't care. Her whole life had stuttered to a halt. From now on she would have to exist at second hand. All her time and energy would have to be devoted to the little life growing inside her. She could feel motherhood closing in on her like the walls of her room.

Several centuries later, she heard a car drive away. It was only one car, and it lacked the high-class purr of Etienne's pulling machine. She waited, expecting him to leave too. Instead, she heard slow, heavy footsteps come up the stairs. He was coming back. She braced herself for a confrontation. It was only a matter of feet across the landing to her bedroom. Gwen did not move as she sensed Etienne reach her threshold. There was no point. He would have a face like thunder, and the smallest movement from her would unleash his fury. She tried to concentrate on the hum of bees, busy in the thyme flowers growing on the sun-drenched terrace. It was supposed to be a diversion. Instead it reminded her of the buzz of disapproval this news would provoke among all her relatives back home.

'How do you feel?'

Gwen's head jerked up before she could stop it. She had expected anger. Strained compassion was the last thing she anticipated. His expression was impassive. She knew he must have been fighting to keep his true feelings under control, exactly as she was.

'Terrible. I've ruined everything,' she muttered, dropping her gaze back to the rag rug.

She heard him take a step towards her. The room

wasn't very big, but he was still as far away from her as it was possible to be while still sharing the same space. After a pause, he took another step, and then a third. Now the tips of his leather shoes intruded into her narrow field of vision. She waited. Eventually, a shadow moved and she felt his touch. It fell lightly against her shoulder. When she did not move, he dropped its full weight on her, stiff and unyielding. She couldn't be sure if it was meant as a comforting gesture. His fingers felt like wood. *Like my heart,* she thought bleakly.

'You aren't entirely to blame, Gwen. It took two of us.'

It was an admission wrung from him like blood, she could tell.

'I must have been mad when I agreed to stay with you. I've never done anything like that before. What was I thinking of?' Her voice was an agonised whisper. The pressure of his hand released and then fell again in something that was supposed to be a reassuring pat. Gwen was beyond appreciating his efforts.

'I'm always scrupulous about…' the hand on her shoulder twitched with his discomfort '…precautions. I don't understand how this can possibly have happened—'

He spoke slowly, but Gwen's response was like quicksilver. 'You aren't trying to deny this baby is yours, are you? You can't control everything—accidents happen, Etienne.'

Pulling away his hand, Etienne looked down on her with naked scorn.

'You must believe it!' she said frantically. 'You said as much yourself, to the doctor!'

'Of course I know it's mine,' he growled. 'What do you think I am?'

'I don't know.' Gwen subsided onto the bed again. 'And I don't know what I'm going to do, either.'

At her words he moved more quickly than he had done since entering her house. Sitting down beside her, he whipped out his mobile phone.

'You don't have to do a thing. Not a single, solitary thing. This is my responsibility, so I shall take care of everything.'

Gwen's brain sprang to life. All the news reports she had seen about Angela Webbington rattled through her brain with the urgency of Etienne's fingers on his keypad. With a scream of horror she leapt away from him.

He stopped and stared at her, dismayed at her reaction. 'What is it? What have I done now?'

'Nothing. You aren't going to do anything to me!'

Gwen began to panic. Backing towards a corner, she wrapped her arms tightly around her waist. She stared at him, wild and wide-eyed. Etienne watched her. His expression hardened from alarm to pity. As it did so, he went back to tapping out a number on his phone.

'Oh, yes, I am,' he announced sharply. 'I'm going to marry you.'

CHAPTER EIGHT

GWEN was too amazed to speak. This was the last thing she had expected and she didn't know what to think. There was a moment of relief—he was not threatening her baby—but then panic loomed again as Etienne continued.

'I'm responsible for this situation. I must take the consequences, and pay my dues.'

He made it sound like a parking offence.

'You can't just announce it like that!' She gasped. 'Don't I have any say in the matter?'

'Why would you want anything different?' He stared at her, mystified. 'Our child will be the legitimate heir to the Moreau name. Some day it will inherit my title, and everything I've worked for on my own account. What could be better than that?'

'But…' his reasonable tone left her scrabbling for objections '…I'm a chef…and you're a count!'

'That will make you the perfect wife for me.' Etienne's voice was strained through centuries of breeding. 'Your work at Le Rossignol has shown me how good you are in social situations, however difficult.

You have a decent enough business brain and grace under pressure. You will make the perfect countess,' he said as if there were no question about it. He had spoken, and it would be her duty to obey.

'Have you stopped to consider for one single second that I really might not want to marry you?'

'What?' Etienne stared at her. He looked genuinely surprised. 'No. Of course I haven't.'

Gwen nodded. She should have known. What sort of a relationship was this? They knew nothing about each other beyond the confines of business. She had served him with a coffee. He had given her a lift home. She had fallen into his arms. That was just about the extent of it. They had only one thing in common. It was the whirlwind excitement of one passionate night. An hour earlier, the thought of marrying Etienne would have been an impossible fantasy—something she had not dared admit to herself. Unconsciously, her hand strayed to her stomach, curving protectively. Now the fantasy had suddenly become a cold-hearted business deal.

'What is the matter, Gwen? Why are you looking at me like that? You can't honestly be about to refuse.' His voice was gently mocking. 'I've never known a woman who wouldn't jump at the chance to become a countess.'

Gwen thought of his stepmother, the odious Sophie, and her poor, nervous niece.

'Well, you know one now,' she announced.

Etienne hit back with an equally solid response. 'This isn't about what either of us wants as individuals. This is about *my* heir, *your* pregnancy, and *our* baby. We have to stop thinking about ourselves and put all our energy into preparing for the future.'

He sounded so aristocratic, so certain. 'Our lifestyles are so different,' she said faintly. 'What about your future?'

'My future is never in any doubt. Let me handle this, Gwen.' He moved as though to put an arm around her shoulder. At the last moment, he hesitated and turned the movement into just a reassuring touch of his hand.

When it came to keeping Le Rossignol afloat, Etienne had been as good as his word. He had not interfered. Gwen wondered whether he would be content to throw money at parenthood in a similar way. She didn't know whether he would back off or take compete control. With her mind in a whirl and no idea how she would set about raising a child, she didn't know which would be worse. That alarmed her.

She searched his face, trying to see the emotions behind his dark eyes. It was so tempting to give in— simply to let him take control and sweep her away.

'I don't have a clue about babies, and there's so much to do if we're going to get married before I'm...' Instinctively, she looked down at her waist. It was still neatly defined, but for how much longer?

'That's the great thing about being a member of the aristocracy. Contingency plans for all the major life events are permanently in place. They only need a few phone calls to set them in motion. And relax—I don't know anything about babies either. I doubt if many first-time parents do. And we'll have more than enough help.'

Gwen watched him tap numbers into his phone and start mobilising his staff. He was oblivious to everything else, so she could observe him in detail. He was still the gloriously handsome, detached figure who had walked into her life on that fateful first evening. This cool professionalism had always been one of his attractions. He shared her need to be in control of every situation. With a surge of desire she saw he was determined to be a part of her baby's future. Etienne barely noticed her interest in him. He was a man in a hurry. The moment he closed his call, he picked up her handbag and set off downstairs. 'Come on. Let's discuss this on neutral territory.'

'Where are you going with my bag?'

'We're going for a drive. This is the bait to get you into my car.' He dangled her bag from his fingers as he opened the passenger door of his Ferrari for her. Gwen came to a halt on her front doorstep.

'Where are we going?'

He gave her a smile that was almost encouraging. 'There's no need to look so suspicious. I know a little bistro right out in the country. The owners are very discreet. We won't be troubled and we can talk freely. There's no risk of being overheard.'

'I'm going to have a baby. What is there left to say?' Gwen concentrated on the ground as she walked towards the car.

'We're going to be married; there are many things to discuss. And let's get one thing straight from the beginning. You're not having *a* baby. You are carrying my child. There is a difference. It means you aren't alone.'

Everything had changed, yet some things were still the same. Etienne was looking at her in the same way he had done over the conference table on *The*

Windflower. He was perfectly composed and in control. And he was still as spectacular as ever. A treacherous suspicion of hunger stirred within her, sealing her fate.

'OK. A discussion over lunch. I can handle that,' she said, trying to gain some control over her dangerous emotions. It would not be a good time to let her feelings get the better of her. She was too confused to know what they were.

Etienne's mouth tightened. 'Yes. There are things I must talk to you about.'

'In the same way you "talked" to Angela Webbington?' Gwen queried, remembering the coverage she had seen of their stormy relationship. Her accusation did not have the effect she expected. Instead of exploding with rage or denial, Etienne simply nodded.

'*Oui.* In exactly that way. Only this time, each of us is going to listen to what the other has to say, Gwen.'

She fell silent. Angela had vanished from his life. Gwen couldn't help wondering if the same thing might happen to her, if she refused to toe his line. She thought of being responsible for a tiny new baby and never seeing Etienne again. Suddenly, a fierce wave of longing engulfed her. Marrying Etienne would give her child a safe, secure life and keep them both within his orbit.

'So…if I marry you, it's a guarantee that everything will be all right?'

Staring resolutely through the windscreen, he eased his car into gear and pulled away. Unusually the Ferrari moved off with dignity, rather than in a shower of gravel.

'Not even I can promise that, Gwen. Nobody can predict what the future holds. But I can promise you one thing. We are going to do this together. My child will be raised to take his place as the next count. He is owed the best of everything, and I intend to see that he gets it, whatever that takes. My responsibility for him began the moment I got you—' he waved a hand in the general direction of her lap '—the moment all this happened. I would never abandon a woman to bring up a child of mine alone—least of all you. We're partners in business. This is a joint effort, too.' He glanced across at her with an encouraging smile.

'Did you talk to your ex-fiancée in this deeply romantic way?' Gwen sent the question spinning towards him like a guided missile. Etienne flicked it aside with a grimace.

'You are not Angela, and you never will be,' he said with such painful restraint Gwen wondered again what Angela had really been like to have had such an effect on this man. 'Things are going to be very different this time.'

Gwen had been warning herself for weeks that it was a bad idea to bring her feelings into this business partnership. Now he would be increasing his influence over her personal, as well as her professional, life. If she agreed to marry him, she might soon be unable to afford the luxury of any emotions at all.

He drove on. His silence was as arid as the countryside flashing past the car. When they stopped, Etienne took his time in going around to open the door for her. She blinked in the harsh sunlight. They were in a little village square, sleepy with heat. Luckily, there were few people around. No one would recognise her when she was this far out in the wilds, but that didn't mean she wanted people to see her at a time of total turmoil.

The bistro's proprietor rushed out, wreathed in smiles. He met them like visiting royalty. In spite of herself, Gwen's heart fluttered a little to see Etienne greeted so kindly, and by his title. Then she thought back to the Internet coverage she had seen of his past. Etienne was famous for his vast number of female 'friends'. He must have brought dozens of girls here in the past. How could marriage change a man like that?

They were led away from the public areas of the restaurant to a secluded table set beneath a bower of vines and creepers. Spectacular passion flowers studded the greenery, their pure white flowers pencilled with blue and yellow detail.

'Gwen will drink fresh orange juice over ice, she'll start with melon and strawberries, followed by the poached fish and salad. And make sure everything is well washed in Evian,' Etienne announced to the waiter.

Gwen said nothing until they were alone together.

'Don't I get any choice in my food?'

'Was there anything you particularly wanted?'

'No, but—'

'Then relax!' He tried to smile. This time his efforts were slightly more successful. 'I've simply saved you the task of choosing the healthiest options. My child will have only the best.'

Gwen heard nothing after that. She tried to listen, but it quickly became obvious Etienne's mind was made up with regard to every detail regarding her, his child, his heritage and his future. Etienne was laying out his big ideas as they applied to her baby, and life in general. Her function was to listen, and presumably nod in all the right places. Unable to think about the implications, she concentrated on her meal. Her earlier wave of sickness was a distant memory, and now she was ravenous. As it turned out, Etienne had made all the right choices for her. Her food was totally delicious. *Damn the man*, she thought mutinously.

'And what do you have to say to all this, Gwen?'

Etienne's question caught her completely off guard.

'I—I don't know. The only thing I know about motherhood is that I'm not cut out for it,' she said hopelessly. 'I've only just managed to escape one family. This taste of freedom after being suffocated for so long has been incredible. Le Rossignol is my life now. How can I sacrifice that, when I've worked so hard to get it? I've only had a few weeks to enjoy it. I've hardly begun to live. Now I'll have to spend the rest of my life running around after…somebody else.'

Etienne did not answer, but his face darkened and he summoned the bill. 'Let's get home. The doctor should have your results by the time we get there.'

Gwen let him lead her back to the car. As he held the door open for her she saw a perfect illustration of what her future might hold. It was trailing across that pretty little village square.

'Gwen—what is it?' Etienne's voice sharpened. Afraid she might be about to faint, he reached out and caught her by the shoulders. Pulling her towards him, he was ready with reassurances, but they died on his lips.

She wasn't looking at him. She was staring over his shoulder. He raked the village square with a glare, but couldn't be expected to see it in the same way she did. It was practically deserted. A few white doves pecked around the feet of some old men enjoying the afternoon in the shade of an ancient walnut tree. Meanwhile, a screaming toddler was being dragged across the cobblestones by a harassed young woman weighed down with shopping. She was struggling on alone, with no one to help her.

Gwen saw, and understood. She was alone and pregnant in a foreign country. But Etienne had helped her once before and, whatever had happened in his past, she did have complete faith in his ability to protect her and her baby. Who was she to jeopardise her child's future simply through fear for her own heart?

'It's nothing. I'm fine,' she reassured him with a wan smile. 'I just caught a glimpse of what life might be like on my own, that's all.'

'I must get you back to the chateau,' he said with concern. 'You look exhausted. It's been a hectic few weeks. You need rest—whatever the outcome of your tests.'

The doctor delivered her results in person. They were positive, as both Gwen and Etienne had known they would be.

'I shall need a full report on my…*fiancée's*—' Etienne spoke the word with difficulty '—condition, and written lists of your recommendations for her care and diet,' he began, then spent the next half an hour grilling the doctor about what would happen, minute by minute. Locked inside her own thoughts, Gwen hardly heard a word he said.

'I'm not up to this, Etienne,' she said miserably. 'I don't know how to be a mother! And what about the restaurant? I need some time to get used to all this—'

'Haven't you been listening? You don't need to do anything. From now on, I shall be taking care of absolutely everything for you.'

Gwen felt again the stirrings of unease. Her life was spinning entirely out of her control. Etienne's words tailed off, his smile fading as he saw her expression.

As he sensed that she was wavering his voice became soothing, a velvet glove encasing cold, hard steel. 'I keep telling you. This is a team effort. Between us, we're going to give our baby the best of everything.' When she did not answer, he continued, in an appeasing tone, 'You've often said how traditional your family are. I could ask your father's permission to marry you, if you like.'

Any colour Gwen might have regained disappeared as she saw Etienne pulling out his mobile. 'No! My parents must never know I got things back to front!' She was adamant. 'As you said, they're old-fashioned. It's wedding first, babies later as far as they're concerned.'

Etienne tucked his phone away again. 'Fine. Just as you like. My people will get all the paperwork sorted out. The moment it's complete, we'll marry with the minimum of fuss. Then we'll fly straight to your parents. You may not want me to ask their permission formally, but they will be the first to know. It's the least

I can do. Trust me, Gwen. Everything will be over and done with in a few signatures,' he assured her. 'My people will do everything, including the catering—for once, you will not need to lift a finger.' Gwen's head was whirling, filled with so many panicked thoughts that she could hardly muster a single straight sentence. One thought, however, was clear.

'So…I'm not going to have a hand in catering for my own wedding?' she said slowly.

Etienne looked puzzled. 'Why would you want to? It's your big day. You'll want to mingle with my friends and family. I've seen how much you enjoy the social aspect of your work at the restaurant.'

'But I hate all that, Etienne! I only do it for the sake of my business!'

'I'm not so sure, Gwen. No one could fake the way you handle yourself in a crowd, and deal with the diners. You'll be the new public face of the house of Malotte. It's about time we had an injection of brains and beauty. The Moreau family has cornered the market in fighters and philanderers for centuries. I'm going to turn our little accident into the best thing that has ever happened to my family.'

Gwen was silent for a long time. If she married Etienne, would there be any room left for her? It already felt as if she were drifting away—dwindling into someone smaller and weaker. But what were her options here? She didn't want an abortion, her family certainly had no money to spare and would be horrified by her predicament…and here was Etienne, determined to take care of everything. Was it such a high price to pay? It

was his duty to do the best for his ancient family. He
wanted it to do more than simply survive. He wanted it
to thrive, and that was exactly what she wanted for her
baby. It was an unromantic basis for a marriage, but, to
use his executive-speak, it ticked all the right boxes for
both of them. Not simply practical boxes either.
Looking at Etienne now, she saw his eyes glowing with
enthusiasm for his latest project. Unable to help herself,
she thought back to the one unforgettable night they had
shared. She felt the memory warm her like a caress.

'When you put it like that, who am I to refuse?' she
said at last.

CHAPTER NINE

FROM that moment, Etienne would not let Gwen lift a finger or take any decisions. His staff swung into action. Within hours most of her belongings had been moved out of the *gite* and installed in the chateau. He supervised everything, including Gwen. Whenever he saw her, he complained if she wasn't sitting down, eating something nourishing or preferably doing both at once. The whole estate became a visible whirlwind of activity. Wherever Gwen went, it felt as though she was in the way. A constant procession of gardeners brought flowers into the house for the indoor staff to arrange. The building was filled with the sounds of curtains being pulled back and squadrons of cleaners opening up long-locked rooms. When the racket finally stopped and Gwen escaped to her new bedroom that evening, she fell asleep within seconds. Doing nothing was turning out to be more exhausting than working for a living.

She woke next morning into a glorious delusion. Opening her eyes to see the unfamiliar surroundings, for a few seconds she imagined Etienne must have swept her into his bed again. Then she realised she was alone. Almost straight away, a feeling of nausea threw her out of bed. It shredded her dreams with the efficiency of a *demi-lune*. Already exhausted, she dragged herself into the shower room. The surroundings of cool green marble revived her a little, and she managed to summon up enough energy to check its cupboards. Her bathroom, like Etienne's, was stocked with a staggering array of soaps, gels and moisturising milks. The whole place hummed gently with a cocktail of organic, plant-based fragrances. She settled on a bottle of invigorating shower gel allegedly chock-full of sea minerals. Ten minutes beneath a spray head the size of a dinner plate was enough to start her thinking about breakfast. In the time it took her to dress in a black skirt and simple white blouse, she was ravenous. Despite her dread of meeting anyone who might tell her to sit down or go back to bed, she set off in search of food.

The chateau was enormous, but the silence of its sunlit halls meant the smallest sound travelled for many metres. She soon found her way to a spectacular vaulted room on the ground floor, overlooking a courtyard garden.

Etienne was already seated at the head of a long dining table. When he saw her enter the room, he folded his newspaper and stood up with a smile.

'*Bonjour*, Gwen. I hope you enjoyed a restful night?' His voice was resonant with concern.

'Thank you. It was wonderful.' *But lonely*, she added to herself. She headed towards the breakfast display, set out on an enormous antique sideboard like the one she remembered from that first fateful night.

'Take a seat. The waitress will fetch anything you need.' Etienne indicated the far end of the table, remote from him. Sure enough, a woman in a severe black dress and white apron moved soundlessly into position.

'But the food is only a few yards away!' Gwen protested.

'You need to have a break, Gwen.' Etienne dismissed her protest with a shrug. 'You've been working too hard, and you are run-down and tired. That is not good for a pregnant woman. So you will be pampered for a while—enjoy it. *Both* of you.'

Far away in a distant part of Etienne's cavernous house, a mason's drill hummed into life. As she gave her order for fresh fruit salad and tea Gwen frowned, and not only at the idea of someone fetching and carrying for her over such a short distance.

'This house seems perfect to me, Etienne. Why does it have to be put under attack by builders?'

'I bought it for its position, beauty and history. It was always going to be too large for a single man, especially while I was dividing my time between so many other properties. It only makes more work for the staff, so I concentrated the restoration work on my suite and the few rooms I needed downstairs. Now you will be a permanent resident here, we shall need every inch of space. You will want to entertain,' he explained.

Gwen was not convinced. 'You said this place was your bolt hole. It's supposed to be somewhere you can escape, and get away from people.'

'Yes, but that was before you became pregnant.'

He made it sound like an accusation. She reddened angrily. 'Don't try and make out it's all my fault!'

'I'm not. There's no point in trying to apportion blame. The damage has been done, so I'm adapting to it. I can't expect you and my baby to live like hermits.'

At his direct mention of the baby, Gwen panicked. Scrabbling for a sheet anchor, she looked at her watch. 'Look at the time! I'll have to hurry if I'm going to get to Le Rossignol before the florist delivers—'

'There's no need. Relax!' Etienne said solicitously. 'You employ plenty of staff there now. Let them deal with it. If you want something to do, why don't you try a makeover of the chateau menus? I'm sure Chef would be willing to negotiate.'

Gwen pulled back as though she had been burned. She couldn't imagine a life without her work. It defined her, and gave her a purpose in life.

'That's very kind of you, Etienne, but I'd rather we stuck to our usual arrangement when it comes to the restaurant.' It was all she could do to hide the panic in her voice. '*Laissez-faire*—isn't that what it's called?'

'Why worry about the place when you don't have to?' He laughed off her concern. 'You have a new role now. I'm not going to let you out of my sight for an instant.' He was starting to look quite pleased with himself. 'We will elect a temporary manager. He can be in charge of the day-to-day running of the restaurant while you're distracted. You told me you were happy enough just to cook. Use my investment to make it easy for yourself. You need rest and supervision to make sure my heir gets the very best possible start in life.'

'Are you suggesting this because you think I can't manage?' she said slowly.

'No partner of mine should be content to merely "manage". I want you to be completely relaxed and happy, Gwen. That is an entirely different state of mind. Look at the difference our business partnership has made to you in only a few weeks. You've been freed from the treadmill, you've had time to rest, and concentrate on the part of the job you love best.' His voice dropped to an appreciative whisper. 'You are a completely different woman from the one I met all those weeks ago.'

'For better, or worse?' Gwen put her head in her hands.

Etienne shot a meaningful look at the maid. She took the hint and evaporated from the room. After a suitable silence, Gwen heard Etienne stand up and walk slowly towards her. She did not move a muscle. When he reached her end of the table, he pulled out the nearest chair. He dropped into the seat. His arms in their smart, dark business suit intruded into her line of sight. He was ready for work. She didn't feel ready for anything— especially when he reached out and gently pulled her hands away from her face. Clasping them in his, he looked deep into her eyes. Once again, she was trapped in the smouldering intensity of his gaze. He was studying her in a way that laid her feelings bare. It redirected the heat of her anger in a way that scared her. Surely, mothers weren't supposed to feel desire. They were supposed to be down-to-earth, and sensible.

'Gwen, I have made some terrible mistakes in the past.' His words were heavy with something she assumed was reassurance. 'I realise that now, and don't intend to repeat *any* of them. I won't allow you to face this alone. That's why things must be like this. My son is going to have the best possible start in life. Believe me.'

She watched him, watching her. His eyes were dark with determination, and the set of his jaw was totally resolute.

With the delicacy she remembered so well, his thumb began to draw slow shapes over the back of her hand.

'It's all in hand. Flowers, food, stationery, ceremony— the whole show is already on the road, as you say. My people have organised everything. You don't have to do a thing—except edit your part of the guest list.' He went on, oblivious to her growing horror. 'When I came into your room late last night to see if you wanted anything, I saw your address book on the bedside table. My PA put it straight onto a database.'

Gwen found herself totally unable to speak. That didn't matter. Etienne was more than happy to do that for her—along with everything else, apparently.

'You looked so peaceful—' he began with a smile, but 'peaceful' was the last thing Gwen felt. Rigid with rage and furious at the effect he continued to have on her, she wrenched her hands from his grasp.

'So you took my address book in the same way you've taken over the rest of my life?' She stood up, shaking. 'It hardly sounds like you need me at all. In fact, I might as well say goodbye to you right now, Etienne, rather than clutter up your itinerary any further!' She heard him call her name, but did not look back.

Twenty minutes later, Gwen was pacing back and

forwards in her room, going over arguments to use against him and trying to calm herself before going back down, when she heard a familiar sound. It was Etienne's car prowling along beneath her window. He was leaving for the office, without saying goodbye. The realisation sliced into her heart. For the first time, the full horror of the situation swept over her. Independence was so important to her that she had travelled halfway across Europe to find it, and ended up *pregnant* by a man who knew nothing about her—who, she now realised, saw her as nothing but a ticket to his heir.

She buried her face in her pillow, but there was no time for tears. She had made her choice. For the sake of her baby, she was determined to make the best of this. However much she might ache inside.

Efficient as ever, Etienne had already put his staff to work. Within moments, Gwen got a text from his PA. An appointment had been made for her at Malotte's most fashionable beautician. All she had to do was turn up. Everything else was in hand. Sure enough, as she was reading the text she heard one of the estate's limousines being drawn up outside the main villa doors.

She went down to tell the chauffeur she would drive herself, in her own car. It was hopeless. Etienne's system didn't allow for alterations. From now on, she would ring for a chauffeur whenever she wanted to go anywhere at all. Gwen bit her tongue, and counted to ten. She couldn't rail at the staff. It was hardly their fault if the Count of Malotte wanted to dictate her every move. Bottling up her anger, she tried to console herself.

She wouldn't have the hassle of driving through Malotte's narrow, twisting streets, or finding a parking space. There might be advantages to Etienne's guilty conscience after all.

A shame they didn't make up for the loss of her freedom.

Summer was flying away. The nightingales had already vanished from the overgrown margins of the chateau grounds. They had escaped before the chill of winter. How Gwen wished she could follow them. She gazed out of the window as the assistant put the finishing touches to her makeover. The village square was drenched in sunshine. Outside, in flickering shadows cast by the lime trees, life was going on in all its noisy variety. In spite of her resolution, she craved the chance to escape the shadow of Etienne's claustrophobic care. She needed to strike out on her own, if only for an hour or two.

The contrast between the air-conditioned comfort indoors and the oven of Malotte in late summer gave her quite a shock. Straight away, she realised that walking anywhere in this heat would make quite a statement. For the first few hundred metres, everything was fine. Then she left the town behind. Without the shadows cast by the buildings of Malotte, the feeling of heat increased. The road out of town was barren and dusty, making her journey more and more of a trial. The red-hot road reflected heat up into her face in a way the *maquis* would not, so she quickly abandoned the highway for a short cut across country. A sheep track ran diagonally up the slope towards the chateau. She suddenly knew where she was heading. She needed to be somewhere outside Etienne's influence—to escape, just for a short while. Trying to ignore the crippling heat, she headed towards the *gite*.

It looked dusty and deserted. It was nowhere near the luxury and comfort of Etienne's chateau, and yet the small bedroom, with all its lack of glamour, was one of the most wonderful things she'd seen for days. Exhausted, emotionally and physically drained, Gwen walked over to the bed and lay down in the wonderful, solitary silence.

She opened her eyes to find them filled with Etienne. 'What have you done to my baby?' he roared.

Gwen put a hand to her temple. 'Stop shouting… what on earth are you talking about?'

Dragging herself into a sitting position, her head full of cotton wool, she had the feeling his words wouldn't have made much more sense if she had been wide awake.

'I've been searching everywhere! Where have you been?'

He was furious. When she realised how the shadows had crept out of the corners of her bedroom, she knew why. She'd been sleeping for hours.

'Here, of course.'

That obviously wasn't the right answer. Etienne threw himself away from her bed and started pacing. Finally shaking herself free from sleep, Gwen shuffled her thoughts into order. 'And at the beautician's. That's all.'

Etienne was beside himself. He strode backwards and forwards, waving his arms in wordless fury.

'You never called a car!' he managed eventually. 'So I visited the salon to give you a lift myself. They said you'd left hours before. I tried Le Rossignol. They hadn't seen you. For all I knew, that meant you were trying to get back to Wales. You might have had an accident, or been picked up, or murdered, or worse… What were you thinking of? Why didn't you ring and tell me what you were doing? I drove up and down that road! Gwen, I've been—!' He lifted his arms into the air again, but the words wouldn't come. He let them drop with a bang.

Gwen looked at him in shock. She had never seen him like this. She hadn't been gone for long enough to deserve this level of anger, surely? Pushed beyond endurance, she opened her mouth to tell him what an arrogant, controlling, unbearable man he was when something in his eyes—some emotion quickly masked—stopped her. Suddenly, she remembered his first question.

'Hang on—*what* did you say about the baby, Etienne?' she asked abruptly.

Etienne's face froze. He seemed to be battling with himself. When he finally spoke, his voice was a whisper.

'Are you still pregnant?'

'Of course I am. You're not making sense. What are you talking about?'

'I was told you'd gone home. I assumed that meant Wales. You wanted to work, you didn't want to be a mother.' His voice was a crackle of fury. 'I thought you'd gone off to have an abortion.'

The word hit her like a slap in the face. Slowly, the real reason for his anger and the state of his appearance filtered through to her.

He was scared.

The only difference between them was that Etienne hadn't spent the last two days putting his fear into words. He had been trying to support her.

'No,' she said quietly. 'No, I'd never do that—especially not without telling you. How could you think such a thing?'

His hands were working, clenching and unclenching at his sides. She could tell he was building up to something terrible, long before he was able to put it into words.

'Because,' he said at last, and then had to draw in a ragged breath before continuing. 'Because of Angela.'

CHAPTER TEN

WITH those few words, Etienne pushed the final piece of jigsaw into place. Gwen remembered what she had read. She knelt up on the bed, facing him.

'Etienne,' she said carefully, 'please tell me the truth. What happened with her?'

He stared at her for a long, long time. Gwen stared back. She watched him work through more emotions than he could possibly name. Then suddenly, she saw him come to a decision. Whirling around, he strode towards the door.

Gwen got there just before he did. She could hardly hope to contain him. As she put a hand on either side of the doorframe she fully expected him to lift her straight out of his way. Instead he stopped. This time he refused to look at her.

'I can't talk about it.'

The coldness in his voice would have been enough of a warning for any other woman. Gwen stood her ground.

'I don't want to talk about it either—but we must.'

His silence spoke to her as loudly as the taut immobility of his body. It was obvious he did not know where to start. It was left to her to walk forward, her steps slow and hesitant. Every moment she expected him to turn away. He didn't. When she was as close as she could get, she put her hand up to his face. Still he did not move. With the pad of her thumb she stroked away the crease between his dark brows. As she did so, she felt the brush of his thick dark lashes against her palm. He had closed his eyes. Then he nodded.

Gwen took the initiative. 'I was telling the truth, Etienne. I really didn't know anything about your association with Angela before you mentioned her name. That led me to the Internet, but it was hard to recognise you from the reports I read. Your reaction to—' she looked down at her waist awkwardly, unwilling to put it into words '—well, all *this* was so different from what I expected, given what was supposed to have happened back then. I don't know what to think,' she said softly.

'I would never want to get rid of a baby,' he announced. 'Then, or now.'

That explained a lot. Gwen's sympathy for Angela Webbington began to waver. There was indeed more to this story than she had been able to uncover before she lost her nerve.

'All my life I had everything, except a real family. My father merely did his duty in providing a Malotte heir. That was the extent of it,' Etienne began with difficulty. He was tracking back over an unbearably painful time and considering each word. 'I knew there had to be more to life than that. I searched far and wide for something to fill that emptiness. Angela was beautiful, successful, and totally unlike anything the House of

Malotte had seen in its entire history. When I got engaged to her, I assumed we would have the perfect partnership. I was wrong. That one error of judgement still haunts me. Angela wanted the Moreau lifestyle, but none of its responsibilities. She could spend and party as hard as I could, but it was beyond her to be faithful. She was neither loyal, nor even honest. Our relationship soon hit the rocks. Finally, she went behind my back and terminated that pregnancy before bothering to inform me she was carrying a child. She called the baby "a body-wrecking disruption to my career".' He stopped as his voice twisted with emotion.

Gwen couldn't begin to imagine what living through that showdown must have felt like. Nothing she could say would ease his pain, so she kept quiet.

'I had always given her a totally free rein,' he continued. 'She did what she liked, and never stopped to think about me or the baby. At the end, she taunted me that she couldn't be sure the baby was even mine. When I found out you were—' He stopped and opened his eyes, clearly wondering what her reaction would be if he said the word.

'*Pregnant*.' She supplied it for him. 'It's OK. I can take it now.'

'I was so determined the same thing was not going to happen again,' he continued grimly. 'I wanted things done properly this time, right from the beginning. Yet that has turned out to be wrong, too.'

'Yes, it has!' Gwen burst out. She couldn't keep quiet any longer. 'You've been heavy-handed, but I should have thought about you as well as myself—should have realised something was wrong. But now we know more about what has pulled us apart, we can work at getting back together. Can't we?' She looked searchingly into his face.

Etienne's expression was guarded.

'That's up to you,' he said at length.

It was a start.

'OK,' Gwen said slowly, feeling her way towards a conversation they should have had long ago. 'Get the doctor back in, and I'll promise to listen to his advice this time, as long as he's a little nicer to me and minds his manners!' She smiled softly and then went on. 'Pregnancy has been the biggest shock of my life—you can't imagine what it's been like. But I'm getting used to it,' she said, still trying to convince herself. 'And I'm going to take the greatest care of our baby, believe me. But in return, I need something to do. I can't sit around all day, being waited on hand, foot and finger. It will drive me mad, Etienne!'

He put a hand tentatively on her shoulder. 'If I let you go back to Le Rossignol, you'll overdo it.'

'Of course I won't!' she scoffed, sliding her arms around his waist and giving him a reassuring squeeze. They both knew taking it easy would be a struggle for her. There was another long, uncomfortable silence.

'Perhaps I could prove it to you,' she offered eventually. 'If you came to work with me, you could enjoy yourself in the restaurant while I'm fiddling about in my kitchens. You'll be on hand to make sure I don't lift anything heavier than a paring knife, and I'll have one eye on you, watching for the first signs of boredom. You can be the one who says when it's time to go home. I might even let you drive me, in my car!' She threw his old insolence back at him archly. 'But only when I get too big to fit behind the wheel.'

Etienne looked down at her with a sudden spark. 'You called the chateau "home"!'

Gwen looked equally startled. 'I did, didn't I? Am I allowed to do that?' She tried to coax a smile from him. 'Do you mind?'

'Of course I don't,' he whispered into the fragrant silk of her hair. 'I went overboard in trying to do the right thing, but it was only when I thought I'd lost you that I realised why. It isn't only the baby, Gwen. I want you, pure and simple—you, and our own family, and our real, living home.'

'That's what I want, too,' she said. 'If only we had both realised from the start what that word meant, it would have saved us all this heartache.'

She had felt so helpless in the face of Etienne's relentless efficiency. Now she saw she had been deaf and blind to his feelings, too.

He looked into her eyes. His expression was filled with such uncomplicated emotion that she held her breath.

'Gwen, I thought Angela had killed all the human parts of me. Then you came along, and showed me how to live again. I never imagined you would leave me. When you seemed to walk out of my life, I realised that love is like sand. The harder you try and hold onto it, the faster it slips away between your fingers.'

Gwen knew this was as close as he would come to opening his heart to her. His skin felt warm and firm beneath her fingers. She felt his soft breath stir her hair.

It tickled, but nothing would have tempted her to move. For long, wonderful moments she relaxed against him. They were together again, and she was in his arms. That was all she cared about. And then something he had said filtered back through the misty happiness filling her mind.

'Love?' she repeated. 'Etienne…?' She paused—unable to summon the courage to finish the sentence.

He stirred. She felt it through the creased, damp ruin of his designer shirt. When he spoke, she realised it was the movement of a restless spirit trying to settle.

'That depends on you.' He spoke with an alien hesitancy. She laid her head against his chest again, and listened to the familiar sound of his heart beating. It had lost the hectic rhythm of a few moments before, and now her own pulse quickened.

With her face safely hidden from him, Gwen allowed herself a small smile. 'No, it doesn't. I was a victim of my heart the first moment I saw you, Etienne. I didn't know it then, but one look at you across that crowded restaurant and I was lost. You came and found me, and that was it. Although I never thought you could feel for me in the way I feel for you now.'

When she said that his arms tightened around her, but he said nothing. She smiled and closed her eyes. Silently, he was giving her all the reassurance she needed.

'My body took control that night. To become anything more than your mistress was a hopeless dream. I realised that. It was why I had to end things. We were opposites in everything.'

'Well, they do say opposites attract,' he said quietly.

Gwen nuzzled against him. She was so happy words

were barely necessary but Etienne had exposed his soul to her. It only made her love him more, and she wanted to make the next time easier for him.

'Could we begin all over again?' she said softly. 'Can we start looking forward as a couple now?'

In answer, he bent and kissed her. He did it so reverently she could hardly believe he was the same vigorous lover who had blazed through her life like a comet. She melted against him. Her response fired him with all the passion that had waited so long to be released.

'Does this reaction mean there's one part of our past you might still want to remember?' he murmured huskily into her neck. At the touch of his lips, Gwen quivered and went limp in his arms.

'That was an incredible night, Etienne,' she breathed.

He was holding her captive against his hard, hot body. She had dreamed of this moment for so long. Now it was here, she could not wait.

'I need you, Etienne…' Her voice was a long, slow gasp of desire.

'How much?' he growled. 'As much as when I gave you our baby?'

'More,' she moaned. 'More…'

His hand moved to cradle her ripening breast. As his thumb described slow, thoughtful circles over her nipple it reacted by swelling to a full peak.

'Your body delights me more and more each day,' he murmured into her ear. Then without another word he lifted her up and carried her back to the bed. Sculpting pillows into soft shapes beneath her tender body, he lay down beside her. His eyes were soft, but his voice was hoarse with anticipation. 'I've missed you so much, Gwen.'

She chuckled. 'If you've missed anyone, it's that girl in four-inch heels and the beautiful dress. Not Our Gwen from the valley with her morning sickness and a desperate need to get back to work.'

'You're wrong. Knowing that you're far too stubborn to change is one of the many things I love about you. One of the things that makes you so special.' He silenced her with another kiss, this time as light as this-tledown. 'And now…I want to see you naked again. It has been such a long, lonely time for both of us. Let me look at you.'

Without a word he undid her blouse, one button at a time. His movements were slow and considered. Anticipation rose up in her like a fountain. Flicking the sides of her shirt apart, he looked down with pride at the taut white lace of her bra. With movements so slow they made Gwen want to scream with urgency, he slid his hands beneath her arching body and unclipped the strap. Lifting the bra up, he exposed her breasts. Both showed the delicate tracery of pressure marks where their in-creasing size had been compressed.

'Oh, poor baby,' he murmured, and Gwen knew he wasn't speaking to the tiny creature growing inside her. Lowering his head, he started by laying a gentle network of kisses over each breast in turn. Then, as the warm fra-grance of her femininity aroused him, his foreplay quickened. His fingers were greedy for the experience of her body. His skill made her writhe beneath him. As he towered over her she prepared for the onslaught her body craved but Etienne had other ideas. He rolled over onto his back.

'You do it. You're in charge.' His words were ragged with desire. 'I don't want to hurt either of you.'

'I won't let you,' Gwen whispered, sliding over his body until they connected with a mutual moan of pleasure.

Etienne's delight in Gwen's body increased her hunger for him. Their lovemaking excited her beyond the point of distraction. She forgot everything except what he meant to her. It was only hours later, when she woke in his bed at the chateau, that it all came flooding back on a tide of morning sickness.

Etienne sat up the moment he felt her stir. Instantly, he hit the remote control to pull the curtains right back from his tall windows.

'Is that enough light for you to reach the bathroom?'

Nodding, Gwen made a bolt for anonymity. His cool and luxurious wet room was a perfect sanctuary. When she felt better, she had a shower and washed her hair. Emerging refreshed, she revelled in the sight of Etienne gazing at her like a connoisseur admiring his latest treasure. There was something about being desired when she felt so unlovable that warmed Gwen's soul. Hot summer sunshine pouring through his windows thawed her still further. Padding back to his big, wide bed, she stretched out across it like a cat.

Etienne smiled as though he were the one who had been at the cream. 'Flaunt yourself like that, Miss Williams, and I shall make you *very* late for work,' he drawled.

'Good,' Gwen said smartly.

'You're humouring me.' He chuckled. 'From now on, I'm never going to forget what Le Rossignol means to you.'

She reached out, trailing a finger around the outline of the face she loved so much. 'Myself, I'm beginning to wonder. You've opened my eyes, Etienne. While I was working all hours, I kept telling myself it was the most important thing in my life. It was only when I realised what you'd been through that I began to get things into perspective. I was kidding myself. You are the only thing I truly can't live without. But I still don't know how I'm going to cope with a family of our own—'

'We're a team, Gwen,' he said hoarsely. 'I want to make things better for you, but I don't always know how.' As he spoke he gathered her up, wet hair, damp towels and all.

'Talk to me. Tell me things, Etienne. Give me something to think about outside of work, and I'll do the same for you. Up until now I've sacrificed my social life and worked extra hard, because I thought no one could love me as much as my family did. Then I found you, but it went wrong and I missed out on all the romance of a proposal. You took control, and that was that. I wanted to be wooed and won, not organised out of existence. That was why I needed that break after my spell at the beautician's!'

With a gasp of relief, Etienne seized on her words and pulled himself onto firmer ground. 'You want romance, *mon amour*? I can at least manage that, in one small way.' Slipping from her arms, he went to find his jacket. It was on the floor, where he had dropped it the night before in the throes of passion. Rifling through his pockets, he pulled out a small leather box and returned to the bedside.

'You appeared in my life like a dream, Gwen, and I want to keep that feeling alive,' he whispered softly. 'That's why I want to give you this. It's a family heirloom. I was going to present it to you at the exact moment our baby is born. That's why I've been carrying it everywhere, in my pocket. But I think it would be much better to give it to you now…'

'What is it?' she probed, like a surgeon looking for trouble.

He raised one eyebrow, mocking her gently. 'I'm going to make at least one of your dreams come true right now.'

Before Gwen knew what was happening, he went down on one knee in front of her. Then he held out the little box.

'Would you do me the honour of becoming my wife, Gwen?'

'But, Etienne…you've already decided that's going to happen…' she said, teasingly.

'I know, and that was wrong of me. I want us to start again, too. This is my proposal. When you accept—'

'*When?*' She laughed, ruffling his hair playfully. 'You still sound very sure of yourself!'

'*If* you accept,' he corrected himself gravely, 'then I shall sweep you off to Wales, where you can have such a big church wedding and lavish reception that it will be talked about for years to come. Then we'll have a honeymoon. When and where is entirely up to you. I want it to be this instant, but when it comes to our life together, Gwen, I've issued my last direct order.'

She was floating on a cloud of disbelief. 'Are you sure? After all, ordering people about is what you do.'

He had a swift answer for that. 'And so do you, when you're at work. That was part of the problem. I underestimated how much you enjoy being in control.'

She smiled. 'I moved away from my family to get a taste of independence. Once I had it, I didn't want to let go. That's why I was so unhappy. You changed so much once we found out I was pregnant.'

'That's why I want you to feel we're together because it's what we *both* want, Gwen. Now I know what makes you so independent, I can allow for that. We may have got things out of sequence but this can be our second chance. What do you say?'

She put her slender, pale hands over his wide brown ones and drew him to his feet.

'I can't think of anything I would like more than to be your wife, Etienne.'

She wanted to say a lot more, but he was in no mood to listen. Pulling her into his arms, he kissed her until she was breathless and laughing with delight.

'Then you'll need this.'

Taking a stunning diamond solitaire from the little ring box, he placed it gently on her finger. With a gasp, Gwen watched it split the sunlight into a rainbow of colours. Then she looked at him with eyes full of longing.

'This ring is absolutely wonderful, Etienne, but all I *really* need is you!'

Merry Christmas

& A Happy New Year!

Thank you for a wonderful 2013...

Special Offers

Every month we put together collections and longer reads written by your favourite authors.

Here are some of next month's highlights— and don't miss our fabulous discount online!

On sale 3rd January On sale 3rd January On sale 20th December

Save 20%
on all Special Releases

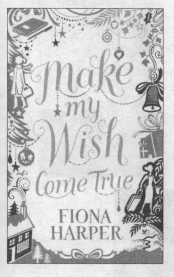

Meet The Sullivans...

ONLY £3.99

Over 1 MILLION Books Sold

BELLA ANDRE

The Look of Love

THE SULLIVANS Over 1 MILLION Books Sold

BELLA ANDRE

From This Moment On

BELLA ANDRE

Can't Help Falling in Love

Over 1 million books sold worldwide!

Stay tuned for more from **The Sullivans** in 2014

Available from:

www.millsandboon.co.uk